D0896489

HENRY JAMES

SELECTED SHORT STORIES

HENRY JAMES

SELECTED SHORT STORIES

EDITED WITH AN INTRODUCTION
BY QUENTIN ANDERSON

REVISED

NEW YORK   *Rinehart & Co., Inc.*   TORONTO

"The Beast in the Jungle" and "The Birthplace" from THE BETTER SORT by Henry James, copyright 1903 by Charles Scribner's Sons, 1931 by Henry James. Reprinted by permission of the publisher.

Permission to distribute this volume in Canada and the Philippine Islands granted by Harper & Brothers for "The Middle Years" and "An International Episode"; by Charles Scribner's Sons for "The Beast in the Jungle" and "The Birthplace"; and by John Farquharson Ltd. (for the Estate of Henry James) for "The Real Thing," "The Pupil," "The Jolly Corner," and "Four Meetings."

Introduction copyright 1950, © 1957, by Quentin Anderson
Philippines copyright, 1957, by Quentin Anderson
Typography and Cover Design by Stefan Salter
Printed in the United States of America
Library of Congress Catalog Card Number: 57-9369

INTRODUCTION

THE list of things Henry James will not do for you, his reader, is rather forbidding. He will not help you to recall past pleasures nor picture the fulfillment of your desires; he is even less likely to nourish your convictions about politics, the arts, or your family and friends. These things, he would feel, are the issue of *your* art —they are your rendering of experience—and he does not wish to be your collaborator. To the readers who insist that fiction do these things he has nothing to say. In his view they have put a high price on their own perceptions and convictions, but they have skipped the very process which might make these interesting: they have not shown us how they came to render experience in this way, nor do they wish to be shown how anyone else has reckoned up his account with the world. This is what James seeks to do. His art exhibits his mind at play within the framework of the imagined situation, yet the effect on the reader never seems arbitrary; on the contrary, it seems the result of rigorous analysis, because each step he takes not only adds to our sense of the situation but makes James's method in tackling it clearer. We can never separate the question, What has he done in this story? from the question, How has he done it?

Everything turns on the "how," on the manner in which we address ourselves to the things we see. Some manners or styles are less compelling than others. When Mark Twain created Huck Finn, and Dickens Sam Weller, they made available to us a mode of seeing, of taking life, that we find pleasurable, and the pleasure is one we seek to prolong. So the world of boyhood comes to remind us of Huck's ways of dealing with men and the river. We are delighted by Huck's method, though we seldom reflect that the essence of his method is Mark Twain's manner. But Henry James does not for a moment permit us the illusion that we can employ his manner. He does not put his characters at our service. He drives us on and on, past barrier after barrier of expectation, until we are penned in the fold—the situation he has contrived is a world which may be compared with ours, but it cannot be broken up and used for our own imaginative purposes. May Bartram of *The Beast in the Jungle* and Morris Gedge of *The Birthplace* do not answer our expectations, or act as we would in a similar situation; they seem, curiously enough, to defeat our expectations, to transcend them; they supply other reasons for their being than those that had occurred to us. James's account of the social scene is similarly intractable. He does not supply us with usable generalizations about genius in *The Birthplace*, or about the repatriated American in *The Jolly Corner*.

Some critics have felt that this was a consequence of the admirable purity of James's artistic intention—the intention to treat of the world precisely as his sensibility demanded, never making the least concession to the interests or beliefs of others. His exclusive devotion to the craft of fiction is thought to have freed him from the burden of prose conventions associated with particular themes and subject matters. As a technical innovator (the account runs) he needed this freedom; he could not serve the fiction-consuming mob. On the basis of these assumptions James is made out to be a writer's saint. This view of James is quite inadequate if it be taken to suggest that he stood aloof from his readers and invented techniques without reference to a conception of human nature. The emphasis ought to be reversed. James is an innovator because he conceives of human beings in a certain way. Investigation of the links between his techniques and his moral view does not give us the secret of his genius, but it is an indispensable part of any account of its workings.

James not only defeats your expectations and drives you toward his conclusions; he does so consciously, and this covert struggle with his reader is the central fact about his fiction. I do not mean that he is writing about you, his reader, but that he is always aware of the arc which separates the reader and himself as both view the situation in the story or novel. He seeks to diminish that arc, so that the end of the story takes place at the moment when your position coincides with his. The reader's initial assumptions are quite as much the matter of his story as the situation itself. His prose, no matter what complexity it takes on, reads like the spoken word because he deeply feels the dialectic character of storytelling—almost hears the questions, exclamations, and objections of the imagined reader.

The Real Thing is both a story and a parable about the process of undermining our assumptions. Both the artist in the story and the reader are tempted to conclude that "the real thing" is indeed what is required to illustrate a great novel. But James makes it very plain that Major and Mrs. Monarch, the models who offer themselves, though they are in fact members of the class with which the novel deals, will not serve to illustrate anything but themselves—they cannot be employed to figure a particular dramatic situation, because they have made themselves general or public persons who cannot be used to suggest perceptions or actions not required of week-end visitors to a great house. Their pathos is the pathos of nullity; they have succeeded in making themselves indistinguishable from their kind, like second-rate works of art.

The artist in the story does not regret having been deceived, feels rather that he has learned something of value. For the author of this parable, James himself, the capacity to recognize and sympathize with such people is of the highest importance. Without this awareness and sympathy he could not write fiction, for he would not know what attitudes held by his readers must be dissolved in the course of telling a particular story. Major and Mrs. Monarch are fictional cousins of Mr. and Mrs. Everybody, who wish to be seen as they see themselves and act as they have always acted. James knows that for most people stories are, so to speak, over before they begin; that our desires, habitual judgments, and memories serve to interpret the particular situation without regard to its particularity, its difference, its interest, and its charm. He is an innovator in fiction chiefly (though not alone) because he speaks in calculated fashion to each of our blindnesses, and uses the barriers we have set up, the resistances of the commonplace, as the material of his fiction.

Four Meetings, the earliest story reprinted here, is nonetheless one of James's best on the theme of Americans and European experience. We are easily led to feel that Miss Spencer's rather indiscriminate hunger for the picturesque is charming and pathetic; we must in the end acknowledge that her greed for "Europe" has been the source of her troubles, not simply her seedy poseur of a cousin, or his ever so European lady. The school-teacher had thought Europe her oyster; she was quite unprepared to be seen as a resource herself.

In *The Real Thing* James is almost explicitly training you, his reader, to read. Like the ideal anthropologist, he has caught the intention of your gestures, your stylized responses, and is suggesting that to enter into his fiction you must be prepared to concede that *in the given situation* another set of responses is appropriate. I note that two results of the creative process are emphasized in this parable: the situation is isolated so that everything that occurs has significance and points to a conclusion, and the reader is seduced into surrendering the assumptions or preconceptions which would make him incapable of sharing James's view of the situation at the end of the story.

The first of these results is achieved by every master of fiction, and if we try, on this basis, to distinguish James from other writers, we find ourselves discussing a variety of ways of doing the same thing. But the second result, secured through what I have called a covert struggle with his reader, distinguishes James's method and accounts for some of his highest achievements (and most of his notable failures). To make his fiction akin to the art of persuasion James employed a sensitive awareness of the imaginative climate of his time, a theory about the forces in individuals and peoples which had bred this climate, and a set of value judgments in accord with his theory. He was subject to a rigid condition: he must never acknowledge the struggle with the reader, nor let the reader discover his intensely American passion for moral theory and moral judgment. When, toward the end of his career, his efforts not to violate this condition became desperate in the face of his ever-mounting moral zeal, he developed an art hypertrophied as to artistry—the "late manner" which has so often been questioned on aesthetic grounds. Attempts to understand this manner as a development of James's technique alone have failed because they have not reckoned with the fact that it is an attempt to incorporate in his fiction assertions, not simply ethical, but also theological in character.

The reader of this collection may be assured that, although the effort to reconcile fiction and persuasion is perennial in James, all the stories reprinted here show his capacity to control it and turn it to fruitful ends. (It would be possible to make a somewhat inferior collection in which this effort would barely appear.) *The Birthplace* (1903), a relatively late story, and a very great one, exemplifies my chief points: that James's manner is extraordinarily compelling and that his capacity to give his situation those manifold connections and firm outlines which make it a world in miniature is allied with a capacity to persuade the reader to substitute James's moral conclusions for commonplace or conventional ones.

Lucidity, ease, force, and a surplusage of glancing lights of suggestion and interconnection inform this story. It appears that James has done much that he need not have done to get the story told, yet each touch illumines others and the whole has the imaginative density found in great poetry. One might say of this story, as of *Hamlet* or of the Don Juan legend, that it is not the work that is difficult of apprehension; it is the theme itself. The theme here is nothing less than the splendid mystery of creation. James exhibits it in such a way that we cannot escape a sense both of the splendor and the mystery. Moreover, he succeeds in conveying something about art (a perception which in Proust awaits you after reading many volumes)—a sense of its growth out of the soil of the commonplace, out of the very rituals of everyday which seem to preclude the possibility of delighted discovery. We may think of the story as a great avenue leading toward life from which

James has cleared the obstacles. My comments must be brief, but an account of James's devices for clearing the approach to his theme will illustrate much of what has already been said.

Morris Gedge and his wife have first of all a fairy-tale success —he is poor but honest, she is patient and loyal; they seem the very drudges of fiction, conventionally fitted to bear an unexpected good fortune, which is, moreover, deliciously apt, since it consists not of a mass of money but of a secure recognition of their pale intellectual pretensions. The position as custodians and guides at Shakespeare's birthplace, offered by Grant-Jackson on behalf of the ineffably respectable Body which administers it, appears to afford the very niche which the Gedges have sought all their lives. By our pleased response to their good fortune, James holds us and proceeds to make us confront a looming anomaly. What can Grant-Jackson, what can Morris Gedge do or be in relation to Shakespeare? The hollow booming success and the gray thin failure seem alike unthinkable, except as moths playing in the light of his work. But there is another anomaly behind. The world is not after all Shakespeare's to command; it is Grant-Jackson's, the Body's, it belongs to the faceless horde of questioning trippers who come to chip off bits of Shakespeare for their very own. So James turns our curiosity about the poet against us—makes us dislike our lust for details which would pin him down and make his imagination less overwhelming. It seems best to take, as Gedge does, the sternest scholarly view, and despise the obscuring shellwork of legend. Yet is not Shakespeare somewhere? Gedge's vigils in the birthplace convince him and us that he is not (though he may be, as Mrs. Hayes says, everywhere).

Shakespeare has proved not to be an intellectual capital on which Gedge can rely, and his awakened "critical sense" begins to threaten his bread and butter; it appears that it will end by getting him fired and wholly detaching him from the crowds of visitors, that is, from humanity at large. He will in fact be farther from Shakespeare than ever, since, though he and Mr. and Mrs. Hayes agree that Shakespeare is not a "Person," it is nonetheless clear that Shakespeare had somehow recognized the world of persons (a world in which your identity is more important than your work) in the act of creating his characters. When the Hayeses return they discover that Gedge has achieved his recognition, has become popular, and is about to get a raise. His worldly fortune is made, and he has in the same breath become a humble fellow to the great poet: he is an artist! At this point some readers are likely to balk (I have known one or two to refuse to go on) because they feel that this is a cheat. How can Gedge take the very legends which he had earlier found contemptible, the very tourists whom he had earlier despised and turn the first into enthralling speeches, the second into enthralled listeners? The proper reply is of course: What else can any artist take, and whom else can he get to listen? The experiences we share, the tattered anecdotes which pass current among the visitors to Stratford, this is the very dross which the artist transmutes into gold. It is not another world of which the poet writes, but this one. Grant-Jackson and his Body have tried hard to turn Shakespeare into a Person, themselves into personages, but Gedge fools them magnificently by proving daily that the best thing to do with experience is not to make it enhance your sense of prestige (that, after all, is what the tourists of the story seem to want of Shakespeare) but to turn it into something enduring, into art. It is pleasant to reflect that the tourists have been surprised into a salutary submission. Though they have come to view the remains of the dead Person, and enhance their own self-esteem as tourists, they find themselves confronted by a live artist, who instead of allowing them to imagine that they have somehow taken possession of Shakespeare, captures their imaginations, indeed, takes possession of them!

Curiously enough, the great event in *The Birthplace* is not explained, nor, we come to see, is it explicable. How did Gedge become an artist? Whence came his style? No one can say. We know that in Shakespeare's supposed birthplace an artist has in fact been born—but we know not how any more than in the case of Shakespeare. Gedge, too, humble though he is, abides our question, and the great theme, the splendid mystery, remains just that.

What this story does tell us is that James's struggle with the reader, though not characteristic of all his work, is at the heart of much of his best work. We find it wherever we find the antithesis between the possible uses of experience: that which characterizes the tourist who has "done" Stratford-on-Avon as against Shakespeare's use of his own experience in his plays. In James's hands this distinction becomes the chief basis for moral discrimination and expands in significance. It is not simply a basis for judging art; it is primarily a principle governing conduct. How does a man regard his experience? This is the chief question. If he seeks to possess it, to monopolize it, that is evil; if he seeks to give it form, to communicate it, that is good. There are, as James remarks in *The Tragic Muse,* two "affections," that which "isolates and simplifies its object" and that which "seeks communications and contacts for it." It is as simple as that, but the ramifications of the principle are endless.

On occasion, and with increasing frequency after the eighties, Henry James elaborated his use of this combined moral and aesthetic antithesis into a full-dress account of the nature and dynamics of providence, borrowing freely from his father's psychology and theology, which the elder Henry James had set forth in such works as *Substance and Shadow* and *Society, the Redeemed Form of Man.* These works are built on an analysis of human nature (recently revived by the novelist, Koestler) as an uneasy balance between the self-assertive and the self-transcendent aspects of personality. Most of what the elder James has to say is as old as Plato or Saint Augustine, but his scheme of salvation has certain novel emphases which his son found irresistible. Although not in any ordinary sense a religious man, the younger Henry James was clearly not satisfied with an immediate moral judgment as to who, in a particular situation, was displaying his self-assertive side or the greedy kind of affection, or, on the other hand, who was exhibiting the self-transcendent or selfless love. A single moral triumph is enough of a "moral" for a story, but it gives us no assurance of the ultimate value of either selfless love or art. Moreover, in the view of the novelist's father, all men move between the poles of selfishness and charity; we are all double, and our triumph in a particular situation does not mean that we are one of God's elect. Divine grace, according to the elder James, is not conferred on certain individuals but on all alike. It follows that salvation must come to society as a whole.

We may now see why the younger Henry James was prone to accept this analysis. It gives to our distinctive use of our experience, our manner or style, a peculiar value. Through the exercise of his art an artist makes his experience part of the consciousness, indeed we may say, of the conscience, of his society. His achievement is not that of a person seeking recognition—to seek recognition as a person is foolishly and wickedly to deny your own doubleness—it is the achievement of the divine love in mankind which will one day succeed in abolishing the idea of particular persons altogether. We shall then be like the souls who have returned to God in the system of the medieval theologian, Scotus Erigena: mere points of light in the divine consciousness, or perhaps (since we retain our style) instruments in a divine orchestra.

It is now apparent that *The Real Thing* and *The Birthplace* are of central importance in defining Henry James's moral horizon and emphasizing what I am obliged to call the *metaphysical* role which the creative imagination plays in his work. A universe in which style is the source of all moral discrimination, and in which the creator is manifested only through the works of his creatures, is a universe which grows, as does Blake's, through the acts of the imagination and in no other way. A detailed examination of this system is not necessary here. Its elements are apparent in *The Jolly Corner* where the distinction between the selfish and selfless ways of taking experience which appears in *The Birthplace* is rendered as a distinction between two aspects of Spencer Brydon's soul. The other self he finds so hateful had, of course, been in the ascendant during the years of his sojourn in Europe. He finds the strength to confront *himself* in Alice Staverton's love—and having done so, he learns to make a selfless use of his experience. When we note that the struggle takes place in a beautiful mansion, a "house of life," we complete the list of James's primary symbols,

although a list of their elaborations in this single story would involve much exegesis. The two selves, the divine love, and the
house, the scene of human experience, come straight from the
elder Henry James, along with much more which the reader of
The Wings of the Dove and *The Golden Bowl* must know if he is
to understand these novels.

More important in this place than an account of this system
of symbolism is the question of the importance to the reader of
James's general moral intention.

In one obvious sense it is important to him who simply reads
the stories contained in this volume, for all of them (save perhaps *An International Episode* and *The Pupil*) clearly exhibit
the antithesis we have been discussing. But we may put the question in another way. The reader might ask: Since I will either find
his stories interesting because of the felt life and the separate
moral judgments they imply, or I will not, and in either case I
must judge each story as an independent whole, must I, as a
responsible reader, seek a precise measure of James's intention?

F. R. Leavis, the English critic, in commenting on James's intention, says two important things on this point. The first has to
do with the self-sufficiency of a given work.

The analysis and judgment of works of literary art belongs to the literary critic, who *is* one in so far as he observes a disciplined relevance in
response, comment and determination of significance. He is concerned
with the work in front of him as something that should contain within
itself the reason why it is so and not otherwise.

We will see in a moment under what conditions the critic or reader
is free to do this, but I wish, before I go on, to quote Mr. Leavis's
conclusion about the part that James's general moral intention
plays in his work:

The system of symbolism, in short, doesn't represent the structure of
interests behind his operative sensibility; it doesn't belong with his
creativeness.

The reader already knows that I find the principles which give
rise to the system of symbolism to which Mr. Leavis refers, in

James's best work as well as his worst, and that I believe that the struggle with the reader—an attempt to find modes of converting us through an aesthetic experience—is observable in the construction of James's stories. I must on these grounds insist that the "system of symbolism" and the principles for which it stands do somehow belong with James's creativeness.

To see how, we must glance at the much-discussed question of James's relation to America. Everyone concedes that, although James spent much of his adult life in Europe, his American traits are very important and probably more likely to afford an understanding of the character of his work than are the effects of his European sojourn. Yet there is much confusion as to what these American traits are. Mr. Leavis feels that when James's father is influencing him he shows a species of "American optimism." Earlier discussions have usually begun with a description of the cultural poverty of James's America, which he has himself described in a classic passage in his biography of Hawthorne. I think it sounder to begin, not with what his America lacked, but with what it had, in the persons not simply of his father or Emerson, but in those of his greatest predecessors in American fiction, Hawthorne and Melville. What these representative American men of letters had, whether for good or ill, was an inveterate tendency to play the prophet in the Old Testament sense. With this tendency the "operative sensibility" of both Hawthorne and Melville had to come to terms if they were to function as creative writers. Mr. Leavis's critic (or, we may add, a properly disciplined reader), schooled in a literary tradition in which each work must justify itself, tells us that it is illicit to introduce a measure of the artist's intention which is derived from the whole body of his work or a judgment of his relation to the American scene *when we are engaged in evaluating a particular work*. The unspoken premise is simply this: since both writer and critic have been disciplined by previous responses to works of art which fall within a certain tradition, they bring to the acts of creation and response their full moral equipment—in other words both writer and critic share a system of values, and if the writer has somehow been untrue to the essential elements of this system the critic is in a position to call him to account.

What Mr. Leavis fails to perceive is that this moral universe created by the English tradition was not Henry James's home. He was only a visitor there, and much of his best work employs the American equivalent for tradition: a general moral intention expressed in a system of symbolism, just as in Hawthorne and Melville. It was precisely because these three writers felt it necessary to be prophets that their works must be read in connection with one another. They could not, as Mr. Leavis does, take the values expressed in literary tradition for granted. They had somehow to announce them. *The Scarlet Letter, Moby Dick,* and *The Portrait of a Lady* all aim at schooling and enriching the moral imaginations of their readers; each is part of a prophetic enterprise which no one book could singly contain or alone justify. None of these writers plays fair in the sense that George Eliot plays fair by restricting herself to a situation in which the reader is a full participant, a moral climate governed by his previous experience, particularly of works of art. No such moral climate could be assumed by an American, even by Henry James, who was a passionate and discriminating admirer of European fiction. Since these three Americans could not assume such a climate they had to find and proclaim its elements for themselves. They may always be charged with having taken it upon themselves to define the very values by which they wished to be judged. But that these American versions of tradition lie at the very root of the creative capacity of these three, there can, I think, be no question.

It is no wonder that Henry James does not appear to belong to this company, for he often gives one the sense that he is a shrewd and sure judge of the wide range of European manners with which he was acquainted; that he needs no hidden sanction for his values because his cultural comparisons, subtle and forceful as they are, have made him wise and confident in his wisdom. Without the hypothesis that there were periods when he wrote without reference to his own version of tradition—when, that is, he tacitly subscribed to another tradition, I could not adequately account for the books which Mr. Leavis and those who share his view of the body of James's work particularly admire: *The Europeans, The Bostonians, Washington Square,* and certain others. However, it will not do to define James's virtues as a writer in a fashion which excludes so much of his work, work of the order of *The Beast in the Jungle, The Birthplace, The Jolly Corner, The Princess Casamassima,* and so on. These are works which have the prophetic reference; which to the eyes of the reader of George Eliot are morally venturesome; which seek to establish within the work the very values which the reader is required to use in assessing its outcome. To say this is to return by a roundabout road to the point made at the outset—that the struggle with the reader is at the heart of James's work.

Moreover, it is to a strong though indistinct sense of this side of James on the part of contemporary readers that he owes his present popularity. The critic's duty has not been fulfilled if he fails to recognize the very aspect of the work to which his age responds. The curious fact is that after thirty years of earnest discussion of James as the discoverer and adapter of certain important technical devices in fiction (the point of view, the stream of consciousness, and so on), in short, the creator of his own convention, we have only begun to realize that this sort of innovation carries with it a necessary corollary: James is the creator of his own moral convention as well. The fact that his father provided the psychological skeleton is far less important than the discovery made by many quite unsophisticated readers that a story by Henry James carries a burden of conviction about the nature of human values that the Steinbecks and the O'Haras cannot supply. We are in fact hungrier than we acknowledge; hungry to the point of undiscriminating excess, for the substance of the moral life. What would it be like so to act that each thought, each gesture, floated on the tide of passionate conviction; that the very shapes and colors of our day were judged and assigned a place in the measure that they contributed to our unique yet communicable sense of the world? The texture of the prose of Henry James answers this question. It is the result of just such a passionate absorption and conviction.

His compelling manner, his capacity for undermining our attitudes, gives him some of the unmatched authority which nursery tales once had for us; he leaves no loophole for contrast or comparison, and makes such figures as John Marcher momentous beyond all proportion to their external circumstances. That a writer who dealt with characters whose situation is materially so easy, whose manners so readily clear paths for their intelligence, who so seldom dedicate themselves to ends high, heroic and public, should at the same time be a writer who has a radical grasp of the problems of human character and destiny is a seeming paradox. James was far ahead of us here. He saw more than half a century ago that if he wished to be a great storyteller, to exercise a real dominion over the imaginations of his readers, he must avoid the very themes which were coming to the fore in fiction: money-making, social reform, the patient exploration of the average, and the celebration of the familiar, and, in general, whatever circumscribed the possible effects of his work by reinforcing our sense of the diminishing importance of individuals. He was as anxious as the present-day existentialist to establish the belief that men create themselves by their acts, and he saw that it would be fatal to occupy himself with those contemporary figures who were, in the eyes of his readers, finished products, told stories, parts of the great romance of the commonplace of which the newspapers tell us at breakfast. Since persons of cultivation and intelligence might be thought capable of facing their problems directly, because they were not caught up in a largely impersonal world, James chose to write about such persons: the world he takes us into is one in which people are wholly responsible for what they do or fail to do, and in which artistic accomplishment contributes to the growth of moral order. The crux of the moral convention which rules this world is, as we have noted, simply our accountability for our experience. What, in the end, have we made of it? This is the bitter question which John Marcher must answer in

The Beast in the Jungle, and Spencer Brydon in *The Jolly Corner.*

A writer working within such a convention must actively contend with the competing conventions, the fictions which pass for reality among his readers. His readers are momentarily his subjects, perhaps even potential proselytes. That the moral convention James employs is, in some final sense, better than yours and mine, I should hardly maintain. It may very well be worse. What must be understood if we wish to evaluate James and establish his position in literature is that his moral convention and his technical innovations are two sides of the same coin: the story that is freshly told has, for its readers, a fresh moral insight. In examining James's position we cannot stay within the bounds of the English tradition in fiction, or content ourselves with comparisons based on fiction alone. We must find comparisons which will set James's moral universe in a clearer light. Dante, Bunyan, Blake, and Hawthorne may help us to dispel the provincial notion that the poet who writes of our world shares our convictions about it. James was moved to create his own version of tradition by American circumstances, but the body of his work is not provincial, except in the sense that he occupies, as do the writers I have named, one of the provinces of the imagination. We have been tourists there, and judicious admirers of the scenery; it is time we inquired into how men are governed in this realm, and investigated its natural resources.

QUENTIN ANDERSON

Columbia College
Columbia University
March, 1950

A NOTE ON THE REVISED EDITION

Some very good readers have felt that this collection would be better balanced if James's explicit concern with Americans and

Europe were more fully represented, and the editor has come to agree with them. In this edition *Four Meetings* has been substituted for *A Bundle of Letters; An International Episode* has been added—although being a *nouvelle* it rather belies the title of the volume—and *The Death of the Lion* has been dropped. The Introduction has been slightly altered in consequence. The editor feels that extended comment on *An International Episode* is out of place here. Its meanings and its delights seem accessible without any help from him. James was never firmer or more at ease about his Americans and his Europeans than he is in this long story—the whole thing ripples with delicate, pointed fun.

March, 1957   Q. A.

A NOTE ON JAMES'S LIFE

HENRY JAMES was born in New York in 1843. His father was independently wealthy and had no profession. The elder James's avocation was theology, preferably homemade, and he was incapable of putting down roots. These characteristics made the education of his five children a geographical and intellectual adventure. Henry James had two intervals of schooling abroad before he enrolled in the Harvard Law School in 1862. At about this time he suffered an injury while fighting a fire. Thus service in the Civil War was impossible. He had little interest in the law. In these circumstances his "visiting mind" took command, and he became a writer, publishing reviews and stories in the *Atlantic Monthly* and elsewhere. By the time of his first adult journey to Europe (1869) he had a modest reputation. His letters during this trip reflect a passionate response to Europe, which a second visit (1872–1874) deepened and confirmed. He was persuaded that he could work best abroad, and in 1875 took up his residence there; first in Paris where he knew Turgenev, Flaubert, and Zola, and then in London. Here and in Sussex he lived the greater part of the remainder of his life, although he was to visit America four times and often spent a part of the year on the Continent. His first substantial novel, *Roderick Hudson,* was published in 1877; the appearance of *Daisy Miller* in 1879 brought him fame. Although fame persisted, his popularity did not really survive the eighties. But, in general, the history of the period between 1877 and 1909 (when he had a serious illness) is a chronicle of his works, his rather formal friendships, and his active social life. It is tempting, though not quite true, to say that he was either dining out or working; he never married and the entire middle ground of domesticity which so nearly fills the days of most men he never had. He was literally a devoted man who buried the meaning of his life in his art. The visit to America which gave rise to *The American Scene* took place in 1904 and 1905. It marks a period, for he afterward undertook to revise and comment on the body of his work for the New York edition. But although he completed no more novels and did nothing on the scale of his last ambitious triad, *The Ambassadors, The Wings of the Dove,* and *The Golden Bowl,* he continued to do extraordinary stories, and to tinker with play writing, which, in the period 1889–1895, had taken altogether too much of his supremely valuable time. The first World War came as a terrible fulfillment of many of his insights and fears, and it was with indignation over the American failure to enter it at the outset that he became a British subject in 1915. He died in 1916.

The best critical biography of James is Frederick W. Dupee's *Henry James* in the American Men of Letters Series (New York: 1951). Fresh material about James's early years is to be found in Léon Edel's *Henry James, The Untried Years: 1843–1870* (New York and Philadelphia: 1953). Among the other works which cast light on James's life are Ralph Barton Perry's biography, *The Thought and Character of William James* (Boston: 1935), F. O. Matthiessen's *The James Family* (New York: 1947), Simon Nowell-Smith's *The Legend of the Master: Henry James* (New York: 1948), and the journal of James's sister, published as *Alice James: Her Brothers—Her Journal* (New York: 1934).

BIBLIOGRAPHICAL NOTE

The stories in this volume follow the text of *The Novels and Tales of Henry James* (New York: 1907–1917, 26 vols.). James's prefaces to this edition have been reprinted as *The Art of the Novel: Critical Prefaces*, with an introduction by R. P. Blackmur (New York: 1934). A second collected edition contains additional stories and novels which James failed to include in the carefully revised first ("New York") edition (London: 1921–1923, 35 vols.). James's important book on America, *The American Scene* (1907) was reissued (New York: 1946). *The Letters of Henry James* (New York: 1920, 2 vols.) was edited by Percy Lubbock. *A Small Boy and Others* (1913) and *Notes of a Son and Brother* (1914) contain reminiscences of James's childhood and early maturity. *The Notebooks of Henry James* was edited by F. O. Matthiessen and K. B. Murdock (New York: 1947). His plays were edited by Léon Edel (New York: 1949). *Henry James: Representative Selections . . .* , edited by Lyon N. Richardson (New York: 1941), contains a useful bibliography, which may be supplemented by reference to the bibliography in the third volume of the *Literary History of the United States* (New York: 1948, 3 vols.). Richardson's bibliography is reprinted in Frederick W. Dupee's anthology of criticism of Henry James, *The Question of Henry James* (New York: 1945). Among the most interesting essays in this collection are those by William Dean Howells, T. S. Eliot, Percy Lubbock, Joseph Warren Beach, and Edmund Wilson. To the reader approaching Henry James for the first time I especially recommend Lionel Trilling's "Introduction" to *The Princess Casamassima* (New York: 1948, 2 vols.) and R. P. Blackmur's difficult but informative chapter on James in the second volume of *The Literary History*. The essay by F. R. Leavis, "Henry James and the Function of Criticism," quoted in the Introduction, appears in *The Common Pursuit* (London: 1952). The present editor's account of James as a moralist, and of the relation of his work to his father's theology, may be found in *The American Henry James* (Rutgers University Press: 1957).

The best guide for the reader who seeks orientation in the extensive body of writing about James is Morton Dauwen Zabel's *Portable Henry James* (New York: 1951; reissued with some additions, 1956).

Some of James's fiction is still hard to obtain. The following novels are (1957) in print: *The Portrait of a Lady, The Turn of the Screw* and *The Lesson of the Master, Washington Square, The Wings of the Dove* are in the Modern Library; New Directions has reprinted *The Other House* and *The Spoils of Poynton; What Maisie Knew* has appeared in the Doubleday Anchor series; The Grove Press has done *The Golden Bowl* and *The Sacred Fount;* Harper's Modern Classics includes *The Ambassadors* and a volume containing both *Daisy Miller* and *Washington Square.*

CONTENTS

FOUR MEETINGS

I SAW her but four times, though I remember them vividly; she made her impression on me. I thought her very pretty and very interesting—a touching specimen of a type with which I had had other and perhaps less charming associations. I'm sorry to hear of her death, and yet when I think of it why *should* I be? The last time I saw her she was certainly not—! But it will be of interest to take our meetings in order.

I

THE FIRST was in the country, at a small tea-party, one snowy night some seventeen years ago. My friend Latouche, going to spend Christmas with his mother, had insisted on my company, and the good lady had given in our honour the entertainment of which I speak. To me it was really full of savour—it had all the right marks: I had never been in the depths of New England at that season. It had been snowing all day and the drifts were knee-high. I wondered how the ladies had made their way to the house; but I inferred that just those general rigours rendered any assembly offering the attraction of two gentlemen from New York worth a desperate effort.

Mrs. Latouche in the course of the evening asked me if I "didn't want to" show the photographs to some of the young ladies. The photographs were in a couple of great portfolios, and had been brought home by her son, who, like myself, was lately returned from Europe. I looked round and was struck with the fact that most of the young ladies were provided with an object of interest more absorbing than the most vivid sun-picture. But there was a person alone near the mantelshelf who looked round the room with a small vague smile, a discreet, a disguised yearning, which seemed somehow at odds with her isolation. I looked at her a moment and then chose. "I should like to show them to that young lady."

"Oh yes," said Mrs. Latouche, "she's just the person. She doesn't care for flirting—I'll speak to her." I replied that if she didn't care for flirting she wasn't perhaps just the person; but Mrs. Latouche had already, with a few steps, appealed to her participation. "She's delighted," my hostess came back to report; "and she's just the person—so quiet and so bright." And she told me the young lady was by name Miss Caroline Spencer—with which she introduced me.

Miss Caroline Spencer was not quite a beauty, but was none the less, in her small odd way, formed to please. Close upon thirty, by every presumption, she was made almost like a little girl and had the complexion of a child. She had also the prettiest head, on which her hair was arranged as nearly as possible like the hair of a Greek bust, though indeed it was to be doubted if she had ever seen a Greek bust. She was "artistic," I suspected, so far as the polar influences of North Verona could allow for such yearnings or could minister to them. Her eyes were perhaps just too round and too inveterately surprised, but her lips had a certain mild decision and her teeth, when she showed them, were charming. About her neck she wore what ladies call, I believe, a "ruche" fastened with a very small pin of pink coral, and in her hand she carried a fan made of plaited straw and adorned with pink ribbon. She wore a scanty black silk dress. She spoke with slow soft neatness, even without smiles showing the prettiness of her teeth, and she seemed extremely pleased, in fact quite fluttered, at the prospect of my demonstrations. These went forward very smoothly after I had moved the portfolios out of their corner and placed a couple of chairs near a lamp. The photographs were usually things I knew—large views of Switzerland, Italy and Spain, landscapes, reproductions of famous buildings, pictures and statues. I said what I could for them, and my companion, looking at them as I held them up, sat perfectly still, her straw fan raised to her under-lip and gently, yet, as I could feel, almost excitedly, rubbing it. Occasionally, as I laid one of the pictures down, she said without confidence, which would have been too much: "Have you seen that place?" I usually answered that I had seen it several times—I had been a great traveller, though I was somehow particularly admonished not to swagger —and then I felt her look at me askance for a moment with her pretty eyes. I had asked her at the outset whether she had been to Europe; to this she had answered "No, no, no"—almost as much below her breath as if the image of such an event scarce, for solemnity, brooked phrasing. But after that, though she never took her eyes off the pictures, she said so little that I feared she was at last bored. Accordingly when we had finished one portfolio I offered, if she desired it, to desist. I rather guessed the exhibition really held her, but her reticence puzzled me and I wanted to make her speak. I turned round to judge better and then saw a faint flush in each of her cheeks. She kept waving her little fan to and fro. Instead of looking at me she fixed her eyes on the remainder of the collection, which leaned, in its receptacle, against the table.

"Won't you show me that?" she quavered, drawing the long breath of a person launched and afloat but conscious of rocking a little.

"With pleasure," I answered, "if you're really not tired."

"Oh I'm not tired a bit. I'm just fascinated." With which as I took up the other portfolio she laid her hand on it, rubbing it softly. "And have you been here too?"

On my opening the portfolio it appeared I had indeed been there. One of the first photographs was a large view of the Castle of Chillon by the Lake of Geneva. "Here," I said, "I've been many a time. Isn't it beautiful?" And I pointed to the perfect reflexion of the rugged rocks and pointed towers in the clear still water. She didn't say "Oh enchanting!" and push it away to see the next picture. She looked a while and then asked if it weren't where Bonnivard, about whom Byron wrote, had been confined.

I assented, trying to quote Byron's verses, but not quite bringing it off.

She fanned herself a moment and then repeated the lines correctly, in a soft flat voice but with charming conviction. By the time she had finished, she was nevertheless blushing. I complimented her and assured her she was perfectly equipped for visiting Switzerland and Italy. She looked at me askance again, to see if I might be serious, and I added that if she wished to recognise Byron's descriptions she must go abroad speedily—Europe was getting sadly dis-Byronised. "How soon must I go?" she thereupon enquired.

"Oh I'll give you ten years."

"Well, I guess I can go in *that* time," she answered as if measuring her words.

"Then you'll enjoy it immensely," I said; "you'll find it of the highest interest." Just then I came upon a photograph of some nook in a foreign city which I had been very fond of and which recalled tender memories. I discoursed (as I suppose) with considerable spirit; my companion sat listening breathless.

"Have you been *very* long over there?" she asked some time after I had ceased.

"Well, it mounts up, put all the times together."

"And have you travelled everywhere?"

"I've travelled a good deal. I'm very fond of it and happily have been able."

Again she turned on me her slow shy scrutiny. "Do you know the foreign languages?"

"After a fashion."

"Is it hard to speak them?"

"I don't imagine you'd find it so," I gallantly answered.

"Oh I shouldn't want to speak—I should only want to listen." Then on a pause she added: "They say the French theatre's so beautiful."

"Ah the best in the world."

"Did you go there very often?"

"When I was first in Paris I went every night."

"Every night!" And she opened her clear eyes very wide. "That to me is"—and her expression hovered—"as if you tell me a fairy-tale." A few minutes later she put to me: "And which country do you prefer?"

"There's one I love beyond any. I think you'd do the same."

Her gaze rested as on a dim revelation and then she breathed "Italy?"

"Italy," I answered softly too; and for a moment we communed over it. She looked as pretty as if instead of showing her photographs I had been making love to her. To increase the resemblance she turned off blushing. It made a pause which she broke at last by saying: "That's the place which—in particular —I thought of going to."

"Oh that's the place—that's the place!" I laughed.

She looked at two or three more views in silence. "They say it's not very dear."

"As some other countries? Well, one gets back there one's money. That's not the least of the charms."

"But it's *all* very expensive, isn't it?"

"Europe, you mean?"

"Going there and travelling. That has been the trouble. I've very little money. I teach, you know," said Miss Caroline Spencer.

"Oh of course one must have money," I allowed; "but one can manage with a moderate amount judiciously spent."

"I think I should manage. I've saved and saved up, and I'm always adding a little to it. It's all for that." She paused a moment, and then went on with suppressed eagerness, as if telling me the story were a rare, but possibly an impure satisfaction. "You see it hasn't been only the money—it has been everything. Everything has acted against it. I've waited and waited. It has been my castle in the air. I'm almost afraid to talk about it. Two or three times it has come a little nearer, and then I've talked about it and it has melted away. I've talked about it too much," she said hypocritically—for I saw such talk was now a small tremulous ecstasy. "There's a lady who's a great friend of mine —she doesn't want to go, but I'm always at her about it. I think

I must tire her dreadfully. She told me just the other day she didn't know what would become of me. She guessed I'd go crazy if I didn't sail, and yet certainly I'd go crazy if I did."

"Well," I laughed, "you haven't sailed up to now—so I suppose you *are* crazy."

She took everything with the same seriousness. "Well, I guess I must be. It seems as if I couldn't think of anything else—and I don't require photographs to work me up! I'm always right *on* it. It kills any interest in things nearer home—things I ought to attend to. That's a kind of craziness."

"Well then the cure for it's just to go," I smiled—"I mean the cure for this kind. Of course you may have the other kind worse," I added—"the kind you get over there."

"Well, I've a faith that I'll go *some* time all right!" she quite elatedly cried. "I've a relative right there on the spot," she went on, "and I guess he'll know how to control me." I expressed the hope that he would, and I forget whether we turned over more photographs; but when I asked her if she had always lived just where I found her, "Oh no sir," she quite eagerly replied; "I've spent twenty-two months and a half in Boston." I met it with the inevitable joke that in this case foreign lands might prove a disappointment to her, but I quite failed to alarm her. "I know more about them than you might think"—her earnestness resisted even that. "I mean by reading—for I've really read considerable. In fact I guess I've prepared my mind about as much as you *can*—in advance. I've not only read Byron—I've read histories and guide-books and articles and lots of things. I know I shall rave about everything."

" 'Everything' is saying much, but I understand your case," I returned. "You've the great American disease, and you've got it 'bad'—the appetite, morbid and monstrous, for colour and form, for the picturesque and the romantic at any price. I don't know whether we come into the world with it—with the germs implanted and antecedent to experience; rather perhaps we catch it early, almost before developed consciousness—we *feel,* as we look about, that we're going (to save our souls, or at least our senses) to be thrown back on it hard. We're like travellers in the desert—deprived of water and subject to the terrible mirage, the torment of illusion, of the thirst-fever. They hear the plash of fountains, they see green gardens and orchards that are hundreds of miles away. So we with *our* thirst—except that with us it's *more* wonderful: we have before us the beautiful old things we've never seen at all, and when we do at last see them—if we're lucky!—we simply recognise them. What experience does is merely to confirm and consecrate our confident dream."

She listened with her rounded eyes. "The way you express it's too lovely, and I'm sure it will be just like that. I've dreamt of everything—I'll know it all!"

"I'm afraid," I pretended for harmless comedy, "that you've wasted a great deal of time."

"Oh yes, that has been my great wickedness!" The people about us had begun to scatter; they were taking their leave. She got up and put out her hand to me, timidly, but as if quite shining and throbbing.

"I'm going back there—one *has* to," I said as I shook hands with her. "I shall look out for you."

Yes, she fairly glittered with her fever of excited faith. "Well, I'll tell you if I'm disappointed." And she left me, fluttering all expressively her little straw fan.

II

A FEW MONTHS after this I crossed the sea eastward again and some three years elapsed. I had been living in Paris and, toward the end of October, went from that city to the Havre, to meet a pair of relatives who had written me they were about to arrive there. On reaching the Havre I found the steamer already docked —I was two or three hours late. I repaired directly to the hotel, where my travellers were duly established. My sister had gone to bed, exhausted and disabled by her voyage; she was the unsteadiest of sailors and her sufferings on this occasion had been extreme. She desired for the moment undisturbed rest and was able to see me but five minutes—long enough for us to agree to stop over, restoratively, till the morrow. My brother-in-law, anxious about his wife, was unwilling to leave her room; but she insisted on my taking him a walk for aid to recovery of his spirits and his land-legs.

The early autumn day was warm and charming, and our stroll through the bright-coloured busy streets of the old French seaport beguiling enough. We walked along the sunny noisy quays and then turned into a wide pleasant street which lay half in sun and half in shade—a French provincial street that resembled an old water-colour drawing: tall grey steep-roofed red-gabled many-storied houses; green shutters on windows and old scrollwork above them; flower-pots in balconies and white-capped women in doorways. We walked in the shade; all this stretched away on the sunny side of the vista and made a picture. We looked at it as we passed along; then suddenly my companion stopped—pressing my arm and staring. I followed his gaze and saw that we had paused just before reaching a café where, under an awning, several tables and chairs were disposed upon the pavement. The windows were open behind; half a dozen plants in tubs were ranged beside the door; the pavement was besprinkled with clean bran. It was a dear little quiet old-world café; inside, in the comparative dusk, I saw a stout handsome woman, who had pink ribbons in her cap, perched up with a mirror behind her back and smiling at some one placed out of sight. This, to be exact, I noted afterwards; what I first observed was a lady seated alone, outside, at one of the little marble-topped tables. My brother-in-law had stopped to look at her. Something had been put before her, but she only leaned back, motionless and with her hands folded, looking down the street and away from us. I saw her but in diminished profile; nevertheless I was sure I knew on the spot that we must already have met.

"The little lady of the steamer!" my companion cried.

"Was she on your steamer?" I asked with interest.

"From morning till night. She was never sick. She used to sit perpetually at the side of the vessel with her hands crossed that way, looking at the eastward horizon."

"And are you going to speak to her?"

"I don't know her. I never made acquaintance with her. I wasn't in form to make up to ladies. But I used to watch her and—I don't know why—to be interested in her. She's a dear little Yankee woman. I've an idea she's a school-mistress taking a holiday—for which her scholars have made up a purse."

She had now turned her face a little more into profile, looking at the steep grey house-fronts opposite. On this I decided. "I shall speak to her myself."

"I wouldn't—she's very shy," said my brother-in-law.

"My dear fellow, I know her. I once showed her photographs at a tea-party." With which I went up to her, making her, as she turned to look at me, leave me in no doubt of her identity. Miss Caroline Spencer had achieved her dream. But she was less quick to recognise me and showed a slight bewilderment. I pushed a chair to the table and sat down. "Well," I said, "I hope you're not disappointed!"

She stared, blushing a little—then gave a small jump and placed me. "It was you who showed me the photographs—at North Verona."

"Yes, it was I. This happens very charmingly, for isn't it quite proper for me to give you a formal reception here—the official welcome? I talked to you so much about Europe."

"You didn't say too much. I'm so intensely happy!" she declared.

Very happy indeed she looked. There was no sign of her being older; she was as gravely, decently, demurely pretty as before. If she had struck me then as a thin-stemmed, mild-hued flower of Puritanism it may be imagined whether in her present situation this clear bloom was less appealing. Beside her an old gentleman was drinking absinthe; behind her the *dame de comptoir* in the pink ribbons called "Alcibiade, Alcibiade!" to the long-aproned waiter. I explained to Miss Spencer that the gentleman with me had lately been her shipmate, and my brother-in-law came up and was introduced to her. But she looked at him as if she had never so much as seen him, and I remembered he had told me her eyes were always fixed on the eastward horizon. She had evidently not noticed him, and, still timidly smiling, made no attempt whatever to pretend the contrary. I stayed with her on the little terrace of the café while he went back to the hotel and to his wife. I remarked to my friend that this meeting of ours at the first hour of her landing partook, among all chances, of the miraculous, but that I was delighted to be there and receive her first impressions.

"Oh I can't tell you," she said—"I feel so much in a dream. I've been sitting here an hour and I don't want to move. Everything's so delicious and romantic. I don't know whether the coffee has gone to my head—it's *so* unlike the coffee of my dead past."

"Really," I made answer, "if you're so pleased with this poor prosaic Havre you'll have no admiration left for better things. Don't spend your appreciation all the first day—remember it's your intellectual letter of credit. Remember all the beautiful places and things that are waiting for you. Remember that lovely Italy we talked about."

"I'm not afraid of running short," she said gaily, still looking at the opposite houses. "I could sit here all day—just saying to myself that here I am at last. It's so dark and strange—so old and different."

"By the way then," I asked, "how come you to be encamped in this odd place? Haven't you gone to one of the inns?" For I was half-amused, half-alarmed at the good conscience with which this delicately pretty woman had stationed herself in conspicuous isolation on the edge of the sidewalk.

"My cousin brought me here and—a little while ago—left me," she returned. "You know I told you I had a relation over here. He's still here—a real cousin. Well," she pursued with unclouded candour, "he met me at the steamer this morning."

It was absurd—and the case moreover none of my business; but I felt somehow disconcerted. "It was hardly worth his while to meet you if he was to desert you so soon."

"Oh he has only left me for half an hour," said Caroline Spencer. "He has gone to get my money."

I continued to wonder. "Where *is* your money?"

She appeared seldom to laugh, but she laughed for the joy of this. "It makes me feel very fine to tell you! It's in circular notes."

"And where are your circular notes?"

"In my cousin's pocket."

This statement was uttered with such clearness of candour that—I can hardly say why—it gave me a sensible chill. I couldn't at all at the moment have justified my lapse from ease, for I knew nothing of Miss Spencer's cousin. Since he stood in that relation to her—dear respectable little person—the presumption was in his favour. But I found myself wincing at the thought that half an hour after her landing her scanty funds should have passed into his hands. "Is he to travel with you?" I asked.

"Only as far as Paris. He's an art-student in Paris—I've always thought that so splendid. I wrote to him that I was coming, but I never expected him to come off to the ship. I supposed he'd only just meet me at the train in Paris. It's very kind of him. But he *is*," said Caroline Spencer, "very kind—and very bright."

I felt at once a strange eagerness to see this bright kind cousin who was an art-student. "He's gone to the banker's?" I enquired.

"Yes, to the banker's. He took me to an hotel—such a queer quaint cunning little place, with a court in the middle and a gallery all round, and a lovely landlady in such a beautifully fluted cap and such a perfectly fitting dress! After a while we came out to walk to the banker's, for I hadn't any French money. But I was very dizzy from the motion of the vessel and I thought I had better sit down. He found this place for me here—then he went off to the banker's himself. I'm to wait here till he comes back."

Her story was wholly lucid and my impression perfectly wanton, but it passed through my mind that the gentleman would never come back. I settled myself in a chair beside my friend and determined to await the event. She was lost in the vision and the imagination of everything near us and about us—she observed, she recognised and admired, with a touching intensity.

She noticed everything that was brought before us by the movement of the street—the peculiarities of costume, the shapes of vehicles, the big Norman horses, the fat priests, the shaven poodles. We talked of these things, and there was something charming in her freshness of perception and the way her book-nourished fancy sallied forth for the revel.

"And when your cousin comes back what are you going to do?" I went on.

For this she had, a little oddly, to think. "We don't quite know."

"When do you go to Paris? If you go by the four o'clock train I may have the pleasure of making the journey with you."

"I don't think we shall do that." So far she was prepared. "My cousin thinks I had better stay here a few days."

"Oh!" said I—and for five minutes had nothing to add. I was wondering what our absentee was, in vulgar parlance, "up to." I looked up and down the street, but saw nothing that looked like a bright and kind American art-student. At last I took the liberty of observing that the Havre was hardly a place to choose as one of the æsthetic stations of a European tour. It was a place of convenience, nothing more; a place of transit, through which transit should be rapid. I recommended her to go to Paris by the afternoon train and meanwhile to amuse herself by driving to the ancient fortress at the mouth of the harbour—that remarkable circular structure which bore the name of Francis the First and figured a sort of small Castle of Saint Angelo. (I might really have foreknown that it was to be demolished.)

She listened with much interest—then for a moment looked grave. "My cousin told me that when he returned he should have something particular to say to me, and that we could do nothing or decide nothing till I should have heard it. But I'll make him tell me right off, and then we'll go to the ancient fortress. Francis the First, did you say? Why, that's lovely. There's no hurry to get to Paris; there's plenty of time."

She smiled with her softly severe little lips as she spoke those last words, yet, looking at her with a purpose, I made out in her eyes, I thought, a tiny gleam of apprehension. "Don't tell me," I said, "that this wretched man's going to give you bad news!"

She coloured as if convicted of a hidden perversity, but she was soaring too high to drop. "Well I guess it's a *little* bad, but I don't believe it's *very* bad. At any rate I must listen to it."

I usurped an unscrupulous authority. "Look here; you didn't come to Europe to listen—you came to *see!*" But now I was sure her cousin would come back; since he had something disagreeable to say to her he'd infallibly turn up. We sat a while longer and I asked her about her plans of travel. She had them on her fingers' ends and told over the names as solemnly as a daughter of another faith might have told over the beads of a rosary: from Paris to Dijon and to Avignon, from Avignon to Marseilles and the Cornice road; thence to Genoa, to Spezia, to Pisa, to Florence, to Rome. It apparently had never occurred to her that there could be the least incommodity in her travelling alone; and since she was unprovided with a companion I of course civilly abstained from disturbing her sense of security.

At last her cousin came back. I saw him turn toward us out of a side-street, and from the moment my eyes rested on him I knew he could but be the bright, if not the kind, American art-student. He wore a slouch hat and a rusty black velvet jacket, such as I had often encountered in the Rue Bonaparte. His shirt-collar displayed a stretch of throat that at a distance wasn't strikingly statuesque. He was tall and lean, he had red hair and freckles. These items I had time to take in while he approached the café, staring at me with natural surprise from under his romantic brim. When he came up to us I immediately introduced myself as an old acquaintance of Miss Spencer's, a character she serenely permitted me to claim. He looked at me hard with a pair of small sharp eyes, then he gave me a solemn wave, in the "European" fashion, of his rather rusty sombrero.

"You weren't on the ship?" he asked.

"No, I wasn't on the ship. I've been in Europe these several years."

He bowed once more, portentously, and motioned me to be

seated again. I sat down, but only for the purpose of observing him an instant—I saw it was time I should return to my sister. Miss Spencer's European protector was, by my measure, a very queer quantity. Nature hadn't shaped him for a Raphaelesque or Byronic attire, and his velvet doublet and exhibited though not columnar throat weren't in harmony with his facial attributes. His hair was cropped close to his head; his ears were large and ill-adjusted to the same. He had a lackadaisical carriage and a sentimental droop which were peculiarly at variance with his keen conscious strange-coloured eyes—of a brown that was almost red. Perhaps I was prejudiced, but I thought his eyes too shifty. He said nothing for some time; he leaned his hands on his stick and looked up and down the street. Then at last, slowly lifting the stick and pointing with it, "That's a very nice bit," he dropped with a certain flatness. He had his head to one side— he narrowed his ugly lids. I followed the direction of his stick; the object it indicated was a red cloth hung out of an old window. "Nice bit of colour," he continued; and without moving his head transferred his half-closed gaze to me. "Composes well. Fine old tone. Make a nice thing." He spoke in a charmless vulgar voice.

"I see you've a great deal of eye," I replied. "Your cousin tells me you're studying art." He looked at me in the same way, without answering, and I went on with deliberate urbanity: "I suppose you're at the studio of one of those great men." Still on this he continued to fix me, and then he named one of the greatest of that day; which led me to ask him if he liked his master.

"Do you understand French?" he returned.

"Some kinds."

He kept his little eyes on me; with which he remarked: "Je suis fou de la peinture!"

"Oh I understand that kind!" I replied. Our companion laid her hand on his arm with a small pleased and fluttered movement; it was delightful to be among people who were on such easy terms with foreign tongues. I got up to take leave and asked her where, in Paris, I might have the honour of waiting on her. To what hotel would she go?

She turned to her cousin enquiringly and he favoured me again with his little languid leer. "Do you know the Hôtel des Princes?"

"I know where it is."

"Well, that's the shop."

"I congratulate you," I said to Miss Spencer. "I believe it's the best inn in the world; but, in case I should still have a moment to call on you here, where are you lodged?"

"Oh it's such a pretty name," she returned gleefully. "À la Belle Normande."

"I guess I know my way round!" her kinsman threw in; and as I left them he gave me with his swaggering head-cover a great flourish that was like the wave of a banner over a conquered field.

III

MY RELATIVE, as it proved, was not sufficiently restored to leave the place by the afternoon train; so that as the autumn dusk began to fall I found myself at liberty to call at the establishment named to me by my friends. I must confess that I had spent much of the interval in wondering what the disagreeable thing was that the less attractive of these had been telling the other. The *auberge* of the Belle Normande proved an hostelry in a shady by-street, where it gave me satisfaction to think Miss Spencer must have encountered local colour in abundance. There was a crooked little court, where much of the hospitality of the house was carried on; there was a staircase climbing to bedrooms on the outer side of the wall; there was a small trickling fountain with a stucco statuette set in the midst of it; there was a little boy in a white cap and apron cleaning copper vessels at a conspicuous kitchen door; there was a chattering landlady, neatly laced, arranging apricots and grapes into an artistic pyramid upon a pink plate. I looked about, and on a green bench outside of an open door labelled Salle-à-Manger, I distinguished Caroline Spencer. No sooner had I looked at her than I was sure something had happened since the morning. Supported by the back of her bench, with her hands clasped in her lap, she kept her eyes on the other side of the court, where the landlady manipulated the apricots.

But I saw that, poor dear, she wasn't thinking of apricots or even of landladies. She was staring absently, thoughtfully; on a nearer view I could have certified she had been crying. I had seated myself beside her before she was aware; then, when she had done so, she simply turned round without surprise and showed me her sad face. Something very bad indeed had happened; she was completely changed, and I immediately charged her with it. "Your cousin has been giving you bad news. You've had a horrid time."

For a moment she said nothing, and I supposed her afraid to speak lest her tears should again rise. Then it came to me that even in the few hours since my leaving her she had shed them all —which made her now intensely, stoically composed. "My poor cousin has been having one," she replied at last. "He has had great worries. His news was bad." Then after a dismally conscious wait: "He was in dreadful want of money."

"In want of yours, you mean?"

"Of any he could get—honourably of course. Mine *is* all—well, that's available."

Ah it was as if I had been sure from the first! "And he has taken it from you?"

Again she hung fire, but her face meanwhile was pleading. "I gave him what I had."

I recall the accent of those words as the most angelic human sound I had ever listened to—which is exactly why I jumped up almost with a sense of personal outrage. "Gracious goodness, madam, do you call that his getting it 'honourably'?"

I had gone too far—she coloured to her eyes. "We won't speak of it."

"We *must* speak of it," I declared as I dropped beside her again. "I'm your friend—upon my word I'm your protector; it seems to me you need one. What's the matter with this extraordinary person?"

She was perfectly able to say. "He's just badly in debt."

"No doubt he is! But what's the special propriety of your—in such tearing haste!—paying for that?"

"Well, he has told me all his story. I *feel* for him so much."

"So do I, if you come to that! But I hope," I roundly added, "he'll give you straight back your money."

As to this she was prompt. "Certainly he will—as soon as ever he can."

"And when the deuce will that be?"

Her lucidity maintained itself. "When he has finished his great picture."

It took me full in the face. "My dear young lady, damn his great picture! Where is this voracious man?"

It was as if she must let me feel a moment that I did push her!—though indeed, as appeared, he was just where he'd naturally be. "He's having his dinner."

I turned about and looked through the open door into the salle-à-manger. There, sure enough, alone at the end of a long table, was the object of my friend's compassion—the bright, the kind young art-student. He was dining too attentively to notice me at first, but in the act of setting down a well-emptied wineglass he caught sight of my air of observation. He paused in his repast and, with his head on one side and his meagre jaws slowly moving, fixedly returned my gaze. Then the landlady came brushing lightly by with her pyramid of apricots.

"And that nice little plate of fruit is for him?" I wailed.

Miss Spencer glanced at it tenderly. "They seem to arrange everything so nicely!" she simply sighed.

I felt helpless and irritated. "Come now, really," I said; "do you think it right, do you think it decent, that that long strong fellow should collar your funds?" She looked away from me—I was evidently giving her pain. The case was hopeless; the long strong fellow had "interested" her.

"Pardon me if I speak of him so unceremoniously," I said. "But you're really too generous, and he hasn't, clearly, the rudiments of delicacy. He made his debts himself—he ought to pay them himself."

"He has been foolish," she obstinately said—"of course I know that. He has told me everything. We had a long talk this morning —the poor fellow threw himself on my charity. He has signed notes to a large amount."

"The more fool he!"

"He's in real distress—and it's not only himself. It's his poor young wife."

"Ah he has a poor young wife?"

"I didn't know—but he made a clean breast of it. He married two years since—secretly."

"Why secretly?"

My informant took precautions as if she feared listeners. Then with low impressiveness: "She was a Countess!"

"Are you very sure of that?"

"She has written me the most beautiful letter."

"Asking you—whom she has never seen—for money?"

"Asking me for confidence and sympathy"—Miss Spencer spoke now with spirit. "She has been cruelly treated by her family—in consequence of what she has done for him. My cousin has told me every particular, and she appeals to me in her own lovely way in the letter, which I've here in my pocket. It's such a wonderful old-world romance," said my prodigious friend. "She was a beautiful young widow—her first husband was a Count, tremendously high-born, but really most wicked, with whom she hadn't been happy and whose death had left her ruined after he had deceived her in all sorts of ways. My poor cousin, meeting her in that situation and perhaps a little too recklessly pitying her and charmed with her, found her, don't you see?"—Caroline's appeal on this head was amazing!—"but too ready to trust a better man after all she had been through. Only when her 'people,' as he says—and I do like the word!—understood she *would* have him, poor gifted young American art-student though he simply was, because she just adored him, her great-aunt, the old Marquise, from whom she had expectations of wealth which she could yet sacrifice for her love, utterly cast her off and wouldn't so much as speak to her, much less to *him*, in their dreadful haughtiness and pride. They *can* be haughty over here, it seems," she ineffably developed—"there's no mistake about that! It's like something in some famous old book. The family, my cousin's wife's," she by this time almost complacently wound up, "are of the oldest Provençal noblesse."

I listened half-bewildered. The poor woman positively found it so interesting to be swindled by a flower of that stock—if stock or flower or solitary grain of truth was really concerned in the matter—as practically to have lost the sense of what the forfeiture of her hoard meant for her. "My dear young lady," I groaned, "you don't want to be stripped of every dollar for such a rigmarole!"

She asserted, at this, her dignity—much as a small pink shorn lamb might have done. "It isn't a rigmarole, and I shan't be stripped. I shan't live any worse than I *have* lived, don't you see? And I'll come back before long to stay with them. The Countess —he still gives her, he says, her title, as they do to noble widows, that is to 'dowagers,' don't you know? in England—insists on a visit from me *some* time. So I guess for *that* I can start afresh— and meanwhile I'll have recovered my money."

It was all too heart-breaking. "You're going home then at once?"

I felt the faint tremor of voice she heroically tried to stifle. "I've nothing left for a tour."

"You gave it *all* up?"

"I've kept enough to take me back."

I uttered, I think, a positive howl, and at this juncture the hero of the situation, the happy proprietor of my little friend's sacred savings and of the infatuated *grande dame* just sketched for me, reappeared with the clear consciousness of a repast bravely earned and consistently enjoyed. He stood on the threshold an instant, extracting the stone from a plump apricot he had fondly retained; then he put the apricot into his mouth and, while he let it gratefully dissolve there, stood looking at us with his long legs apart and his hands thrust into the pockets of his velvet coat. My companion got up, giving him a thin glance that

I caught in its passage and which expressed at once resignation
and fascination—the last dregs of her sacrifice and with it an
anguish of upliftedness. Ugly vulgar pretentious dishonest as I
thought him, and destitute of every grace of plausibility, he had
yet appealed successfully to her eager and tender imagination.
I was deeply disgusted, but I had no warrant to interfere, and
at any rate felt that it would be vain. He waved his hand meanwhile with a breadth of appreciation. "Nice old court. Nice mellow
old place. Nice crooked old staircase. Several pretty things."

Decidedly I couldn't stand it, and without responding I gave
my hand to my friend. She looked at me an instant with her little
white face and rounded eyes, and as she showed her pretty teeth
I suppose she meant to smile. "Don't be sorry for me," she sublimely pleaded; "I'm very sure I shall see something of this dear
old Europe yet."

I refused however to take literal leave of her—I should find a
moment to come back next morning. Her awful kinsman, who had
put on his sombrero again, flourished it off at me by way of a
bow—on which I hurried away.

On the morrow early I did return, and in the court of the inn
met the landlady, more loosely laced than in the evening. On my
asking for Miss Spencer, "*Partie,* monsieur," the good woman
said. "She went away last night at ten o'clock, with her—her—not
her husband, eh?—in fine her Monsieur. They went down to the
American ship." I turned off—I felt the tears in my eyes. The
poor girl had been some thirteen hours in Europe.

IV

I MYSELF, more fortunate, continued to sacrifice to opportunity
as I myself met it. During this period—of some five years—I
lost my friend Latouche, who died of a malarious fever during
a tour in the Levant. One of the first things I did on my return
to America was to go up to North Verona on a consolatory visit
to his poor mother. I found her in deep affliction and sat with her
the whole of the morning that followed my arrival—I had come
in late at night—listening to her tearful descant and singing the

praises of my friend. We talked of nothing else, and our conversation ended only with the arrival of a quick little woman who drove herself up to the door in a "carry-all" and whom I saw toss the reins to the horse's back with the briskness of a startled sleeper throwing off the bedclothes. She jumped out of the carry-all and she jumped into the room. She proved to be the minister's wife and the great town-gossip, and she had evidently, in the latter capacity, a choice morsel to communicate. I was as sure of this as I was that poor Mrs. Latouche was not absolutely too bereaved to listen to her. It seemed to me discreet to retire, and I described myself as anxious for a walk before dinner.

"And by the way," I added, "if you'll tell me where my old friend Miss Spencer lives, I think I'll call on her."

The minister's wife immediately responded. Miss Spencer lived in the fourth house beyond the Baptist church; the Baptist church was the one on the right, with that queer green thing over the door; they called it a portico, but it looked more like an old-fashioned bedstead swung in the air. "Yes, do look up poor Caroline," Mrs. Latouche further enjoined. "It will refresh her to see a strange face."

"I should think she had had enough of strange faces!" cried the minister's wife.

"To see, I mean, a charming visitor"—Mrs. Latouche amended her phrase.

"I should think she had had enough of charming visitors!" her companion returned. "But *you* don't mean to stay ten years," she added with significant eyes on me.

"Has she a visitor of that sort?" I asked in my ignorance.

"You'll make out the sort!" said the minister's wife. "She's easily seen; she generally sits in the front yard. Only take care what you say to her, and be very sure you're polite."

"Ah she's so sensitive?"

The minister's wife jumped up and dropped me a curtsey—a most sarcastic curtsey. "That's what she is, if you please. 'Madame la Comtesse!'"

And pronouncing these titular words with the most scathing

accent, the little woman seemed fairly to laugh in the face of the lady they designated. I stood staring, wondering, remembering.

"Oh I shall be very polite!" I cried; and, grasping my hat and stick, I went on my way.

I found Miss Spencer's residence without difficulty. The Baptist church was easily identified, and the small dwelling near it, of a rusty white, with a large central chimney-stack and a Virginia creeper, seemed naturally and properly the abode of a withdrawn old maid with a taste for striking effects inexpensively obtained. As I approached I slackened my pace, for I had heard that some one was always sitting in the front yard, and I wished to reconnoitre. I looked cautiously over the low white fence that separated the small garden-space from the unpaved street, but I descried nothing in the shape of a Comtesse. A small straight path led up to the crooked door-step, on either side of which was a little grass-plot fringed with currant-bushes. In the middle of the grass, right and left, was a large quince-tree, full of antiquity and contortions, and beneath one of the quince-trees were placed a small table and a couple of light chairs. On the table lay a piece of unfinished embroidery and two or three books in bright-coloured paper covers. I went in at the gate and paused halfway along the path, scanning the place for some further token of its occupant, before whom—I could hardly have said why—I hesitated abruptly to present myself. Then I saw the poor little house to be of the shabbiest and felt a sudden doubt of my right to penetrate, since curiosity had been my motive and curiosity here failed of confidence. While I demurred a figure appeared in the open doorway and stood there looking at me. I immediately recognized Miss Spencer, but she faced me as if we had never met. Gently, but gravely and timidly, I advanced to the door-step, where I spoke with an attempt at friendly banter.

"I waited for you over there to come back, but you never came."

"Waited where, sir?" she quavered, her innocent eyes rounding themselves as of old. She was much older; she looked tired and wasted.

"Well," I said, "I waited at the old French port."

She stared harder, then recognised me, smiling, flushing, clasping her two hands together. "I remember you now—I remember that day." But she stood there, neither coming out nor asking me to come in. She was embarrassed.

I too felt a little awkward while I poked at the path with my stick. "I kept looking out for you year after year."

"You mean in Europe?" she ruefully breathed.

"In Europe of course! Here apparently you're easy enough to find."

She leaned her hand against the unpainted door-post and her head fell a little to one side. She looked at me thus without speaking, and I caught the expression visible in women's eyes when tears are rising. Suddenly she stepped out on the cracked slab of stone before her threshold and closed the door. Then her strained smile prevailed and I saw her teeth were as pretty as ever. But there had been tears too. "Have you been there ever since?" she lowered her voice to ask.

"Until three weeks ago. And you—you never came back?"

Still shining at me as she could, she put her hand behind her and reopened the door. "I'm not very polite," she said. "Won't you come in?"

"I'm afraid I incommode you."

"Oh no!"—she wouldn't hear of it now. And she pushed back the door with a sign that I should enter.

I followed her in. She led the way to a small room on the left of the narrow hall, which I supposed to be her parlour, though it was at the back of the house, and we passed the closed door of another apartment which apparently enjoyed a view of the quince-trees. This one looked out upon a small wood-shed and two clucking hens. But I thought it pretty until I saw its elegance to be of the most frugal kind; after which, presently, I thought it prettier still, for I had never seen faded chintz and old mezzotint engravings, framed in varnished autumn leaves, disposed with so touching a grace. Miss Spencer sat down on a very small section of the sofa, her hands tightly clasped in her lap. She looked ten years older, and I needn't now have felt called to insist on the facts of her person. But I still thought them interesting, and at any rate I was moved by them. She was peculiarly agitated. I tried to appear not to notice it; but suddenly, in the most inconsequent fashion—it was an irresistible echo of our concentrated passage in the old French port—I said to her: "I do incommode you. Again you're in distress."

She raised her two hands to her face and for a moment kept it buried in them. Then taking them away, "It's because you remind me," she said.

"I remind you, you mean, of that miserable day at the Havre?"

She wonderfully shook her head. "It wasn't miserable. It was delightful."

Ah was it? my manner of receiving this must have commented. "I never was so shocked as when, on going back to your inn the next morning, I found you had wretchedly retreated."

She waited an instant, after which she said: "Please let us not speak of that."

"Did you come straight back here?" I nevertheless went on.

"I was back here just thirty days after my first start."

"And here you've remained ever since?"

"Every minute of the time."

I took it in; I didn't know what to say, and what I presently said had almost the sound of mockery. "When then are you going to make that tour?" It might be practically aggressive; but there was something that irritated me in her depths of resignation, and I wished to extort from her some expression of impatience.

She attached her eyes a moment to a small sun-spot on the carpet; then she got up and lowered the window-blind a little to obliterate it. I waited, watching her with interest—as if she had still something more to give me. Well, presently, in answer to my last question, she gave it. "Never!"

"I hope at least your cousin repaid you that money," I said.

At this again she looked away from me. "I don't care for it now."

"You don't care for your money?"

"For ever going to Europe."

"Do you mean you wouldn't go if you could?"

"I can't—I can't," said Caroline Spencer. "It's all over. Everything's different. I never think of it."

"The scoundrel never repaid you then!" I cried.

"Please, please—!" she began.

But she had stopped—she was looking toward the door. There had been a rustle and a sound of steps in the hall.

I also looked toward the door, which was open and now admitted another person—a lady who paused just within the threshold. Behind her came a young man. The lady looked at me with a good deal of fixedness—long enough for me to rise to a vivid impression of herself. Then she turned to Caroline Spencer and, with a smile and a strong foreign accent, *"Pardon, ma chère!* I didn't know you had company," she said. "The gentleman came in so quietly." With which she again gave me the benefit of her attention. She was very strange, yet I was at once sure I had seen her before. Afterwards I rather put it that I had only seen ladies remarkably like her. But I had seen them very far away from North Verona, and it was the oddest of all things to meet one of them in that frame. To what quite other scene did the sight of her transport me? To some dusky landing before a shabby Parisian *quatrième*—to an open door revealing a greasy antechamber and to Madame leaning over the banisters while she holds a faded wrapper together and bawls down to the portress to bring up her coffee. My friend's guest was a very large lady, of middle age, with a plump dead-white face and hair drawn back *à la chinoise*. She had a small penetrating eye and what is called in French *le sourire agréable*. She wore an old pink cashmere dressing-gown covered with white embroideries, and, like the figure in my momentary vision, she confined it in front with a bare and rounded arm and a plump and deeply-dimpled hand.

"It's only to spick about my café," she said to her hostess with her *sourire agréable*. "I should like it served in the garden under the leetle tree."

The young man behind her had now stepped into the room,

where he also stood revealed, though with rather less of a challenge. He was a gentleman of few inches but a vague importance, perhaps the leading man of the world of North Verona. He had a small pointed nose and a small pointed chin; also, as I observed, the most diminutive feet and a manner of no point at all. He looked at me foolishly and with his mouth open.

"You shall have your coffee," said Miss Spencer as if an army of cooks had been engaged in the preparation of it.

"C'est bien!" said her massive inmate. "Find your bouk"— and this personage turned to the gaping youth.

He gaped now at each quarter of the room. "My grammar, d' ye mean?"

The large lady however could but face her friend's visitor while persistently engaged with a certain laxity in the flow of her wrapper. "Find your bouk," she more absently repeated.

"My poetry, d' ye mean?" said the young man, who also couldn't take his eyes off me.

"Never mind your bouk"—his companion reconsidered. "To-day we'll just talk. We'll make some conversation. But we mustn't interrupt Mademoiselle's. Come, come"—and she moved off a step. "Under the leetle tree," she added for the benefit of Mademoiselle. After which she gave me a thin salutation, jerked a measured "Monsieur!" and swept away again with her swain following.

I looked at Miss Spencer, whose eyes never moved from the carpet, and I spoke, I fear, without grace. "Who in the world's that?"

"The Comtesse—that *was:* my *cousine* as they call it in French."

"And who's the young man?"

"The Countess's pupil, Mr. Mixter." This description of the tie uniting the two persons who had just quitted us must certainly have upset my gravity; for I recall the marked increase of my friend's own as she continued to explain. "She gives lessons in French and music, the simpler sorts—"

"The simpler sorts of French?" I fear I broke in.

But she was still impenetrable, and in fact had now an intonation that put me vulgarly in the wrong. "She has had the worst reverses—with no one to look to. She's prepared for any exertion —and she takes her misfortunes with gaiety."

"Ah well," I returned—no doubt a little ruefully, "that's all I myself am pretending to do. If she's determined to be a burden to nobody, nothing could be more right and proper."

My hostess looked vaguely, though I thought quite wearily enough, about: she met this proposition in no other way. "I must go and get the coffee," she simply said.

"Has the lady many pupils?" I none the less persisted.

"She has only Mr. Mixter. She gives him all her time." It might have set me off again, but something in my whole impression of my friend's sensibility urged me to keep strictly decent. "He pays very well," she at all events inscrutably went on. "He's not very bright—as a pupil; but he's very rich and he's very kind. He has a buggy—with a back, and he takes the Countess to drive."

"For good long spells I hope," I couldn't help interjecting— even at the cost of her so taking it that she had still to avoid my eyes. "Well, the country's beautiful for miles," I went on. And then as she was turning away: "You're going for the Countess's coffee?"

"If you'll excuse me a few moments."

"Is there no one else to do it?"

She seemed to wonder who there should be. "I keep no servants."

"Then can't I help?" After which, as she but looked at me, I bettered it. "Can't she wait on herself?"

Miss Spencer had a slow headshake—as if that too had been a strange idea. "She isn't used to *manual* labour."

The discrimination was a treat, but I cultivated decorum. "I see—and you *are*." But at the same time I couldn't abjure curiosity. "Before you go, at any rate, please tell me this: who *is* this wonderful lady?"

"I told you just who in France—that extraordinary day. She's the wife of my cousin, whom you saw there."

"The lady disowned by her family in consequence of her marriage?"

"Yes; they've never seen her again. They've completely broken with her."

"And where's her husband?"

"My poor cousin's dead."

I pulled up, but only a moment. "And where's your money?"

The poor thing flinched—I kept her on the rack. "I don't know," she woefully said.

I scarce know what it didn't prompt me to—but I went step by step. "On her husband's death this lady at once came to you?"

It was as if she had had too often to describe it. "Yes, she arrived one day."

"How long ago?"

"Two years and four months."

"And has been here ever since?"

"Ever since."

I took it all in. "And how does she like it?"

"Well, not *very* much," said Miss Spencer divinely.

That too I took in. "And how do *you*—?"

She laid her face in her two hands an instant as she had done ten minutes before. Then, quickly, she went to get the Countess's coffee.

Left alone in the little parlour I found myself divided between the perfection of my disgust and a contrary wish to see, to learn more. At the end of a few minutes the young man in attendance on the lady in question reappeared as for a fresh gape at me. He was inordinately grave—to be dressed in such parti-coloured flannels; and he produced with no great confidence on his own side the message with which he had been charged. "She wants to know if you won't come right out."

"Who wants to know?"

"The countess. That French lady."

"She has asked you to bring me?"

"Yes sir," said the young man feebly—for I may claim to have surpassed him in stature and weight.

I went out with him, and we found his instructress seated under one of the small quince-trees in front of the house; where she was engaged in drawing a fine needle with a very fat hand through a piece of embroidery not remarkable for freshness. She pointed graciously to the chair beside her and I sat down. Mr. Mixter glanced about him and then accommodated himself on the grass at her feet; whence he gazed upward more gapingly than ever and as if convinced that between us something wonderful would now occur.

"I'm sure you spick French," said the Countess, whose eyes were singularly protuberant as she played over me her agreeable smile.

"I do, madam—*tant bien que mal*," I replied, I fear, more dryly.

"Ah voilà!" she cried as with delight. "I knew it as soon as I looked at you. You've been in my poor dear country."

"A considerable time."

"You love it then, *mon pays de France?*"

"Oh it's an old affection." But I wasn't exuberant.

"And you know Paris well?"

"Yes, *sans me vanter*, madam, I think I really do." And with a certain conscious purpose I let my eyes meet her own.

She presently, hereupon, moved her own and glanced down at Mr. Mixter. "What are we talking about?" she demanded of her attentive pupil.

He pulled his knees up, plucked at the grass, stared, blushed a little. "You're talking French," said Mr. Mixter.

"*La belle découverte!*" mocked the Countess. "It's going on ten months," she explained to me, "since I took him in hand. Don't put yourself out not to say he's *la bêtise même*," she added in fine style. "He won't in the least understand you."

A moment's consideration of Mr. Mixter, awkwardly sporting at our feet, quite assured me that he wouldn't. "I hope your other pupils do you more honour," I then remarked to my entertainer.

"I have no others. They don't know what French—or what anything else—is in this place; they don't want to know. You may therefore imagine the pleasure it is to me to meet a person who speaks it like yourself." I could but reply that my own pleasure wasn't less, and she continued to draw the stitches through her embroidery with an elegant curl of her little finger. Every few moments she put her eyes, near-sightedly, closer to her work—this as if for elegance too. She inspired me with no more confidence than her late husband, if husband he was, had done, years before, on the occasion with which this one so destestably matched: she was coarse, common, affected, dishonest—no more a Countess than I was a Caliph. She had an assurance—based clearly on experience; but this couldn't have been the experience of "race." Whatever it was indeed it did now, in a yearning fashion, flare out of her. "Talk to me of Paris, *mon beau Paris* that I'd give my eyes to see. The very name of it *me fait languir*. How long since you were there?"

"A couple of months ago."

"*Vous avez de la chance!* Tell me something about it. What were they doing? Oh for an hour of the Boulevard!"

"They were doing about what they're always doing—amusing themselves a good deal."

"At the theatres, *hein?*" sighed the Countess. "At the cafés-concerts? *sous ce beau ciel*—at the little tables before the doors? *Quelle existence!* You know I'm a Parisienne, monsieur," she added, "to my finger-tips."

"Miss Spencer was mistaken then," I ventured to return, "in telling me you're a Provençale."

She stared a moment, then put her nose to her embroidery, which struck me as having acquired even while we sat a dingier and more desultory air. "Ah I'm a Provençale by birth, but a Parisienne by—inclination." After which she pursued: "And by the saddest events of my life—as well as by some of the happiest, hélas!"

"In other words by a varied experience!" I now at last smiled.

She questioned me over it with her hard little salient eyes. "Oh experience!—I could talk of that, no doubt, if I wished. *On en a de toutes les sortes*—and I never dreamed that mine, for example, would ever have *this* in store for me." And she indicated with her large bare elbow and with a jerk of her head all surrounding objects; the little white house, the pair of quince-trees, the rickety paling, even the rapt Mr. Mixter.

I took them all bravely in. "Ah if you mean you're decidedly in exile—!"

"You may imagine what it is. These two years of my *épreuve* —*elles m'en ont données, des heures, des heures!* One gets used to things"—and she raised her shoulders to the highest shrug ever accomplished at North Verona; "so that I sometimes think I've got used to this. But there are some things that are always beginning again. For example my coffee."

I so far again lent myself. "Do you always have coffee at this hour?"

Her eyebrows went up as high as her shoulders had done. "At what hour would you propose to me to have it? I must have my little cup after breakfast."

"Ah you breakfast at this hour?"

"At mid-day—*comme cela se fait*. Here they breakfast at a quarter past seven. That 'quarter past' is charming!"

"But you were telling me about your coffee," I observed sympathetically.

"My *cousine* can't believe in it; she can't understand it. C'est une fille charmante, but that little cup of black coffee with a drop of '*fine*,' served at this hour—they exceed her comprehension. So I have to break the ice each day, and it takes the coffee the time you see to arrive. And when it does arrive, monsieur—! If I don't press it on *you*—though monsieur here sometimes joins me!—it's because you've drunk it on the Boulevard."

I resented extremely so critical a view of my poor friend's exertions, but I said nothing at all—the only way to be sure of my civility. I dropped my eyes on Mr. Mixter, who, sitting cross-legged and nursing his knees, watched my companion's foreign graces with an interest that familiarity had apparently done little

to restrict. She became aware, naturally, of my mystified view
of him and faced the question with all her boldness. "He adores
me, you know," she murmured with her nose again in her tapestry
—"he dreams of becoming *mon amoureux*. Yes, *il me fait une cour
acharnée*—such as you see him. That's what we've come to. He
has read some French novel—it took him six months. But ever
since that he has thought himself a hero and me—such as I am,
monsieur—*je ne sais quelle dévergondée!*"

Mr. Mixter may have inferred that he was to that extent the
object of our reference; but of the manner in which he was han-
dled he must have had small suspicion—preoccupied as he was,
as to my companion, with the ecstasy of contemplation. Our
hostess moreover at this moment came out of the house, bearing
a coffee-pot and three cups on a neat little tray. I took from her
eyes, as she approached us, a brief but intense appeal—the mute
expression as I felt, conveyed in the hardest little look she had yet
addressed me, of her longing to know what, as a man of the world
in general and of the French world in particular, I thought of
these allied forces now so encamped on the stricken field of her
life. I could only "act" however, as they said at North Verona,
quite impenetrably—only make no answering sign. I couldn't
intimate, much less could I frankly utter, my inward sense of the
Countess's probable past, with its measure of her virtue, value
and accomplishments, and of the limits of the consideration to
which she could properly pretend. I couldn't give my friend a hint
of how I myself personally "saw" her interesting pensioner—
whether as the runaway wife of a too-jealous hair-dresser or of a
too-morose pastry-cook, say; whether as a very small bourgeoise,
in fine, who had vitiated her case beyond patching up, or even
as some character, of the nomadic sort, less edifying still. I
couldn't let in, by the jog of a shutter, as it were, a hard informing
ray and then, washing my hands of the business, turn my back
for ever. I could on the contrary but save the situation, my own
at least, for the moment, by pulling myself together with a master
hand and appearing to ignore everything but that the dreadful
person between us *was* a "grande dame." This effort was possible

indeed but as a retreat in good order and with all the forms of courtesy. If I couldn't speak, still less could I stay, and I think I must, in spite of everything, have turned black with disgust to see Caroline Spencer stand there like a waiting-maid. I therefore won't answer for the shade of success that may have attended my saying to the Countess, on my feet and as to leave her: "You expect to remain some time in these *parages?*"

What passed between us, as from face to face, while she looked up at me, *that* at least our companion may have caught, that at least may have sown, for the aftertime, some seed of revelation. The Countess repeated her terrible shrug. "Who knows? I don't see my way—! It isn't an existence, but when one's in misery—! *Chère belle,*" she added as an appeal to Miss Spencer, "you've gone and forgotten the *'fine'!*"

I detained that lady as, after considering a moment in silence the small array, she was about to turn off in quest of this article. I held out my hand in silence—I had to go. Her wan set little face, severely mild and with the question of a moment before now quite cold in it, spoke of extreme fatigue, but also of something else strange and conceived—whether a desperate patience still, or at last some other desperation, being more than I can say. What was clearest on the whole was that she was glad I was going. Mr. Mixter had risen to his feet and was pouring out the Countess's coffee. As I went back past the Baptist church I could feel how right my poor friend had been in her conviction at the other, the still intenser, the now historic crisis, that she should still see something of that dear old Europe.

AN INTERNATIONAL EPISODE

I

FOUR YEARS AGO—in 1874—two young Englishmen had occasion to go to the United States. They crossed the ocean at midsummer and, arriving in New York on the first day of August, were much struck with the high, the torrid temperature. Disembarking upon the wharf they climbed into one of the huge high-hung coaches that convey passengers to the hotels, and with a great deal of bouncing and bumping they took their course through Broadway. The midsummer aspect of New York is doubtless not the most engaging, though nothing perhaps could well more solicit an alarmed attention. Of quite other sense and sound from those of any typical English street was the endless rude channel, rich in incongruities, through which our two travellers advanced—looking out on either side at the rough animation of the sidewalks, at the high-coloured heterogeneous architecture, at the huge white marble façades that, bedizened with gilded lettering, seemed to glare in the strong crude light, at the multifarious awnings, banners and streamers, at the extraordinary number of omnibuses, horse-cars and other democratic vehicles, at the vendors of cooling fluids, the white trousers and big straw hats of the policemen, the tripping gait of the modish young persons on the pavement, the general brightness, newness, juvenility, both of people and things. The young men had exchanged few observations, but in crossing Union Square, in front of the monument to Washington—in the very shadow indeed projected by the image of the *pater patriae*—one of them remarked to the other: "Awfully rum place."

"Ah very odd, very odd," said the other, who was the clever man of the two.

"Pity it's so beastly hot," resumed the first speaker after a pause.

"You know we're in a low latitude," said the clever man.

"I dare say," remarked his friend.

"I wonder," said the second speaker presently, "if they can give one a bath."

"I dare say not," the other returned.

"Oh I say!" cried his comrade.

This animated discussion dropped on their arrival at the hotel, recommended to them by an American gentleman whose acquaintance they had made—with whom, indeed, they had become very intimate—on the steamer and who had proposed to accompany them to the inn and introduce them in a friendly way to the proprietor. This plan, however, had been defeated by their friend's finding his "partner" in earnest attendance on the wharf, with urgent claims on his immediate presence of mind. But the two Englishmen, with nothing beyond their national prestige and personal graces to recommend them, were very well received at the hotel, which had an air of capacious hospitality. They found a bath not unattainable and were indeed struck with the facilities for prolonged and reiterated immersion with which their apartment was supplied. After bathing a good deal—more indeed than they had ever done before on a single occasion—they made their way to the dining-room of the hotel, which was a spacious restaurant with a fountain in the middle, a great many tall plants in ornamental tubs and an array of French waiters. The first dinner on land, after a sea-voyage, is in any connexion a delightful hour, and there was much that ministered to ease in the general situation of our young men. They were formed for good spirits and addicted and appointed to hilarity; they were more observant than they appeared; they were, in an inarticulate accidentally dissimulative fashion, capable of high appreciation. This was perhaps especially the case with the elder, who was also, as I have said, the man of talent. They sat down at a little table which was a very different affair from the great clattering see-saw in the saloon of the steamer. The wide doors and windows of the restaurant stood open, beneath large awnings, to a wide expanse studded with other plants in tubs and rows of spreading trees— beyond which appeared a large shady square without palings and with marble-paved walks. And above the vivid verdure rose other façades of white marble and of pale chocolate-coloured stone, squaring themselves against the deep blue sky. Here, outside, in the light and the shade and the heat, was a great tinkling of the bells of innumerable street-cars and a constant strolling and shuf-fling and rustling of many pedestrians, extremely frequent among whom were young women in Pompadour-looking dresses. The place within was cool and vaguely-lighted; with the plash of water, the odour of flowers and the flitting of French waiters, as I have said, on soundless carpets.

"It's rather like Paris, you know," said the younger of our two travellers.

"It's like Paris—only more so," his companion returned.

"I suppose it's the French waiters," said the first speaker. "Why don't they have French waiters in London?"

"Ah but fancy a French waiter at a London club!" said his friend.

The elder man stared as if he couldn't fancy it. "In Paris I'm very apt to dine at a place where there's an English waiter. Don't you know, what's-his-name's, close to the thingumbob? They always set an English waiter at me. I suppose they think I can't speak French."

"No more you can!" And this candid critic unfolded his napkin.

The other paid no heed whatever to his candour. "I say," the latter resumed in a moment, "I suppose we must learn to speak American. I suppose we must take lessons."

"I can't make them out, you know," said the clever man.

"What the deuce is *he* saying?" asked his comrade, appealing from the French waiter.

"He's recommending some soft-shell crabs," said the clever man.

And so, in a desultory view of the mysteries of the new world bristling about them, the young Englishmen proceeded to dine—

going in largely, as the phrase is, for cooling draughts and dishes, as to which their attendant submitted to them a hundred alternatives. After dinner they went out and slowly walked about the neighbouring streets. The early dusk of waning summer was at hand, but the heat still very great. The pavements were hot even to the stout boot-soles of the British travellers, and the trees along the kerb-stone emitted strange exotic odours. The young men wandered through the adjoining square—that queer place without palings and with marble walks arranged in black and white lozenges. There were a great many benches crowded with shabby-looking people, and the visitors remarked very justly that it wasn't much like Grosvenor Square. On one side was an enormous hotel, lifting up into the hot darkness an immense array of open and brightly-lighted windows. At the base of this populous structure was an eternal jangle of horse-cars, and all round it, in the upper dusk, a sinister hum of mosquitoes. The ground-floor of the hotel, figuring a huge transparent cage, flung a wide glare of gaslight into the street, of which it formed a public adjunct, absorbing and emitting the passers-by promiscuously. The young Englishmen went in with every one else, from curiosity, and saw a couple of hundred men sitting on divans along a great marble-paved corridor, their legs variously stretched out, together with several dozen more standing in a cue, as at the ticket-office of a railway station, before a vast marble altar of sacrifice, a thing shaped like the counter of a huge shop. These latter persons, who carried portmanteaux in their hands, had a dejected exhausted look; their garments were not fresh, as if telling of some rush, or some fight, for life, and they seemed to render mystic tribute to a magnificent young man with a waxed moustache and a shirt front adorned with diamond buttons, who every now and then dropped a cold glance over their multitudinous patience. They were American citizens doing homage to an hotel-clerk.

"I'm glad he didn't tell us to go there," said one of our Englishmen, alluding to their friend on the steamer, who had told them so many things. They walked up the Fifth Avenue, where he had for instance told them all the first families lived. But the first families were out of town, and our friends had but the satisfaction of seeing some of the second—or perhaps even the third—taking the evening air on balconies and high flights of doorsteps in streets at right angles to the main straight channel. They went a little way down one of these side-streets and there saw young ladies in white dresses—charming-looking persons—seated in graceful attitudes on the chocolate-coloured steps. In one or two places these young ladies were conversing across the street with other young ladies seated in similar postures and costumes in front of the opposite houses, and in the warm night air their colloquial tones sounded strangely in the ears of the young Englishmen. One of the latter, nevertheless—the younger—betrayed a disposition to intercept some stray item of this interchange and see what it would lead to; but his companion observed pertinently enough that he had better be careful. They mustn't begin by making mistakes.

"But he told us, you know—he told us," urged the young man, alluding again to the friend on the steamer.

"Never mind what he told us!" answered his elder, who, if he had more years and a more developed wit, was also apparently more of a moralist.

By bedtime—in their impatience to taste of a terrestrial couch again our seafarers went to bed early—it was still insufferably hot, and the buzz of the mosquitoes at the open windows might have passed for an audible crepitation of the temperature. "We can't stand this, you know," the young Englishmen said to each other; and they tossed about all night more boisterously than they had been tossed by Atlantic billows. On the morrow their first thought was that they would re-embark that day for England, but it then occurred to them they might find an asylum nearer at hand. The cave of Æolus became their ideal of comfort, and they wondered where the Americans went when wishing to cool off. They hadn't the least idea, and resolved to apply for information to Mr. J. L. Westgate. This was the name inscribed in a bold hand on the back of a letter carefully preserved in the pocket-book of our younger gentleman. Beneath the address, in the left-hand corner of the envelope, were the words "Introducing Lord Lambeth and Percy Beaumont Esq." The letter had been given to the two Englishmen by a good friend of theirs in London, who had been in America two years previously and had singled out Mr. J. L. Westgate from the many friends he had left there as the consignee, as it were, of his compatriots. "He's really very decent," the Englishman in London had said, "and he has an awfully pretty wife. He's tremendously hospitable—he'll do everything in the world for you, and as he knows every one over there it's quite needless I should give you any other introduction. He'll make you see every one—trust him for the right kick-off. He has a tremendously pretty wife." It was natural that in the hour of tribulation Lord Lambeth and Mr. Percy Beaumont should have bethought themselves of so possible a benefactor; all the more so that he lived in the Fifth Avenue and that the Fifth Avenue, as they had ascertained the night before, was contiguous to their hotel. "Ten to one he'll be out of town," said Percy Beaumont; "but we can at least find out where he has gone and can at once give chase. He can't possibly have gone to a hotter place, you know."

"Oh there's only one hotter place," said Lord Lambeth, "and I hope he hasn't gone there."

They strolled along the shady side of the street to the number indicated by the precious letter. The house presented an imposing chocolate-coloured expanse, relieved by facings and window-cornices of florid sculpture and by a couple of dusty rose-trees which clambered over the balconies and the portico. This last-mentioned feature was approached by a monumental flight of steps.

"Rather better than a dirty London thing," said Lord Lambeth, looking down from this altitude after they had rung the bell.

"It depends upon what London thing you mean," replied his companion. "You've a tremendous chance to get wet between the house-door and your carriage."

"Well," said Lord Lambeth, glancing at the blaze of the sky, "I 'guess' it doesn't rain so much here!"

The door was opened by a long negro in a white jacket, who grinned familiarly when Lord Lambeth asked for Mr. Westgate. "He ain't at home, sir; he's down town at his o'fice."

"Oh at his office?" said the visitors. "And when will he be at home?"

"Well, when he goes out dis way in de mo'ning he ain't liable to come home all day."

This was discouraging; but the address of Mr. Westgate's office was freely imparted by the intelligent black and was taken down by Percy Beaumont in his pocket-book. The comrades then returned, languidly enough, to their hotel and sent for a hackney-coach; and in this commodious vehicle they rolled comfortably down town. They measured the whole length of Broadway again and found it a path of fire; and then, deflecting to the left, were deposited by their conductor before a fresh light ornamental structure, ten stories high, in a street crowded with keen-faced light-limbed young men who were running about very nimbly and stopping each other eagerly at corners and in doorways. Passing under portals that were as the course of a twofold torrent, they were introduced by one of the keen-faced young men—he was a charming fellow in wonderful cream-coloured garments and a hat with a blue ribbon, who had evidently recognised them as aliens and helpless—to a very snug hydraulic elevator, in which they took their place with many other persons and which, shooting upward in its vertical socket, presently projected them into the seventh heaven, as it were, of the edifice. Here, after brief delay, they found themselves face to face with the friend of their friend in London. His office was composed of several conjoined rooms, and they waited very silently in one of these after they had sent in their letter and their cards. The letter was not one it would take Mr. Westgate very long to read, but he came out to speak to them more instantly than they could have expected; he had evidently jumped up from work. He was a tall lean personage and was dressed all in fresh white linen; he had a thin sharp familiar face, a face suggesting one of the ingenious modern objects with alternative uses, good as a blade or as a hammer, good for the deeps and for the shallows. His forehead was high but expressive, his eyes sharp but amused, and a large brown moustache, which concealed his mouth, made his chin, beneath it, look small. Relaxed though he was at this moment Lord Lambeth judged him on the spot tremendously clever.

"How do you do, Lord Lambeth, how do you do, sir?"—he held the open letter in his hand. "I'm very glad to meet you—I hope you're very well. You had better come in here—I think it's cooler"; and he led the way into another room, where there were law-books and papers and where windows opened wide under striped awnings. Just opposite one of the windows, on a line with his eyes, Lord Lambeth observed the weather-vane of a church-steeple. The uproar of the street sounded infinitely far below, and his lordship felt high indeed in the air. "I say it's cooler," pursued their host, "but everything's relative. How do you stand the heat?"

"I can't say we like it," said Lord Lambeth; "but Beaumont likes it better than I."

"Well, I guess it will break," Mr. Westgate cheerfully declared; "there's never anything bad over here but it does break. It was very hot when Captain Littledale was here; he did nothing but drink sherry-cobblers. He expresses some doubt in his letter whether I shall remember him—as if I don't remember once mixing six sherry-cobblers for him in about fifteen minutes. I hope you left him well. I'd be glad to mix him some more."

"Oh yes, he's all right—and without *them*," said Lord Lambeth.

"I'm always very glad to see your countrymen," Mr. Westgate pursued. "I thought it would be time some of you should be coming along. A friend of mine was saying to me only a day or two ago 'It's time for the water-melons and the Englishmen.'"

"The Englishmen and the water-melons just now are about the same thing," Percy Beaumont observed with a wipe of his dripping forehead.

"Ah well, we'll put you on ice as we do the melons. You must go down to Newport."

"We'll go anywhere!" said Lord Lambeth.

"Yes, you want to go to Newport; that's what you want to do." Mr. Westgate was very positive. "But let's see—when did you get here?"

"Only yesterday," said Percy Beaumont.

"Ah yes, by the *Russia*. Where are you staying?"

"At the Hanover, I think they call it."

"Pretty comfortable?" enquired Mr. Westgate.

"It seems a capital place, but I can't say we like the gnats," said Lord Lambeth.

Mr. Westgate stared and laughed. "Oh no, of course you don't like the gnats. We shall expect you to like a good many things over here, but we shan't insist on your liking the gnats; though certainly you'll admit that, as gnats, they're big things, eh? But you oughtn't to remain in the city."

"So we think," said Lord Lambeth. "If you'd kindly suggest something—"

"Suggest something, my dear sir?"—and Mr. Westgate looked him over with narrowed eyelids. "Open your mouth and shut your eyes! Leave it to me and I'll fix you all right. It's a matter of national pride with me that all Englishmen should have a good time, and as I've been through a good deal with them I've learned to minister to their wants. I find they generally want the true thing. So just please consider yourselves my property; and if any one should try to appropriate you please say 'Hands off—too late for the market.' But let's see," continued the American with his face of toil, his voice of leisure and his general intention, apparently, of everything; "let's see: are you going to make something of a stay, Lord Lambeth?"

"Oh dear no," said the young Englishman; "my cousin was to make this little visit, so I just came with him at an hour's notice, for the lark."

"Is it your first time over here?"

"Oh dear yes."

"I was obliged to come on some business," Percy Beaumont explained, "and I brought Lambeth along for company."

"And *you* have been here before, sir?"

"Never, never!"

"I thought from your referring to business—" Mr. Westgate threw off.

"Oh you see I'm just acting for some English shareholders by way of legal advice. Some of my friends—well, if the truth must be told" Mr. Beaumont laughed—"have a grievance against one of your confounded railways, and they've asked me to come and judge, if possible, on the spot, what they can hope."

Mr. Westgate's amused eyes grew almost tender. "What's your railroad?" he asked.

"The Tennessee Central."

The American tilted back his chair and poised it an instant. "Well, I'm sorry you want to attack one of our institutions. But I guess you had better enjoy yourself *first!*"

"I'm certainly rather afraid I can't work in this weather," the young emissary confessed.

"Leave that to the natives," said Mr. Westgate. "Leave the Tennessee Central to me, Mr. Beaumont. I guess I can tell you more about it than most any one. But I didn't know you Englishmen ever did any work—in the upper classes."

"Oh we do a lot of work, don't we, Lambeth?" Percy Beaumont appealed.

"I must certainly be back early for *my* engagements," said his companion irrelevantly but gently.

"For the shooting, eh? or is it the yachting or the hunting or the fishing?" enquired his entertainer.

"Oh I must be in Scotland,"—and Lord Lambeth just amiably blushed.

"Well then," Mr. Westgate returned, "you had better amuse yourself first also. You must go right down and see Mrs. Westgate."

"We should be so happy—if you'd kindly tell us the train," said Percy Beaumont.

"You don't take any train. You take a boat."

"Oh I see. And what is the name of—a—the—a—town?"

"It's a regular old city—don't you let them hear you call it a village or a hamlet or anything of that kind. They'd half-kill you. Only it's a city of pleasure—of lawns and gardens and verandahs and views and, above all, of good Samaritans," Mr. Westgate developed. "But you'll see what Newport is. It's cool. That's the principal thing. You'll greatly oblige me by going down there and putting yourself in the hands of Mrs. Westgate. It isn't perhaps for me to say it, but you couldn't be in better ones. Also in those of her sister, who's staying with her. She's half-crazy about Englishmen. She thinks there's nothing like them."

"Mrs. Westgate or—a—her sister?" asked Percy Beaumont modestly, yet in the tone of a collector of characteristic facts.

"Oh I mean my wife," said Mr. Westgate. "I don't suppose my sister-in-law knows much about them yet. You'll show her anyhow. She has always led a very quite life. She has lived in Boston."

Percy Beaumont listened with interest. "That, I believe, is the most intellectual centre."

"Well, yes—Boston knows it's central and feels it's intellectual. I don't go there much—I stay round here," Mr. Westgate more loosely pursued.

"I say, you know, *we* ought to go there," Lord Lambeth broke out to his companion.

"Oh Lord Lambeth, wait till the great heat's over!" Mr. Westgate interposed. "Boston in this weather would be very trying; it's not the temperature for intellectual exertion. At Boston, you know, you have to pass an examination at the city limits, and when you come away they give you a kind of degree."

Lord Lambeth flushed himself, in his charming way, with wonder, though his friend glanced to make sure he wasn't looking too credulous—they had heard so much about American practices. He decided in time, at any rate, to take a safe middle course. "I dare say it's very jolly."

"I dare say it is," Mr. Westgate returned. "Only I must impress on you that at present—to-morrow morning at an early hour—you'll be expected at Newport. We have a house there—many of our most prominent citizens and society leaders go there for the summer. I'm not sure that at this very moment my wife can take you in—she has a lot of people staying with her. I don't know who they all are—only she may have no room. But you can begin with the hotel and meanwhile you can live at my house. In that way—simply sleeping at the hotel—you'll find it tolerable. For the rest you must make yourself at home at my place. You mustn't be shy, you know; if you're only here for a month that will be a great waste of time. Mrs. Westgate won't neglect you, and you had better not undertake to resist her. I know something about that. I guess you'll find some pretty girls on the premises. I shall write to my wife by this afternoon's mail, and to-morrow she and Miss Alden will look out for you. Just walk right in and get into touch. Your steamer leaves from this part of the city, and I'll send right out and get you a cabin. Then at half-past four o'clock just call for me here, and I'll go with you and put you on board. It's a big boat; you might get lost. A few days hence, at the end of the week, I don't know but I'll come down myself and see how you are."

The two young Englishmen inaugurated the policy of not resisting Mrs. Westgate by submitting, with great docility and thankfulness, to her husband. He was evidently a clear thinker, and he made an impression on his visitors; his hospitality seemed to recommend itself consciously—with a friendly wink, as might be, hinting judicially that you couldn't make a better bargain. Lord Lambeth and his cousin left their entertainer to his labours and returned to their hotel, where they spent three or four hours in their respective shower-baths. Percy Beaumont had suggested that they ought to see something of the town, but "Oh damn the town!" his noble kinsman had rejoined. They returned to Mr. Westgate's office in a carriage, with their luggage, very punctually; but it must be reluctantly recorded that this time he so kept them waiting that they felt themselves miss their previous escape and were deterred only by an amiable modesty from dispensing with his attendance and starting on a hasty scramble to embark. But when at last he appeared and the carriage plunged into the purlieus of Broadway they jolted and jostled to such good purpose that they reached the huge white vessel while the bell for departure was still ringing and the absorption of passengers still active. It was indeed, as Mr. Westgate had said, a big boat, and his leadership in the innumerable and interminable corridors and cabins, with which he seemed perfectly acquainted and of which any one and every one appeared to have the *entrée*, was very grateful to the slightly bewildered voyagers. He showed them their state-room—a luxurious retreat embellished with gas-lamps, mirrors *en pied* and florid furniture—and then, long after they had been intimately convinced that the steamer was in motion and launched upon the unknown stream they were about to navigate, he bade them a sociable farewell.

"Well good-bye, Lord Lambeth," he said. "Good-bye, Mr. Percy Beaumont. I hope you'll have a good time. Just let them do what they want with you. Take it as it's meant. Renounce your own personality. I'll come down by and by and enjoy what's left of you."

II

THE YOUNG Englishmen emerged from their cabin and amused themselves with wandering about the immense labyrinthine ship, which struck them as a monstrous floating hotel or even as a semi-submerged kindergarten. It was densely crowded with passengers, the larger number of whom appeared to be ladies and very young children; and in the big saloons, ornamented in white and gold, which followed each other in surprising succession, beneath the swinging gas-lights and among the small side-passages where the negro domestics of both sexes assembled with an air of amused criticism, every one was moving to and fro and exchanging loud and familiar observations. Eventually, at the instance of a blackamoor more closely related to the scene than his companions, our friends went and had "supper" in a wonderful place arranged like a theatre, where, from a gilded gallery upon which little boxes appeared to open, a large orchestra played operatic selections and, below, people handed about bills of fare in the manner of programmes. All this was sufficiently curious; but the agreeable thing, later, was to sit out on one of the great white decks in the warm breezy darkness and, the vague starlight aiding, make out the line of low mysterious coast. Our travellers tried American cigars—those of Mr. Westgate—and conversed, as they usually conversed, with many odd silences, lapses of logic and incongruities of transition; like a pair who have grown old together and learned to guess each other's sense; or, more especially, like persons so conscious of a common point of view that missing links and broken lights and loose ends, the unexpressed and the understood, could do the office of talk.

"We really seem to be going out to sea," Percy Beaumont observed. "Upon my honour we're going back to England. He has shipped us off again. I call that 'real mean.' "

"I dare say it's all right," said Lord Lambeth. "I want to see those pretty girls at Newport. You know he told us the place was an island, and aren't all islands in the sea?"

"Well," resumed the elder traveller after a while, "if his house is as good as his cigars I guess we shall muddle through."

"I fancy he's awfully 'prominent,' you know, and I rather liked him," Lord Lambeth pursued as if this appreciation of Mr. Westgate had but just glimmered on him.

His comrade, however, engaged in another thought, didn't so much as appear to catch it. "I say, I guess we had better remain at the inn. I don't think I like the way he spoke of his house. I rather object to turning in with such a tremendous lot of women."

"Oh I don't mind," said Lord Lambeth. And then they smoked a while in silence. "Fancy his thinking we do no work in England!" the young man resumed.

But it didn't rouse his friend, who only replied: "I dare say he didn't really a bit think so."

"Well, I guess they don't know much about England over here!" his lordship humorously sighed. After which there was another long pause. "He *has* got us out of a hole," observed the young nobleman.

Percy Beaumont genially assented. "Nobody certainly could have been more civil."

"Littledale said his wife was great fun," Lord Lambeth then contributed.

"Whose wife—Littledale's?"

"Our benefactor's. Mrs. Westgate. What's his name? J. L. It 'kind of' sounds like a number. But I guess it's a high number," he continued with freshened gaiety.

The same influences appeared, however, with Mr. Beaumont to make rather for anxiety. "What was fun to Littledale," he said at last a little sententiously, "may be death to us."

"What do you mean by that?" his companion asked. "I'm as good a man as Littledale."

"My dear boy, I hope you won't begin to flirt," said the elder man.

His friend smoked acutely. "Well, I dare say I shan't *begin*."

"With a married woman, if she's bent upon it, it's all very well," Mr. Beaumont allowed. "But our friend mentioned a young lady—a sister, a sister-in-law. For God's sake keep free of her."

"How do you mean, 'free'?"

"Depend upon it she'll try to land you."

"Oh rot!" said Lord Lambeth.

"American girls are very 'cute,'" the other urged.

"So much the better," said the young man.

"I fancy they're always up to some wily game," Mr. Beaumont developed.

"They can't be worse than they are in England," said Lord Lambeth judicially.

"Ah but in England you've got your natural protectors. You've got your mother and sisters."

"My mother and sisters—!" the youth began with a certain energy. But he stopped in time, puffing at his cigar.

"Your mother spoke to me about it with tears in her eyes," said his monitor. "She said she felt very nervous. I promised to keep you out of mischief."

"You had better take care of yourself!" cried Mr. Beaumont's charge.

"Ah," the responsible party returned, "I haven't the expectation of—whatever it is you expect. Not to mention other attractions."

"Well," said Lord Lambeth, "don't cry out before you're hurt!"

It was certainly very much cooler at Newport, where the travellers found themselves assigned to a couple of diminutive bedrooms in a far-away angle of an immense hotel. They had gone ashore in the early summer twilight and had very promptly put themselves to bed; thanks to which circumstance and to their having, during the previous hours, in their commodious cabin, slept the sleep of youth and health, they began to feel, towards eleven o'clock, very alert and inquisitive. They looked out of their windows across a row of small green fields, bordered with low stone dykes of rude construction, and saw a deep blue ocean lying beneath a deep blue sky and flecked now and then with scintillating patches of foam. A strong fresh breeze came in through the curtainless apertures and prompted our young men to observe generously that it didn't seem half a bad climate. They made other observations after they had emerged from their rooms in pursuit of breakfast—a meal of which they partook in a huge bare hall where a hundred negroes in white jackets shuffled about on an uncarpeted floor; where the flies were superabundant and the tables and dishes covered over with a strange voluminous integument of coarse blue gauze; and where several little boys and girls, who had risen late, were seated in fastidious solitude at the morning repast. These young persons had not the morning paper before them, but were engaged in languid perusal of the bill of fare.

This latter document was a great puzzle to our friends, who, on reflecting that its bewildering categories took account of breakfast alone, had the uneasy prevision of an encyclopaedic dinner-list. They found copious diversion at their inn, an enormous wooden structure for the erection of which it struck them the virgin forests of the West must have been quite laid waste. It was perforated from end to end with immense bare corridors, through which a strong draught freely blew, bearing along wonderful figures of ladies in white morning-dresses and clouds of Valenciennes lace, who floated down the endless vistas on expanded furbelows very much as angels spread their wings. In front was a gigantic verandah on which an army might have encamped—a vast wooden terrace with a roof as high as the nave of a cathedral. Here our young men enjoyed, as they supposed, a glimpse of American society, which was distributed over the measureless expanse in a variety of sedentary attitudes and appeared to consist largely of pretty young girls, dressed as for a *fête champêtre,* swaying to and fro in rocking-chairs, fanning themselves with large straw fans and enjoying an enviable exemption from social cares. Lord Lambeth had a theory, which it might be interesting to trace to its origin, that it would be not only agreeable, but easily possible, to enter into relations with one of these young ladies; and his companion found occasion to check his social yearning.

"You had better take care—else you'll have an offended father or brother pulling out a bowie-knife."

"I assure you it's all right," Lord Lambeth replied. "You know the Americans come to these big hotels to make acquaintances."

"I know nothing about it, and neither do you," said his comrade, who, like a clever man, had begun to see that the observation of American society demanded a readjustment of their standard.

"Hang it then, let's find out!" he cried with some impatience. "You know I don't want to miss anything."

"We *will* find out," said Percy Beaumont very reasonably. "We'll go and see Mrs. Westgate and make all the proper enquiries."

And so the enquiring pair, who had this lady's address inscribed in her husband's hand on a card, descended from the verandah of the big hotel and took their way, according to direction, along a large straight road, past a series of fresh-looking villas, embosomed in shrubs and flowers and enclosed in an in-genious variety of wooden palings. The morning shone and flut-tered, the villas stood up bravely in their smartness, and the walk of the young travellers turned all to confidence. Every-thing looked as if it had received a coat of fresh paint the day before—the red roofs, the green shutters, the clean bright browns and buffs of the house-fronts. The flower-beds on the little lawns sparkled in the radiant air and the gravel in the short carriage-sweeps flashed and twinkled. Along the road came a hundred little basket-phaetons in which, almost always, a couple of ladies were sitting—ladies in white dresses and long white gloves, hold-ing the reins and looking at the two Englishmen, whose nation-ality was not elusive, through fine blue veils, tied tightly about their faces as if to guard their complexions. At last the visitors came within sight of the sea again, and then, having interrogated a gardener over the paling of a villa, turned into an open gate. Here they found themselves face to face with the ocean and with a many-pointed much-balconied structure, resembling a magni-fied châlet, perched on a green embankment just above it. The house had a verandah of extraordinary width all round, and a great many doors and windows standing open to the verandah. These various apertures had, together, such an accessible hos-pitable air, such a breezy flutter, within, of light curtains, such expansive thresholds and reassuring interiors, that our friends hardly knew which was the regular entrance and, after hesitating a moment, presented themselves at one of the windows. The room within was indistinct, but in a moment a graceful figure vaguely shaped itself in the rich-looking gloom—a lady came to meet them. Then they saw she had been seated at a table writ-ing, and that, hearing them, she had got up. She stepped out into the light; she wore a frank charming smile, with which she held out her hand to Percy Beaumont.

"Oh you must be Lord Lambeth and Mr. Beaumont. I've heard from my husband that you were coming. I make you warmly welcome." And she shook hands with each of her guests. Her guests were a little shy, but they made a gallant effort; they responded with smiles and exclamations, they apologised for not knowing the front door. The lady returned with vivacity that when she wanted to see people very much she didn't insist on those distinctions, and that Mr. Westgate had written to her of his English friends in terms that made her really anxious. "He says you're so terribly prostrated," she reported.

"Oh you mean by the heat?"—Percy Beaumont rose to it. "We were rather knocked up, but we feel wonderfully better. We had such a jolly—a—voyage down here. It's so very good of you to mind."

"Yes, it's so very kind of you," murmured Lord Lambeth.

Mrs. Westgate stood smiling; Mrs. Westgate was pretty. "Well, I did mind, and I thought of sending for you this morning to the Ocean House. I'm very glad you're better, and I'm charmed you're really with us. You must come round to the other side of the piazza." And she led the way, with a light smooth step, looking back at the young men and smiling.

The other side of the piazza was, as Lord Lambeth presently remarked, a very jolly place. It was of the most liberal proportions and, with its awnings, its fanciful chairs, its cushions and rugs, its view of the ocean close at hand and tumbling along the base of the low cliffs whose level tops intervened in lawnlike smoothness, formed a charming complement to the drawing-room. As such it was in course of employment at the present hour; it was occupied by a social circle. There were several ladies and two or three gentlemen, to whom Mrs. Westgate proceeded to introduce the distinguished strangers. She mentioned a great many names, very freely and distinctly; the young Englishmen, shuffling about and bowing, were rather bewildered. But at last they were provided with chairs—low wicker chairs, gilded and tied with a great many ribbons—and one of the ladies (a very young person with a little snub nose and several dimples) offered Percy Beaumont a fan. The fan was also adorned with pink love-knots, but the more guarded of our couple declined it, though he was very hot. Presently, however, everything turned to ease; the breeze from the sea was delicious and the view charming; the people sitting about looked fresh and fair. Several of the younger ladies were clearly girls, and the gentlemen slim bright youths such as our friends had seen the day before in New York. The ladies were working on bands of tapestry, and one of the young men had an open book in his lap. Percy afterwards learned from a lady that this young man had been reading aloud—that he was from Boston and was very fond of reading aloud. Percy pronounced it a great pity they had interrupted him; he should like so much (from all he had heard) to listen to a Bostonian read. Couldn't the young man be induced to go on?

"Oh no," said this informant very freely; "he wouldn't be able to get the young ladies to attend to him now."

There was something very friendly, Beaumont saw, in the attitude of the company; they looked at their new recruits with an air of animated sympathy and interest; they smiled, brightly and unanimously, at everything that dropped from either. Lord Lambeth and his companion felt they were indeed made cordially welcome. Mrs. Westgate seated herself between them, and while she talked continuously to each they had occasion to observe that she came up to their friend Littledale's promise. She was thirty years old, with the eyes and the smile of a girl of seventeen, and was light and graceful—elegant, exquisite. Mrs. Westgate was, further, what she had occasion to describe some person, among her many winged words, as being, all spontaneity. Frank and demonstrative, she appeared always—while she looked at you delightedly with her beautiful young eyes—to be making sudden confessions and concessions, breaking out after momentary wonders.

"We shall expect to see a great deal of you," she said to Lord Lambeth with her bland intensity. "We're very fond of Englishmen here; that is there are a great many we've been fond of. After a day or two you must come and stay with us; we hope you'll stay a nice long while. Newport's quite attractive when you come really to know it, when you know plenty of people. Of course you and Mr. Beaumont will have no difficulty about that. Englishmen are very well received here; there are almost always two or three of them about. I think they always like it, and I must say I should think they would. They receive particular attention—I must say I think they sometimes get spoiled; but I'm sure you and Mr. Beaumont are proof against that. My husband tells me you're friends of Captain Littledale's; he was such a charming man. He made himself so agreeable here that I wonder he didn't stay. That would have carried out his system. It couldn't have been pleasanter for him in his own country. Though I suppose it's very pleasant in England too—for English people. I don't know myself; I've been there very little. I've been a great deal abroad, but I always cling to the Continent. I must say I'm extremely fond of Paris; you know we Americans always are; we go there when we die. Did you ever hear that before?—it was said by a great wit. I mean the good Americans; but we're all good—you'll see that for yourself. All I know of England is London, and all I know of London is that place—on that little corner, you know—where you buy jackets, jackets with that coarse braid and those big buttons. They make very good jackets in London, I'll do you the justice to say that. And some people like the hats. But about the hats I was always a heretic; I always got my hats in Paris. You can't wear an English hat—at least, I never could—unless you dress your hair à l'anglaise; and I must say that's a talent I never possessed. In Paris they'll make things to suit your peculiarities; but in England I think you like much more to have—how shall I say it?—one thing for everybody. I mean as regards dress. I don't know about other things; but I've always supposed that in other things everything was different. I mean according to the people —according to the classes and all that. I'm afraid you'll think I don't take a very favourable view; but you know you can't take a very favourable view in Dover Street and the month of November. That has always been my fate. Do you know Jones's Hotel in Dover Street? That's all I know of England. Of course every one admits that the English hotels are your weak point. There was always the most frightful fog—I couldn't see to try my things on. When I got over to America—into the light—I usually found they were twice too big. The next time I mean to go at the right season; I guess I'll go next year. I want very much to take my sister; she has never been to England. I don't know whether you know what I mean by saying that the Englishmen who come here sometimes get spoiled. I mean they take things as a matter of course—things that are done for them. Now naturally anything's a matter of course only when the Englishmen are very nice. But you'll say—oh yes you will, or you would if some of you ever did say much!—they're almost always very nice. You can't expect this to be nearly such an interesting country as England; there are not nearly so many things to see, and we haven't your country life. I've never seen anything of your country life; when I'm in Europe I'm always on the Continent. But I've heard a great deal about it; I know that when you're among yourselves in the country you have the most beautiful time. Of course we've nothing of that sort, we've nothing on that scale. I don't apologise, Lord Lambeth; some Americans are always apologising; you must have noticed that. We've the reputation of always boasting and 'blowing' and waving the American flag; but I must say that what strikes me is that we're perpetually making excuses and trying to smooth things over. The American flag has quite gone out of fashion; it's very carefully folded up, like a table-cloth the worse for wear. Why should we apologise? The English never apologise—do they? No, I must say *I* never apologise. You must take us as we come—with all our imperfections on our heads. Of course we haven't your country life and your old ruins and your great estates and your leisure-class and all that—though I don't really know anything about them, because when I go over I always cling to the Continent. But if we haven't I should think you might find it a pleasant change—I think any country's pleasant where they have pleasant manners. Captain Littledale told me he had never seen such pleasant manners as at Newport, and he had been a great deal in European society. Hadn't he been in the diplomatic service? He told me the dream of his life was to get appointed to a diplomatic post in Washington. But he doesn't seem to have succeeded. Perhaps that was only a part of *his* pleasant manners. I suppose at any rate that in England promotion—and all that sort of thing—is fearfully slow. With us, you know, it's a great deal too quick. You see I admit our drawbacks. But I must confess I think Newport an ideal place. I don't know anything like it anywhere. Captain Littledale told me *he* didn't know anything like it anywhere. It's entirely different from most watering-places; it's a much more refined life. I must say I think that when one goes to a foreign country one ought to enjoy the differences. Of course there are differences; otherwise what did one come abroad for? Look for your pleasure in the differences, Lord Lambeth; that's the way to do it; and then I am sure you'll find American society—at least the Newport phase—quite unique. I wish very much Mr. Westgate were here; but he's dreadfully confined to New York. I suppose you think that's very strange—for a gentleman. Only you see we haven't any leisure-class."

Mrs. Westgate's discourse was delivered with a mild merciless monotony, a paucity of intonation, an impartial flatness that suggested a flowery mead scrupulously "done over" by a steam roller that had reduced its texture to that of a drawing-room carpet. Lord Lambeth listened to her with, it must be confessed, a rather ineffectual attention, though he summoned to his aid such a show as he might of discriminating motions and murmurs. He had no great faculty for apprehending generalisations. There were some three or four indeed which, in the play of his own intelligence, he had originated and which had sometimes appeared to meet the case—any case; yet he felt he had never known such a case as Mrs. Westgate or as her presentation of *her* cases. But at the present time he could hardly have been said to follow this exponent as she darted fish-like through the sea of speculation. Fortunately she asked for no special rejoinder, since she looked about at the rest of the company as well and smiled at Mr. Beaumont on the other side of her as if he too must understand her and agree with her. He was measurably more successful than his companion; for besides being, as we know, cleverer, his attention was not vaguely distracted by close vicinity to a remarkably interesting young person with dark hair and blue eyes. This was the situation of Lord Lambeth, to whom it occurred after a while that the young person with blue eyes and dark hair might be the pretty sister of whom Mrs. Westgate had spoken. She presently turned to him with a remark establishing her identity.

"It's a great pity you couldn't have brought my brother-in-law with you. It's a great shame he should be in New York on such days as these."

"Oh yes—it's very stuffy," said Lord Lambeth.

"It must be dreadful there," said the pretty sister.

"I dare say he's immensely taken up," the young man returned with a sense of conscientiously yearning toward American realities.

"The gentlemen in America work too much," his friend went on.

"Oh do they? Well, I dare say they like it," he hopefully threw out.

"*I* don't like it. One never sees them."

"Don't you really?" asked Lord Lambeth. "I shouldn't have fancied that."

"Have you come to study American manners?" the blue eyes and dark hair went on.

"Oh I don't know. I just came over for the joke of it. I haven't got long." Then occurred a pause, after which he began again. "But he *will* turn up here, won't he?"

"I certainly hope he will. He must help to entertain you and Mr. Beaumont."

Lord Lambeth looked at her from handsome eyes that were brown. "Do you suppose he'd have come down with us if we had pressed it?"

The pretty girl treated this as rather an easy conundrum. "I dare say he would," she smiled.

"Really!" said the young Englishman. "Well, he was no end civil."

His young woman seemed much amused; this at least was in her eyes, which freely met Lord Lambeth's. "He *would* be. He's a perfect husband. But all Americans are that," she confidently continued.

"Really!" Lord Lambeth exclaimed again; and wondered whether all American ladies had such a passion for generalising as these two.

III

HE SAT THERE a good while: there was a great deal of talk; it was all pitched in a key of expression and emphasis rather new to him. Every one present, the cool maidens not least, personally addressed him, and seemed to make a particular point of doing so by the friendly repetition of his name. Three or four other persons came in, and there was a shifting of seats, a changing of places; the gentlemen took, individually, an interest in the visitors, putting somehow more imagination and more "high comedy" into this effort than the latter had ever seen displayed save in a play or a story. These well-wishers feared the two Britons mightn't be comfortable at their hotel—it being, as one of them said, "not so private as those dear little English inns of yours." This last gentleman added that as yet perhaps, alas, privacy wasn't quite so easily obtained in America as might be desired; still, he continued, you could generally get it by paying for it; in fact you could get everything in America nowadays by paying for it. The life was really growing more private; it was growing greatly to resemble European—which wasn't to be wondered at when two thirds of the people leading it were so awfully much at home in Europe. Europe, in the course of this conversation, was indeed, as Lord Lambeth afterwards remarked to his compatriot, rather bewilderingly rubbed into them: did they pretend to be European, and when had they ever been entered under that head? Everything at Newport, at all events, was described to them as thoroughly private; they would probably find themselves, when all was said, a good deal struck with that. It was also represented to the strangers that it mattered very little whether their hotel was agreeable, as every one would want them to "visit round," as somebody called it: they would stay with other people and in any case would be constantly at Mrs.

Westgate's. They would find that charming; it was the pleasantest house in Newport. It was only a pity Mr. Westgate was never there—he being a tremendously fine man, one of the finest they had. He worked like a horse and left his wife to play the social part. Well, she played it all right, if that was all he wanted. He liked her to enjoy herself, and she did know how. She was highly cultivated and a splendid converser—the sort of converser people would come miles to hear. But some preferred her sister, who was in a different style altogether. Some even thought her prettier, but decidedly Miss Alden wasn't so smart. She was more in the Boston style—the *quiet* Boston; she had lived a great deal there and was very highly educated. Boston girls, it was intimated, were more on the English model.

Lord Lambeth had presently a chance to test the truth of this last proposition; for, the company rising in compliance with a suggestion from their hostess that they should walk down to the rocks and look at the sea, the young Englishman again found himself, as they strolled across the grass, in proximity to Mrs. Westgate's sister. Though Miss Alden was but a girl of twenty she appeared conscious of the weight of expectation—unless she quite wantonly took on duties she might have let alone; and this was perhaps the more to be noticed as she seemed by habit rather grave and backward, perhaps even proud, with little of the other's free fraternising. She might have been thought too deadly thin, not to say also too deadly pale; but while she moved over the grass, her arms hanging at her sides, and, seriously or absently, forgot expectations, though again brightly to remember them and to look at the summer sea as if that was what she really cared for, her companion judged her at least as pretty as Mrs. Westgate and reflected that if this was the Boston style, "the quiet Boston," it would do very well. He could fancy her very clever, highly educated and all the rest of it; but clearly also there were ways in which she could spare a fellow—could ease him; she wouldn't keep him so long on the stretch at once. For all her cleverness moreover he felt she had to think a little what to say; she didn't say the first thing that came into her head: he had come from a different part of the world, from a different society, and she was trying to adapt her conversation. The others were scattered about the rocks; Mrs. Westgate had charge of Percy Beaumont.

"Very jolly place for this sort of thing," Lord Lambeth said. "It must do beautifully to sit."

"It does indeed; there are cosy nooks and there are breezy ones, which I often try—as if they had been made on purpose."

"Ah I suppose you've had a lot made," he fell in.

She seemed to wonder. "Oh no, we've had nothing made. It's all pure nature."

"I should think you'd have a few little benches—rustic seats and that sort of thing. It might really be so jolly to 'develop' the place," he suggested.

It made her thoughtful—even a little rueful. "I'm afraid we haven't so many of those things as you."

"Ah well, if you go in for pure nature, as you were saying, there's nothing like that. Nature, over here, must be awfully grand." And Lord Lambeth looked about him.

The little coast-line that contributed to the view melted away, but it too much lacked presence and character—a fact Miss Alden appeared to rise to a perception of. "I'm afraid it seems to you very rough. It's not like the coast-scenery in Kingsley's novels."

He wouldn't let her, however, undervalue it. "Ah the novels always overdo everything, you know. You mustn't go by the novels."

They wandered a little on the rocks; they stopped to look into a narrow chasm where the rising tide made a curious bellowing sound. It was loud enough to prevent their hearing each other, and they stood for some moments in silence. The girl's eyes took in her companion, observing him attentively but covertly, as those of women even in blinking youth know how to do. Lord Lambeth repaid contemplation; tall straight and strong, he was handsome as certain young Englishmen, and certain young

Englishmen almost alone, are handsome; with a perfect finish of feature and a visible repose of mind, an inaccessibility to questions, somehow stamped in by the same strong die and pressure that nature, designing a precious medal, had selected and applied. It was not that he looked stupid; it was only, we assume, that his perceptions didn't show in his face for restless or his imagination for irritable. He was not, as he would himself have said, tremendously clever; but, though there was rather a constant appeal for delay in his waiting, his perfectly patient eye, this registered simplicity had its beauty as well and, whatever it might have appeared to plead for, didn't plead in the name of indifference or inaction. This most searching of his new friends thought him the handsomest young man she had ever seen; and Bessie Alden's imagination, unlike that of her companion, was irritable. He, however, had already made up his mind, quite originally and without aid, that she had a grace exceedingly her own.

"I dare say it's very gay here—that you've lots of balls and parties," he said; since, though not tremendously clever, he rather prided himself on having with women a strict sufficiency of conversation.

"Oh yes, there's a great deal going on. There are not so many balls, but there are a good many other pleasant things," Bessie Alden explained. "You'll see for yourself; we live rather in the midst of it."

"It will be very kind of you to let us see. But I thought you Americans were always dancing."

"I suppose we dance a good deal, though I've never seen much of it. We don't do it much at any rate in summer. And I'm sure," she said, "that we haven't as many balls as you in England."

He wondered—these so many prompt assumptions about his own country made him gape a little. "Ah in England it all depends, you know."

"You'll not think much of our gaieties," she said—though she seemed to settle it for him with a quaver of interrogation. The interrogation sounded earnest indeed and the decision arch; the mixture, at any rate, was charming. "Those things with us are much less splendid than in England."

"I fancy you don't really mean that," her companion laughed.

"I assure you I really mean everything I say," she returned. "Certainly from what I've read about English society it is very different."

"Ah well, you know," said Lord Lambeth, who appeared to cling to this general theory, "those things are often described by fellows who know nothing about them. You mustn't mind what you read."

"Ah what a blasphemous speech—I *must* mind what I read!" our young woman protested. "When I read Thackeray and George Eliot how can I help minding?"

"Oh well, Thackeray and George Eliot"—and her friend pleasantly bethought himself. "I'm afraid I haven't read much of them."

"Don't you suppose they knew about society?" asked Bessie Alden.

"Oh I dare say they knew; they must have got up their subject. Good writers do, don't they? But those fashionable novels are mostly awful rot, you know."

His companion rested on him a moment her dark blue eyes; after which she looked down into the chasm where the water was tumbling about. "Do you mean Catherine Grace Gore for instance?" she then more aspiringly asked.

But at this he broke down—he coloured, laughed, gave up. "I'm afraid I haven't read that either. I'm afraid you'll think I'm not very intellectual."

"Reading Mrs. Gore is no proof of intellect. But I like reading everything about English life—even poor books. I'm so curious about it," said Bessie Alden.

"Aren't ladies curious about everything?" he asked with continued hilarity.

"I don't think so. I don't think we're enough so—that we

care about many things. So it's all the more of a compliment," she added, "that I should want to know so much about England."

The logic here seemed a little close; but Lord Lambeth, advised of a compliment, found his natural modesty close at hand. "I'm sure you know a great deal more than I do."

"I really think I know a great deal—for a person who has never been there."

"Have you really never been there?" cried he. "Fancy!"

"Never—except in imagination. And I *have* been to Paris," she admitted.

"Fancy," he repeated with gaiety—"fancy taking those brutes first! But you *will* come soon?"

"It's the dream of my life!" Bessie Alden brightly professed.

"Your sister at any rate seems to know a tremendous lot about us," Lord Lambeth went on.

She appeared to take her view of this. "My sister and I are two very different persons. She has been a great deal in Europe. She has been in England a little—not intimately. But she has met English people in other countries, and she arrives very quickly at conclusions."

"Ah I guess she does," he laughed. "But you must have known some too."

"No—I don't think I've ever spoken to one before. You're the first Englishman that—to my knowledge—I've ever talked with."

Bessie Alden made this statement with a certain gravity—almost, as it seemed to the young man, an impressiveness. The impressive always made him feel awkward, and he now began to laugh and swing his stick. "Ah you'd have been sure to know!" And then he added after an instant: "I'm sorry I'm not a better specimen."

The girl looked away, but taking it more gaily. "You must remember you're only a beginning." Then she retraced her steps, leading the way back to the lawn, where they saw Mrs. Westgate come toward them with Percy Beaumont still at her side. "Perhaps I shall go to England next year," Miss Alden continued;

"I want to immensely. My sister expects to cross about then, and she has asked me to go with her. If I do I shall make her stay as long as possible in London."

"Ah, you must come early in July," said Lord Lambeth. "That's the time when there's most going on."

"I don't think I can wait even till early in July," his friend returned. "By the first of May I shall be very impatient." They had gone further, and Mrs. Westgate and her companion were near. "Kitty," said the younger sister, "I've given out that we go to London next May. So please to conduct yourself accordingly."

Percy Beaumont wore a somewhat animated—even a slightly irritated—air. He was by no means of so handsome an effect as his comrade, though in the latter's absence he might, with his manly stature and his fair dense beard, his fresh clean skin and his quiet outlook, have pleased by a due affirmation of the best British points. Just now Beaumont's clear eyes had a rather troubled light, which, after glancing at Bessie Alden while she spoke, he turned with some intensity on Lord Lambeth. Mrs. Westgate's beautiful radiance of interest and dissent fell meanwhile impartially everywhere.

"You had better wait till the time comes," she said to her sister. "Perhaps next May you won't care so much for London. Mr. Beaumont and I," she went on, smiling at her companion, "have had a tremendous discussion. We don't agree about anything. It's perfectly delightful."

"Oh I say, Percy!" exclaimed Lord Lambeth.

"I disagree," said Beaumont, raising his eyebrows and stroking down his back hair, "even to the point of thinking it *not* delightful."

"Ah you *must* have been getting it!" cried his friend.

"I don't see anything delightful in my disagreeing with Mrs. Westgate," said Percy Beaumont.

"Well, I do!" Mrs. Westgate declared as she turned again to her sister. "You know you've to go to town. There must be something at the door for you. You had better take Lord Lambeth."

Mr. Beaumont, at this point, looked straight at his comrade, trying to catch his eye. But Lord Lambeth wouldn't look at him; his own eyes were better occupied. "I shall be very happy"— Bessie Alden rose straight to their hostess's suggestion. "I'm only going to some shops. But I'll drive you about and show you the place."

"An American woman who respects herself," said Mrs. Westgate, turning to the elder man with her bright expository air, "must buy something every day of her life. If she can't do it herself she must send out some member of her family for the purpose. So Bessie goes forth to fulfil my mission."

The girl had walked away with Lord Lambeth by her side, to whom she was talking still; and Percy Beaumont watched them as they passed toward the house. "She fulfils her own mission," he presently said; "that of being very attractive."

But even here Mrs. Westgate discriminated. "I don't know that I should precisely say attractive. She's not so much that as she's charming when you really know her. She's very shy."

"Oh indeed?" said Percy Beaumont with evident wonder. And then as if to alternate with a certain grace the note of scepticism: "I guess your shyness, in that case, is different from ours."

"Everything of ours is different from yours," Mrs. Westgate instantly returned. "But my poor sister's given over, I hold, to a fine Boston *gaucherie* that has rubbed off on her by being there so much. She's a dear good girl, however; she's a charming type of girl. She is not in the least a flirt; that isn't at all her line; she doesn't know the alphabet of any such vulgarity. She's very simple, very serious, very *true*. She has lived, however, rather too much in Boston with another sister of mine, the eldest of us, who married a Bostonian. Bessie's very cultivated, not at all like me—I'm not in the least cultivated and am called so only by those who don't know what true culture is. But Bessie does; she has studied Greek; she has read everything; she's what they call in Boston 'thoughtful.' "

"Ah well, it only depends on what one thinks *about*," said Mr. Beaumont, who appeared to find her zeal for distinctions catching.

"I really believe," Mrs. Westgate pursued, "that the most charming girl in the world is a Boston superstructure on a New York *fond*, or perhaps a New York superstructure on a Boston *fond*. At any rate it's the mixture," she declared, continuing to supply her guest with information and to do him the honours of the American world with a zeal that left nothing to be desired.

Lord Lambeth got into a light low pony-cart with Bessie Alden, and she drove him down the long Avenue, whose extent he had measured on foot a couple of hours before, into the ancient town, as it was called in that part of the world, of Newport. The ancient town was a curious affair—a collection of fresh-looking little wooden houses, painted white, scattered over a hillside and clustering about a long straight street paved with huge old cobbles. There were plenty of shops, a large allowance of which appeared those of fruit-vendors, with piles of huge watermelons and pumpkins stacked in front of them; while, drawn up before the shops or bumping about on the round stones, were innumerable other like or different carts freighted with ladies of high fashion who greeted each other from vehicle to vehicle and conversed on the edge of the pavement in a manner that struck Lord Lambeth as of the last effusiveness: with a great many "Oh my dears" and little quick sounds and motions—obscure native words, shibboleths and signs. His companion went into seventeen shops—he amused himself with counting them—and accumulated at the bottom of the trap a pile of bundles that hardly left the young Englishman a place for his feet. As she had no other attendant he sat in the phaeton to hold the pony; where, though not a particularly acute observer, he saw much harmlessly to divert him—especially the ladies just mentioned, who wandered up and down with an aimless intentness, as if looking for something to buy, and who, tripping in and out of their vehicles, displayed remarkably pretty feet. It all seemed to Lord Lambeth very odd and bright and gay. And he felt by the time they got back to the villa that he had made a stride in intimacy with Miss Alden.

The young Englishmen spent the whole of that day and the whole of many successive days in the cultivation, right and left, far and near, of this celerity of social progress. They agreed that it was all extremely jolly—that they had never known anything more agreeable. It is not proposed to report the detail of their sojourn on this charming shore; though were it convenient I might present a record of impressions none the less soothing that they were not exhaustively analysed. Many of them still linger in the minds of our travellers, attended by a train of harmonious images—images of early breezy shining hours on lawns and piazzas that overlooked the sea; of innumerable pretty girls saying innumerable quaint and familiar things; of infinite lounging and talking and laughing and flirting and lunching and dining; of a confidence that broke down, of a freedom that pulled up, nowhere; of an idyllic ease that was somehow too ordered for a primitive social consciousness and too innocent for a developed; of occasions on which they so knew every one and every thing that they almost ached with reciprocity; of drives and rides in the late afternoon, over gleaming beaches, on long sea-roads, beneath a sky lighted up by marvellous sunsets; of tea-tables, on the return, informal, irregular, agreeable; of evenings at open windows or on the perpetual verandahs, in the summer starlight, above the warm Atlantic and amid irrelevant outbursts of clever minstrelsy. The young Englishmen were introduced to everybody, entertained by everybody, intimate with everybody, and it was all the book of life, of American life, at least; with the chapter of "complications" bodily omitted. At the end of three days they had removed their luggage from the hotel and had gone to stay with Mrs. Westgate—a step as to which Percy Beaumont at first took up an attitude of mistrust apparently founded on some odd and just a little barbaric talk forced on him, he would have been tempted to say, and very soon after their advent, by Miss Alden. He had indeed been aware of her occasional approach or appeal, since she wasn't

literally always in conversation with Lord Lambeth. He had
meditated on Mrs. Westgate's account of her sister and discovered for himself that the young lady was "sharp" (Percy's critical categories remained few and simple) and appeared to have
read a great deal. She seemed perfectly well-bred, though he
couldn't make out that, as Mrs. Westgate funnily insisted, she
was shy. If she was shy she carried it off with an ease—!

"Mr. Beaumont," she had said, "please tell me something
about Lord Lambeth's family. How would you say it in England?—his position."

"His position?" Percy's instinct was to speak as if he had
never heard of such a matter.

"His rank—or whatever you call it. Unfortunately we haven't
got a 'Peerage,' like the people in Thackeray."

"That's a great pity," Percy pleaded. "You'd find the whole
matter in black and white, and upon my honour I know very
little about it."

The girl seemed to wonder at this innocence. "You know at
least whether he's what they call a great noble."

"Oh yes, he's in that line."

"Is he a 'peer of the realm'?"

"Well, as yet—very nearly."

"And has he any other title than Lord Lambeth?"

"His title's the Marquis of Lambeth." With which the fountain of Bessie's information appeared to run a little dry. She
looked at him, however, with such interest that he presently
added: "He's the son of the Duke of Bayswater."

"The eldest—?"

"The only one."

"And are his parents living?"

"Naturally—as to his father. If *he* weren't living Lambeth
would be a duke."

"So that when 'the old lord' dies"—and the girl smiled with
more simplicity than might have been expected in one so "sharp"
—"he'll become Duke of Bayswater?"

"Of course," said their common friend. "But his father's in
excellent health."

"And his mother?"

Percy seemed amused. "The Duchess is built to last!"

"And has he any sisters?"

"Yes, there are two."

"And what are they called?"

"One of them's married. She's the Countess of Pimlico."

"And the other?"

"The other's unmarried—she's plain Lady Julia."

Bessie entered into it all. "Is she very plain?"

He began to laugh again. "You wouldn't find her so handsome as her brother," he said; and it was after this that he attempted to dissuade the heir of the Duke of Bayswater from accepting Mrs. Westgate's invitation. "Depend upon it," he said, "that girl means to have a go at you."

"It seems to me you're doing your best to make a fool of me," the modest young nobleman answered.

"She has been asking me," his friend imperturbably pursued, "all about your people and your possessions."

"I'm sure it's very good of her!" Lord Lambeth returned.

"Well then," said Percy, "if you go straight into it, if you hurl yourself bang upon the spears, you do so with your eyes open."

"Damn my eyes!" the young man pronounced. "If one's to be a dozen times a day at the house it's a great deal more convenient to sleep there. I'm sick of travelling up and down this beastly Avenue."

Since he had determined to go Percy would of course have been very sorry to allow him to go alone; he was a man of many scruples—in the direction in which he had any at all—and he remembered his promise to the Duchess. It was obviously the memory of this promise that made Mr. Beaumont say to his companion a couple of days later that he rather wondered he should be so fond of such a girl.

"In the first place how do you know how fond I am?" asked Lord Lambeth. "And in the second why shouldn't I be fond of her?"

"I shouldn't think she'd be in your line."

"What do you call my 'line'? You don't set her down, I suppose, as 'fast'?"

"Exactly so. Mrs. Westgate tells me that there's no such thing as the fast girl in America; that it's an English invention altogether and that the term has no meaning here."

"All the better. It's an animal I detest," said Lord Lambeth.

"You prefer then rather a priggish American *précieuse?*"

Lord Lambeth took his time. "Do you call Miss Alden all that?"

"Her sister tells me," said Percy Beaumont, "that she's tremendously literary."

"Well, why shouldn't she be? She's certainly very clever and has every appearance of a well-stored mind."

Percy for an instant watched his young friend, who had turned away. "I should rather have supposed you'd find her stores oppressive."

The young man, after this, faced him again. "Why, do you think me such a dunce?" And then as his friend but vaguely protested: "The girl's all right," he said—and quite as if this judgement covered all the ground. It wasn't that there was no ground—but he knew what he was about.

Percy, for a while further, and a little uncomfortably flushed with the sense of his false position—that of presenting culture in a "mean" light, as they said at Newport—Percy kept his peace; but on August 10th he wrote to the Duchess of Bayswater. His conception of certain special duties and decencies, as I have said, was strong, and this step wholly fell in with it. His companion meanwhile was having much talk with Miss Alden—on the red sea-rocks beyond the lawn; in the course of long island rides, with a slow return in the glowing twilight; on the deep verandah, late in the evening. Lord Lambeth, who had stayed at many houses, had never stayed at one in which it was possible for a young man to converse so freely and frequently with a young lady. This young lady no longer applied to their other guest for information concerning his lordship. She addressed herself directly to the young nobleman. She asked him a great many questions, some of which did, according to Mr. Beaumont's term, a little oppress him; for he took no pleasure in talking about himself.

"Lord Lambeth"—this had been one of them—"are you an hereditary legislator?"

"Oh I say," he returned, "don't make me call myself such names as that."

"But you're natural members of Parliament."

"I don't like the sound of that either."

"Doesn't your father sit in the House of Lords?" Bessie Alden went on.

"Very seldom," said Lord Lambeth.

"Is it a very august position?" she asked.

"Oh dear no," Lord Lambeth smiled.

"I should think it would be very grand"—she serenely kept it up, as the female American, he judged, would always keep anything up—"to possess simply by an accident of birth the right to make laws for a great nation."

"Ah but one doesn't make laws. There's a lot of humbug about it."

"I don't believe that," the girl unconfusedly declared. "It must be a great privilege, and I should think that if one thought of it in the right way—from a high point of view—it would be very inspiring."

"The less one thinks of it the better, I guess!" Lord Lambeth after a moment returned.

"I think it's tremendous"—this at least she kept up; and on another occasion she asked him if he had any tenantry. Hereupon it was that, as I have said, he felt a little the burden of her earnestness.

But he took it good-humouredly. "Do you want to buy up their leases?"

"Well—have you got any 'livings'?" she demanded as if the word were rich and rare.

"Oh I say!" he cried. "Have *you* got a pet clergyman looking out?" But she made him plead guilty to his having, in prospect, a castle; he confessed to but one. It was the place in which he had been born and brought up, and, as he had an old-time liking for it, he was beguiled into a few pleasant facts about it and into pronouncing it really very jolly. Bessie listened with great interest, declaring she would give the world to see such a place. To which he charmingly made answer: "It would be awfully kind of you to come and stay there, you know." It was not inconvenient to him meanwhile that Percy Beaumont hadn't happened to hear him make this genial remark.

Mr. Westgate, all this time, hadn't, as they said at Newport, "come on." His wife more than once announced that she expected him on the morrow; but on the morrow she wandered about a little, with a telegram in her jewelled fingers pronouncing it too "fiendish" he should let his business so dreadfully absorb him that he could but platonically hope, as she expressed it, his two Englishmen were having a good time. "I must say," said Mrs. Westgate, "that it's no thanks to him if you are!" And she went on to explain, while she kept up that slow-paced circulation which enabled her well-adjusted skirts to display themselves so advantageously, that unfortunately in America there was no leisure-class and that the universal passionate surrender of the men to business-questions and business-questions only, as if they were the all in all of life, was a tide that would have to be stemmed. It was Lord Lambeth's theory, freely propounded when the young men were together, that Percy was having a very good time with Mrs. Westgate and that under the pretext of meeting for the purpose of animated discussion they were indulging in practices that imparted a shade of hypocrisy to the lady's regret for her husband's absence.

"I assure you we're always discussing and differing," Mr. Beaumont however asseverated. "She's awfully argumentative. American ladies certainly don't mind contradicting you flat. Upon my word I don't think I was ever treated so by a woman before. We have ours ever so much more in hand. She's so devilish positive."

The superlative degree so variously affirmed, however, was evidently a source of attraction in Mrs. Westgate, for the elder man was constantly at his hostess's side. He detached himself one day to the extent of going to New York to talk over the Tennessee Central with her husband; but he was absent only forty-eight hours, during which, with that gentleman's assistance, he completely settled this piece of business. "They know how to put things—and put people—'through' in New York," he subsequently and quite breathlessly observed to his comrade; and he added that Mr. Westgate had seemed markedly to fear his wife might suffer for loss of her guest—he had been in such an awful hurry to send him back to her. "I'm afraid you'll never come up to an American husband—if that's what the wives expect," he said to Lord Lambeth.

Mrs. Westgate, however, was not to enjoy much longer the entertainment with which an indulgent husband had desired to keep her provided. August had still a part of its course to run when his lordship received from his mother the disconcerting news that his father had been taken ill and that he had best at once come home. The young nobleman concealed his chagrin with no great success. "I left the Duke but the other day absolutely all right—so what the deuce does it mean?" he asked of his comrade. "What's a fellow to do?"

Percy Beaumont was scarce less annoyed; he had deemed it his duty, as we know, to report faithfully to the Duchess, but had not expected this distinguished woman to act so promptly on his hint. "It means," he said, "that your father is somehow, and rather suddenly, laid up. I don't suppose it's anything serious, but you've no option. Take the first steamer, but take it without alarm."

This really struck Lord Lambeth as meaning that he essentially needn't take it, since alarm would have been his only good motive; yet he nevertheless, after an hour of intenser irritation than he could quite have explained to himself, made his farewells; in the course of which he exchanged a few last words with Bessie Alden that are the only ones making good their place in our record. "Of course I needn't assure you that if you should come to England next year I expect to be the very first person notified of it."

She looked at him in that way she had which never quite struck him as straight and clear, yet which always struck him as kind and true. "Oh if we come to London I should think you'd sufficiently hear of it."

Percy Beaumont felt it his duty also to embark, and this same rigour compelled him one windless afternoon, in mid-Atlantic, to say to his friend that he suspected the Duchess's telegram to have been in part the result of something he himself had written her. "I wrote her—as I distinctly warned you I had promised in general to do—that you were extremely interested in a little American girl."

The young man, much upset by this avowal, indulged for some moments in the strong and simple language of resentment. But if I have described him as inclined to candour and to reason I can give no better proof of it than the fact of his being ready to face the truth by the end of half an hour. "You were quite right after all. I'm very much interested in her. Only, to be fair," he added, "you should have told my mother also that she's not—at all seriously—interested in poor me."

Mr. Beaumont gave the rein to mirth and mockery. "There's nothing so charming as modesty in a young man in the position of 'poor' you. That speech settles for me the question of what's the matter with you."

Lord Lambeth's handsome eyes turned rueful and queer. "Is anything so flagrantly the matter with me?"

"Everything, my dear boy," laughed his companion, passing a hand into his arm for a walk.

"Well, *she* isn't interested—she isn't!" the young man insisted.

"My poor friend," said Percy Beaumont rather gravely, "you're very far gone!"

IV

IN POINT OF FACT, as the latter would have said, Mrs. Westgate disembarked by the next mid-May on the British coast. She was accompanied by her sister, but unattended by any other member of her family. To the lost comfort of a husband respectably to produce, as she phrased it, she was now habituated; she had made half a dozen journeys to Europe under this drawback of looking ill-temperedly separated and yet of being thanklessly enslaved, and she still decently accounted for her spurious singleness to wondering friends on this side of the Atlantic by formulating the grim truth —the only grimness indeed in all her view—that in America there is no leisure-class. The two ladies came up to London and alighted at Jones's Hotel, where Mrs. Westgate, who had made on former occasions the most agreeable impression at this establishment, received an obsequious greeting. Bessie Alden had felt much excited about coming to England; she had expected the "associations" would carry her away and counted on the joy of treating her eyes and her imagination to all the things she had read of in poets and historians. She was very fond of the poets and historians, of the picturesque, of the past, of associations, of relics and reverberations of greatness; so that on coming into the great English world, where strangeness and familiarity would go hand in hand, she was prepared for a swarm of fresh emotions. They began very promptly—these tender fluttering sensations; they began with the sight of the beautiful English landscape, whose dark richness was quickened and brightened by the season; with the carpeted fields and flowering hedge-rows, as she looked at them from the window of the train; with the spires of the rural churches peeping above the rook-haunted tree-tops; with the oak-studded, deer-peopled parks, the ancient homes, the cloudy light, the speech, the manners, all the significant differences. Mrs. Westgate's response was of course less quick and less extravagant, and she gave but a wandering attention to her sister's ejaculations and rhapsodies.

"You know my enjoyment of England's not so intellectual as Bessie's," she said to several of her friends in the course of her visit to this country. "And yet if it's not intellectual I can't say it's in the least sensual. I don't think I can quite say what it is, my enjoyment of England." When once it was settled that the two ladies should come abroad and should spend a few weeks in London and perhaps in other parts of the celebrated island on their way to the Continent, they of course exchanged a good many allusions to their English acquaintance.

"It will certainly be much nicer having friends there," was a remark that had one day dropped from Bessie while she sat on the sunny deck of the steamer, at her sister's feet, from under which spread conveniently a large soft rug.

"Whom do you mean by friends?" Mrs. Westgate had then invited the girl to say.

"All those English gentlemen you've known and entertained. Captain Littledale, for instance. And Lord Lambeth and Mr. Beaumont," the girl further mentioned.

"Do you expect them to give us a very grand reception?"

She reflected a moment; she was addicted, as we know, to fine reflexion. "Well—to be nice."

"My poor sweet child!" murmured her sister.

"What have I said that's so silly?" Bessie asked.

"You're a little too simple; just a little. It's very becoming, but it pleases people at your expense."

"I'm certainly too simple to understand you," said our young lady.

Mrs. Westgate had an ominous pause. "Shall I tell you a story?"

"If you'd be so good. That's what's frequently done to amuse simple people."

Mrs. Westgate consulted her memory while her companion sat at gaze of the shining sea. "Did you ever hear of the Duke of Green-Erin?"

"I think not," said Bessie.

"Well, it's no matter," her sister went on.

"It's a proof of my simplicity."

"My story's meant to illustrate that of some other people," said Mrs. Westgate. "The Duke of Green-Erin's what they call in England a great swell, and some five years ago he came to America. He spent most of his time in New York, and in New York he spent his days and his nights at the Butterworths'. You've heard at least of the Butterworths. *Bien*. They did everything in the world for him—the poor Butterworths—they turned themselves inside out. They gave him a dozen dinner-parties and balls, and were the means of his being invited to fifty more. At first he used to come into Mrs. Butterworth's box at the opera in a tweed travelling-suit, but some one stopped that. At any rate he had a beautiful time and they parted the best friends in the world. Two years elapse and the Butterworths come abroad and go to London. The first thing they see in all the papers—in England those things are in the most prominent place—is that the Duke of Green-Erin has arrived in town for the season. They wait a little, and then Mr. Butterworth—as polite as ever—goes and leaves a card. They wait a little more; the visit's not returned; they wait three weeks: *silence de mort,* the Duke gives no sign. The Butterworths see a lot of other people, put down the Duke of Green-Erin as a rude ungrateful man and forget all about him. One fine day they go to Ascot Races—where they meet him face to face. He stares a moment and then comes up to Mr. Butterworth, taking something from his pocket-book—something which proves to be a bank-note. 'I'm glad to see you, Mr. Butterworth,' he says, 'so that I can pay you that ten pounds I lost to you in New York. I saw the other day you remembered our bet; here are the ten pounds, Mr. Butterworth. Good-bye Mr. Butterworth.' And off he goes, and that's the last they see of the Duke of Green-Erin."

"Is that your story?" asked Bessie Alden.

"Don't tell me you don't think it interesting!" her sister replied.

"I don't think I believe it," said the girl.

"Ah then," cried Mrs. Westgate, "mademoiselle isn't of such an unspotted *candeur!* Believe it or not as you like. There's at any rate no smoke without fire."

"Is that the way," asked Bessie after a moment, "that you expect your friends to treat you?"

"I defy them to treat me very ill, for the simple reason that I shall never give them the opportunity. With the best will in the world, in that case, they can't be very disobliging."

Our young lady for a time said nothing. "I don't see what makes you talk that way," she then resumed. "The English are a great people."

"Exactly; and that's just the way they've grown great—by dropping you when you've ceased to be useful. People say they aren't clever, but I find them prodigiously clever."

"You know you've liked them—all the Englishmen you've seen," Bessie brought up.

"They've liked *me*," her sister returned; "so I think I'd rather put it. And of course one likes that."

Bessie pursued for some moments her studies in sea-green. "Well," she said, "whether they like me or not, I mean to like them. And happily," she wound up, "Lord Lambeth doesn't owe me ten pounds."

During the first few days after their arrival at Jones's Hotel our charming Americans were much occupied with what they would have called looking about them. They found occasion to make numerous purchases, and their opportunities for enquiry and comment were only those supplied by the deferential London shopmen. Bessie Alden, even in driving from the station, felt to intensity the many-voiced appeal of the capital of the race from which she had sprung, and, at the risk of exhibiting her as a person of vulgar tastes, it must be recorded that for many days she desired no higher pleasure than to roll about the crowded streets in the public conveyances. They presented to her attentive eyes strange pictures and figures, and it's at least beneath the dignity of our historic muse to enumerate the trivial objects and incidents in which the imagination of this simple young lady from Boston lost itself. It may be freely mentioned, however, that whenever, after a round of visits in Bond Street and Regent Street, she was about to return with her sister to Jones's Hotel, she desired they should, at whatever cost to convenience, be driven home by way of Westminster Abbey. She had begun by asking if it wouldn't be possible to take the Tower en route to their lodgings; but it happened that at a more primitive stage of her culture Mrs. Westgate had paid a visit to this venerable relic, which she spoke of ever afterwards, vaguely, as a dreadful disappointment. She thus expressed the liveliest disapproval of any attempt to combine historical researches with the purchase of hair-brushes and note-paper. The most she would consent to do in the line of backward brooding was to spend half an hour at Madame Tussaud's, where she saw several dusty wax effigies of members of the Royal Family. It was made clear to Bessie that if she wished to go to the Tower she must get some one else to take her. Bessie expressed hereupon an earnest disposition to go alone; but in respect to this proposal as well Mrs. Westgate had the cold sense of complications.

"Remember," she said, "that you're not in your innocent little Boston. It's not a question of walking up and down Beacon Street." With which she went on to explain that there were two classes of American girls in Europe—those who walked about alone and those who didn't. "You happen to belong, my dear," she said to her sister, "to the class that doesn't."

"It's only," laughed Bessie, though all yearningly, "because you happen quite arbitrarily to place me." And she devoted much private meditation to this question of effecting a visit to the Tower of London.

Suddenly it seemed as if the problem might be solved; the two ladies at Jones's Hotel received a visit from Willie Woodley. So was familiarly designated a young American who had sailed from New York a few days after their own departure and who, enjoying some freedom of acquaintance with them in that city, had lost no time, on his arrival in London, in coming to pay them his respects. He had in fact gone to see them directly after going to see his tailor; than which there can be no greater exhibition of promptitude on the part of a young American just installed at the Charing Cross Hotel. He was a slight mild youth, without high colour but with many elegant forms, famous for the authority with which he led the "German" in New York. He was indeed, by the young ladies who habitually figured in such evolutions, reckoned "the best dancer in the world"; it was in those terms he was always spoken of and his pleasant identity indicated. He was the most convenient gentle young man, for almost any casual light purpose, it was possible to meet; he was beautifully dressed—"in the English style"—and knew an immense deal about London. He had been at Newport during the previous summer, at the time of our young Englishmen's visit, and he took extreme pleasure in the society of Bessie Alden, whom he never addressed but as "Miss Bessie." She immediately arranged with him, in the presence of her sister, that he should guide her to the scene of Lady Jane Grey's execution.

"You may do as you please," said Mrs. Westgate. "Only—if you desire the information—it is not the custom here for young ladies to knock about London with wild young men."

"Miss Bessie has waltzed with me so often—not to call it so wildly," the young man returned, "that she can surely go out with me in a jog-trot cab."

"I consider public waltzing," said Mrs. Westgate, "the most innocent, because the most guarded and regulated, pleasure of our time."

"It's a jolly compliment to our time!" Mr. Woodley cried with a laugh of the most candid significance.

"I don't see why I should regard what's done here," Bessie pursued. "Why should I suffer the restrictions of a society of which I enjoy none of the privileges?"

"That's very good—very good," her friend applauded.

"Oh go to the Tower and feel the axe if you like!" said Mrs. Westgate. "I consent to your going with Mr. Woodley; but I wouldn't let you go with an Englishman."

"Miss Bessie wouldn't care to go with an Englishman!" Mr. Woodley declared with an asperity doubtless not unnatural in a young man who, dressing in a manner that I have indicated and knowing a great deal, as I have said, about London, saw no reason for drawing these sharp distinctions. He agreed upon a day with Miss Bessie—a day of that same week; while an ingenious mind might perhaps have traced a connexion between the girl's reference to her lack of social privilege or festal initiation and a question she asked on the morrow as she sat with her sister at luncheon.

"Don't you mean to write to—to any one?"

"I wrote this morning to Captain Littledale," Mrs. Westgate replied.

"But Mr. Woodley believes Captain Littledale away in India."

"He said he thought he had heard so; he knows nothing about it."

For a moment Bessie said nothing more; then at last, "And don't you intend to write to—to Mr. Beaumont?" she enquired.

Her sister waited with a look at her. "You mean to Lord Lambeth."

"I said Mr. Beaumont because he was—at Newport—so good a friend of yours."

Mrs. Westgate prolonged the attitude of sisterly truth. "I don't really care two straws for Mr. Beaumont."

"You were certainly very nice to him."

"I'm very nice to every one," said Mrs. Westgate simply.

Nothing indeed could have been simpler save perhaps the way Bessie smiled back: "To every one but me."

Her sister continued to look at her. "Are you in love with Lord Lambeth?"

Our young woman stared a moment, and the question was too unattended with any train even to make her shy. "Not that I know of."

"Because if you are," Mrs. Westgate went on, "I shall certainly not send for him."

"That proves what I said," Bessie gaily insisted—"that you're not really nice to me."

"It would be a poor service, my dear child," said her sister.

"In what sense? There's nothing *against* Lord Lambeth that I know of."

Mrs. Westgate seemed to cover much country in a few moments. "You *are* in love with him then?"

Bessie stared again, but this time blushing a little. "Ah if you'll not be serious we won't mention him again."

For some minutes accordingly Lord Lambeth was shrouded in silence, and it was Mrs. Westgate who, at the end of this period, removed the ban. "Of course I shall let him know we're here. I think he'd be hurt—justly enough—if we should go away without seeing him. It's fair to give him a chance to come and thank me for the kindness we showed him. But I don't want to seem eager."

"Neither do I," said Bessie very simply.

"Though I confess," her companion added, "that I'm curious to see how he'll behave."

"He behaved very well at Newport."

"Newport isn't London. At Newport he could do as he liked; but here it's another affair. He has to have an eye to consequences."

"If he had more freedom then at Newport," argued Bessie, "it's the more to his credit that he behaved well; and if he has to be so careful here it's possible he'll behave even better."

"Better, better?" echoed her sister a little impatiently. "My dear child, what do you mean by better and what's your point of view?"

Bessie wondered. "What do *you* mean by my point of view?"

"Don't you care for Lord Lambeth—a tiny speck?" Mrs. Westgate demanded.

This time Bessie Alden took it with still deeper reserve. She slowly got up from table, turning her face away. "You'll oblige me by not talking so."

Mrs. Westgate sat watching her for some moments as she moved slowly about the room and went and stood at the window. "I'll write to him this afternoon," she said at last.

"Do as you please!" Bessie answered; after which she turned round. "I'm not afraid to say I like Lord Lambeth. I like him very much."

Mrs. Westgate bethought herself. "He's not clever."

"Well, there have been clever people whom I've disliked," the girl said; "so I suppose I may like a stupid one. Besides, Lord Lambeth's no stupider than any one else."

"No stupider than he gives you warning of," her sister smiled.

"If I were in love with him as you said just now," Bessie returned, "it would be bad policy on your part to abuse him."

"My dear child, don't give me lessons in policy!" cried Mrs. Westgate. "The policy I mean to follow is very deep."

The girl began once more to walk about; then she stopped before her companion. "I've never heard in the course of five minutes so many hints and innuendos. I wish you'd tell me in plain English what you mean."

"I mean you may be much annoyed."

"That's still only a hint," said Bessie.

Her sister just hesitated. "It will be said of you that you've come after him—that you followed him."

Bessie threw back her pretty head much as a startled hind, and a look flashed into her face that made Mrs. Westgate get up. "Who says such things as that?"

"People here."

"I don't believe it."

"You've a very convenient faculty of doubt. But my policy will be, as I say, very deep. I shall leave you to find out as many things as possible for yourself."

Bessie fixed her eyes on her sister, and Mrs. Westgate could have believed there were tears in them. "Do they talk that way here?"

"You'll see. I shall let you alone."

"Don't let me alone," said Bessie Alden. "Take me away."

"No; I want to see what you make of it," her sister continued.

"I don't understand."

"You'll understand after Lord Lambeth has come," said Mrs. Westgate with a persistence of private amusement.

The two ladies had arranged that on this afternoon Willie Woodley should go with them to Hyde Park, where Bessie expected it would prove a rich passage to have sat on a little green chair under the great trees and beside Rotten Row. The want of a suitable escort had hitherto hampered this adventure; but no escort, now, for such an expedition, could have been more suitable than their devoted young countryman, whose mission in life, it might almost be said, was to find chairs for ladies and who appeared on the stroke of half-past five adorned with every superficial grace that could qualify him for the scene.

"I've written to Lord Lambeth, my dear," Mrs. Westgate mentioned on coming into the room where Bessie, drawing on long grey gloves, had given their visitor the impression that she was particularly attuned. Bessie said nothing, but Willie Woodley exclaimed that his lordship was in town; he had seen his name in the *Morning Post*. "Do you read the *Morning Post?*" Mrs. Westgate thereupon asked.

"Oh yes; it's great fun." Mr. Woodley almost spoke as if the pleasure were attended with physical risk.

"I want so to see it," said Bessie, "there's so much about it in Thackeray."

"I'll send it to you every morning!" cried the young man with elation.

He found them what Bessie thought excellent places under the great trees and beside the famous avenue the humours of which had been made familiar to the girl's childhood by the pictures in *Punch*. The day was bright and warm and the crowd of riders and spectators, as well as the great procession of carriages, proportionately dense and many-coloured. The scene bore the stamp of the London social pressure at its highest, and it made our young woman think of more things than she could easily express to her companions. She sat silent, under her parasol, while her imagination, according to its wont, kept pace with the deep strong tide of the exhibition. Old impressions and preconceptions became living things before the show, and she found herself, amid the crowd of images, fitting a history to this person and a theory to that, and making a place for them all in her small private museum of types. But if she said little her sister on one side and Willie Woodley on the other delivered themselves in lively alternation.

"Look at that green dress with blue flounces. Quelle toilette!" said Mrs. Westgate.

"That's the Marquis of Blackborough," the young man was

able to contribute—"the one in the queer white coat. I heard him speak the other night in the House of Lords; it was something about ramrods; he called them *wamwods*. He's an awful swell."

"Did you ever see anything like the way they're pinned back?" Mrs. Westgate resumed. "They never know where to stop."

"They do nothing but stop," said Willie Woodley. "It prevents them from walking. Here comes a great celebrity—Lady Beatrice Bellevue. She's awfully fast; see what little steps she takes."

"Well, my dear," Mrs. Westgate pursued to Bessie, "I hope you're getting some ideas for your couturière?"

"I'm getting plenty of ideas," said Bessie, "but I don't know that my couturière would particularly appreciate them."

Their companion presently perceived a mounted friend who drew up beside the barrier of the Row and beckoned to him. He went forward and the crowd of pedestrians closed about him, so that for some minutes he was hidden from sight. At last he reappeared, bringing a gentleman with him—a gentleman whom Bessie at first supposed to be his friend dismounted. But at a second glance she found herself looking at Lord Lambeth, who was shaking hands with her sister.

"I found him over there," said Willie Woodley, "and I told him you were here."

And then Lord Lambeth, raising his hat afresh, shook hands with Bessie—"Fancy your being here!" He was blushing and smiling; he looked very handsome and he had a note of splendour he had not had in America. The girl's free fancy, as we know, was just then in marked exercise; so that the tall young Englishman, as he stood there looking down at her, had the benefit of it. "He's handsomer and more splendid than anything I've ever seen," she said to herself. And then she remembered he was a Marquis and she thought he somehow looked a Marquis. "Really, you know," he cried, "you ought to have let a fellow know you've come!"

"I wrote to you an hour ago," said Mrs. Westgate.

"Doesn't all the world know it?" smiled Bessie.

"I assure you I didn't know it!" he insisted. "Upon my honour I hadn't heard of it. Ask Woodley now; had I, Woodley?"

"Well, I think you're rather a humbug," this gentleman brought forth.

"You don't believe that—do you, Miss Alden?" asked his lordship. "You don't believe I'm rather a humbug, eh?"

"No," said Bessie after an instant, but choosing and conferring a grace on the literal—"I don't."

"You're too tall to stand up, Lord Lambeth," Mrs. Westgate pronounced. "You approach the normal only when you sit down. Be so good as to get a chair."

He found one and placed it sidewise, close to the two ladies. "If I hadn't met Woodley I should never have found you," he went on. "Should I, Woodley?"

"Well, I guess not," said the young American.

"Not even with my letter?" asked Mrs. Westgate.

"Ah well, I haven't got your letter yet; I suppose I shall get it this evening. It was awfully kind of you to write."

"So I said to Bessie," the elder lady observed.

"*Did* she say so, Miss Alden?" Lord Lambeth a little pointlessly enquired. "I dare say you've been here a month."

"We've been here three," mocked Mrs. Westgate.

"*Have* you been here three months?" the young man asked again of Bessie.

"It seems a long time," Bessie answered.

He had but a brief wonder—he found something. "I say, after that you had better not call me a humbug! I've only been in town three weeks, but you must have been hiding away. I haven't seen you anywhere."

"Where should you have seen us—where should we have gone?" Mrs. Westgate fairly put to him.

It found Willy Woodley at least ready. "You should have gone to Hurlingham."

"No, let Lord Lambeth tell us," Mrs. Westgate insisted.

"There are plenty of places to go to," he said—"each one stupider than the other. I mean people's houses. They send you cards."

"No one has sent us a scrap of a card," Bessie laughed.

Mrs. Westgate attenuated. "We're very quiet. We're here as travellers."

"We've been to Madame Tussaud's," Bessie further mentioned.

"Oh I say!" cried Lord Lambeth.

"We thought we should find your image there," said Mrs. Westgate—"yours and Mr. Beaumont's."

"In the Chamber of Horrors?" laughed the young man.

"It did duty very well for a party," said Mrs. Westgate. "All the women were *décolletées,* and many of the figures looked as if they could almost speak."

"Upon my word," his lordship returned, "you see people at London parties who look a long way from that!"

"Do you think Mr. Woodley could find us Mr. Beaumont?" asked the elder of the ladies.

He stared and looked about. "I dare say he could. Percy sometimes comes here. Don't you think you could find him, Woodley? Make a dive or a dash for it."

"Thank you; I've had enough of violent movement," said Willie Woodley. "I'll wait till Mr. Beaumont comes to the surface."

"I'll bring him to see you," said Lord Lambeth. "Where are you staying?"

"You'll find the address in my letter—Jones's Hotel."

"Oh one of those places just out of Piccadilly? Beastly hole, isn't it?" Lord Lambeth enquired.

"I believe it's the best hotel in London," said Mrs. Westgate.

"But they give you awful rubbish to eat, don't they?" his lordship went on.

Mrs. Westgate practised the same serenity. "Awful."

"I always feel so sorry for people who come up to town and go to live in those dens," continued the young man. "They eat nothing but filth."

"Oh I say!" cried Willie Woodley.

"Well, and how do you like London, Miss Alden?" Lord Lambeth asked, unperturbed by this ejaculation.

The girl was prompt. "I think it grand."

"My sister likes it, in spite of the 'filth'!" Mrs. Westgate recorded.

"I hope then you're going to stop a long time."

"As long as I can," Bessie replied.

"And where's wonderful Mr. Westgate?" asked Lord Lambeth of this gentleman's wife.

"He's where he always is—in that tiresome New York."

"He must have staying power," said the young man.

She appeared to consider. "Well, he stays ahead of every one else."

Lord Lambeth sat nearly an hour with his American friends; but it is not our purpose to relate their conversation in full. He addressed a great many remarks to the younger lady and finally turned toward her altogether, while Willie Woodley wasted a certain amount of effort to regale Mrs. Westgate. Bessie herself was sparing of effusion; she thought, on her guard, of what her sister had said to her at luncheon. Little by little, however, she interested herself again in her English friend very much as she had done at Newport; only it seemed to her he might here become more interesting. He would be an unconscious part of the antiquity, the impressiveness, the picturesqueness of England; of all of which things poor Bessie Alden, like most familiars of the overciphered *tabula rasa,* was terribly at the mercy.

"I've often wished I were back at Newport," the young man candidly stated. "Those days I spent at your sister's were awfully jolly."

"We enjoyed them very much; I hope your father's better."

"Oh dear yes. When I got to England the old humbug was out grouse-shooting. It was what you call in America a gigantic fraud. My mother had got nervous. My three weeks at Newport seemed a happy dream."

"America certainly is very different from England," said Bessie.

"I hope you like England better, eh?" he returned almost persuasively.

"No Englishman can ask that seriously of a person of another country."

He turned his cheerful brown eyes on her. "You mean it's a matter of course?"

"If I were English," said Bessie, "it would certainly seem to me a matter of course that every one should be a good patriot."

"Oh dear, yes; patriotism's everything." He appeared not quite to follow, but was clearly contented. "Now what are you going to do here?"

"On Thursday I'm going to the Tower."

"The Tower?"

"The Tower of London. Did you never hear of it?"

"Oh yes, I've been there," said Lord Lambeth. "I was taken there by my governess when I was six years old. It's a rum idea your going there."

"Do give me a few more rum ideas then. I want to see everything of that sort. I'm going to Hampton Court and to Windsor and to the Dulwich Gallery."

He seemed greatly amused. "I wonder you don't go to Rosherville Gardens."

Bessie yearned. "Are they interesting?"

"Oh wonderful!"   .

"Are they weirdly old? That's all I care for," she said.

"They're tremendously old; they're all falling to ruins."

The girl rose to it. "I think there's nothing so charming as an old ruinous garden. We must certainly go there."

Her friend broke out into mirth. "I say, Woodley, here's Miss Alden wants to go down to Rosherville Gardens! Hang it, they *are* 'weird'!"

Willie Woodley looked a little blank; he was caught in the fact of ignorance of an apparently conspicuous feature of London life. But in a moment he turned it off. "Very well," he said, "I'll write for a permit."

Lord Lambeth's exhilaration increased. " 'Gad, I believe that, to get your money's worth over here, you Americans would go anywhere!"

"We wish to go to Parliament," said Bessie. "That's one of the first things."

"Ah it would bore you to death!" he returned.

"We wish to hear you speak."

"I never speak—except to young ladies."

She looked at him from under the shade of her parasol. "You're very strange," she then quietly concluded. "I don't think I approve of you."

"Ah now don't be severe, Miss Alden!" he cried with the note of sincerity. "Please don't be severe. I want you to like me—awfully."

"To like you awfully? You mustn't laugh at me then when I make mistakes. I regard it as my right—as a free-born American—to make as many mistakes as I choose."

"Upon my word I didn't laugh at you," the young man pleaded.

"And not only that," Bessie went on; "but I hold that all my mistakes should be set down to my credit. You must think the better of me for them."

"I can't think better of you than I do," he declared.

Again, shadily, she took him in. "You certainly speak very well to young ladies. But why don't you address the House?—isn't that what they call it?"

"Because I've nothing to say."

"Haven't you a great position?" she demanded.

He looked a moment at the back of his glove. "I'll set that down as one of your mistakes—to your credit." And as if he disliked talking about his position he changed the subject. "I wish you'd let me go with you to the Tower and to Hampton Court and to all those other places."

"We shall be most happy," said Bessie.

"And of course I shall be delighted to show you the Houses of Parliament—some day that suits you. There are a lot of things I want to do for you. I want you to have a good time. And I should like very much to present some of my friends to you if it wouldn't bore you. Then it would be awfully kind of you to come down to Branches."

"We're much obliged to you, Lord Lambeth," said Bessie. "And what may Branches be?"

"It's a house in the country. I think you might like it."

Willie Woodley and Mrs. Westgate were at this moment sitting in silence, and the young man's ear caught these last words of the other pair. "He's inviting Miss Bessie to one of his castles," he murmured to his companion.

Mrs. Westgate hereupon, foreseeing what she mentally called "complications," immediately got up; and the two ladies, taking leave of their English friend, returned, under conduct of their American, to Jones's Hotel.

V

LORD LAMBETH came to see them on the morrow, bringing Percy Beaumont with him—the latter having at once declared his intention of neglecting none of the usual offices of civility. This declaration, however, on his kinsman's informing him of the advent of the two ladies, had been preceded by another exchange.

"Here they are then and you're in for it."

"And what am I in for?" the younger man had enquired.

"I'll let your mother give it a name. With all respect to whom," Percy had added, "I must decline on this occasion to do any more police duty. The Duchess must look after you yourself."

"I'll give her a chance," the Duchess's son had returned a trifle grimly. "I shall make her go and see them."

"She won't do it, my boy."

"We'll see if she doesn't," said Lord Lambeth.

But if Mr. Beaumont took a subtle view of the arrival of the fair strangers at Jones's Hotel he was sufficiently capable of a still deeper refinement to offer them a smiling countenance. He fell into animated conversation—conversation animated at least on *her* side—with Mrs. Westgate, while his companion appealed more confusedly to the younger lady. Mrs. Westgate began confessing and protesting, declaring and discriminating.

"I must say London's a great deal brighter and prettier just now than it was when I was here last—in the month of November. There's evidently a great deal going on, and you seem to have a good many flowers. I've no doubt it's very charming for all you people and that you amuse yourselves immensely. It's very good of you to let Bessie and me come and sit and look at you. I suppose you'll think I'm very satirical, but I must confess that that's the feeling I have in London."

"I'm afraid I don't quite understand to what feeling you allude," said Percy Beaumont.

"The feeling that it's all very well for you English people. Everything's beautifully arranged for you."

"It seems to me it's very well arranged here for some Americans sometimes," Percy plucked up spirit to answer.

"For some of them, yes—if they like to be patronised. But I must say I don't like to be patronised. I may be very eccentric and undisciplined and unreasonable, but I confess I never was fond of patronage. I like to associate with people on the same terms as I do in my own country; that's a peculiar taste that I have. But here people seem to expect something else—really I can't make out quite what. I'm afraid you'll think I'm very ungrateful, for I certainly have received in one way and another a great deal of attention. The last time I was here a lady sent me a message that I was at liberty to come and pay her my respects."

"Dear me, I hope you didn't go," Mr. Beaumont cried.

"You're deliciously naïf, I must say that for you!" Mrs. Westgate promptly pursued. "It must be a great advantage to you here in London. I suppose that if I myself had a little more naïveté—of your blessed national lack of any approach to a sense for shades—I should enjoy it more. I should be content to sit on a chair in the Park and see the people pass, to be told that this is the Duchess of Suffolk and that the Lord Chamberlain, and that I must be thankful for the privilege of beholding them. I dare say it's very peevish and critical of me to ask for anything else. But I was always critical—it's the joy of my life—and I freely confess to the sin of being fastidious. I'm told there's some remarkably superior second-rate society provided here for strangers. *Merci!* I don't want any superior second-rate society. I want the society I've been accustomed to."

Percy mustered a rueful gaiety. "I hope you don't call Lambeth and me second-rate!"

"Oh I'm accustomed to you!" said Mrs. Westgate. "Do you know you English sometimes make the most wonderful speeches? The first time I came to London I went out to dine—as I told you, I've received a great deal of attention. After dinner, in the drawing-room, I had some conversation with an old lady—no, you mustn't look that way: I assure you I had! I forget what we talked about, but she presently said, in allusion to something we were discussing: 'Oh, you know, the aristocracy do so-and-so, but in one's own class of life it's very different.' In one's own class of life! What's a poor unprotected American woman to do in a country where she is liable to have that sort of thing said to her?"

"I should say she's not to mind, not a rap—though you seem to get hold of some very queer old ladies. I compliment you on your acquaintance!" Percy pursued. "If you're trying to bring me to admit that London's an odious place you'll not succeed. I'm extremely fond of it and think it the jolliest place in the world."

"Pour vous autres—I never said the contrary," Mrs. Westgate retorted—an expression made use of, this last, because both interlocutors had begun to raise their voices. Mr. Beaumont naturally didn't like to hear the seat of his existence abused, and Mrs. Westgate, no less naturally, didn't like a stubborn debater.

"Hallo!" said Lord Lambeth; "what are they up to now?" And he came away from the window, where he had been standing with Bessie.

"I quite agree with a very clever countrywoman of mine," the elder lady continued with charming ardour even if with imperfect relevancy. She smiled at the two gentlemen for a moment with terrible brightness, as if to toss at their feet—upon their native heath—the gauntlet of defiance. "For me there are only two social positions worth speaking of—that of an American lady and that of the Emperor of Russia."

"And what do you do with the American gentlemen?" asked Lord Lambeth.

"She leaves them in America!" said his comrade.

On the departure of their visitors Bessie mentioned that Lord Lambeth would come the next day, to go with them to the Tower, and that he had kindly offered to bring his "trap" and drive them all through the city. Mrs. Westgate listened in silence to this news and for some time afterwards also said nothing. But at last, "If you hadn't requested me the other day not to speak of it," she began, "there's something I'd make bold to ask you." Bessie frowned a little; her dark blue eyes grew more dark than blue. But her sister went on. "As it is I'll take the risk. You're not in love with Lord Lambeth: I believe it perfectly. Very good. But is there by chance any danger of your becoming so? It's a very simple question—don't take offence. I've a particular reason," said Mrs. Westgate, "for wanting to know."

Bessie for some moments said nothing; she only looked displeased. "No; there's no danger," she at last answered with a certain dryness.

"Then I should like to frighten them!" cried her sister, clasping jewelled hands.

"To frighten whom?"

"All these people. Lord Lambeth's family and friends."

The girl wondered. "How should you frighten them?"

"It wouldn't be I—it would be you. It would frighten them to suppose you holding in thrall his lordship's young affections."

Our young lady, her clear eyes still overshadowed by her dark brows, continued to examine it. "Why should that frighten them?"

Mrs. Westgate winged her shaft with a smile before launching it. "Because they think you're not good enough. You're a charming girl, beautiful and amiable, intelligent and clever, and as *bien-élevée* as it is possible to be; but you're not a fit match for Lord Lambeth."

Bessie showed again a coldness. "Where do you get such extraordinary ideas? You've said some such odd things lately. My dear Kitty, where do you collect them?"

But Kitty, unabashed, held to her idea. "Yes, it would put them on pins and needles, and it wouldn't hurt *you*. Mr. Beaumont's already most uneasy. I could soon see that."

The girl turned it over. "Do you mean they spy on him, that they interfere with him?"

"I don't know what power they have to interfere, but I know that a British *materfamilias*—and when she's a Duchess into the bargain—is often a force to be reckoned with."

It has already been intimated that before certain appearances of strange or sinister cast our young woman was apt to shy off into scepticism. She abstained on the present occasion from expressing disbelief, for she wished not to irritate her sister. But she said to herself that Kitty had been misinformed—that this was a traveller's tale. Though she was a girl of quick imagination there could in the nature of things be no truth for her in the attribution to her of a vulgar identity. Only the form she gave her doubt was: "I must say that in that case I'm very sorry for Lord Lambeth."

Mrs. Westgate, more and more exhilarated by her own scheme, irradiated interest. "If I could only believe it was safe! But when you begin to pity him I, on my side, am afraid."

"Afraid of what?"

"Of your pitying him too much."

Bessie turned impatiently off—then at the end of a minute faced about. "What if I *should* pity him too much?"

Mrs. Westgate hereupon averted herself, but after a moment's reflexion met the case. "It would come, after all, to the same thing."

Lord Lambeth came the next day with his trap, when the two ladies, attended by Willie Woodley, placed themselves under his guidance and were conveyed eastward, through some of the most fascinating, as Bessie called them, even though the duskiest districts, to the great turreted donjon that overlooks the London shipping. They alighted together to enter the famous fortress, where they secured the services of a venerable beef-eater, who, ignoring the presence of other dependants on his leisure, made a fine exclusive party of them and marched them through courts and corridors, through armouries and prisons. He delivered his usual peripatetic discourse, and they stopped and stared and peeped and stooped according as he marshalled and directed them. Bessie appealed to this worthy—even on more heads than he seemed aware of; she overtaxed, in her earnestness, his learnt lesson and found the place, as she more than once mentioned to him, quite delirious. Lord Lambeth was in high good-humour; his delirium at least was gay and he betrayed afresh that aptitude for the simpler forms of ironic comment that the girl had noted in him. Willie Woodley kept looking at the ceilings and tapping the walls with the knuckle of a pearl-grey glove; and Mrs. West-gate, asking at frequent intervals to be allowed to sit down and wait till they came back, was as frequently informed that they would never do anything so weak. When it befell that Bessie's glowing appeals, chiefly on collateral points of English history, but left the warder gaping she resorted straight to Lord Lambeth. His lordship then pleaded gross incompetence, declaring he knew nothing about that sort of thing and greatly diverted, to all appearance, at being treated as an authority.

"You can't honestly expect people to know as awfully much as you," he said.

"I should expect you to know a great deal more," Bessie Alden returned.

"Well, women always know more than men about names and dates and historical characters," he said. "There was Lady Jane Grey we've just been hearing about, who went in for Latin and Greek and all the learning of her age."

"*You* have no right to be ignorant at all events," Bessie argued with all her freedom.

"Why haven't I as good a right as any one else?"

"Because you've lived in the midst of all these things."

"What things do you mean? Axes and blocks and thumb-screws?"

"All these historical things. You belong to an historical family."

"Bessie really harks back too much to the dead past—she

makes too much of it," Mrs. Westgate opined, catching the sense of this colloquy.

"Yes, you hark back," the young man laughed, thankful for a formula. "You do make too much of the dead past."

He went with the ladies a couple of days later to Hampton Court, Willie Woodley being also of the party. The afternoon was charming, the famous horse-chestnuts blossomed to admiration, and Lord Lambeth, who found in Miss Alden the improving governess, he declared, of his later immaturity, as Mademoiselle Boquet, dragging him by the hand to view all lions, had been that of his earliest, pronounced the old red palace not half so beastly as he had supposed. Bessie herself rose to raptures; she went about murmuring and "raving." "It's too lovely; it's too enchanting; it's too exactly what it ought to be!"

At Hampton Court the tinkling flocks are not provided with an official bellwether, but are left to browse at discretion on the tough herbage of History. It happened in this manner that, in default of another informant, our young woman, who on doubtful questions was able to suggest a great many alternatives, found herself again apply for judicious support to Lord Lambeth. He, however, could but once more declare himself a broken reed and that his education, in such matters, had been sadly neglected.

"And I'm sorry it makes you so wretched," he further professed.

"You're so disappointing, you know," she returned; but more in pity—pity for herself—than in anger.

"Ah now don't say that! That's the worst thing you could possibly say."

"No"—she spoke with a sad lucidity—"it's not so bad as to say that I had expected nothing of you."

"I don't know"—and he seemed to rejoice in a chance to demur. "Give me a notion of the sort of thing you expected."

"Well, that you'd be more what I should like to be—what I should try to be—in your place."

"Ah my place!" he groaned. "You're always talking about my place."

The girl gave him a look; he might have thought she coloured; and for a little she made no rejoinder. "Does it strike you that I'm always talking about your place?"

"I'm sure you do it a great honour," he said as if fearing he had sounded uncivil.

"I've often thought about it," she went on after a moment. "I've often thought of your future as an hereditary legislator. An hereditary legislator ought to know so many things, oughtn't he?"

"Not if he doesn't legislate."

"But you *will* legislate one of these days—you may have to at any time; it's absurd your saying you won't. You're very much looked up to here—I'm assured of that."

"I don't know that I ever noticed it."

"It's because you're used to it then. You ought to fill the place."

"How do you mean, fill it?" asked Lord Lambeth.

"You ought to be very clever and brilliant—to be 'up' in almost everything."

He turned on her his handsome young face of profane wonder. "Shall I tell you something? A young man in my position, as you call it—"

"I didn't invent the term," she interposed. "I've seen it in a great many books."

"Hang it, you're always at your books! A fellow in my position then does well enough at the worst—he muddles along whatever he does. That's about what I mean to say."

"Well, if your own people are content with you," Bessie laughed, "it's not for me to complain. But I shall always think that properly you should have a great mind—a great character."

"Ah that's very theoretic!" the young man promptly brought out. "Depend upon it, that's a Yankee prejudice."

"Happy the country then," she as eagerly declared, "where people's prejudices make so for light."

He stopped short, with his slightly strained gaiety, as for the pleasantness of high argument. "What it comes to then is that we're all here a pack of fools and me the biggest of the lot?"

"I said nothing so rude of a great people—and a great person. But I must repeat that you personally are—in your representative capacity that's to be—disappointing."

"My dear Miss Alden," he simply cried at this, "I'm the best fellow in the world!"

"Ah if it were not for that!" she beautifully smiled.

Mrs. Westgate had many more friends in London than she pretended, and before long had renewed acquaintance with most of them. Their hospitality was prompt, so that, one thing leading to another, she began, as the phrase is, to go out. Bessie Alden, in this way, saw a good deal of what she took great pleasure in calling to herself English society. She went to balls and danced, she went to dinners and talked, she went to concerts and listened—at concerts Bessie always listened—she went to exhibitions and wondered. Her enjoyment was keen and her curiosity insatiable, and, grateful in general for all her opportunities, she especially prized the privilege of meeting certain celebrated persons, authors and artists, philosophers and statesmen, of whose renown she had been a humble and distant beholder and who now, as part of the frequent furniture of London drawing-rooms, struck her as stars fallen from the firmament and become palpable—revealing also sometimes on contact qualities not to have been predicted of bodies sidereal. Bessie, who knew so many of her contemporaries by reputation, lost in this way certain fond illusions; but on the other hand she had innumerable satisfactions and enthusiasms, and she laid bare the wealth of her emotions to a dear friend of her own sex in Boston, with whom she was in voluminous correspondence. Some of her sentiments indeed she sought mildly to flash upon Lord Lambeth, who came almost every day to Jones's Hotel and whom Mrs. Westgate admitted to be really devoted. Captain Littledale, it appeared, had gone to India; and of several others of this lady's ex-pensioners—gentlemen who, as she said, had made, in New York, a club-house of her drawing-room—no tidings were to be obtained; but this particular friend of other days was certainly attentive enough to make up for the accidental absences, the short memories, the remarked lapses, of every one else. He drove the sisters in the Park, took them to visit private collections of pictures and, having a house of his own, invited them to luncheon, to tea, to dinner, to supper even after the arduous German opera. Mrs. Westgate, following the fashion of many of her countrywomen, caused herself and her companion to be presented at the English Court by her diplomatic representative—for it was in this manner that she alluded to the American Minister to England, enquiring what on earth he was put there for if not to make the proper arrangements for her reception at Court.

Lord Lambeth expressed a hatred of Courts, but he had social privileges or exercised some court function—these undiscriminated attributes, dim backgrounds where old gold seemed to shine through transparent conventions, were romantically rich to our young heroine—that involved his support of his sovereign on the day on which the two ladies at Jones's Hotel repaired to Buckingham Palace in a remarkable coach sent by his lordship to fetch them. He appeared in a gorgeous uniform, and Bessie Alden was particularly struck with his glory—especially when on her asking him, rather foolishly as she felt, if he were a loyal subject, he replied that he was a loyal subject to herself. This pronouncement was emphasized by his dancing with her at a royal ball to which the two ladies afterwards went, and was not impaired by the fact that she thought he danced very ill. He struck her as wonderfully kind; she asked herself with growing vivacity why he should be so kind. It was just his character—that seemed the natural reply. She had told her relative how much she liked him, and now that she liked him more she wondered at her excess. She liked him for his clear nature; to this question as well that seemed the natural answer. The truth was that when once the impressions of London life began to crowd thickly upon her she completely forgot her subtle sister's warning on the cynicism of public opinion. It had given her great pain at the moment; but there was no particular reason why she should remember it: it corresponded too little with any sensible reality. Besides which there was her habit, her beautiful system, of consenting to know nothing of human baseness or of the vulgar side. There were things, just as there were people, that were as nought from the moment one ignored them. She was accordingly not haunted with the sense of a low imputation. She wasn't in love with Lord Lambeth—she assured herself of that. It will immediately be observed that when such assurances become necessary the state of a young lady's affections is already ambiguous; and indeed the girl made no attempt to dissimulate (to her finer intelligence) that "appeal of type"—she had a ready name for it—to which her gallant hovering gentleman caused her wonderingly to respond. She was fully aware that she liked it, this so unalloyed image of the simple candid manly healthy English temperament. She spoke to herself of it as if she liked the man for it instead of her liking it for the man. She cherished the thought of his bravery, which she had never in the least seen tested, enjoyed a fond view in him of the free and instinctive range of the "gentlemanly" character, and was as familiar with his good looks as if she habitually handed him out his neckties. She was perfectly conscious moreover of privately dilating on his more adventitious merits—of the effect on her imagination of the large opportunities of so splendid a person; opportunities she hardly knew for what, but, as she supposed, for doing great things, for setting an example, for exerting an influence, for conferring happiness, for encouraging the arts. She had an ideal of conduct for a young man who should find himself in this grand position, and she tried to adapt it to her friend's behaviour as you might attempt to fit a silhouette in cut paper over a shadow projected on a wall. Bessie Alden's silhouette, however, refused to coincide at all points with his lordship's figure; a want of harmony that she sometimes deplored beyond discretion. It was his own affair she at moments told herself—it wasn't *her* concern the least in the world. When he was absent it was of course less striking—then he might have seemed sufficiently to unite high responsibilities with high braveries. But when he sat there within sight, laughing and talking with his usual effect of natural salubrity and mental mediocrity, she took the measure of his shortcoming and felt acutely that if his position was, so to speak, heroic, there was little of that large line in the young man himself. Then her imagination wandered away from him—very far away; for it was an incontestable fact that at these moments he lagged ever so much behind it. He affected her as on occasion, dreadful to say, almost *actively* stupid. It may have been that while she so curiously enquired and so critically brooded *her* personal wit, her presence of mind, made no great show—though it is also possible that she sometimes positively charmed, or at least interested, her friend by this very betrayal of the frequent, the distant and unreported, excursion. So it would have hung together that a part of her unconscious appeal to him from the first had been in his feeling her judge and appraise him more freely and irresponsibly—more at her ease and her leisure, as it were—than several young ladies with whom he had passed for adventurously intimate. To be convinced of her "cleverness" and yet also to be aware of her appreciation—when the cleverness might have been after all but dangerous and complicating—all made, to Lord Lambeth's sense, for convenience and cheer. Hadn't he compassed the satisfaction, that high aim of young men greatly placed and greatly moneyed, of being liked for himself? It was true a cynical counsellor might have whispered to him: "Liked for yourself? Ah not so very awfully *much!*" He had at any rate the constant hope of adding to that quantity.

It may not seem to fit in—but the truth was strange—that Bessie Alden, when he struck her as "deficient," found herself aspiring by that very reason to some finer way of liking him. This was fairly indeed on grounds of conscience—because she felt he had been thoroughly "nice" to her sister and so deemed it no more than fair that she should think as well of him as he thought of her. The effort in question was possibly sometimes not so successful as it might have been, the result being at moments an irritation, which, though consciously vague, was yet, with inconsequence, acute enough to express itself in hostile criticism of several British institutions. Bessie went to entertainments at which she met Lord Lambeth, but also to others at which he was neither actually nor imaginably present; and it was chiefly at these latter that she encountered those literary and artistic celebrities of whom mention has been made. After a while she reduced the matter to a principle. If he should appear anywhere she might take it for a flat sign that there would be neither poets nor philosophers; and as a result—for it was almost a direct result—she used to enumerate to the young man these objects of her admiration.

"You seem to be awfully fond of that sort of people," he said one day as if the idea had just occurred to him.

"They're the people in England I'm most curious to see," she promptly replied.

"I suppose that's because you've read so much," Lord Lambeth gallantly threw off.

"I've *not* read so much. It's because we think so much of them at home."

"Oh I see! In your so awfully clever Boston."

"Not only in our awfully clever Boston, but in our just commonly clever everywhere. We hold them in great honour," said Bessie. "It's they who go to the best dinner-parties."

"I dare say you're right. I can't say I know many of them."

"It's a pity you don't," she returned. "It would do you some good."

"I dare say it would," said the young man very humbly. "But I must say I don't like the looks of some of them."

"Neither do I—of some of them. But there are all kinds, and many of them are charming."

"I've talked with two or three of them," Lord Lambeth went on, "and I thought they had a kind of fawning manner."

"Why should they fawn?" Bessie demanded.

"I'm sure I don't know. Why indeed?"

"Perhaps you only thought so," she suggested.

"Well, of course," her companion allowed, "that's a kind of thing that can't be proved."

"In America they don't fawn," she went on.

"Don't they? Ah well then they must be better company."

She had a pause. "That's one of the few things I don't like about England,—your keeping the distinguished people apart."

"How do you mean, apart?"

"Why letting them come only to certain places. You never see them."

All his pleasant face wondered—he seemed to take it as another of her rather stiff riddles. "What people do you mean?"

"The eminent people; the authors and artists; the clever people."

"Oh there are other eminent people besides those!" said Lord Lambeth.

"Well, you certainly keep them apart," Bessie earnestly contended.

"And there are plenty of other clever people."

It was spoken with a fine simple faith, yet the tone of it made her laugh. "'Plenty'? How many?"

On another occasion—just after a dinner-party—she mentioned something else in England she didn't like.

"Oh I say!" he cried; "haven't you abused us enough?"

"I've never abused you at all," said Bessie; "but I don't like your 'precedence.'"

She was to feel relieved at his not taking it solemnly. "It isn't *my* precedence!"

"Yes, it's yours—just exactly yours; and I think it's odious," she insisted.

"I never saw such a young lady for discussing things! Has some one had the impudence to go before you?" Lord Lambeth asked.

"It's not the going before me I object to," said Bessie; "it's their pretending they've a right to do it—a right I should grovellingly recognise."

"I never saw such a person, either, for not 'recognising,' let alone for not 'grovelling.' Every one here has to grovel to somebody or to something—and no doubt it's all beastly. But one takes the thick with the thin, and it saves a lot of trouble."

"It *makes* a lot of trouble, by which I mean a lot of ugliness. It's horrid!" Bessie maintained.

"But how would you have the first people go?" the young man asked. "They can't go last, you know."

"Whom do you mean by the first people?"

"Ah if you mean to question first principles!" said Lord Lambeth.

"If those are your first principles no wonder some of your arrangements are horrid!" she cried with a charming but not wholly sincere ferocity. "I'm a silly chit, no doubt, so of course I go last; but imagine what Kitty must feel on being informed that she's not at liberty to budge till certain other ladies have passed out!"

"Oh I say, she's not 'informed'!" he protested. "No one would do such a thing as that."

"She's made to feel it—as if they were afraid she'd make a rush for the door. No, you've a lovely country"—she clung as for consistency to her discrimination—"but your precedence is horrid."

"I certainly shouldn't think your sister would like it," Lord Lambeth said with even exaggerated gravity. But she couldn't induce him—amused as he almost always was at the effect of giving her, as he called it, her head—to join her in more formal reprobation of this repulsive custom, which he spoke of as a convenience she would destroy without offering a better in its place.

VI

PERCY BEAUMONT had all this time been a very much less frequent visitor at Jones's Hotel than his former fellow traveller; he had in fact called but twice on the two Ameircan ladies. Lord Lambeth, who often saw him, reproached him with his neglect and declared that though Mrs. Westgate had said nothing about it he made no doubt she was secretly wounded by it. "She suffers too much to speak," said his comrade.

"That's all gammon," Percy returned; "there's a limit to what people can suffer!" And though sending no apologies to Jones's Hotel he undertook in a manner to explain his absence. "You're always there yourself, confound you, and that's reason enough for my not going."

"I don't see why. There's enough for both of us."

"Well, I don't care to be a witness of your reckless passion," said Percy Beaumont.

His friend turned on him a cold eye and for a moment said nothing, presently, however, speaking a little stiffly. "My passion doesn't make such a show as you might suppose, considering what a demonstrative beggar I am."

"I don't want to know anything about it—anything whatever,"

said Beaumont. "Your mother asks me every time she sees me whether I believe you're really lost—and Lady Pimlico does the same. I prefer to be able to answer that I'm in complete ignorance, that I never go there. I stay away for consistency's sake. As I said the other day they must look after you themselves."

"Well, you're wonderfully considerate," the young man returned. "They never question *me*."

"They're afraid of you. They're afraid of annoying you and making you worse. So they go to work very cautiously, and, somewhere or other, they get their information. They know a great deal about you. They know you've been with those ladies to the dome of Saint Paul's and—where was the other place?—to the Thames Tunnel."

"If all their knowledge is as accurate as that it must be very valuable," said Lord Lambeth.

"Well, at any rate, they know you've been visiting the 'sights of the metropolis.' They think—very naturally, as it seems to me —that when you take to visiting the sights of the metropolis with a little nobody of an American girl something may be supposed to be 'up.'" The young man met this remark with scornful laughter, but his companion continued after a pause: "I told you just now that I cultivate my ignorance, but I find I can no longer stand my suspense. I confess I do want to know whether you propose to marry Miss Alden."

On this point Lord Lambeth gave his questioner no prompt satisfaction; he only mused—frowningly, portentously. "By Jove they go rather too far. They *shall* have cause to worry—I promise them."

Percy Beaumont, however, continued to aim at lucidity. "You don't, it's true, quite redeem your threats. You said the other day you'd make your mother call."

Lord Lambeth just hung fire. "Well, I asked her to."

"And she declined?"

"Yes, but she shall do it yet."

"Upon my word," said Percy, "if she gets much more scared I verily believe she will." His friend watched him on this, and he went on. "She'll go to the girl herself."

"How do you mean 'go' to her?"

"She'll try to get 'at' her—to square her. She won't care what she does."

Lord Lambeth turned away in silence; he took twenty steps and slowly returned. "She had better take care what she does. I've invited Mrs. Westgate and Miss Alden to Branches, and this evening I shall name a day."

"And shall you invite your mother and your sisters to meet them?"

Lord Lambeth indulged in one of his rare discriminations. "I shall give them the opportunity."

"That will touch the Duchess up," said Percy Beaumont. "I 'guess' she'll come."

"She may do as she pleases."

"Then you do really propose to marry the little sister?"

"I like the way you talk about it!" the young man cried. "She won't gobble me down. Don't be afraid."

"She won't leave you on your knees," Percy declared. "What the devil's the inducement?"

"You talk about proposing—wait till I *have* proposed," Lord Lambeth went on.

His friend looked at him harder. "That's right, my dear chap. Think of *all* the bearings."

"She's a charming girl," pursued his lordship.

"Of course she's a charming girl. I don't know a girl more charming—in a very quiet way. But there are other charming girls—charming in all sorts of ways—nearer home."

"I particularly like her spirit," said Bessie's admirer—almost as on a policy of aggravation.

"What's the peculiarity of her spirit?"

"She's not afraid, and she says things out and thinks herself as good as any one. She's the only girl I've ever seen," Lord Lambeth explained, "who hasn't seemed to me dying to marry me."

Mr. Beaumont considered it. "How do you know she isn't dying if you haven't felt her pulse? I mean if you haven't asked her?"

"I don't know how; but I know it."

"I'm sure she asked *me*—over there—questions enough about your property and your titles," Percy declared.

"She has done that to me too—again and again," his friend returned. "But she wants to know about everything."

"Everything? Ah I'll warrant she wants to know. Depend upon it she's dying to marry you just as much, and just by the same law, as all the rest of them."

It appeared to give the young man, for a moment, something rather special to think of. "I shouldn't like her to refuse me—I shouldn't like that."

"If the thing would be so disagreeable then, both to you and to her, in heaven's name leave it alone." Such was the moral drawn by Mr. Beaumont; which left him practically the last word in the discussion.

Mrs. Westgate, on her side, had plenty to say to her sister about the rarity of the latter's visits and the non-appearance at their own door of the Duchess of Bayswater. She confessed, however, to taking more pleasure in this hush of symptoms than she could have taken in the most lavish attentions on the part of that great lady. "It's unmistakeable," she said, "delightfully unmistakeable; a most interesting sign that we've made them wretched. The day we dined with him I was really sorry for the poor boy." It will have been gathered that the entertainment offered by Lord Lambeth to his American friends had been graced by the presence of no near relation. He had invited several choice spirits to meet them, but the ladies of his immediate family were to Mrs. Westgate's sense—a sense perhaps morbidly acute—conspicuous by their hostile absence.

"I don't want to work you up any further," Bessie at last ventured to remark, "but I don't know why you should have so many theories about Lord Lambeth's poor mother. You know a great many young men in New York without knowing their mothers."

Mrs. Westgate rested deep eyes on her sister and then turned away. "My dear Bessie, you're superb!"

"One thing's certain"—the girl continued not to blench at her irony. "If I believed I were a cause of annoyance, however unwitting, to Lord Lambeth's family I should insist—"

"Insist on my leaving England?" Mrs. Westgate broke in.

"No, not that. I want to go to the National Gallery again; I want to see Stratford-on-Avon and Canterbury Cathedral. But I should insist on his ceasing relations with us."

"That would be very modest and very pretty of you—but you wouldn't do it at this point."

"Why do you say 'at this point'?" Bessie asked. "Have I ceased to be modest?"

"You care for him too much. A month ago, when you said you didn't, I believe it was quite true. But at present, my dear child," said Mrs. Westgate, "you wouldn't find it quite so simple a matter never to see Lord Lambeth again. I've watched it come on."

"You're mistaken," Bessie declared. "You don't understand."

"Ah you poor proud thing, don't be perverse!" her companion returned.

The girl gave the matter, thus admonished, some visible thought. "I know him better certainly, if you mean that. And I like him very much. But I don't like him enough to make trouble for him with his family. However, I don't believe in that."

"I like the way you say 'however'!" Mrs. Westgate commented. "Do you pretend you wouldn't be glad to marry him?"

Again Bessie calmly considered. "It would take a great deal more than is at all imaginable to make me marry him."

Her relative showed an impatience. "And what's the great difficulty?"

"The great difficulty is that I shouldn't care to," said Bessie Alden.

The morning after Lord Lambeth had had with his own frankest critic that exchange of ideas which has just been narrated, the ladies at Jones's Hotel received from him a written invitation to pay their projected visit to Branches Castle on the following Tuesday. "I think I've made up a very pleasant party," his lordship went on. "Several people whom you know, and my mother and sisters, who have been accidentally prevented from making your acquaintance sooner." Bessie at this lost no time in calling her sister's attention to the injustice she had done the Duchess of Bayswater, whose hostility was now proved to be a vain illusion.

"Wait till you see if she comes," said Mrs. Westgate. "And if she's to meet us at her son's house the obligation's all the greater for her to call on us."

Bessie hadn't to wait long, for it appeared that her friend's parent now descried the direction in which, according to her companion's observation, courtesy pointed. On the morrow, early in the afternoon, two cards were brought to the apartment of the American ladies—one of them bearing the name of the Duchess of Bayswater and the other that of the Countess of Pimlico. Mrs. Westgate glanced at the clock. "It isn't yet four," she said; "they've come early; they want really to find us. We'll receive them." And she gave orders that her visitors should be admitted. A few moments later they were introduced and a solemn exchange of amenities took place. The Duchess was a large lady with a fine fresh colour; the Countess of Pimlico was very pretty and elegant.

The Duchess looked about her as she sat down—looked not especially at Mrs. Westgate. "I dare say my son has told you that I've been wanting to come to see you," she dropped—and from no towering nor inconvenient height.

"You're very kind," said Mrs. Westgate vaguely—her conscience not allowing her to assent to this proposition, and indeed not permitting her to enunciate her own with any appreciable emphasis.

"He tells us you were so kind to him in America," said the Duchess.

"We're very glad," Mrs. Westgate replied, "to have been able to make him feel a little more—a little less—a little at home."

"I think he stayed at your house," the visitor more heavily breathed, but as an overture, across to Bessie Alden.

Mrs. Westgate intercepted the remark. "A very short time indeed."

"Oh!" said the Duchess; and she continued to address her interest to Bessie, who was engaged in conversation with her daughter.

"Do you like London?" Lady Pimlico had asked of Bessie, after looking at her a good deal—at her face and her hands, her dress and her hair.

The girl was prompt and clear. "Very much indeed."

"Do you like this hotel?"

"It's very comfortable."

"Do you like stopping at hotels?" Lady Pimlico asked after a pause.

"I'm very fond of travelling, and I suppose hotels are a necessary part of it. But they're not the part I'm fondest of," Bessie without difficulty admitted.

"Oh I hate travelling!" said Lord Lambeth's sister, who transferred her attention to Mrs. Westgate.

"My son tells me you're going to Branches," the Duchess presently resumed.

"Lord Lambeth has been so good as to ask us," said Mrs. Westgate, who felt herself now under the eyes of both visitors and who had her customary happy consciousness of a distinguished appearance. The only mitigation of her felicity on this point was that, having taken in every item of that of the Duchess, she said to herself: "She won't know how well I'm dressed!"

"He has been so good as to tell me he expects me, but I'm not quite sure of what I can do," the noble lady exhaled.

"He had offered us the p—the prospect of meeting you," Mrs. Westgate further contributed.

"I hate the country at this season," the Duchess went on.

Her hostess melted to sweetness. "I delight in it at all seasons. And I think it now above all pleasanter than London."

But the Duchess's eyes were absent again; she was looking very fixedly at Bessie. In a minute she slowly rose, passed across the room with a great rustle and an effect of momentous displacement, reached a chair that stood empty at the girl's right hand and silently seated herself. As she was a majestic voluminous woman this little transaction had inevitably an air of somewhat impressive intention. It diffused a certain awkwardness, which Lady Pimlico, as a sympathetic daughter, perhaps desired to rectify in turning to Mrs. Westgate. "I suppose you go out immensely."

"No, very little. We're strangers, and we didn't come for the local society."

"I see," said Lady Pimlico. "It's rather nice in town just now."

"I've known it of course duskier and dingier. But we only go to see a few people," Mrs. Westgate added—"old friends or persons we particularly like."

"Of course one can't like every one," Lady Pimlico conceded.

"It depends on one's society," Mrs. Westgate returned.

The Duchess meanwhile had addressed herself to Bessie. "My son tells me the young ladies in America are so clever."

"I'm glad they made so good an impression on him," our heroine smiled.

The Duchess took the case, clearly, as no matter for grimacing; there reigned in her large pink face a meridian calm. "He's very susceptible. He thinks every one clever—and sometimes they are."

"Sometimes," Bessie cheerfully assented.

The Duchess continued all serenely and publicly to appraise her. "Lambeth's very susceptible, but he's very volatile too."

"Volatile?" Bessie echoed.

"He's very inconstant. It won't do to depend on him."

"Ah," the girl returned, "I don't recognise that description. We've depended on him greatly, my sister and I, and have found him so faithful. He has never disappointed us."

"He'll disappoint you yet," said her Grace with a certain rich force.

Bessie gave a laugh of amusement as at such a contention from such a quarter. "I suppose it will depend on what we expect of him."

"The less you expect the better," said her massive monitress.

"Well, we expect nothing unreasonable."

The Duchess had a fine contemplative pause—evidently with more to say. She made, in the quantity, her next selection. "Lambeth says he has seen so much of you."

"He has been with us very often—he has been a ministering angel," Bessie hastened to put on record.

"I dare say you're used to that. I'm told there's a great deal of that in America."

"A great deal of angelic ministering?" the girl laughed again.

"Is that what you call it? I know you've different expressions."

"We certainly don't always understand each other," said Mrs. Westgate, the termination of whose interview with Lady Pimlico had allowed her to revert to their elder visitor.

"I'm speaking of the young men calling so much on the young ladies," the Duchess explained.

"But surely in England," Mrs. Westgate appealed, "the young ladies don't call on the young men?"

"Some of them do—almost!" Lady Pimlico declared. "When a young man's a great *parti*."

"Bessie, you must make a note of that," said Mrs. Westgate. "My sister"—she gave their friends the benefit of the knowledge —"is a model traveller. She writes down all the curious facts she hears in a little book she keeps for the purpose."

The Duchess took it, with a noble art of her own, as if she hadn't heard it; and while she was so occupied—for this involved a large deliberation—her daughter turned to Bessie. "My brother has told us of your being so clever."

"He should have said my sister," Bessie returned—"when she treats you to such flights as that."

"Shall you be long at Branches?" the Duchess abruptly asked of her.

Bessie was to have afterwards a vivid remembrance of wondering what her Grace (she was so glad Duchesses had that predicate) would mean by "long." But she might as well somehow have wondered what the occupants of the planet Mars would. "He has invited us for three days."

"I think I must really manage it," the Duchess declared—"and my daughter too."

"That will be charming!"

"Delightful!" cried Mrs. Westgate.

"I shall expect to see a deal of you," the Duchess continued. "When I go to Branches I monopolise my son's guests."

"They must give themselves up to you," said Mrs. Westgate all graciously.

"I quite yearn to see it—to see the Castle," Bessie went on to the larger lady. "I've never seen one—in England at least; and you know we've none in America."

"Ah you're fond of castles?"—her Grace quite took it up.

"Of the idea of them—which is all I know—immensely." And the girl's pale light deepened for the assurance. "It has been the dream of my life to live in one."

The Duchess looked at her as if hardly knowing how to take such words, which, from the ducal point of view, had either to be very artless or very aggressive. "Well," she said, rising, "I'll show you Branches myself." And upon this the noble ladies took their departure.

"What did they mean by it?" Mrs. Westgate sought to know when they had gone.

"They meant to do the friendly thing," Bessie surmised, "because we're going to meet them."

"It's too late to do the friendly thing," Mrs. Westgate replied almost grimly. "They meant to overawe us by their fine manners and their grandeur; they meant to make you *lâcher prise*."

"*Lâcher prise?* What strange things you say!" the girl sighed as fairly for pain.

"They meant to snub us so that we shouldn't dare to go to Branches," Mrs. Westgate substituted with confidence.

"On the contrary," said Bessie, "the Duchess offered to show me the place herself."

"Yes, you may depend upon it she won't let you out of her sight. She'll show you the place from morning till night."

"You've a theory for everything," our young woman a little more helplessly allowed.

"And you apparently have none for anything."

"I saw no attempt to 'overawe' us," Bessie nevertheless persisted. "Their manners weren't fine."

"They were not even good!" Mrs. Westgate declared.

Her sister had a pause, but in a few moments claimed the possession of an excellent theory. "They just came to look at me!" she brought out as with much ingenuity. Mrs. Westgate did the idea justice; she greeted it with a smile and pronounced it a credit to a fresh young mind; while in reality she felt that the girl's scepticism, or her charity, or, as she had sometimes called it appropriately, her idealism, was proof against irony. Bessie, however, remained meditative all the rest of that day and well on into the morrow. She privately ached—almost as under a dishonour—with the aftersense of having been inspected in that particular way.

On the morrow before luncheon Mrs. Westgate, having occasion to go out for an hour, left her sister writing a letter. When she came back she met Lord Lambeth at the door of the hotel and in the act of leaving it. She thought he looked considerably embarrassed; he certainly, she said to herself, had no spring. "I'm sorry to have missed you. Won't you come back?" she asked.

"No—I can't. I've seen your sister. I can never come back." Then he looked at her a moment and took her hand. "Good-bye, Mrs. Westgate—you've been very kind to me." And with what she thought a strange sad air on his handsome young face he turned away.

She went in only to find Bessie still writing her letter; find her, that is, seated at the table with the arrested pen in her hand. She put her question after a moment. "Lord Lambeth has been here?"

Then Bessie got up and showed her a pale serious face—bending it on her for some time, confessing silently and, a little, pleading. "I told him," the girl said at last, "that we couldn't go to Branches."

Mrs. Westgate gave a gasp of temporary disappointment. "He might have waited," she nevertheless smiled, "till one had seen the Castle." An hour afterwards she spoke again. "I do wish, you know, you might have accepted him."

"I couldn't," said Bessie with the slowest gravest gentlest of headshakes.

"He's really such a dear," Mrs. Westgate pursued.

"I couldn't," Bessie repeated.

"If it's only," her sister added, "because those women will think they succeeded—that they paralysed us!"

Our young lady turned away, but presently added: "They were interesting. I should have liked to see them again."

"So should I!" cried Mrs. Westgate with much point.

"And I should have liked to see the Castle," said Bessie. "But now we must leave England."

Her sister's eyes studied her. "You won't wait to go to the National Gallery?"

"Not now."

"Nor to Canterbury Cathedral?"

Bessie lost herself for a little in this. "We can stop there on our way to Paris," she then said.

Lord Lambeth didn't tell Percy Beaumont that the contingency he was not prepared at all to like had occurred; but that gentleman, on hearing that the two ladies had left London, wondered with some intensity what had happened; wondered, that is, till the Duchess of Bayswater came a little to his assistance. The two ladies went to Paris—when Mrs. Westgate beguiled the journey by repeating several times: "That's what I regret; they'll think they petrified us." But Bessie Alden, strange and charming girl, seemed to regret nothing.

THE REAL THING

~~~~

I

WHEN the porter's wife, who used to answer the house-bell, announced "A gentleman and a lady, sir," I had, as I often had in those days—the wish being father to the thought—an immediate vision of sitters. Sitters my visitors in this case proved to be; but not in the sense I should have preferred. There was nothing at first however to indicate that they mightn't have come for a portrait. The gentleman, a man of fifty, very high and very straight, with a moustache slightly grizzled and a dark grey walking-coat admirably fitted, both of which I noted professionally—I don't mean as a barber or yet as a tailor—would have struck me as a celebrity if celebrities often were striking. It was a truth of which I had for some time been conscious that a figure with a good deal of frontage was, as one might say, almost never a public institution. A glance at the lady helped to remind me of this paradoxical law: she also looked too distinguished to be a "personality." Moreover one would scarcely come across two variations together.

Neither of the pair immediately spoke—they only prolonged the preliminary gaze suggesting that each wished to give the other a chance. They were visibly shy; they stood there letting me take them in—which, as I afterwards perceived, was the most practical thing they could have done. In this way their embarrassment served their cause. I had seen people painfully reluctant to mention that they desired anything so gross as to be represented on canvas; but the scruples of my new friends appeared almost insurmountable. Yet the gentleman might have said "I should like a portrait of my wife," and the lady might have said "I should like a portrait of my husband." Perhaps they weren't husband and wife—this naturally would make the matter more delicate. Perhaps they wished to be done together—in which case they ought to have brought a third person to break the news.

"We come from Mr. Rivet," the lady finally said with a dim smile that had the effect of a moist sponge passed over a "sunk" piece of painting, as well as of a vague allusion to vanished beauty. She was as tall and straight, in her degree, as her companion, and with ten years less to carry. She looked as sad as a woman could look whose face was not charged with expression; that is her tinted oval mask showed waste as an exposed surface shows friction. The hand of time had played over her freely, but to an effect of elimination. She was slim and stiff, and so well-dressed, in dark blue cloth, with lappets and pockets and buttons, that it was clear she employed the same tailor as her husband. The couple had an indefinable air of prosperous thrift—they evidently got a good deal of luxury for their money. If I was to be one of their luxuries it would behove me to consider my terms.

"Ah Claude Rivet recommended me?" I echoed; and I added that it was very kind of him, though I could reflect that, as he only painted landscape, this wasn't a sacrifice.

The lady looked very hard at the gentleman, and the gentleman looked round the room. Then staring at the floor a moment and stroking his moustache, he rested his pleasant eyes on me with the remark: "He said you were the right one."

"I try to be, when people want to sit."

"Yes, we should like to," said the lady anxiously.

"Do you mean together?"

My visitors exchanged a glance. "If you could do anything with *me* I suppose it would be double," the gentleman stammered.

"Oh yes, there's naturally a higher charge for two figures than for one."

"We should like to make it pay," the husband confessed.

"That's very good of you," I returned, appreciating so unwonted a sympathy—for I supposed he meant pay the artist.

A sense of strangeness seemed to dawn on the lady. "We mean for the illustrations—Mr. Rivet said you might put one in."

"Put in—an illustration?" I was equally confused.

"Sketch her off, you know," said the gentleman, colouring.

It was only then that I understood the service Claude Rivet had rendered me; he had told them how I worked in black-and-white, for magazines, for storybooks, for sketches of contemporary life, and consequently had copious employment for models. These things were true, but it was not less true—I may confess it now; whether because the aspiration was to lead to everything or to nothing I leave the reader to guess—that I couldn't get the honours, to say nothing of the emoluments, of a great painter of portraits out of my head. My "illustrations" were my pot-boilers; I looked to a different branch of art—far and away the most interesting it had always seemed to me—to perpetuate my fame. There was no shame in looking to it also to make my fortune; but that fortune was by so much further from being made from the moment my visitors wished to be "done" for nothing. I was disappointed; for in the pictorial sense I had immediately *seen* them. I had seized their type—I had already settled what I would do with it. Something that wouldn't absolutely have pleased them, I afterwards reflected.

"Ah you're—you're—a—?" I began as soon as I had mastered my surprise. I couldn't bring out the dingy word "models": it seemed so little to fit the case.

"We haven't had much practice," said the lady.

"We've got to *do* something, and we've thought that an artist in your line might perhaps make something of us," her husband threw off. He further mentioned that they didn't know many artists and that they had gone first, on the off-chance—he painted views of course, but sometimes put in figures; perhaps I remembered—to Mr. Rivet, whom they had met a few years before at a place in Norfolk where he was sketching.

"We used to sketch a little ourselves," the lady hinted.

"It's very awkward, but we absolutely *must* do something," her husband went on.

"Of course we're not so *very* young," she admitted with a wan smile.

With the remark that I might as well know something more

about them the husband had handed me a card extracted from a neat new pocket-book—their appurtenances were all of the freshest—and inscribed with the words "Major Monarch." Impressive as these words were they didn't carry my knowledge much further; but my visitor presently added: "I've left the army and we've had the misfortune to lose our money. In fact our means are dreadfully small."

"It's awfully trying—a regular strain," said Mrs. Monarch.

They evidently wished to be discreet—to take care not to swagger because they were gentlefolk. I felt them willing to recognise this as something of a drawback, at the same time that I guessed at an underlying sense—their consolation in adversity—that they *had* their points. They certainly had; but these advantages struck me as preponderantly social; such for instance as would help to make a drawing-room look well. However, a drawing-room was always, or ought to be, a picture.

In consequence of his wife's allusion to their age Major Monarch observed: "Naturally it's more for the figure that we thought of going in. We can still hold ourselves up." On the instant I saw that the figure was indeed their strong point. His "naturally" didn't sound vain, but it lighted up the question. *"She* has the best one," he continued, nodding at his wife with a pleasant after-dinner absence of circumlocution. I could only reply, as if we were in fact sitting over our wine, that this didn't prevent his own from being very good; which led him in turn to make answer: "We thought that if you ever have to do people like us we might be something like it. *She* particularly—for a lady in a book, you know."

I was so amused by them that, to get more of it, I did my best to take their point of view; and though it was an embarrassment to find myself appraising physically, as if they were animals on hire or useful blacks, a pair whom I should have expected to meet only in one of the relations in which criticism is tacit, I looked at Mrs. Monarch judicially enough to be able to exclaim after a moment with conviction: "Oh yes, a lady in a book!" She was singularly like a bad illustration.

"We'll stand up, if you like," said the Major; and he raised himself before me with a really grand air.

I could take his measure at a glance—he was six feet two and a perfect gentleman. It would have paid any club in process of formation and in want of a stamp to engage him at a salary to stand in the principal window. What struck me at once was that in coming to me they had rather missed their vocation; they could surely have been turned to better account for advertising purposes. I couldn't of course see the thing in detail, but I could see them make somebody's fortune—I don't mean their own. There was something in them for a waistcoat-maker, an hotel-keeper or a soap-vendor. I could imagine "We always use it" pinned on their bosoms with the greatest effect; I had a vision of the brilliancy with which they would launch a table d'hôte.

Mrs. Monarch sat still, not from pride but from shyness, and presently her husband said to her: "Get up, my dear, and show how smart you are." She obeyed, but she had no need to get up to show it. She walked to the end of the studio and then came back blushing, her fluttered eyes on the partner of her appeal. I was reminded of an incident I had accidentally had a glimpse of in Paris—being with a friend there, a dramatist about to produce a play, when an actress came to him to ask to be entrusted with a part. She went through her paces before him, walked up and down as Mrs. Monarch was doing. Mrs. Monarch did it quite as well, but I abstained from applauding. It was very odd to see such people apply for such poor pay. She looked as if she had ten thousand a year. Her husband had used the word that described her: she was in the London current jargon essentially and typically "smart." Her figure was, in the same order of ideas, conspicuously and irreproachably "good." For a woman of her age her waist was surprisingly small; her elbow moreover had the orthodox crook. She held her head at the conventional angle, but why did she come to *me?* She ought to have tried on jackets at a big shop. I feared my visitors were not only destitute but "artistic"—which would be a great complication. When she sat down again I thanked her, observing that what a draughtsman most valued in his model was the faculty of keeping quiet.

"Oh *she* can keep quiet," said Major Monarch. Then he added jocosely: "I've always kept her quiet."

"I'm not a nasty fidget, am I?" It was going to wring tears from me, I felt, the way she hid her head, ostrich-like, in the other broad bosom.

The owner of this expanse addressed his answer to me. "Perhaps it isn't out of place to mention—because we ought to be quite business-like, oughtn't we?—that when I married her she was known as the Beautiful Statue."

"Oh dear!" said Mrs. Monarch ruefully.

"Of course I should want a certain amount of expression," I rejoined.

"Of *course!*"—and I had never heard such unanimity.

"And then I suppose you know that you'll get awfully tired."

"Oh we *never* get tired!" they eagerly cried.

"Have you had any kind of practice?"

They hesitated—they looked at each other. "We've been photographed—*immensely,*" said Mrs. Monarch.

"She means the fellows have asked us themselves," added the Major.

"I see—because you're so good-looking."

"I don't know what they thought, but they were always after us."

"We always got our photographs for nothing," smiled Mrs. Monarch.

"We might have brought some, my dear," her husband remarked.

"I'm not sure we have any left. We've given quantities away," she explained to me.

"With our autographs and that sort of thing," said the Major.

"Are they to be got in the shops?" I enquired as a harmless pleasantry.

"Oh yes, *hers*—they used to be."

"Not now," said Mrs. Monarch with her eyes on the floor.

II

I COULD fancy the "sort of thing" they put on the presentation copies of their photographs, and I was sure they wrote a beautiful hand. It was odd how quickly I was sure of everything that concerned them. If they were now so poor as to have to earn shillings and pence they could never have had much of a margin. Their good looks had been their capital, and they had good-humouredly made the most of the career that this resource marked out for them. It was in their faces, the blankness, the deep intellectual repose of the twenty years of country-house visiting that had given them pleasant intonations. I could see the sunny drawing-rooms, sprinkled with periodicals she didn't read, in which Mrs. Monarch had continuously sat; I could see the wet shrubberies in which she had walked, equipped to admiration for either exercise. I could see the rich covers the Major had helped to shoot and the wonderful garments in which, late at night, he repaired to the smoking-room to talk about them. I could imagine their leggings and waterproofs, their knowing tweeds and rugs, their rolls of sticks and cases of tackle and neat umbrellas; and I could evoke the exact appearance of their servants and the compact variety of their luggage on the platforms of country stations.

They gave small tips, but they were liked; they didn't do anything themselves, but they were welcome. They looked so well everywhere; they gratified the general relish for stature, complexion and "form." They knew it without fatuity or vulgarity, and they respected themselves in consequence. They weren't superficial; they were thorough and kept themselves up—it had been their line. People with such a taste for activity had to have some line. I could feel how even in a dull house they could have been counted on for the joy of life. At present something had happened —it didn't matter what, their little income had grown less, it had grown least—and they had to do something for pocket-money. Their friends could like them, I made out, without liking to support them. There was something about them that represented credit—their clothes, their manners, their type; but if credit is a

large empty pocket in which an occasional chink reverberates,
the chink at least must be audible. What they wanted of me was
to help to make it so. Fortunately they had no children—I soon
divined that. They would also perhaps wish our relations to be
kept secret: this was why it was "for the figure"—the reproduc-
tion of the face would betray them.

I liked them—I felt, quite as their friends must have done—
they were so simple; and I had no objection to them if they would
suit. But somehow with all their perfections I didn't easily believe in them. After all they were amateurs, and the ruling passion
of my life was the detestation of the amateur. Combined with this
was another perversity—an innate preference for the represented
subject over the real one: the defect of the real one was so apt to
be a lack of representation. I liked things that appeared; then one
was sure. Whether they *were* or not was a subordinate and almost
always a profitless question. There were other considerations, the
first of which was that I already had two or three recruits in
use, notably a young person with big feet, in alpaca, from Kilburn,
who for a couple of years had come to me regularly for my illustrations and with whom I was still—perhaps ignobly—satisfied.
I frankly explained to my visitors how the case stood, but they
had taken more precautions than I supposed. They had reasoned
out their opportunity, for Claude Rivet had told them of the projected *édition de luxe* of one of the writers of our day—the rarest
of the novelists—who, long neglected by the multitudinous vulgar
and dearly prized by the attentive (need I mention Philip Vin-
cent?) had had the happy fortune of seeing, late in life, the dawn
and then the full light of a higher criticism; an estimate in which
on the part of the public there was something really of expiation.
The edition preparing, planned by a publisher of taste, was practically an act of high reparation; the wood-cuts with which it was
to be enriched were the homage of English art to one of the most
independent representatives of English letters. Major and Mrs.
Monarch confessed to me they had hoped I might be able to work
them into my branch of the enterprise. They knew I was to do the

first of the books, "Rutland Ramsay," but I had to make clear
to them that my participation in the rest of the affair—this first
book was to be a test—must depend on the satisfaction I should
give. If this should be limited my employers would drop me with
scarce common forms. It was therefore a crisis for me, and naturally I was making special preparations, looking about for new
people, should they be necessary, and securing the best types. I
admitted however that I should like to settle down to two or three
good models who would do for everything.

"Should we have often to—a—put on special clothes?" Mrs.
Monarch timidly demanded.

"Dear yes—that's half the business."

"And should we be expected to supply our own costumes?"

"Oh no; I've got a lot of things. A painter's models put on—
or put off—anything he likes."

"And you mean—a—the same?"

"The same?"

Mrs. Monarch looked at her husband again.

"Oh she was just wondering," he explained, "if the costumes
are in *general* use." I had to confess that they were, and I mentioned further that some of them—I had a lot of genuine greasy
last-century things—had served their time, a hundred years ago,
on living world-stained men and women; on figures not perhaps
so far removed, in that vanished world, from *their* type, the Monarchs', *quoi!* of a breeched and bewigged age. "We'll put on anything that *fits*," said the Major.

"Oh I arrange that—they fit in the pictures."

"I'm afraid I should do better for the modern books. I'd come
as you like," said Mrs. Monarch.

"She has got a lot of clothes at home: they might do for contemporary life," her husband continued.

"Oh I can fancy scenes in which you'd be quite natural." And
indeed I could see the slipshod rearrangements of stale properties
—the stories I tried to produce pictures for without the exasperation of reading them—whose sandy tracts the good lady might

help to people. But I had to return to the fact that for this sort of work—the daily mechanical grind—I was already equipped: the people I was working with were fully adequate.

"We only thought we might be more like *some* characters," said Mrs. Monarch mildly, getting up.

Her husband also rose; he stood looking at me with a dim wistfulness that was touching in so fine a man. "Wouldn't it be rather a pull sometimes to have—a—to have—?" He hung fire; he wanted me to help him by phrasing what he meant. But I couldn't —I didn't know. So he brought it out awkwardly: "The *real* thing; a gentleman, you know, or a lady." I was quite ready to give a general assent—I admitted that there was a great deal in that. This encouraged Major Monarch to say, following up his appeal with an unacted gulp: "It's awfully hard—we've tried everything." The gulp was communicative; it proved too much for his wife. Before I knew it Mrs. Monarch had dropped again upon a divan and burst into tears. Her husband sat down beside her, holding one of her hands; whereupon she quickly dried her eyes with the other, while I felt embarrassed as she looked up at me. "There isn't a confounded job I haven't applied for—waited for—prayed for. You can fancy we'd be pretty bad first. Secretaryships and that sort of thing? You might as well ask for a peerage. I'd be *anything*—I'm strong; a messenger or a coalheaver. I'd put on a gold-laced cap and open carriage-doors in front of the haberdasher's; I'd hang about a station to carry portmanteaux; I'd be a postman. But they won't *look* at you; there are thousands as good as yourself already on the ground. *Gentlemen,* poor beggars, who've drunk their wine, who've kept their hunters!"

I was as reassuring as I knew how to be, and my visitors were presently on their feet again while, for the experiment, we agreed on an hour. We were discussing it when the door opened and Miss Churm came in with a wet umbrella. Miss Churm had to take the omnibus to Maida Vale and then walk half a mile. She looked a trifle blowsy and slightly splashed. I scarcely ever saw her come in without thinking afresh how odd it was that, being so little in herself, she should yet be so much in others. She was a meagre little Miss Churm, but was such an ample heroine of romance. She was only a freckled cockney, but she could represent everything, from a fine lady to a shepherdess; she had the faculty as she might have had a fine voice or long hair. She couldn't spell and she loved beer, but she had two or three "points," and practice, and a knack, and mother-wit, and a whimsical sensibility, and a love of the theatre, and seven sisters, and not an ounce of respect, especially for the *h*. The first thing my visitors saw was that her umbrella was wet, and in their spotless perfection they visibly winced at it. The rain had come on since their arrival.

"I'm all in a soak; there *was* a mess of people in the 'bus. I wish you lived near a stytion," said Miss Churm. I requested her to get ready as quickly as possible, and she passed into the room in which she always changed her dress. But before going out she asked me what she was to get into this time.

"It's the Russian princess, don't you know?" I answered; "the one with the 'golden eyes,' in black velvet, for the long thing in the *Cheapside*."

"Golden eyes? I *say!*" cried Miss Churm, while my companions watched her with intensity as she withdrew. She always arranged herself, when she was late, before I could turn round; and I kept my visitors a little on purpose, so that they might get an idea, from seeing her, what would be expected of themselves. I mentioned that she was quite my notion of an excellent model—she was really very clever.

"Do you think she looks like a Russian princess?" Major Monarch asked with lurking alarm.

"When I make her, yes."

"Oh if you have to *make* her—!" he reasoned, not without point.

"That's the most you can ask. There are so many who are not makeable."

"Well now, *here's* a lady"—and with a persuasive smile he passed his arm into his wife's—"who's already made!"

"Oh I'm not a Russian princess," Mrs. Monarch protested a little coldly. I could see she had known some and didn't like them.

There at once was a complication of a kind I never had to fear with Miss Churm.

This young lady came back in black velvet—the gown was rather rusty and very low on her lean shoulders—and with a Japanese fan in her red hands. I reminded her that in the scene I was doing she had to look over some one's head. "I forget whose it is; but it doesn't matter. Just look over a head."

"I'd rather look over a stove," said Miss Churm; and she took her station near the fire. She fell into position, settled herself into a tall attitude, gave a certain backward inclination to her head and a certain forward droop to her fan, and looked, at least to my prejudiced sense, distinguished and charming, foreign and dangerous. We left her looking so while I went downstairs with Major and Mrs. Monarch.

"I believe I could come about as near it as that," said Mrs. Monarch.

"Oh you think she's shabby, but you must allow for the alchemy of art."

However, they went off with an evident increase of comfort founded on their demonstrable advantage in being the real thing. I could fancy them shuddering over Miss Churm. She was very droll about them when I went back, for I told her what they wanted.

"Well, if *she* can sit I'll tyke to book-keeping," said my model.

"She's very ladylike," I replied as an innocent form of aggravation.

"So much the worse for *you*. That means she can't turn round."

"She'll do for the fashionable novels."

"Oh yes, she'll *do* for them!" my model humorously declared. "Ain't they bad enough without her?" I had often sociably denounced them to Miss Churm.

III

IT WAS for the elucidation of a mystery in one of these works that I first tried Mrs. Monarch. Her husband came with her, to be useful if necessary—it was sufficiently clear that as a general thing he would prefer to come with her. At first I wondered if this were for "propriety's" sake—if he were going to be jealous and meddling. The idea was too tiresome, and if it had been confirmed it would speedily have brought our acquaintance to a close. But I soon saw there was nothing in it and that if he accompanied Mrs. Monarch it was—in addition to the chance of being wanted—simply because he had nothing else to do. When they were separate his occupation was gone and they never *had* been separate. I judged rightly that in their awkward situation their close union was their main comfort and that this union had no weak spot. It was a real marriage, an encouragement to the hesitating, a nut for pessimists to crack. Their address was humble—I remember afterwards thinking it had been the only thing about them that was really professional—and I could fancy the lamentable lodgings in which the Major would have been left alone. He could sit there more or less grimly with his wife—he couldn't sit there anyhow without her.

He had too much tact to try and make himself agreeable when he couldn't be useful; so when I was too absorbed in my work to talk he simply sat and waited. But I liked to hear him talk—it made my work, when not interrupting it, less mechanical, less special. To listen to him was to combine the excitement of going out with the economy of staying at home. There was only one hindrance—that I seemed not to know any of the people this brilliant couple had known. I think he wondered extremely, during the term of our intercourse, whom the deuce I *did* know. He hadn't a stray sixpence of an idea to fumble for, so we didn't spin it very fine; we confined ourselves to questions of leather and even of liquor—saddlers and breeches-makers and how to get excellent claret cheap—and matters like "good trains" and the habits of small game. His lore on these last subjects was astonishing—he managed to interweave the station-master with the ornithologist. When he couldn't talk about greater things he could talk cheerfully about smaller, and since I couldn't accompany him into reminiscences of the fashionable world he could lower the conversation without a visible effort to my level.

So earnest a desire to please was touching in a man who could so easily have knocked one down. He looked after the fire and had an opinion on the draught of the stove without my asking him, and I could see that he thought many of my arrangements not half knowing. I remember telling him that if I were only rich I'd offer him a salary to come and teach me how to live. Sometimes he gave a random sigh of which the essence might have been: "Give me even such a bare old barrack as *this*, and I'd do something with it!" When I wanted to use him he came alone; which was an illustration of the superior courage of women. His wife could bear her solitary second floor, and she was in general more discreet; showing by various small reserves that she was alive to the propriety of keeping our relations markedly professional— not letting them slide into sociability. She wished it to remain clear that she and the Major were employed, not cultivated, and if she approved of me as a superior, who could be kept in his place, she never thought me quite good enough for an equal.

She sat with great intensity, giving the whole of her mind to it, and was capable of remaining for an hour almost as motionless as before a photographer's lens. I could see she had been photographed often, but somehow the very habit that made her good for that purpose unfitted her for mine. At first I was extremely pleased with her ladylike air, and it was a satisfaction, on coming to follow her lines, to see how good they were and how far they could lead the pencil. But after a little skirmishing I began to find her too insurmountably stiff; do what I would with it my drawing looked like a photograph or a copy of a photograph. Her figure had no variety of expression—she herself had no sense of variety. You may say that this was my business and was only a question of placing her. Yet I placed her in every conceivable position and she managed to obliterate their differences. She was always a lady certainly, and into the bargain was always the same lady. She was the real thing, but always the same thing. There were moments when I rather writhed under the serenity of her confidence that she *was* the real thing. All her dealings with me and all her husband's were an implication that this was lucky for *me*. Meanwhile I found myself trying to invent types that approached her own, instead of making her own transform itself—in the clever way that was not impossible for instance to poor Miss Churm. Arrange as I would and take the precautions I would, she always came out, in my pictures, too tall—landing me in the dilemma of having represented a fascinating woman as seven feet high, which (out of respect perhaps to my own very much scantier inches) was far from my idea of such a personage.

The case was worse with the Major—nothing I could do would keep *him* down, so that he became useful only for the representation of brawny giants. I adored variety and range, I cherished human accidents, the illustrative note; I wanted to characterise closely, and the thing in the world I most hated was the danger of being ridden by a type. I had quarrelled with some of my friends about it; I had parted company with them for maintaining that one *had* to be, and that if the type was beautiful—witness Raphael and Leonardo—the servitude was only a gain. I was neither Leonardo nor Raphael—I might only be a presumptuous young modern searcher; but I held that everything was to be sacrificed sooner than character. When they claimed that the obsessional form could easily *be* character I retorted, perhaps superficially, "Whose?" It couldn't be everybody's—it might end in being nobody's.

After I had drawn Mrs. Monarch a dozen times I felt surer even than before that the value of such a model as Miss Churm resided precisely in the fact that she had no positive stamp, combined of course with the other fact that what she did have was a curious and inexplicable talent for imitation. Her usual appearance was like a curtain which she could draw up at request for a capital performance. This performance was simply suggestive; but it was a word to the wise—it was vivid and pretty. Sometimes even I thought it, though she was plain herself, too insipidly pretty; I made it a reproach to her that the figures drawn from her were monotonously (*bêtement,* as we used to say) graceful. Nothing made her more angry; it was so much her pride to feel she could sit for characters that had nothing in common with each other. She would accuse me at such moments of taking away her "reputytion."

It suffered a certain shrinkage, this queer quantity, from the repeated visits of my new friends. Miss Churm was greatly in demand, never in want of employment, so I had no scruple in putting her off occasionally, to try them more at my ease. It was certainly amusing at first to do the real thing—it was amusing to do Major Monarch's trousers. They *were* the real thing, even if he did come out colossal. It was amusing to do his wife's back hair—it was so mathematically neat—and the particular "smart" tension of her tight stays. She lent herself especially to positions in which the face was somewhat averted or blurred; she abounded in ladylike back views and *profils perdus*. When she stood erect she took naturally one of the attitudes in which court-painters represent queens and princesses; so that I found myself wondering whether, to draw out this accomplishment, I couldn't get the editor of the *Cheapside* to publish a really royal romance, "A Tale of Buckingham Palace." Sometimes however the real thing and the make-believe came into contact; by which I mean that Miss Churm, keeping an appointment or coming to make one on days when I had much work in hand, encountered her invidious rivals. The encounter was not on their part, for they noticed her no more than if she had been the housemaid; not from intentional loftiness, but simply because as yet, professionally, they didn't know how to fraternise, as I could imagine they would have liked—or at least that the Major would. They couldn't talk about the omnibus —they always walked; and they didn't know what else to try— she wasn't interested in good trains or cheap claret. Besides, they must have felt—in the air—that she was amused at them, secretly derisive of their ever knowing how. She wasn't a person to conceal the limits of her faith if she had had a chance to show them. On the other hand Mrs. Monarch didn't think her tidy; for why else did she take pains to say to me—it was going out of the way, for Mrs. Monarch—that she didn't like dirty women?

One day when my young lady happened to be present with my other sitters—she even dropped in, when it was convenient, for a chat—I asked her to be so good as to lend a hand in getting tea, a service with which she was familiar and which was one of a class that, living as I did in a small way, with slender domestic resources, I often appealed to my models to render. They liked to lay hands on my property, to break the sitting, and sometimes the china—it made them feel Bohemian. The next time I saw Miss Churm after this incident she surprised me greatly by making a scene about it—she accused me of having wished to humiliate her. She hadn't resented the outrage at the time, but had seemed obliging and amused, enjoying the comedy of asking Mrs. Monarch, who sat vague and silent, whether she would have cream and sugar, and putting an exaggerated simper into the question. She had tried intonations—as if she too wished to pass for the real thing—till I was afraid my other visitors would take offence.

Oh they were determined not to do this, and their touching patience was the measure of their great need. They would sit by the hour, uncomplaining, till I was ready to use them; they would come back on the chance of being wanted and would walk away cheerfully if it failed. I used to go to the door with them to see in what magnificent order they retreated. I tried to find other employment for them—I introduced them to several artists. But they didn't "take," for reasons I could appreciate, and I became rather anxiously aware that after such disappointments they fell back upon me with a heavier weight. They did me the honour to think me most *their* form. They weren't romantic enough for the painters, and in those days there were few serious workers in black-and-white. Besides, they had an eye to the great job I had mentioned to them—they had secretly set their hearts on supplying the right essence for my pictorial vindication of our fine novelist. They knew that for this undertaking I should want no costume-effects, none of the frippery of past ages—that it was a case in which everything would be contemporary and satirical and presumably genteel. If I could work them into it their future would be assured, for the labour would of course be long and the occupation steady.

One day Mrs. Monarch came without her husband—she explained his absence by his having had to go to the City. While she sat there in her usual relaxed majesty there came at the door a knock which I immediately recognised as the subdued appeal of a model out of work. It was followed by the entrance of a young man whom I at once saw to be a foreigner and who proved in fact an Italian acquainted with no English word but my name, which he uttered in a way that made it seem to include all others. I hadn't then visited his country, nor was I proficient in his tongue; but as he was not so meanly constituted—what Italian is?—as to depend only on that member for expression he conveyed to me, in familiar but graceful mimicry, that he was in search of exactly the employment in which the lady before me was engaged. I was not struck with him at first, and while I continued to draw I dropped few signs of interest or encouragement. He stood his ground however—not importunately, but with a dumb dog-like fidelity in his eyes that amounted to innocent impudence, the manner of a devoted servant—he might have been in the house for years—unjustly suspected. Suddenly it struck me that this very attitude and expression made a picture; whereupon I told him to sit down and wait till I should be free. There was another picture in the way he obeyed me, and I observed as I worked that there were others still in the way he looked wonderingly, with his head thrown back, about the high studio. He might have been crossing himself in Saint Peter's. Before I finished I said to myself "The fellow's a bankrupt orange-monger, but a treasure."

When Mrs. Monarch withdrew he passed across the room like a flash to open the door for her, standing there with the rapt pure gaze of the young Dante spellbound by the young Beatrice. As I never insisted, in such situations, on the blankness of the British domestic, I reflected that he had the making of a servant—and I needed one, but couldn't pay him to be only that—as well as of a model; in short I resolved to adopt my bright adventurer if he would agree to officiate in the double capacity. He jumped at my offer, and in the event my rashness—for I had really known nothing about him—wasn't brought home to me. He proved a sympathetic though a desultory ministrant, and had in a wonderful degree the *sentiment de la pose*. It was uncultivated, instinctive, a part of the happy instinct that had guided him to my door and helped him to spell out my name on the card nailed to it. He had had no other introduction to me than a guess, from the shape of my high north window, seen outside, that my place was a studio and that as a studio it would contain an artist. He had wandered to England in search of fortune, like other itinerants, and had embarked, with a partner and a small green hand-cart, on the sale of penny ices. The ices had melted away and the partner had dissolved in their train. My young man wore tight yellow trousers with reddish stripes and his name was Oronte. He was sallow but fair, and when I put him into some old clothes of my own he looked like an Englishman. He was as good as Miss Churm, who could look, when requested, like an Italian.

IV

I THOUGHT Mrs. Monarch's face slightly convulsed when, on her coming back with her husband, she found Oronte installed. It was strange to have to recognise in a scrap of a lazzarone a competitor to her magnificent Major. It was she who scented danger first, for the Major was anecdotically unconscious. But Oronte gave us tea, with a hundred eager confusions—he had never been concerned in so queer a process—and I think she thought better of me for having at last an "establishment." They saw a couple of drawings that I had made of the establishment, and Mrs. Monarch hinted that it never would have struck her he had sat for them. "Now the drawings you make from *us*, they look exactly like us," she reminded me, smiling in triumph; and I recognised that this was indeed just their defect. When I drew

the Monarchs I couldn't anyhow get away from them—get into
the character I wanted to represent; and I hadn't the least desire
my model should be discoverable in my picture. Miss Churm
never was, and Mrs. Monarch thought I hid her, very properly,
because she was vulgar; whereas if she was lost it was only as the
dead who go to heaven are lost—in the gain of an angel the more.

By this time I had got a certain start with "Rutland Ramsay,"
the first novel in the great projected series; that is I had produced
a dozen drawings, several with the help of the Major and his wife,
and I had sent them in for approval. My understanding with the
publishers, as I have already hinted, had been that I was to be
left to do my work, in this particular case, as I liked, with the
whole book committed to me; but my connexion with the rest
of the series was only contingent. There were moments when,
frankly, it *was* a comfort to have the real thing under one's hand;
for there were characters in "Rutland Ramsay" that were very
much like it. There were people presumably as erect as the Major
and women of as good a fashion as Mrs. Monarch. There was a
great deal of country-house life—treated, it is true, in a fine fanciful ironical generalised way—and there was a considerable implication of knickerbockers and kilts. There were certain things I
had to settle at the outset; such things for instance as the exact
appearance of the hero and the particular bloom and figure of the
heroine. The author of course gave me a lead, but there was a
margin for interpretation. I took the Monarchs into my confidence, I told them frankly what I was about, I mentioned my
embarrassments and alternatives. "Oh take *him!*" Mrs. Monarch
murmured sweetly, looking at her husband; and "What could you
want better than my wife?" the Major enquired with the comfortable candour that now prevailed between us.

I wasn't obliged to answer these remarks—I was only obliged
to place my sitters. I wasn't easy in mind, and I postponed a little
timidly perhaps the solving of my question. The book was a large
canvas, the other figures were numerous, and I worked off at first
some of the episodes in which the hero and the heroine were not
concerned. When once I had set *them* up I should have to stick

to them—I couldn't make my young man seven feet high in one place and five feet nine in another. I inclined on the whole to the latter measurement, though the Major more than once reminded me that *he* looked about as young as any one. It was indeed quite possible to arrange him, for the figure, so that it would have been difficult to detect his age. After the spontaneous Oronte had been with me a month, and after I had given him to understand several times over that his native exuberance would presently constitute an insurmountable barrier to our further intercourse, I waked to a sense of his heroic capacity. He was only five feet seven, but the remaining inches were latent. I tried him almost secretly at first, for I was really rather afraid of the judgement my other models would pass on such a choice. If they regarded Miss Churm as little better than a snare what would they think of the representation by a person so little the real thing as an Italian street-vendor of a protagonist formed by a public school?

If I went a little in fear of them it wasn't because they bullied me, because they had got an oppressive foothold, but because in their really pathetic decorum and mysteriously permanent new-ness they counted on me so intensely. I was therefore very glad when Jack Hawley came home: he was always of such good coun-sel. He painted badly himself, but there was no one like him for putting his finger on the place. He had been absent from England for a year; he had been somewhere—I don't remember where—to get a fresh eye. I was in a good deal of dread of any such organ, but we were old friends; he had been away for months and a sense of emptiness was creeping into my life. I hadn't dodged a missile for a year.

He came back with a fresh eye, but with the same old black velvet blouse, and the first evening he spent in my studio we smoked cigarettes till the small hours. He had done no work him-self, he had only got the eye; so the field was clear for the pro-duction of my little things. He wanted to see what I had produced for the *Cheapside,* but he was disappointed in the exhibition. That at least seemed the meaning of two or three comprehensive groans which, as he lounged on my big divan, his leg folded under him,

looking at my latest drawings, issued from his lips with the smoke
of the cigarette.

"What's the matter with you?" I asked.

"What's the matter with *you?*"

"Nothing save that I'm mystified."

"You are indeed. You're quite off the hinge. What's the meaning of this new fad?" And he tossed me, with visible irreverence,
a drawing in which I happened to have depicted both my elegant
models. I asked if he didn't think it good, and he replied that it
struck him as execrable, given the sort of thing I had always represented myself to him as wishing to arrive at; but I let that pass
—I was so anxious to see exactly what he meant. The two figures
in the picture looked colossal, but I supposed this was *not* what
he meant, inasmuch as, for aught he knew to the contrary, I might
have been trying for some such effect. I maintained that I was
working exactly in the same way as when he last had done me the
honour to tell me I might do something some day. "Well, there's
a screw loose somewhere," he answered; "wait a bit and I'll discover it." I depended upon him to do so: where else was the fresh
eye? But he produced at last nothing more luminous than "I don't
know—I don't like your types." This was lame for a critic who
had never consented to discuss with me anything but the question
of execution, the direction of strokes and the mystery of values.

"In the drawings you've been looking at I think my types are
very handsome."

"Oh they won't do!"

"I've been working with new models."

"I see you have. *They* won't do."

"Are you very sure of that?"

"Absolutely—they're stupid."

"You mean *I* am—for I ought to get round that."

"You *can't*—with such people. Who are they?"

I told him, so far as was necessary, and he concluded heart-
lessly: "Ce sont des gens qu'il faut mettre à la porte."

"You've never seen them; they're awfully good"—I flew to
their defence.

"Not seen them? Why all this recent work of yours drops to pieces with them. It's all I want to see of them."

"No one else has said anything against it—the *Cheapside* people are pleased."

"Every one else is an ass, and the *Cheapside* people the biggest asses of all. Come, don't pretend at this time of day to have pretty illusions about the public, especially about publishers and editors. It's not for *such* animals you work—it's for those who know, *coloro che sanno;* so keep straight for *me* if you can't keep straight for yourself. There was a certain sort of thing you used to try for—and a very good thing it was. But this twaddle isn't *in* it." When I talked with Hawley later about "Rutland Ramsay" and its possible successors he declared that I must get back into my boat again or I should go to the bottom. His voice in short was the voice of warning.

I noted the warning, but I didn't turn my friends out of doors. They bored me a good deal; but the very fact that they bored me admonished me not to sacrifice them—if there was anything to be done with them—simply to irritation. As I look back at this phase they seem to me to have pervaded my life not a little. I have a vision of them as most of the time in my studio, seated against the wall on an old velvet bench to be out of the way, and resembling the while a pair of patient courtiers in a royal ante-chamber. I'm convinced that during the coldest weeks of the winter they held their ground because it saved them fire. Their newness was losing its gloss, and it was impossible not to feel them objects of charity. Whenever Miss Churm arrived they went away, and after I was fairly launched in "Rutland Ramsay" Miss Churm arrived pretty often. They managed to express to me tacitly that they supposed I wanted her for the low life of the book, and I let them suppose it, since they had attempted to study the work—it was lying about the studio—without discovering that it dealt only with the highest circles. They had dipped into the most brilliant of our novelists without deciphering many passages. I still took an hour from them, now and again, in spite of Jack Hawley's warning: it would be time enough to dismiss them, if dismissal should be necessary, when the rigour of the season was over. Hawley had made their acquaintance—he had met them at my fireside—and thought them a ridiculous pair. Learning that he was a painter they tried to approach him, to show him too that they were the real thing; but he looked at them, across the big room, as if they were miles away: they were a compendium of everything he most objected to in the social system of his country. Such people as that, all convention and patent-leather, with ejaculations that stopped conversation, had no business in a studio. A studio was a place to learn to see, and how could you see through a pair of feather-beds?

The main inconvenience I suffered at their hands was that at first I was shy of letting it break upon them that my artful little servant had begun to sit to me for "Rutland Ramsay." They knew I had been odd enough—they were prepared by this time to allow oddity to artists—to pick a foreign vagabond out of the streets when I might have had a person with whiskers and credentials; but it was some time before they learned how high I rated his accomplishments. They found him in an attitude more than once, but they never doubted I was doing him as an organ-grinder. There were several things they never guessed, and one of them was that for a striking scene in the novel, in which a footman briefly figured, it occurred to me to make use of Major Monarch as the menial. I kept putting this off, I didn't like to ask him to don the livery—besides the difficulty of finding a livery to fit him. At last, one day late in the winter, when I was at work on the despised Oronte, who caught one's idea on the wing, and was in the glow of feeling myself go very straight, they came in, the Major and his wife, with their society laugh about nothing (there was less and less to laugh at); came in like country-callers—they always reminded me of that—who have walked across the park after church and are presently persuaded to stay to luncheon. Luncheon was over, but they could stay to tea—I knew they wanted it. The fit was on me, however, and I couldn't let my ardour cool and my work wait, with the fading daylight, while my model prepared it. So I asked Mrs. Monarch if she would mind laying it out—a request which for an instant brought all the blood to her face. Her eyes were on her husband's for a second, and some mute telegraphy passed between them. Their folly was over the next instant; his cheerful shrewdness put an end to it. So far from pitying their wounded pride, I must add, I was moved to give it as complete a lesson as I could. They bustled about together and got out the cups and saucers and made the kettle boil. I know they felt as if they were waiting on my servant, and when the tea was prepared I said: "He'll have a cup, please—he's tired." Mrs. Monarch brought him one where he stood, and he took it from her as if he had been a gentleman at a party squeezing a crush-hat with an elbow.

Then it came over me that she had made a great effort for me—made it with a kind of nobleness—and that I owed her a compensation. Each time I saw her after this I wondered what the compensation could be. I couldn't go on doing the wrong thing to oblige them. Oh it *was* the wrong thing, the stamp of the work for which they sat—Hawley was not the only person to say it now. I sent in a large number of the drawings I had made for "Rutland Ramsay," and I received a warning that was more to the point than Hawley's. The artistic adviser of the house for which I was working was of opinion that many of my illustrations were not what had been looked for. Most of these illustrations were the subjects in which the Monarchs had figured. Without going into the question of what *had* been looked for, I had to face the fact that at this rate I shouldn't get the other books to do. I hurled myself in despair on Miss Churm—I put her through all her paces. I not only adopted Oronte publicly as my hero, but one morning when the Major looked in to see if I didn't require him to finish a *Cheapside* figure for which he had begun to sit the week before, I told him I had changed my mind—I'd do the drawing from my man. At this my visitor turned pale and stood looking at me. "Is *he* your idea of an English gentleman?" he asked.

I was disappointed, I was nervous, I wanted to get on with my work; so I replied with irritation: "Oh my dear Major—I can't be ruined for *you!*"

It was a horrid speech, but he stood another moment—after which, without a word, he quitted the studio. I drew a long breath, for I said to myself that I shouldn't see him again. I hadn't told him definitely that I was in danger of having my work rejected, but I was vexed at his not having felt the catastrophe in the air, read with me the moral of our fruitless collaboration, the lesson that in the deceptive atmosphere of art even the highest respectability may fail of being plastic.

I didn't owe my friends money, but I did see them again. They reappeared together three days later, and, given all the other facts, there was something tragic in that one. It was a clear proof they could find nothing else in life to do. They had threshed the matter out in a dismal conference—they had digested the bad news that they were not in for the series. If they weren't useful to me even for the *Cheapside* their function seemed difficult to determine, and I could only judge at first that they had come, forgivingly, decorously, to take a last leave. This made me rejoice in secret that I had little leisure for a scene; for I had placed both my other models in position together and I was pegging away at a drawing from which I hoped to derive glory. It had been suggested by the passage in which Rutland Ramsay, drawing up a chair to Artemisia's piano-stool, says extraordinary things to her while she ostensibly fingers out a difficult piece of music. I had done Miss Churm at the piano before—it was an attitude in which she knew how to take on an absolutely poetic grace. I wished the two figures to "compose" together with intensity, and my little Italian had entered perfectly into my conception. The pair were vividly before me, the piano had been pulled out; it was a charming show of blended youth and murmured love, which I had only to catch and keep. My visitors stood and looked at it, and I was friendly to them over my shoulder.

They made no response, but I was used to silent company and went on with my work, only a little disconcerted—even though exhilarated by the sense that *this* was at least the ideal thing— at not having got rid of them after all. Presently I heard Mrs. Monarch's sweet voice beside or rather above me: "I wish her hair were a little better done." I looked up and she was staring with a strange fixedness at Miss Churm, whose back was turned to her. "Do you mind my just touching it?" she went on—a question which made me spring up for an instant as with the instinctive fear that she might do the young lady a harm. But she quieted me with a glance I shall never forget—I confess I should like to have been able to paint *that*—and went for a moment to my model. She spoke to her softly, laying a hand on her shoulder and bending over her; and as the girl, understanding, gratefully assented, she disposed her rough curls, with a few quick passes, in such a way as to make Miss Churm's head twice as charming. It was one of the most heroic personal services I've ever seen rendered. Then Mrs. Monarch turned away with a low sigh and, looking about her as if for something to do, stooped to the floor with a noble humility and picked up a dirty rag that had dropped out of my paint-box.

The Major meanwhile had also been looking for something to do, and, wandering to the other end of the studio, saw before him my breakfast-things neglected, unremoved. "I say, can't I be useful *here?*" he called out to me with an irrepressible quaver. I assented with a laugh that I fear was awkward, and for the next ten minutes, while I worked, I heard the light clatter of china and the tinkle of spoons and glass. Mrs. Monarch assisted her husband—they washed up my crockery, they put it away. They wandered off into my little scullery, and I afterwards found that they had cleaned my knives and that my slender stock of plate had an unprecedented surface. When it came over me, the latent eloquence of what they were doing, I confess that my drawing was blurred for a moment—the picture swam. They had accepted their failure, but they couldn't accept their fate. They had bowed their heads in bewilderment to the perverse and cruel law in virtue of which the real thing could be so much less precious than the unreal; but they didn't want to starve. If my servants were my models, then my models might be my servants. They would reverse the parts—the others would sit for the ladies and gentlemen and *they* would do the work. They would still be in the studio—it was an intense dumb appeal to me not to turn them out. "Take us on," they wanted to say—"we'll do *anything*."

My pencil dropped from my hand; my sitting was spoiled and I got rid of my sitters, who were also evidently rather mystified and awestruck. Then, alone with the Major and his wife I had a most uncomfortable moment. He put their prayer into a single sentence: "I say, you know—just let *us* do for you, can't you?" I couldn't—it was dreadful to see them emptying my slops; but I pretended I could, to oblige them, for about a week. Then I gave them a sum of money to go away, and I never saw them again. I obtained the remaining books, but my friend Hawley repeats that Major and Mrs. Monarch did me a permanent harm, got me into false ways. If it be true I'm content to have paid the price—for the memory.

THE MIDDLE YEARS

I

THE April day was soft and bright, and poor Dencombe, happy in the conceit of reasserted strength, stood in the garden of the hotel, comparing, with a deliberation in which however there was still something of languor, the attractions of easy strolls. He liked the feeling of the south so far as you could have it in the north, he liked the sandy cliffs and the clustered pines, he liked even the colourless sea. "Bournemouth as a health-resort" had sounded like a mere advertisement, but he was thankful now for the commonest conveniences. The sociable country postman, passing through the garden, had just given him a small parcel which he took out with him, leaving the hotel to the right and creeping to a bench he had already haunted, a safe recess in the cliff. It looked to the south, to the tinted walls of the Island, and was protected behind by the sloping shoulder of the down. He was tired enough when he reached it, and for a moment was disappointed; he was better of course, but better, after all, than what? He should never again, as at one or two great moments of the past, be better than himself. The infinite of life was gone, and what remained of the dose a small glass scored like a thermometer by the apothecary. He sat and stared at the sea, which appeared all surface and twinkle, far shallower than the spirit of man. It was the abyss of human illusion that was the real, the tideless deep. He held his packet, which had come by book-post, unopened on his knee, liking, in the lapse of so many joys—his illness had made him feel his age—to know it was there, but taking for granted there could be no complete renewal of the pleasure, dear to young experience, of seeing one's self "just out." Dencombe, who had a reputation, had come out too often and knew too well in advance how he should look.

His postponement associated itself vaguely, after a little, with a group of three persons, two ladies and a young man, whom, beneath him, straggling and seemingly silent, he could see move slowly together along the sands. The gentleman had his head bent over a book and was occasionally brought to a stop by the charm of this volume, which, as Dencombe could perceive even at a distance, had a cover alluringly red. Then his companions, going a little further, waited for him to come up, poking their parasols into the beach, looking around them at the sea and sky and clearly sensible of the beauty of the day. To these things the young man with the book was still more clearly indifferent; lingering, credulous, absorbed, he was an object of envy to an observer from whose connexion with literature all such artlessness had faded. One of the ladies was large and mature; the other had the spareness of comparative youth and of a social situation possibly inferior. The large lady carried back Dencombe's imagination to the age of crinoline; she wore a hat of the shape of a mushroom, decorated with a blue veil, and had the air, in her aggressive amplitude, of clinging to a vanished fashion or even a lost cause. Presently her companion produced from under the folds of a mantle a limp portable chair which she stiffened out and of which the large lady took possession. This act, and something in the movement of either party, at once characterised the performers—they performed for Dencombe's recreation—as opulent matron and humble dependent. Where moreover was the virtue of an approved novelist if one couldn't establish a relation between such figures? the clever theory for instance that the young man was the son of the opulent matron and that the humble dependent, the daughter of a clergyman or an officer, nourished a secret passion for him. Was that not visible from the way she stole behind her protectress to look back at him?—back to where he had let himself come to a full stop when his mother sat down to rest. His book was a novel, it had the catchpenny binding; so that while the romance of life stood neglected at his side he lost himself in that of the circulating library. He moved mechanically to where the sand was softer and ended by plumping down in it to finish his chapter at his ease.

The humble dependent, discouraged by his remoteness, wandered with a martyred droop of the head in another direction, and the exorbitant lady, watching the waves, offered a confused resemblance to a flying-machine that had broken down.

When his drama began to fail Dencombe remembered that he had after all another pastime. Though such promptitude on the part of the publisher was rare he was already able to draw from its wrapper his "latest," perhaps his last. The cover of "The Middle Years" was duly meretricious, the smell of the fresh pages the very odour of sanctity; but for the moment he went no further—he had become conscious of a strange alienation. He had forgotten what his book was about. Had the assault of his old ailment, which he had so fallaciously come to Bournemouth to ward off, interposed utter blankness as to what had preceded it? He had finished the revision of proof before quitting London, but his subsequent fortnight in bed had passed the sponge over colour. He couldn't have chanted to himself a single sentence, couldn't have turned with curiosity or confidence to any particular page. His subject had already gone from him, leaving scarce a superstition behind. He uttered a low moan as he breathed the chill of this dark void, so desperately it seemed to represent the completion of a sinister process. The tears filled his mild eyes; something precious had passed away. This was the pang that had been sharpest during the last few years—the sense of ebbing time, of shrinking opportunity; and now he felt not so much that his last chance was going as that it was gone indeed. He had done all he should ever do, and yet hadn't done what he wanted. This was the laceration—that practically his career was over: it was as violent as a grip at his throat. He rose from his seat nervously—a creature hunted by a dread; then he fell back in his weakness and nervously opened his book. It was a single volume; he preferred single volumes and aimed at a rare compression. He began to read and, little by little, in this occupation, was pacified and reassured. Everything came back to him, but came back with a wonder, came back above all with a high and magnificent beauty. He read his own prose, he turned his own leaves, and had as he sat there with the spring sunshine on the page an emotion peculiar and intense. His career was over, no doubt, but it was over, when all was said, with *that*.

He had forgotten during his illness the work of the previous year; but what he had chiefly forgotten was that it was extraordinarily good. He dived once more into his story and was drawn down, as by a siren's hand, to where, in the dim underworld of fiction, the great glazed tank of art, strange silent subjects float. He recognised his motive and surrendered to his talent. Never probably had that talent, such as it was, been so fine. His difficulties were still there, but what was also there, to his perception, though probably, alas! to nobody's else, was the art that in most cases had surmounted them. In his surprised enjoyment of this ability he had a glimpse of a possible reprieve. Surely its force wasn't spent—there was life and service in it yet. It hadn't come to him easily, it had been backward and roundabout. It was the child of time, the nursling of delay; he had struggled and suffered for it, making sacrifices not to be counted, and now that it was really mature was it to cease to yield, to confess itself brutally beaten? There was an infinite charm for Dencombe in feeling as he had never felt before that diligence *vincit omnia*. The result produced in his little book was somehow a result beyond his conscious intention: it was as if he had planted his genius, had trusted his method, and they had grown up and flowered with this sweetness. If the achievement had been real, however, the process had been painful enough. What he saw so intensely today, what he felt as a nail driven in, was that only now, at the very last, had he come into possession. His development had been abnormally slow, almost grotesquely gradual. He had been hindered and retarded by experience, he had for long periods only groped his way. It had taken too much of his life to produce too little of his art. The art had come, but it had come after everything else. At such a rate a first existence was too short—long enough only to collect material; so that to fructify, to use the material, one should have a second age, an extension. This extension was what poor Dencombe sighed for. As he turned the last leaves of his volume he murmured "Ah for another go, ah for a better chance!"

The three persons drawing his attention to the sands had vanished and then reappeared; they had now wandered up a path, an artificial and easy ascent, which led to the top of the cliff. Dencombe's bench was halfway down, on a sheltered ledge, and the large lady, a massive heterogeneous person with bold black eyes and kind red cheeks, now took a few moments to rest. She wore dirty gauntlets and immense diamond ear-rings; at first she looked vulgar, but she contradicted this announcement in an agreeable off-hand tone. While her companions stood waiting for her she spread her skirts on the end of Dencombe's seat. The young man had gold spectacles, through which, with his finger still in his red-covered book, he glanced at the volume, bound in the same shade of the same colour, lying on the lap of the original occupant of the bench. After an instant Dencombe felt him struck with a resemblance; he had recognised the gilt stamp on the crimson cloth, was reading "The Middle Years" and now noted that somebody else had kept pace with him. The stranger was startled, possibly even a little ruffled, to find himself not the only person favoured with an early copy. The eyes of the two proprietors met a moment, and Dencombe borrowed amusement from the expression of those of his competitor, those, it might even be inferred, of his admirer. They confessed to some resentment—they seemed to say: "Hang it, has he got it *already?* Of course he's a brute of a reviewer!" Dencombe shuffled his copy out of sight while the opulent matron, rising from her repose, broke out: "I feel already the good of this air!"

"I can't say I do," said the angular lady. "I find myself quite let down."

"I find myself horribly hungry. At what time did you order luncheon?" her protectress pursued.

The young person put the question by. "Doctor Hugh always orders it."

"I ordered nothing today—I'm going to make you diet," said their comrade.

"Then I shall go home and sleep. *Qui dort dine!*"

"Can I trust you to Miss Vernham?" asked Doctor Hugh of his elder companion.

"Don't I trust *you?*" she archly enquired.

"Not too much!" Miss Vernham, with her eyes on the ground, permitted herself to declare. "You must come with us at least to the house," she went on while the personage on whom they appeared to be in attendance began to mount higher. She had got a little out of ear-shot; nevertheless Miss Vernham became, so far as Dencombe was concerned, less distinctly audible to murmur to the young man: "I don't think you realise all you owe the Countess!"

Absently, a moment, Doctor Hugh caused his gold-rimmed spectacles to shine at her. "Is that the way I strike you? I see— I see!"

"She's awfully good to us," continued Miss Vernham, compelled by the lapse of the other's motion to stand there in spite of his discussion of private matters. Of what use would it have been that Dencombe should be sensitive to shades hadn't he detected in that arrest a strange influence from the quiet old convalescent in the great tweed cape? Miss Vernham appeared suddenly to become aware of some such connexion, for she added in a moment: "If you want to sun yourself here you can come back after you've seen us home."

Doctor Hugh, at this, hesitated, and Dencombe, in spite of a desire to pass for unconscious, risked a covert glance at him. What his eyes met this time, as happened, was, on the part of the young lady, a queer stare, naturally vitreous, which made her remind him of some figure—he couldn't name it—in a play or a novel, some sinister governess or tragic old maid. She seemed to scan him, to challenge him, to say out of general spite: "What have you got to do with us?" At the same instant the rich humour of the Countess reached them from above: "Come, come, my little lambs; you should follow your old *bergère!*" Miss Vernham turned away for it, pursuing the ascent, and Doctor Hugh, after another mute appeal to Dencombe and a minute's evident demur, deposited his book on the bench as if to keep his place, or even as a gage of earnest return, and bounded without difficulty up the rougher part of the cliff.

Equally innocent and infinite are the pleasures of observation and the resources engendered by the trick of analysing life. It amused poor Dencombe, as he dawdled in his tepid air-bath, to believe himself awaiting a revelation of something at the back of a fine young mind. He looked hard at the book on the end of the bench, but wouldn't have touched it for the world. It served his purpose to have a theory that shouldn't be exposed to refutation. He already felt better of his melancholy; he had, according to his old formula, put his head at the window. A passing Countess could draw off the fancy when, like the elder of the ladies who had just retreated, she was as obvious as the giantess of a caravan. It was indeed general views that were terrible; short ones, contrary to an opinion sometimes expressed, were the refuge, were the remedy. Doctor Hugh couldn't possibly be anything but a reviewer who had understandings for early copies with publishers or with newspapers. He reappeared in a quarter of an hour with visible relief at finding Dencombe on the spot and the gleam of white teeth in an embarrassed but generous smile. He was perceptibly disappointed at the eclipse of the other copy of the book; it made a pretext the less for speaking to the quiet gentleman. But he spoke notwithstanding; he held up his own copy and broke out pleadingly: "*Do* say, if you have occasion to speak of it, that it's the best thing he has done yet!"

Dencombe responded with a laugh: "Done yet" was so amusing to him, made such a grand avenue of the future. Better still, the young man took *him* for a reviewer. He pulled out "The Middle Years" from under his cape, but instinctively concealed any telltale look of fatherhood. This was partly because a person was always a fool for insisting to others on his work. "Is that what you're going to say yourself?" he put to his visitor.

"I'm not quite sure I shall write anything. I don't, as a regular thing—I enjoy in peace. But it's awfully fine."

Dencombe just debated. If the young man had begun to abuse him he would have confessed on the spot to his identity, but there was no harm in drawing out any impulse to praise. He drew it out with such success that in a few moments his new acquaintance, seated by his side, was confessing candidly that the works of the author of the volumes before them were the only ones he could read a second time. He had come the day before from London, where a friend of his, a journalist, had lent him his copy of the last, the copy sent to the office of the journal and already the subject of a "notice" which, as was pretended there—but one had to allow for "swagger"—it had taken a full quarter of an hour to prepare. He intimated that he was ashamed for his friend, and in the case of a work demanding and repaying study, of such inferior manners; and, with his fresh appreciation and his so irregular wish to express it, he speedily became for poor Dencombe a remarkable, a delightful apparition. Chance had brought the weary man of letters face to face with the greatest admirer in the new generation of whom it was supposable he might boast. The admirer in truth was mystifying, so rare a case was it to find a bristling young doctor—he looked like a German physiologist—enamoured of literary form. It was an accident, but happier than most accidents, so that Dencombe, exhilarated as well as confounded, spent half an hour in making his visitor talk while he kept himself quiet. He explained his premature possession of "The Middle Years" by an allusion to the friendship of the publisher, who, knowing he was at Bournemouth for his health, had paid him this graceful attention. He allowed he had been ill, for Doctor Hugh would infallibly have guessed it; he even went so far as to wonder if he mightn't look for some hygienic "tip" from a personage combining so bright an enthusiasm with a presumable knowledge of the remedies now in vogue. It would shake his faith a little perhaps to have to take a doctor seriously who could take *him* so seriously, but he enjoyed this gushing modern youth and felt with an acute pang that there would still be work to do in a world in which such odd combinations were presented. It wasn't true, what he had tried for renunciation's sake to believe, that all the combinations were exhausted. They weren't by any means—they were infinite: the exhaustion was in the miserable artist.

Doctor Hugh, an ardent physiologist, was saturated with the spirit of the age—in other words he had just taken his degree; but he was independent and various, he talked like a man who would have preferred to love literature best. He would fain have made fine phrases, but nature had denied him the trick. Some of the finest in "The Middle Years" had struck him inordinately, and he took the liberty of reading them to Dencombe in support of his plea. He grew vivid, in the balmy air, to his companion, for whose deep refreshment he seemed to have been sent; and was particularly ingenuous in describing how recently he had become acquainted, and how instantly infatuated, with the only man who had put flesh between the ribs of an art that was starving on su-perstitions. He hadn't yet written to him—he was deterred by a strain of respect. Dencombe at this moment rejoiced more in-wardly than ever that he had never answered the photographers. His visitor's attitude promised him a luxury of intercourse, though he was sure a due freedom for Doctor Hugh would depend not a little on the Countess. He learned without delay what type of Countess was involved, mastering as well the nature of the tie that united the curious trio. The large lady, an Englishwoman by birth and the daughter of a celebrated baritone, whose taste *minus* his talent she had inherited, was the widow of a French nobleman and mistress of all that remained of the handsome fortune, the fruit of her father's earnings, that had constituted her dower. Miss Vernham, an odd creature but an accomplished pianist, was attached to her person at a salary. The Countess was generous, independent, eccentric; she travelled with her minstrel and her medical man. Ignorant and passionate she had nevertheless mo-ments in which she was almost irresistible. Dencombe saw her sit for her portrait in Doctor Hugh's free sketch, and felt the picture of his young friend's relation to her frame itself in his mind. This young friend, for a representative of the new psychology, was him-self easily hypnotised, and if he became abnormally communica-tive it was only a sign of his real subjection. Dencombe did ac-cordingly what he wanted with him, even without being known as Dencombe.

Taken ill on a journey in Switzerland the Countess had picked him up at an hotel, and the accident of his happening to please her had made her offer him, with her imperious liberality, terms that couldn't fail to dazzle a practitioner without patients and whose resources had been drained dry by his studies. It wasn't the way he would have proposed to spend his time, but it was time that would pass quickly, and meanwhile she was wonderfully kind. She exacted perpetual attention, but it was impossible not to like her. He gave details about his queer patient, a "type" if there ever was one, who had in connexion with her flushed obesity, and in addition to the morbid strain of a violent and aimless will, a grave organic disorder; but he came back to his loved novelist, whom he was so good as to pronounce more essentially a poet than many of those who went in for verse, with a zeal excited, as all his indiscretion had been excited, by the happy chance of Dencombe's sympathy and the coincidence of their occupation. Dencombe had confessed to a slight personal acquaintance with the author of "The Middle Years," but had not felt himself as ready as he could have wished when his companion, who had never yet encountered a being so privileged, began to be eager for particulars. He even divined in Doctor Hugh's eye at that moment a glimmer of suspicion. But the young man was too inflamed to be shrewd and repeatedly caught up the book to exclaim: "Did you notice this?" or "Weren't you immensely struck with that?" "There's a beautiful passage toward the end," he broke out; and again he laid his hand on the volume. As he turned the pages he came upon something else, while Dencombe saw him suddenly change colour. He had taken up as it lay on the bench Dencombe's copy instead of his own, and his neighbour at once guessed the reason of his start. Doctor Hugh looked grave an instant; then he said: "I see you've been altering the text!" Dencombe was a passionate corrector, a fingerer of style; the last thing he ever arrived at was a form final for himself. His ideal would have been to publish secretly, and then, on the published text, treat himself to the terrified revise, sacrificing always a first edition and beginning for posterity and even for the collectors, poor dears, with a second. This morning, in "The Middle Years," his pencil had pricked a dozen lights. He was amused at the effect of the young man's reproach; for an instant it made him change colour. He stammered at any rate ambiguously, then through a blur of ebbing consciousness saw Doctor Hugh's mystified eyes. He only had time to feel he was about to be ill again—that emotion, excitement, fatigue, the heat of the sun, the solicitation of the air, had combined to play him a trick, before, stretching out a hand to his visitor with a plaintive cry, he lost his senses altogether.

Later he knew he had fainted and that Doctor Hugh had got him home in a Bath-chair, the conductor of which, prowling within hail for custom, had happened to remember seeing him in the garden of the hotel. He had recovered his perception on the way, and had, in bed that afternoon, a vague recollection of Doctor Hugh's young face, as they went together, bent over him in a comforting laugh and expressive of something more than a suspicion of his identity. That identity was ineffaceable now, and all the more that he was rueful and sore. He had been rash, been stupid, had gone out too soon, stayed out too long. He oughtn't to have exposed himself to strangers, he ought to have taken his servant. He felt as if he had fallen into a hole too deep to descry any little patch of heaven. He was confused about the time that had passed—he pieced the fragments together. He had seen his doctor, the real one, the one who had treated him from the first and who had again been very kind. His servant was in and out on tiptoe, looking very wise after the fact. He said more than once something about the sharp young gentleman. The rest was vagueness in so far as it wasn't despair. The vagueness, however, justified itself by dreams, dozing anxieties from which he finally emerged to the consciousness of a dark room and a shaded candle.

"You'll be all right again—I know all about you now," said a voice near him that he felt to be young. Then his meeting with Doctor Hugh came back. He was too discouraged to joke about it yet, but made out after a little that the interest was intense for his visitor. "Of course I can't attend you professionally—you've got your own man, with whom I've talked and who's excellent," Doctor Hugh went on. "But you must let me come to see you as a good friend. I've just looked in before going to bed. You're doing beautifully, but it's a good job I was with you on the cliff. I shall come in early tomorrow. I want to do something for you. I want to do everything. You've done a tremendous lot for me." The young man held his hand, hanging over him, and poor Dencombe, weakly aware of this living pressure, simply lay there and accepted his devotion. He couldn't do anything less—he needed help too much.

The idea of the help he needed was very present to him that night, which he spent in a lucid stillness, an intensity of thought that constituted a reaction from his hours of stupor. He was lost, he was lost—he was lost if he couldn't be saved. He wasn't afraid of suffering, of death, wasn't even in love with life; but he had had a deep demonstration of desire. It came over him in the long quiet hours that only with "The Middle Years" had he taken his flight; only on that day, visited by soundless processions, had he recognised his kingdom. He had had a revelation of his range. What he dreaded was the idea that his reputation should stand on the unfinished. It wasn't with his past but with his future that it should properly be concerned. Illness and age rose before him like spectres with pitiless eyes: how was he to bribe such fates to give him the second chance? He had had the one chance that all men have—he had had the chance of life. He went to sleep again very late, and when he awoke Doctor Hugh was sitting at hand. There was already by this time something beautifully familiar in him.

"Don't think I've turned out your physician," he said; "I'm acting with his consent. He has been here and seen you. Somehow he seems to trust me. I told him how we happened to come together yesterday, and he recognises that I've a peculiar right."

Dencombe felt his own face pressing. "How have you squared the Countess?"

The young man blushed a little, but turned it off. "Oh never mind the Countess!"

"You told me she was very exacting."

Doctor Hugh had a wait. "So she is."

"And Miss Vernham's an *intrigante*."

"How do you know that?"

"I know everything. One *has* to, to write decently!"

"I think she's mad," said limpid Doctor Hugh.

"Well, don't quarrel with the Countess—she's a present help to you."

"I don't quarrel," Doctor Hugh returned. "But I don't get on with silly women." Presently he added: "You seem very much alone."

"That often happens at my age. I've outlived, I've lost by the way."

Doctor Hugh faltered; then surmounting a soft scruple: "Whom have you lost?"

"Every one."

"Ah no," the young man breathed, laying a hand on his arm.

"I once had a wife—I once had a son. My wife died when my child was born, and my boy, at school, was carried off by typhoid."

"I wish I'd been there!" cried Doctor Hugh.

"Well—if you're here!" Dencombe answered with a smile that, in spite of dimness, showed how he valued being sure of his companion's whereabouts.

"You talk strangely of your age. You're not old."

"Hypocrite—so early!"

"I speak physiologically."

"That's the way I've been speaking for the last five years, and it's exactly what I've been saying to myself. It isn't till we *are* old that we begin to tell ourselves we're not."

"Yet I know I myself am young," Doctor Hugh returned.

"Not so well as I!" laughed his patient, whose visitor indeed would have established the truth in question by the honesty with which he changed the point of view, remarking that it must be one of the charms of age—at any rate in the case of high distinction —to feel that one has laboured and achieved. Doctor Hugh employed the common phrase about earning one's rest, and it made poor Dencombe for an instant almost angry. He recovered himself, however, to explain, lucidly enough, that if, ungraciously, he knew nothing of such a balm, it was doubtless because he had wasted inestimable years. He had followed literature from the first, but he had taken a lifetime to get abreast of her. Only today at last had he begun to *see,* so that all he had hitherto shown was a movement without a direction. He had ripened too late and was so clumsily constituted that he had had to teach himself by mistakes.

"I prefer your flowers then to other people's fruit, and your mistakes to other people's successes," said gallant Doctor Hugh. "It's for your mistakes I admire you."

"You're happy—you don't know," Dencombe answered.

Looking at his watch the young man had got up; he named the hour of the afternoon at which he would return. Dencombe warned him against committing himself too deeply, and expressed again all his dread of making him neglect the Countess—perhaps incur her displeasure.

"I want to be like you—I want to learn by mistakes!" Doctor Hugh laughed.

"Take care you don't make too grave a one! But do come back," Dencombe added with the glimmer of a new idea.

"You should have had more vanity!" His friend spoke as if he knew the exact amount required to make a man of letters normal.

"No, no—I only should have had more time. I want another go."

"Another go?"

"I want an extension."

"An extension?" Again Doctor Hugh repeated Dencombe's words, with which he seemed to have been struck.

"Don't you know?—I want to what they call 'live.' "

The young man, for good-bye, had taken his hand, which closed with a certain force. They looked at each other hard. "You *will* live," said Doctor Hugh.

"Don't be superficial. It's too serious!"

"You *shall* live!" Dencombe's visitor declared, turning pale.

"Ah that's better!" And as he retired the invalid, with a troubled laugh, sank gratefully back.

All that day and all the following night he wondered if it mightn't be arranged. His doctor came again, his servant was attentive, but it was to his confident young friend that he felt himself mentally appeal. His collapse on the cliff was plausibly explained and his liberation, on a better basis, promised for the morrow; meanwhile, however, the intensity of his meditations kept him tranquil and made him indifferent. The idea that occupied him was none the less absorbing because it was a morbid fancy. Here was a clever son of the age, ingenious and ardent, who happened to have set him up for connoisseurs to worship. This servant of his altar had all the new learning in science and all the old reverence in faith; wouldn't he therefore put his knowledge at the disposal of his sympathy, his craft at the disposal of his love? Couldn't he be trusted to invent a remedy for a poor artist to whose art he had paid a tribute? If he couldn't the alternative was hard: Dencombe would have to surrender to silence unvindicated and undivined. The rest of the day and all the next he toyed in secret with this sweet futility. Who would work the miracle for him but the young man who could combine such lucidity with such passion? He thought of the fairy-tales of science and charmed himself into forgetting that he looked for a magic that was not of this world. Doctor Hugh was an apparition, and that placed him above the law. He came and went while his patient, who now sat up, followed him with supplicating eyes. The interest of knowing the great author had made the young man begin "The Middle Years" afresh and would help him to find a richer sense between its covers. Dencombe had told him what he "tried for"; with all his intelligence, on a first perusal, Doctor Hugh had failed to guess it. The baffled celebrity wondered then who in the world *would* guess it: he was amused once more at the diffused massive weight that could be thrown into the missing of an intention. Yet he wouldn't rail at the general mind to-day—consoling as that ever had been: the revelation of his own slowness had seemed to make all stupidity sacred.

Doctor Hugh, after a little, was visibly worried, confessing, on enquiry, to a source of embarrassment at home. "Stick to the Countess—don't mind me," Dencombe said repeatedly; for his companion was frank enough about the large lady's attitude. She was so jealous that she had fallen ill—she resented such a breach of allegiance. She paid so much for his fidelity that she must have it all: she refused him the right to other sympathies, charged him with scheming to make her die alone, for it was needless to point out how little Miss Vernham was a resource in trouble. When Doctor Hugh mentioned that the Countess would already have left Bournemouth if he hadn't kept her in bed, poor Dencombe held his arm tighter and said with decision: "Take her straight away." They had gone out together, walking back to the sheltered nook in which, the other day, they had met. The young man, who had given his companion a personal support, declared with emphasis that his conscience was clear—he could ride two horses at once. Didn't he dream for his future of a time when he should have to ride five hundred? Longing equally for virtue, Dencombe replied that in that golden age no patient would pretend to have contracted with him for his whole attention. On the part of the Countess wasn't such an avidity lawful? Doctor Hugh denied it, said there was no contract, but only a free understanding, and that a sordid servitude was impossible to a generous spirit; he liked moreover to talk about art, and that was the subject on which, this time, as they sat together on the sunny bench, he tried most to engage the author of "The Middle Years." Dencombe, soaring again a little on the weak wings of convalescence and still haunted by that happy notion of an organised rescue, found another strain of eloquence to plead the cause of a certain splendid "last manner," the very citadel, as it would prove, of his reputation, the stronghold into which his real treasure would be gathered. While his listener gave up the morning and the great still sea ostensibly waited he had a wondrous explanatory hour. Even for himself he was inspired as he told what his treasure would consist of; the precious metals he would dig from the mine, the jewels rare, strings of pearls, he would hang between the columns of his temple. He was wondrous for himself, so thick his convictions crowded, but still more wondrous for Doctor Hugh, who assured him none the less that the very pages he had just published were already encrusted with gems. This admirer, however, panted for the combinations to come and, before the face of the beautiful day, renewed to Dencombe his guarantee that his profession would hold itself responsible for such a life. Then he suddenly clapped his hand upon his watch-pocket and asked leave to absent himself for half an hour. Dencombe waited there for his return, but was at last recalled to the actual by the fall of a shadow across the ground. The shadow darkened into that of Miss Vernham, the young lady in attendance on the Countess; whom Dencombe, recognising her, perceived so clearly to have come to speak to him that he rose from his bench to acknowledge the civility. Miss Vernham indeed proved not particularly civil; she looked strangely agitated, and her type was now unmistakeable.

"Excuse me if I do ask," she said, "whether it's too much to hope that you may be induced to leave Doctor Hugh alone." Then before our poor friend, greatly disconcerted, could protest: "You ought to be informed that you stand in his light—that you may do him a terrible injury."

"Do you mean by causing the Countess to dispense with his services?"

"By causing her to disinherit him." Dencombe stared at this, and Miss Vernham pursued, in the gratification of seeing she could produce an impression: "It has depended on himself to come into something very handsome. He has had a grand prospect, but I think you've succeeded in spoiling it."

"Not intentionally, I assure you. Is there no hope the accident may be repaired?" Dencombe asked.

"She was ready to do anything for him. She takes great fancies, she lets herself go—it's her way. She has no relations, she's free to dispose of her money, and she's very ill," said Miss Vernham for a climax.

"I'm very sorry to hear it," Dencombe stammered.

"Wouldn't it be possible for you to leave Bournemouth? That's what I've come to see about."

He sank to his bench. "I'm very ill myself, but I'll try!"

Miss Vernham still stood there with her colourless eyes and the brutality of her good conscience. "Before it's too late, please!" she said; and with this she turned her back, in order, quickly, as if it had been a business to which she could spare but a precious moment, to pass out of his sight.

Oh yes, after this Dencombe was certainly very ill. Miss Vernham had upset him with her rough fierce news; it was the sharpest shock to him to discover what was at stake for a penniless young man of fine parts. He sat trembling on his bench, staring at the waste of waters, feeling sick with the directness of the blow. He was indeed too weak, too unsteady, too alarmed; but he would make the effort to get away, for he couldn't accept the guilt of interference and his honour was really involved. He would hobble home, at any rate, and then think what was to be done. He made his way back to the hotel and, as he went, had a characteristic vision of Miss Vernham's great motive. The Countess hated women of course—Dencombe was lucid about that; so the hungry pianist had no personal hopes and could only console herself with the bold conception of helping Doctor Hugh in order to marry him after he should get his money or else induce him to recognise her claim for compensation and buy her off. If she had befriended him at a fruitful crisis he would really, as a man of delicacy—and she knew what to think of that point—have to reckon with her.

At the hotel Dencombe's servant insisted on his going back to bed. The invalid had talked about catching a train and had begun with orders to pack; after which his racked nerves had yielded to a sense of sickness. He consented to see his physician, who immediately was sent for, but he wished it to be understood that his door was irrevocably closed to Doctor Hugh. He had his plan, which was so fine that he rejoiced in it after getting back to bed. Doctor Hugh, suddenly finding himself snubbed without mercy, would, in natural disgust and to the joy of Miss Vernham, renew his allegiance to the Countess. When his physician arrived Dencombe learned that he was feverish and that this was very wrong: he was to cultivate calmness and try, if possible, not to think. For the rest of the day he wooed stupidity; but there was an ache that kept him sentient, the probable sacrifice of his "extension," the limit of his course. His medical adviser was anything but pleased; his successive relapses were ominous. He charged this personage to put out a strong hand and take Doctor Hugh off his mind— it would contribute so much to his being quiet. The agitating name, in his room, was not mentioned again, but his security was a smothered fear, and it was not confirmed by the receipt, at ten o'clock that evening, of a telegram which his servant opened and read him and to which, with an address in London, the signature of Miss Vernham was attached. "Beseech you to use all influence to make our friend join us here in the morning. Countess much the worse for dreadful journey, but everything may still be saved." The two ladies had gathered themselves up and had been capable in the afternoon of a spiteful revolution. They had started for the capital, and if the elder one, as Miss Vernham had announced, was very ill, she had wished to make it clear that she was proportionately reckless. Poor Dencombe, who was not reckless and who only desired that everything should indeed be "saved," sent this missive straight off to the young man's lodging and had on the morrow the pleasure of knowing that he had quitted Bournemouth by an early train.

Two days later he pressed in with a copy of a literary journal in his hand. He had returned because he was anxious and for the pleasure of flourishing the great review of "The Middle Years." Here at least was something adequate—it rose to the occasion; it was an acclamation, a reparation, a critical attempt to place the author in the niche he had fairly won. Dencombe accepted and submitted; he made neither objection nor enquiry, for old complications had returned and he had had two dismal days. He was convinced not only that he should never again leave his bed, so that his young friend might pardonably remain, but that the demand he should make on the patience of beholders would be of the most moderate. Doctor Hugh had been to town, and he tried to find in his eyes some confession that the Countess was pacified and his legacy clinched; but all he could see there was the light of his juvenile joy in two or three of the phrases of the newspaper. Dencombe couldn't read them, but when his visitor had insisted on repeating them more than once he was able to shake an unintoxicated head. "Ah no—but they would have been true of what I *could* have done!"

"What people 'could have done' is mainly what they've in fact done," Doctor Hugh contended.

"Mainly, yes; but I've been an idiot!" Dencombe said.

Doctor Hugh did remain; the end was coming fast. Two days later his patient observed to him, by way of the feeblest of jokes, that there would now be no question whatever of a second chance. At this the young man stared; then he exclaimed: "Why it has come to pass—it has come to pass! The second chance has been the public's—the chance to find the point of view, to pick up the pearl!"

"Oh the pearl!" poor Dencombe uneasily sighed. A smile as cold as a winter sunset flickered on his drawn lips as he added: "The pearl is the unwritten—the pearl is the unalloyed, the *rest*, the lost!"

From that hour he was less and less present, heedless to all appearance of what went on round him. His disease was definitely mortal, of an action as relentless, after the short arrest that had enabled him to fall in with Doctor Hugh, as a leak in a great ship. Sinking steadily, though this visitor, a man of rare resources, now cordially approved by his physician, showed endless art in guarding him from pain, poor Dencombe kept no reckoning of favour or neglect, betrayed no symptom of regret or speculation. Yet toward the last he gave a sign of having noticed how for two days Doctor Hugh hadn't been in his room, a sign that consisted of his suddenly opening his eyes to put a question. Had he spent those days with the Countess?

"The Countess is dead," said Doctor Hugh. "I knew that in a particular contingency she wouldn't resist. I went to her grave."

Dencombe's eyes opened wider. "She left you 'something handsome'?"

The young man gave a laugh almost too light for a chamber of woe. "Never a penny. She roundly cursed me."

"Cursed you?" Dencombe wailed.

"For giving her up. I gave her up for *you*. I had to choose," his companion explained.

"You chose to let a fortune go?"

"I chose to accept, whatever they might be, the consequences of my infatuation," smiled Doctor Hugh. Then as a larger pleasantry: "The fortune be hanged! It's your own fault if I can't get your things out of my head."

The immediate tribute to his humour was a long bewildered moan; after which, for many hours, many days, Dencombe lay motionless and absent. A response so absolute, such a glimpse of a definite result and such a sense of credit, worked together in his mind and, producing a strange commotion, slowly altered and transfigured his despair. The sense of cold submersion left him— he seemed to float without an effort. The incident was extraordinary as evidence, and it shed an intenser light. At the last he signed to Doctor Hugh to listen and, when he was down on his knees by the pillow, brought him very near. "You've made me think it all a delusion."

"Not your glory, my dear friend," stammered the young man.

"Not my glory—what there is of it! It *is* glory—to have been tested, to have had our little quality and cast our little spell. The thing is to have made somebody care. You happen to be crazy of course, but that doesn't affect the law."

"You're a great success!" said Doctor Hugh, putting into his young voice the ring of a marriage-bell.

Dencombe lay taking this in; then he gathered strength to speak once more. "A second chance—*that's* the delusion. There never was to be but one. We work in the dark—we do what we can—we give what we have. Our doubt is our passion and our passion is our task. The rest is the madness of art."

"If you've doubted, if you've despaired, you've always 'done' it," his visitor subtly argued.

"We've done something or other," Dencombe conceded.

"Something or other is everything. It's the feasible. It's *you!*"

"Comforter!" poor Dencombe ironically sighed.

"But it's true," insisted his friend.

"It's true. It's frustration that doesn't count."

"Frustration's only life," said Doctor Hugh.

"Yes, it's what passes." Poor Dencombe was barely audible, but he had marked with the words the virtual end of his first and only chance.

THE PUPIL

I

THE poor young man hesitated and procrastinated: it cost him such an effort to broach the subject of terms, to speak of money to a person who spoke only of feelings and, as it were, of the aristocracy. Yet he was unwilling to take leave, treating his engagement as settled, without some more conventional glance in that direction than he could find an opening for in the manner of the large affable lady who sat there drawing a pair of soiled *gants de Suède* through a fat jewelled hand and, at once pressing and gliding, repeated over and over everything but the thing he would have liked to hear. He would have liked to hear the figure of his salary; but just as he was nervously about to sound that note the little boy came back—the little boy Mrs. Moreen had sent out of the room to fetch her fan. He came back without the fan, only with the casual observation that he couldn't find it. As he dropped this cynical confession he looked straight and hard at the candidate for the honour of taking his education in hand. This personage reflected somewhat grimly that the first thing he should have to teach his little charge would be to appear to address himself to his mother when he spoke to her—especially not to make her such an improper answer as that.

When Mrs. Moreen bethought herself of this pretext for getting rid of their companion Pemberton supposed it was precisely to approach the delicate subject of his remuneration. But it had been only to say some things about her son that it was better a boy of eleven shouldn't catch. They were extravagantly to his advantage save when she lowered her voice to sigh, tapping her left side familiarly, "And all overclouded by *this,* you know; all at the mercy of a weakness—!" Pemberton gathered that the weakness was in the region of the heart. He had known the poor child was not robust: this was the basis on which he had been invited to treat, through an English lady, an Oxford acquaintance, then at Nice, who happened to know both his needs and those of the amiable American family looking out for something really superior in the way of a resident tutor.

The young man's impression of his prospective pupil, who had come into the room as if to see for himself the moment Pemberton was admitted, was not quite the soft solicitation the visitor had taken for granted. Morgan Moreen was somehow sickly without being "delicate," and that he looked intelligent—it is true Pemberton wouldn't have enjoyed his being stupid—only added to the suggestion that, as with his big mouth and big ears he really couldn't be called pretty, he might too utterly fail to please. Pemberton was modest, was even timid; and the chance that his small scholar would prove cleverer than himself had quite figured, to his anxiety, among the dangers of an untried experiment. He reflected, however, that these were risks one had to run when one accepted a position, as it was called, in a private family; when as yet one's university honours had, pecuniarily speaking, remained barren. At any rate when Mrs. Moreen got up as to intimate that, since it was understood he would enter upon his duties within the week she would let him off now, he succeeded, in spite of the presence of the child, in squeezing out a phrase about the rate of payment. It was not the fault of the conscious smile which seemed a reference to the lady's expensive identity, it was not the fault of this demonstration, which had, in a sort, both vagueness and point, if the allusion didn't sound rather vulgar. This was exactly because she became still more gracious to reply: "Oh I can assure you that all that will be quite regular."

Pemberton only wondered, while he took up his hat, what "all that" was to amount to—people had such different ideas. Mrs. Moreen's words, however, seemed to commit the family to a pledge definite enough to elicit from the child a strange little comment in the shape of the mocking foreign ejaculation "Oh la-la!"

Pemberton, in some confusion, glanced at him as he walked

slowly to the window with his back turned, his hands in his pockets and the air in his elderly shoulders of a boy who didn't play. The young man wondered if he should be able to teach him to play, though his mother had said it would never do and that this was why school was impossible. Mrs. Moreen exhibited no discomfiture; she only continued blandly: "Mr. Moreen will be delighted to meet your wishes. As I told you, he has been called to London for a week. As soon as he comes back you shall have it out with him."

This was so frank and friendly that the young man could only reply, laughing as his hostess laughed: "Oh I don't imagine we shall have much of a battle."

"They'll give you anything you like," the boy remarked unexpectedly, returning from the window. "We don't mind what anything costs—we live awfully well."

"My darling, you're too quaint!" his mother exclaimed, putting out to caress him a practised but ineffectual hand. He slipped out of it, but looked with intelligent innocent eyes at Pemberton, who had already had time to notice that from one moment to the other his small satiric face seemed to change its time of life. At this moment it was infantine, yet it appeared also to be under the influence of curious intuitions and knowledges. Pemberton rather disliked precocity and was disappointed to find gleams of it in a disciple not yet in his teens. Nevertheless he divined on the spot that Morgan wouldn't prove a bore. He would prove on the contrary a source of agitation. This idea held the young man, in spite of a certain repulsion.

"You pompous little person! We're not extravagant!" Mrs. Moreen gaily protested, making another unsuccessful attempt to draw the boy to her side. "You must know what to expect," she went on to Pemberton.

"The less you expect the better!" her companion interposed. "But we *are* people of fashion."

"Only so far as *you* make us so!" Mrs. Moreen tenderly mocked. "Well then, on Friday—don't tell me you're superstitious—and mind you don't fail us. Then you'll see us all. I'm so sorry the girls

are out. I guess you'll like the girls. And, you know, I've another
son, quite different from this one."

"He tries to imitate me," Morgan said to their friend.

"He tries? Why he's twenty years old!" cried Mrs. Moreen.

"You're very witty," Pemberton remarked to the child—a proposition his mother echoed with enthusiasm, declaring Morgan's
sallies to be the delight of the house.

The boy paid no heed to this; he only enquired abruptly of the
visitor, who was surprised afterwards that he hadn't struck him
as offensively forward: "Do you *want* very much to come?"

"Can you doubt it after such a description of what I shall
hear?" Pemberton replied. Yet he didn't want to come at all; he
was coming because he had to go somewhere, thanks to the collapse of his fortune at the end of a year abroad spent on the system of putting his scant patrimony into a single full wave of experience. He had had his full wave but couldn't pay the score at
his inn. Moreover he had caught in the boy's eyes the glimpse
of a far-off appeal.

"Well, I'll do the best I can for you," said Morgan; with which
he turned away again. He passed out of one of the long windows;
Pemberton saw him go and lean on the parapet of the terrace. He
remained there while the young man took leave of his mother, who,
on Pemberton's looking as if he expected a farewell from him, interposed with: "Leave him, leave him; he's so strange!" Pemberton supposed her to fear something he might say. "He's a genius
—you'll love him," she added. "He's much the most interesting
person in the family." And before he could invent some civility
to oppose to this she wound up with: "But we're all good, you
know!"

"He's a genius—you'll love him!" were words that recurred
to our aspirant before the Friday, suggesting among many things
that geniuses were not invariably loveable. However, it was all
the better if there was an element that would make tutorship absorbing: he had perhaps taken too much for granted it would only
disgust him. As he left the villa after his interview he looked up

at the balcony and saw the child leaning over it. "We shall have great larks!" he called up.

Morgan hung fire a moment and then gaily returned: "By the time you come back I shall have thought of something witty!"

This made Pemberton say to himself "After all he's rather nice."

II

On the Friday he saw them all, as Mrs. Moreen had promised, for her husband had come back and the girls and the other son were at home. Mr. Moreen had a white moustache, a confiding manner and, in his buttonhole, the ribbon of a foreign order— bestowed, as Pemberton eventually learned, for services. For what services he never clearly ascertained: this was a point—one of a large number—that Mr. Moreen's manner never confided. What it emphatically did confide was that he was even more a man of the world than you might first make out. Ulick, the firstborn, was in visible training for the same profession—under the disadvantage as yet, however, of a buttonhole but feebly floral and a moustache with no pretensions to type. The girls had hair and figures and manners and small fat feet, but had never been out alone. As for Mrs. Moreen Pemberton saw on a nearer view that her elegance was intermittent and her parts didn't always match. Her husband, as she had promised, met with enthusiasm Pemberton's ideas in regard to a salary. The young man had endeavoured to keep these stammerings modest, and Mr. Moreen made it no secret that *he* found them wanting in "style." He further mentioned that he aspired to be intimate with his children, to be their best friend, and that he was always looking out for them. That was what he went off for, to London and other places—to look out; and this vigilance was the theory of life, as well as the real occupation, of the whole family. They all looked out, for they were very frank on the subject of its being necessary. They desired it to be understood that they were earnest people, and also that their fortune, though quite adequate for earnest people, required the most careful administration. Mr. Moreen, as the parent bird, sought sustenance for the nest. Ulick invoked support mainly at the club, where Pemberton guessed that it was usually served on green cloth. The girls used to do up their hair and their frocks themselves, and our young man felt appealed to to be glad, in regard to Morgan's education, that, though it must naturally be of the best, it didn't cost too much. After a little he *was* glad, forgetting at times his own needs in the interest inspired by the child's character and culture and the pleasure of making easy terms for him.

During the first weeks of their acquaintance Morgan had been as puzzling as a page in an unknown language—altogether different from the obvious little Anglo-Saxons who had misrepresented childhood to Pemberton. Indeed the whole mystic volume in which the boy had been amateurishly bound demanded some practice in translation. Today, after a considerable interval, there is something phantasmagoric, like a prismatic reflexion or a serial novel, in Pemberton's memory of the queerness of the Moreens. If it were not for a few tangible tokens—a lock of Morgan's hair cut by his own hand, and the half-dozen letters received from him when they were disjoined—the whole episode and the figures peopling it would seem too inconsequent for anything but dreamland. Their supreme quaintness was their success—as it appeared to him for a while at the time; since he had never seen a family so brilliantly equipped for failure. Wasn't it success to have kept him so hatefully long? Wasn't it success to have drawn him in that first morning at déjeuner, the Friday he came—it was enough to *make* one superstitious—so that he utterly committed himself, and this not by calculation or on a signal, but from a happy instinct which made them, like a band of gipsies, work so neatly together? They amused him as much as if they had really been a band of gipsies. He was still young and had not seen much of the world—his English years had been properly arid; therefore the reversed conventions of the Moreens—for they had *their* desperate proprieties—struck him as topsy-turvy. He had encountered nothing like them at Oxford; still less had any such note been struck to his younger American ear during the four years at Yale in which he had richly supposed himself to be reacting against a Puritan strain. The reaction of the Moreens, at any rate, went ever so much further. He had thought himself very sharp that first day in hitting them all off in his mind with the "cosmopolite" label. Later it seemed feeble and colourless—confessedly helplessly provisional.

He yet when he first applied it felt a glow of joy—for an instructor he was still empirical—rise from the apprehension that living with them would really be to see life. Their sociable strangeness was an intimation of that—their chatter of tongues, their gaiety and good humour, their infinite dawdling (they were always getting themselves up, but it took for ever, and Pemberton had once found Mr. Moreen shaving in the drawing-room), their French, their Italian and, cropping up in the foreign fluencies, their cold tough slices of American. They lived on maccaroni and coffee—they had these articles prepared in perfection—but they knew recipes for a hundred other dishes. They overflowed with music and song, were always humming and catching each other up, and had a sort of professional acquaintance with Continental cities. They talked of "good places" as if they had been pickpockets or strolling players. They had at Nice a villa, a carriage, a piano and a banjo, and they went to official parties. They were a perfect calendar of the "days" of their friends, which Pemberton knew them, when they were indisposed, to get out of bed to go to, and which made the week larger than life when Mrs. Moreen talked of them with Paula and Amy. Their initiations gave their new inmate at first an almost dazzling sense of culture. Mrs. Moreen had translated something at some former period—an author whom it made Pemperton feel *borné* never to have heard of. They could imitate Venetian and sing Neapolitan, and when they wanted to say something very particular communicated with each other in an ingenious dialect of their own, an elastic spoken cipher which Pemberton at first took for some *patois* of one of their countries, but which he "caught on to" as he would not have grasped provincial development of Spanish or German.

"It's the family language—Ultramoreen," Morgan explained to him drolly enough; but the boy rarely condescended to use it himself, though he dealt in colloquial Latin as if he had been a little prelate.

Among all the "days" with which Mrs. Moreen's memory was taxed she managed to squeeze in one of her own, which her friends sometimes forgot. But the house drew a frequented air from the number of fine people who were freely named there and from sevral mysterious men with foreign titles and English clothes whom Morgan called the Princes and who, on sofas with the girls, talked French very loud—though sometimes with some oddity of accent —as if to show they were saying nothing improper. Pemberton wondered how the Princes could ever propose in that tone and so publicly: he took for granted cynically that this was what was desired of them. Then he recognised that even for the chance of such an advantage Mrs. Moreen would never allow Paula and Amy to receive alone. These young ladies were not at all timid, but it was just the safeguards that made them so candidly free. It was a houseful of Bohemians who wanted tremendously to be Philistines.

In one respect, however, certainly, they achieved no rigour— they were wonderfully amiable and ecstatic about Morgan. It was a genuine tenderness, an artless admiration, equally strong in each. They even praised his beauty, which was small, and were as afraid of him as if they felt him of finer clay. They spoke of him as a little angel and a prodigy—they touched on his want of health with long, vague faces. Pemberton feared at first an extravagance that might make him hate the boy, but before this happened he had become extravagant himself. Later, when he had grown rather to hate the others, it was a bribe to patience for him that they were at any rate nice about Morgan, going on tiptoe if they fancied he was showing symptoms, and even giving up somebody's "day" to procure him a pleasure. Mixed with this too was the oddest wish to make him independent, as if they had felt themselves not good enough for him. They passed him over to the new member of their circle very much as if wishing to force some charity of adoption on so free an agent and get rid of their own charge.

They were delighted when they saw Morgan take so to his kind
playfellow, and could think of no higher praise for the young man.
It was strange how they contrived to reconcile the appearance,
and indeed the essential fact, of adoring the child with their eagerness to wash their hands of him. Did they want to get rid of
him before he should find them out? Pemberton was finding them
out month by month. The boy's fond family, however this might
be, turned their backs with exaggerated delicacy, as if to avoid the
reproach of interfering. Seeing in time how little he had in common with them—it was by *them* he first observed it; they pro-
claimed it with complete humility—his companion was moved to
speculate on the mysteries of transmission, the far jumps of hered-
ity. Where his detachment from most of the things they represented had come from was more than an observer could say—it
certainly had burrowed under two or three generations.

As for Pemberton's own estimate of his pupil, it was a good
while before he got the point of view, so little had he been prepared for it by the smug young barbarians to whom the tradition
of tutorship, as hitherto revealed to him, had been adjusted. Morgan was scrappy and surprising, deficient in many properties supposed common to the *genus* and abounding in others that were the
portion only of the supernaturally clever. One day his friend made
a great stride: it cleared up the question to perceive that Morgan
was supernaturally clever and that, though the formula was temporarily meagre, this would be the only assumption on which one
could successfully deal with him. He had the general quality of a
child for whom life had not been simplified by school, a kind of
homebred sensibility which might have been bad for himself but
was charming for others, and a whole range of refinement and perception—little musical vibrations as taking as picked-up airs—
begotten by wandering about Europe at the tail of his migratory
tribe. This might not have been an education to recommend in
advance, but its results with so special a subject were as appreciable as the marks on a piece of fine porcelain. There was at the
same time in him a small strain of stoicism, doubtless the fruit of
having had to begin early to bear pain, which counted for pluck

and made it of less consequence that he might have been thought at school rather a polyglot little beast. Pemberton indeed quickly found himself rejoicing that school was out of the question: in any million of boys it was probably good for all but one, and Morgan was that millionth. It would have made him comparative and superior—it might have made him really require kicking. Pemberton would try to be school himself—a bigger seminary than five hundred grazing donkeys, so that, winning no prizes, the boy would remain unconscious and irresponsible and amusing—amusing, because, though life was already intense in his childish nature, freshness still made there a strong draught for jokes. It turned out that even in the still air of Morgan's various disabilities jokes flourished greatly. He was a pale lean acute undeveloped little cosmopolite, who liked intellectual gymnastics and who also, as regards the behaviour of mankind, had noticed more things than you might suppose, but who nevertheless had his proper playroom of superstitions, where he smashed a dozen toys a day.

III

AT NICE once, toward evening, as the pair rested in the open air after a walk, and looked over the sea at the pink western lights, he said suddenly to his comrade: "Do you like it, you know—being with us all in this intimate way?"

"My dear fellow, why should I stay if I didn't?"

"How do I know you'll stay? I'm almost sure you won't, very long."

"I hope you don't mean to dismiss me," said Pemberton.

Morgan debated, looking at the sunset. "I think if I did right I ought to."

"Well, I know I'm supposed to instruct you in virtue; but in that case don't do right."

"You're very young—fortunately," Morgan went on, turning to him again.

"Oh yes, compared with you!"

"Therefore it won't matter so much if you do lose a lot of time."

"That's the way to look at it," said Pemberton accommodatingly.

They were silent a minute; after which the boy asked: "Do you like my father and my mother very much?"

"Dear me, yes. Charming people."

Morgan received this with another silence; then unexpectedly, familiarly, but at the same time affectionately, he remarked: "You're a jolly old humbug!"

For a particular reason the words made our young man change colour. The boy noticed in an instant that he had turned red, whereupon he turned red himself and pupil and master exchanged a longish glance in which there was a consciousness of many more things than are usually touched upon, even tacitly, in such a relation. It produced for Pemberton an embarrassment; it raised in a shadowy form a question—this was the first glimpse of it—destined to play a singular and, as he imagined, owing to the altogether peculiar conditions, an unprecedented part in his intercourse with his little companion. Later, when he found himself talking with the youngster in a way in which few youngsters could ever have been talked with, he thought of that clumsy moment on the bench at Nice as the dawn of an understanding that had broadened. What had added to the clumsiness then was that he thought it his duty to declare to Morgan that he might abuse him, Pemberton, as much as he liked, but must never abuse his parents. To this Morgan had the easy retort that he hadn't dreamed of abusing them; which appeared to be true: it put Pemberton in the wrong.

"Then why am I a humbug for saying *I* think them charming?" the young man asked, conscious of a certain rashness.

"Well—they're not your parents."

"They love you better than anything in the world—never forget that," said Pemberton.

"Is that why you like them so much?"

"They're very kind to me," Pemberton replied evasively.

"You *are* a humbug!" laughed Morgan, passing an arm into his tutor's. He leaned against him looking off at the sea again and swinging his long thin legs.

"Don't kick my shins," said Pemberton while he reflected "Hang it, I can't complain of them to the child!"

"There's another reason too," Morgan went on, keeping his legs still.

"Another reason for what?"

"Besides their not being your parents."

"I don't understand you," said Pemberton.

"Well, you will before long. All right!"

He did understand fully before long, but he made a fight even with himself before he confessed it. He thought it the oddest thing to have a struggle with the child about. He wondered he didn't hate the hope of the Moreens for bringing the struggle on. But by the time it began any such sentiment for that scion was closed to him. Morgan was a special case, and to know him was to accept him on his own odd terms. Pemberton had spent his aversion to special cases before arriving at knowledge. When at last he did arrive his quandary was great. Against every interest he had attached himself. They would have to meet things together. Before they went home that evening at Nice the boy had said, clinging to his arm:

"Well, at any rate you'll hang on to the last."

"To the last?"

"Till you're fairly beaten."

"*You* ought to be fairly beaten!" cried the young man, drawing him closer.

IV

A YEAR after he had come to live with them Mr. and Mrs. Moreen suddenly gave up the villa at Nice. Pemberton had got used to suddeness, having seen it practised on a considerable scale during two jerky little tours—one in Switzerland the first summer, and the other late in the winter, when they all ran down to Florence and then, at the end of ten days, liking it much less than they had intended, straggled back in mysterious depression. They had returned to Nice "for ever," as they said; but this didn't prevent their squeezing, one rainy muggy May night, into a second-class railway-carriage—you could never tell by which class they would travel—where Pemberton helped them to stow away a wonderful collection of bundles and bags. The explanation of this manœuvre was that they had determined to spend the summer "in some bracing place"; but in Paris they dropped into a small furnished apartment—a fourth floor in a third-rate avenue, where there was a smell on the staircase and the *portier* was hateful—and passed the next four months in blank indigence.

The better part of this baffled sojourn was for the preceptor and his pupil, who, visiting the Invalides and Notre Dame, the Conciergerie and all the museums, took a hundred remunerative rambles. They learned to know their Paris, which was useful, for they came back another year for a longer stay, the general character of which in Pemberton's memory today mixes pitiably and confusedly with that of the first. He sees Morgan's shabby knickerbockers—the everlasting pair that didn't match his blouse and that as he grew longer could only grow faded. He remembers the particular holes in his three or four pair of coloured stockings.

Morgan was dear to his mother, but he never was better dressed than was absolutely necessary—partly, no doubt, by his own fault, for he was as indifferent to his appearance as a German philosopher. "My dear fellow, you *are* coming to pieces," Pemberton would say to him in sceptical remonstrance; to which the child would reply, looking at him serenely up and down: "My dear fellow, so are you! I don't want to cast you in the shade." Pemberton could have no rejoinder for this—the assertion so closely represented the fact. If however the deficiencies of his own wardrobe were a chapter by themselves he didn't like his little charge to look too poor. Later he used to say "Well, if we're poor, why, after all, shouldn't we look it?" and he consoled himself with thinking there was something rather elderly and gentlemanly in Morgan's disrepair—it differed from the untidiness of the urchin who plays and spoils his things. He could trace perfectly the degrees by which, in proportion as her little son confined himself to his tutor for society, Mrs. Moreen shrewdly forbore to renew his garments. She did nothing that didn't show, neglected him because he escaped notice, and then, as he illustrated this clever policy, discouraged at home his public appearances. Her position was logical enough—those members of her family who did show had to be showy.

During this period and several others Pemberton was quite aware of how he and his comrade might strike people; wandering languidly through the Jardin des Plantes as if they had nowhere to go, sitting on the winter days in the galleries of the Louvre, so splendidly ironical to the homeless, as if for the advantage of the *calorifère*. They joked about it sometimes: it was the sort of joke that was perfectly within the boy's compass. They figured themselves as part of the vast vague hand-to-mouth multitude of the enormous city and pretended they were proud of their position in it—it showed them "such a lot of life" and made them conscious of a democratic brotherhood. If Pemberton couldn't feel a sympathy in destitution with his small companion—for after all Morgan's fond parents would never have let him really suffer—the boy would at least feel it with him, so it came to the same thing. He used sometimes to wonder what people would think they were—to fancy they were looked askance at, as if it might be a suspected case of kidnapping. Morgan wouldn't be taken for a young patrician with a preceptor—he wasn't smart enough; though he might pass for his companion's sickly little brother. Now and then he had a five-franc piece, and except once, when they bought a couple of lovely neckties, one of which he made Pemberton accept, they laid it out scientifically in old books. This was sure to be a great day, always spent on the quays, in a rummage of the dusty boxes that garnish the parapets. Such occasions helped them to live, for their books ran low very soon after the beginning of their acquaintance. Pemberton had a good many in England, but he was obliged to write to a friend and ask him kindly to get some fellow to give him something for them.

If they had to relinquish that summer the advantage of the bracing climate the young man couldn't but suspect this failure of the cup when at their very lips to have been the effect of a rude jostle of his own. This had represented his first blow-out, as he called it, with his patrons; his first successful attempt—though there was little other success about it—to bring them to a consideration of his impossible position. As the ostensible eve of a costly journey the moment had struck him as favourable to an earnest protest, the presentation of an ultimatum. Ridiculous as it sounded, he had never yet been able to compass an uninterrupted private inter-view with the elder pair or with either of them singly. They were always flanked by their elder children, and poor Pemberton usually had his own little charge at his side. He was conscious of its being a house in which the surface of one's delicacy got rather smudged; nevertheless he had preserved the bloom of his scruple against an-nouncing to Mr. and Mrs. Moreen with publicity that he shouldn't be able to go on longer without a little money. He was still simple enough to suppose Ulick and Paula and Amy might not know that since his arrival he had only had a hundred and forty francs; and he was magnanimous enough to wish not to compromise their par-ents in their eyes. Mr. Moreen now listened to him, as he listened to every one and to every thing, like a man of the world, and seemed to appeal to him—though not of course too grossly—to try and be a little more of one himself. Pemberton recognised in fact the importance of the character—from the advantage it gave Mr. Moreen. He was not even confused or embarrassed, whereas the young man in his service was more so than there was any rea-son for. Neither was he surprised—at least any more than a gentle-man had to be who freely confessed himself a little shocked—though not perhaps strictly at Pemberton.

"We must go into this, musn't we, dear?" he said to his wife. He assured his young friend that the matter should have his very best attention; and he melted into space as elusively as if, at the door, he were taking an inevitable but deprecatory precedence. When, the next moment, Pemberton found himself alone with Mrs. Moreen it was to hear her say "I see, I see"—stroking the roundness of her chin and looking as if she were only hesitat-ing between a dozen easy remedies. If they didn't make their push

Mr. Moreen could at least disappear for several days. During his absence his wife took up the subject again spontaneously, but her contribution to it was merely that she had thought all the while they were getting on so beautifully. Pemberton's reply to this revelation was that unless they immediately put down something on account he would leave them on the spot and for ever. He knew she would wonder how he would get away, and for a moment expected her to enquire. She didn't, for which he was almost grateful to her, so little was he in a position to tell.

"You won't, you *know* you won't—you're too interested," she said. "You *are* interested, you know you are, you dear kind man!" She laughed with almost condemnatory archness, as if it were a reproach—though she wouldn't insist; and flirted a soiled pocket-handkerchief at him.

Pemberton's mind was fully made up to take his step the following week. This would give him time to get an answer to a letter he had dispatched to England. If he did in the event nothing of the sort—that is if he stayed another year and then went away only for three months—it was not merely because before the answer to his letter came (most unsatisfactory when it did arrive) Mr. Moreen generously counted out to him, and again with the sacrifice to "form" of a marked man of the world, three hundred francs in elegant ringing gold. He was irritated to find that Mrs. Moreen was right, that he couldn't at the pinch bear to leave the child. This stood out clearer for the very reason that, the night of his desperate appeal to his patrons, he had seen fully for the first time where he was. Wasn't it another proof of the success with which those patrons practised their arts that they had managed to avert for so long the illuminating flash? It descended on our friend with a breadth of effect which perhaps would have struck a spectator as comical, after he had returned to his little servile room, which looked into a close court where a bare dirty opposite wall took, with the sound of shrill clatter, the reflexion of lighted back windows. He had simply given himself away to a band of adventurers. The idea, the word itself, wore a romantic horror for him —he had always lived on such safe lines. Later it assumed a more interesting, almost a soothing, sense: it pointed a moral, and Pemberton could enjoy a moral. The Moreens were adventurers not merely because they didn't pay their debts, because they lived on society, but because their whole view of life, dim and confused and instinctive, like that of clever colour-blind animals, was speculative and rapacious and mean. Oh they were "respectable," and that only made them more *immondes!* The young man's analysis, while he brooded, put it at last very simply—they were adventurers because they were toadies and snobs. That was the completest account of them—it was the law of their being. Even when this truth became vivid to their ingenious inmate he remained unconscious of how much his mind had been prepared for it by the extraordinary little boy who had now become such a complication in his life. Much less could he then calculate on the information he was still to owe the extraordinary little boy.

V

BUT it was during the ensuing time that the real problem came up —the problem of how far it was excusable to discuss the turpitude of parents with a child of twelve, of thirteen, of fourteen. Absolutely inexcusable and quite impossible it of course at first appeared; and indeed the question didn't press for some time after Pemberton had received his three hundred francs. They produced a temporary lull, a relief from the sharpest pressure. The young man frugally amended his wardrobe and even had a few francs in his pocket. He thought the Moreens looked at him as if he were almost too smart, as if they ought to take care not to spoil him. If Mr. Moreen hadn't been such a man of the world he would perhaps have spoken of the freedom of such neckties on the part of a subordinate. But Mr. Moreen was always enough a man of the world to let things pass—he had certainly shown that. It was singular how Pemberton guessed that Morgan, though saying nothing about it, knew something had happened. But three hundred francs, especially when one owed money, couldn't last for ever; and when the treasure was gone—the boy knew when it had failed—Morgan did break ground. The party had returned to Nice at the beginning of the winter, but not to the charming villa. They went to an hotel, where they stayed three months, and then moved to another establishment, explaining that they had left the first because, after waiting and waiting, they couldn't get the rooms they wanted. These apartments, the rooms they wanted, were generally very splendid; but fortunately they never *could* get them—fortunately, I mean, for Pemberton, who reflected always that if they had got them there would have been a still scanter educational fund. What Morgan said at last was said suddenly, irrelevantly, when the moment came, in the middle of a lesson, and consisted of the apparently unfeeling words: "You ought to *filer,* you know—you really ought."

Pemberton stared. He had learnt enough French slang from Morgan to know that to *filer* meant to cut sticks. "Ah my dear fellow, don't turn me off!"

Morgan pulled a Greek lexicon toward him—he used a Greek-German—to look out a word, instead of asking it of Pemberton. "You can't go on like this, you know."

"Like what, my boy?"

"You know they don't pay you up," said Morgan, blushing and turning his leaves.

"Don't pay me?" Pemberton stared again and feigned amazement. "What on earth put that into your head?"

"It has been there a long time," the boy replied rummaging his book.

Pemberton was silent, then he went on: "I say, what are you hunting for? They pay me beautifully."

"I'm hunting for the Greek for awful whopper," Morgan dropped.

"Find that rather for gross impertinence and disabuse your mind. What do I want of money?"

"Oh that's another question!"

Pemberton wavered—he was drawn in different ways. The severely correct thing would have been to tell the boy that such a matter was none of his business and bid him go on with his lines. But they were really too intimate for that; it was not the way he was in the habit of treating him; there had been no reason it should be. On the other hand Morgan had quite lighted on the truth—he really shouldn't be able to keep it up much longer; therefore why not let him know one's real motive for forsaking him? At the same time it wasn't decent to abuse to one's pupil the family of one's pupil; it was better to misrepresent than to do that. So in reply to his comrade's last exclamation he just declared, to dismiss the subject, that he had received several payments.

"I say—I say!" the boy ejaculated, laughing.

"That's all right," Pemberton insisted. "Give me your written rendering."

Morgan pushed a copybook across the table, and he began to read the page, but with something running in his head that made it no sense. Looking up after a minute or two he found the child's eyes fixed on him and felt in them something strange. Then Morgan said: "I'm not afraid of the stern reality."

"I haven't yet seen the thing you *are* afraid of—I'll do you that justice!"

This came out with a jump—it was perfectly true—and evidently gave Morgan pleasure. "I've thought of it a long time," he presently resumed.

"Well, don't think of it any more."

The boy appeared to comply, and they had a comfortable and even an amusing hour. They had a theory that they were very thorough, and yet they seemed always to be in the amusing part of lessons, the intervals between the dull dark tunnels, where there were waysides and jolly views. Yet the morning was brought to a violent end by Morgan's suddenly leaning his arms on the table, burying his head in them and bursting into tears: at which Pemberton was the more startled that, as it then came over him, it was the first time he had ever seen the boy cry and that the impression was consequently quite awful.

The next day, after much thought, he took a decision and, believing it to be just, immediately acted on it. He cornered Mr. and

Mrs. Moreen again and let them know that if on the spot they didn't pay him all they owed him he wouldn't only leave their house but would tell Morgan exactly what had brought him to it.

"Oh you *haven't* told him?" cried Mrs. Moreen with a pacifying hand on her well-dressed bosom.

"Without warning you? For what do you take me?" the young man returned.

Mr. and Mrs. Moreen looked at each other; he could see that they appreciated, as tending to their security, his superstition of delicacy, and yet that there was a certain alarm in their relief. "My dear fellow," Mr. Moreen demanded, "what use *can* you have, leading the quiet life we all do, for such a lot of money?" —a question to which Pemberton made no answer, occupied as he was in noting that what passed in the mind of his patrons was something like: "Oh then, if we've felt that the child, dear little angel, has judged us and how he regards us, and we haven't been betrayed, he must have guessed—and in short it's *general!*" an inference that rather stirred up Mr. and Mrs. Moreen, as Pemberton had desired it should. At the same time, if he had supposed his threat would do something towards bringing them round, he was disappointed to find them taking for granted—how vulgar their perception *had* been!—that he had already given them away. There was a mystic uneasiness in their parental breasts, and that had been the inferior sense of it. None the less, however, his threat did touch them; for if they had escaped it was only to meet a new danger. Mr. Moreen appealed to him, on every precedent, as a man of the world; but his wife had recourse, for the first time since his domestication with them, to a fine *hauteur,* reminding him that a devoted mother, with her child, had arts that protected her against gross misrepresentation.

"I should misrepresent you grossly if I accused you of common honesty!" our friend replied; but as he closed the door behind him sharply, thinking he had not done himself much good, while Mr. Moreen lighted another cigarette, he heard his hostess shout after him more touchingly:

"Oh you do, you *do,* put the knife to one's throat!"

The next morning, very early, she came to his room. He recognised her knock, but had no hope she brought him money; as to which he was wrong, for she had fifty francs in her hand. She squeezed forward in her dressing-gown, and he received her in his own, between his bath-tub and his bed. He had been tolerably schooled by this time to the "foreign ways" of his hosts. Mrs. Moreen was ardent, and when she was ardent she didn't care what she did; so she now sat down on his bed, his clothes being on the chairs, and, in her preoccupation, forgot, as she glanced round, to be ashamed of giving him such a horrid room. What Mrs. Moreen's ardour now bore upon was the design of persuading him that in the first place she was very good-natured to bring him fifty francs, and that in the second, if he would only see it, he was really too absurd to expect to be *paid*. Wasn't he paid enough without perpetual money—wasn't he paid by the comfortable luxurious home he enjoyed with them all, without a care, an anxiety, a solitary want? Wasn't he sure of his position, and wasn't that everything to a young man like him, quite unknown, with singularly little to show, the ground of whose exorbitant pretensions it had never been easy to discover? Wasn't he paid above all by the sweet relation he had established with Morgan—quite ideal as from master to pupil—and by the simple privilege of knowing and living with so amazingly gifted a child; than whom really (and she meant literally what she said) there was no better company in Europe? Mrs. Moreen herself took to appealing to him as a man of the world; she said "Voyons, mon cher," and "My dear man, look here now"; and urged him to be reasonable, putting it before him that it was truly a chance for him. She spoke as if, according as he *should* be reasonable, he would prove himself worthy to be her son's tutor and of the extraordinary confidence they had placed in him.

After all, Pemberton reflected, it was only a difference of theory and the theory didn't matter much. They had hitherto gone on that of remunerated, as now they would go on that of gratuitous, service; but why should they have so many words about it? Mrs. Moreen at all events continued to be convincing; sitting there with her fifty francs she talked and reiterated as women reiterate, and bored and irritated him, while he leaned against the wall with his hands in the pockets of his wrapper, drawing it together round his legs and looking over the head of his visitor at the grey negations of his window. She wound up with saying: "You see I bring you a definite proposal."

"A definite proposal?"

"To make our relations regular, as it were—to put them on a comfortable footing."

"I see—it's a system," said Pemberton. "A kind of organised blackmail."

Mrs. Moreen bounded up, which was exactly what he wanted. "What do you mean by that?"

"You practise on one's fears—one's fears about the child if one should go away."

"And pray what would happen to him in that event?" she demanded with majesty.

"Why he'd be alone with *you*."

"And pray with whom *should* a child be but with those whom he loves most?"

"If you think that, why don't you dismiss me?"

"Do you pretend he loves you more than he loves *us?*" cried Mrs. Moreen.

"I think he ought to. I make sacrifices for him. Though I've heard of those *you* make I don't see them."

Mrs. Moreen stared a moment; then with emotion she grasped her inmate's hand. "*Will* you make it—the sacrifice?"

He burst out laughing. "I'll see. I'll do what I can. I'll stay a little longer. Your calculation's just—I *do* hate intensely to give him up; I'm fond of him and he thoroughly interests me, in spite of the inconvenience I suffer. You know my situation perfectly. I haven't a penny in the world and, occupied as you see me with Morgan, am unable to earn money."

Mrs. Moreen tapped her undressed arm with her folded banknote. "Can't you write articles? Can't you translate as *I* do?"

"I don't know about translating; it's wretchedly paid."

"I'm glad to earn what I can," said Mrs. Moreen with prodigious virtue.

"You ought to tell me who you do it for." Pemberton paused a moment, and she said nothing; so he added: "I've tried to turn off some little sketches, but the magazines won't have them—they're declined with thanks."

"You see then you're not such a phœnix," his visitor pointedly smiled—"to pretend to abilities you're sacrificing for our sake."

"I haven't time to do things properly," he ruefully went on. Then as it came over him that he was almost abjectly good-natured to give these explanations he added: "If I stay on longer it must be on one condition—that Morgan shall know distinctly on what footing I am."

Mrs. Moreen demurred. "Surely you don't want to show off to a child?"

"To show *you* off, do you mean?"

Again she cast about, but this time it was to produce a still finer flower. "And *you* talk of blackmail!"

"You can easily prevent it," said Pemberton.

"And *you* talk of practising on fears!" she bravely pushed on.

"Yes, there's no doubt I'm a great scoundrel."

His patroness met his eyes—it was clear she was in straits. Then she thrust out her money at him. "Mr. Moreen desired me to give you this on account."

"I'm much obliged to Mr. Moreen, but we *have* no account."

"You won't take it?"

"That leaves me more free," said Pemberton.

"To poison my darling's mind?" groaned Mrs. Moreen.

"Oh your darling's mind—!" the young man laughed.

She fixed him a moment, and he thought she was going to break out tormentedly, pleadingly: "For God's sake, tell me what *is* in it!" But she checked this impulse—another was stronger. She pocketed the money—the crudity of the alternative was comical—and swept out of the room with the desperate concession: "You may tell him any horror you like!"

VI

A COUPLE of days after this, during which he had failed to profit by so free a permission, he had been for a quarter of an hour walking with his charge in silence when the boy became sociable again with the remark: "I'll tell you how I know it; I know it through Zénobie."

"Zénobie? Who in the world is *she?*"

"A nurse I used to have—ever so many years ago. A charming woman. I liked her awfully, and she liked me."

"There's no accounting for tastes. What is it you know through her?"

"Why what their idea is. She went away because they didn't fork out. She did like me awfully, and she stayed two years. She told me all about it—that at last she could never get her wages. As soon as they saw how much she liked me they stopped giving her anything. They thought she'd stay for nothing—just *because,* don't you know?" And Morgan had a queer little conscious lucid look. "She did stay ever so long—as long as she could. She was only a poor girl. She used to send money to her mother. At last she couldn't afford it any longer, and went away in a fearful rage one night—I mean of course in a rage against *them.* She cried over me tremendously, she hugged me nearly to death. She told me all about it," the boy repeated. "She told me it was their idea. So I guessed, ever so long ago, that they have had the same idea with you."

"Zénobie was very sharp," said Pemberton. "And she made you so."

"Oh that wasn't Zénobie; that was nature. And experience!" Morgan laughed.

"Well, Zénobie was a part of your experience."

"Certainly I was a part of hers, poor dear!" the boy wisely sighed. "And I'm part of yours."

"A very important part. But I don't see how you know I've been treated like Zénobie."

"Do you take me for the biggest dunce you've known?" Morgan asked. "Haven't I been conscious of what we've been through together?"

"What we've been through?"

"Our privations—our dark days."

"Oh our days have been bright enough."

Morgan went on in silence for a moment. Then he said: "My dear chap, you're a hero!"

"Well, you're another!" Pemberton retorted.

"No I'm not, but I ain't a baby. I won't stand it any longer. You must get some occupation that pays. I'm ashamed, I'm ashamed!" quavered the boy with a ring of passion, like some high silver note from a small cathedral chorister, that deeply touched his friend.

"We ought to go off and live somewhere together," the young man said.

"I'll go like a shot if you'll take me."

"I'd get some work that would keep us both afloat," Pemberton continued.

"So would I. Why shouldn't *I* work? I ain't such a beastly little muff as *that* comes to."

"The difficulty is that your parents wouldn't hear of it. They'd never part with you; they worship the ground you tread on. Don't you see the proof of it?" Pemberton developed. "They don't dislike me; they wish me no harm; they're very amiable people, but they're perfectly ready to expose me to any awkwardness in life for your sake."

The silence in which Morgan received his fond sophistry struck Pemberton somehow as expressive. After a moment the child repeated: "You *are* a hero!" Then he added: "They leave me with you altogether. You've all the responsibility. They put me off on you from morning till night. Why then should they object to my taking up with you completely? I'd help you."

"They're not particularly keen about my being helped, and they delight in thinking of you as *theirs*. They're tremendously proud of you."

"I'm not proud of *them*. But you know that," Morgan returned.

"Except for the little matter we speak of they're charming people," said Pemberton, not taking up the point made for his intelligence, but wondering greatly at the boy's own, and especially at this fresh reminder of something he had been conscious of from the first—the strangest thing in his friend's large little composition, a temper, a sensibility, even a private ideal, which made him as privately disown the stuff his people were made of. Morgan had in secret a small loftiness which made him acute about betrayed meanness; as well as a critical sense for the manners immediately surrounding him that was quite without precedent in a juvenile nature, especially when one noted that it had not made this nature "old-fashioned," as the word is of children—quaint or wizened or offensive. It was as if he had been a little gentleman and had paid the penalty by discovering that he was the only such person in his family. This comparison didn't make him vain, but it could make him melancholy and a trifle austere. While Pemberton guessed at these dim young things, shadows of shadows, he was partly drawn on and partly checked, as for a scruple, by the charm of attempting to sound the little cool shallows that were so quickly growing deeper. When he tried to figure to himself the morning twilight of childhood, so as to deal with it safely, he saw it was never fixed, never arrested, that ignorance, at the instant he touched it, was already flushing faintly into knowledge, that there was nothing that at a given moment you could say an intelligent child didn't know. It seemed to him that he himself knew too much to imagine Morgan's simplicity and too little to disembroil his tangle.

The boy paid no heed to his last remark; he only went on: "I'd have spoken to them about their idea, as I call it, long ago, if I hadn't been sure what they'd say."

"And what would they say?"

"Just what they said about what poor Zénobie told me—that it was a horrid dreadful story, that they had paid her every penny they owed her."

"Well, perhaps they had," said Pemberton.

"Perhaps they've paid you!"

"Let us pretend they have, and *n'en parlons plus.*"

"They accused her of lying and cheating"—Morgan stuck to historic truth. "That's why I don't want to speak to them."

"Lest they should accuse me too?" To this Morgan made no answer, and his companion, looking down at him—the boy turned away his eyes, which had filled—saw that he couldn't have trusted himself to utter. "You're right. Don't worry them," Pemberton pursued. "Except for that, they *are* charming people."

"Except for *their* lying and *their* cheating?"

"I say—I say!" cried Pemberton, imitating a little tone of the lad's which was itself an imitation.

"We must be frank, at the last; we *must* come to an understanding," said Morgan with the importance of the small boy who lets himself think he is arranging great affairs—almost playing at shipwreck or at Indians. "I know all about everything."

"I dare say your father has his reasons," Pemberton replied, but too vaguely, as he was aware.

"For lying and cheating?"

"For saving and managing and turning his means to the best account. He has plenty to do with his money. You're an expensive family."

"Yes, I'm very expensive," Morgan concurred in a manner that made his preceptor burst out laughing.

"He's saving for *you,*" said Pemberton. "They think of you in everything they do."

"He might, while he's about it, save a little—" The boy paused, and his friend waited to hear what. Then Morgan brought out oddly: "A little reputation."

"Oh there's plenty of that. That's all right!"

"Enough of it for the people they know, no doubt. The people they know are awful."

"Do you mean the princes? We mustn't abuse the princes."

"Why not? They haven't married Paula—they haven't married Amy. They only clean out Ulick."

"You *do* know everything!" Pemberton declared.

"No I don't after all. I don't know what they live on, or how they live, or *why* they live! What have they got and how did they get it? Are they rich, are they poor, or have they a *modeste aisance?* Why are they always chiveying me about—living one year like ambassadors and the next like paupers? Who are they, anyway, and what are they? I've thought of all that—I've thought of a lot of things. They're so beastly worldly. That's what I hate most—oh I've *seen* it! All they care about is to make an appearance and to pass for something or other. What the dickens do they want to pass for? What *do* they, Mr. Pemberton?"

"You pause for a reply," said Pemberton, treating the question as a joke, yet wondering too and greatly struck with his mate's intense if imperfect vision. "I haven't the least idea."

"And what good does it do? Haven't I seen the way people treat them—the 'nice' people, the ones they want to know? They'll take anything from them—they'll lie down and be trampled on. The nice ones hate that—they just sicken them. You're the only really nice person we know."

"Are you sure? They don't lie down for me!"

"Well, you shan't lie down for them. You've got to go—that's what you've got to do," said Morgan.

"And what will become of you?"

"Oh I'm growing up. I shall get off before long. I'll see you later."

"You had better let me finish you," Pemberton urged, lending himself to the child's strange superiority.

Morgan stopped in their walk, looking up at him. He had to look up much less than a couple of years before—he had grown, in his loose leanness, so long and high. "Finish me?" he echoed.

"There are such a lot of jolly things we can do together yet. I want to turn you out—I want you to do me credit."

Morgan continued to look at him. "To give you credit—do you mean?"

"My dear fellow, you're too clever to live."

"That's just what I'm afraid you think. No, no; it isn't fair—

I can't endure it. We'll separate next week. The sooner it's over the sooner to sleep."

"If I hear of anything—any other chance—I promise to go," Pemberton said.

Morgan consented to consider this. "But you'll be honest," he demanded; "you won't pretend you haven't heard?"

"I'm much more likely to pretend I have."

"But what can you hear of, this way, stuck in a hole with us? You ought to be on the spot, to go to England—you ought to go to America."

"One would think you were *my* tutor!" said Pemberton.

Morgan walked on and after a little had begun again: "Well, now that you know I know and that we look at the facts and keep nothing back—it's much more comfortable, isn't it?"

"My dear boy, it's so amusing, so interesting, that it will surely be quite impossible for me to forego such hours as these."

This made Morgan stop once more. "You *do* keep something back. Oh you're not straight—*I* am!"

"How am I not straight?"

"Oh you've got your idea!"

"My idea?"

"Why that I probably shan't make old—make older—bones, and that you can stick it out till I'm removed."

"You *are* too clever to live!" Pemberton repeated.

"I call it a mean idea," Morgan pursued. "But I shall punish you by the way I hang on."

"Look out or I'll poison you!" Pemberton laughed.

"I'm stronger and better every year. Haven't you noticed that there hasn't been a doctor near me since you came?"

"*I'm* your doctor," said the young man, taking his arm and drawing him tenderly on again.

Morgan proceeded and after a few steps gave a sigh of mingled weariness and relief. "Ah now that we look at the facts it's all right!"

VII

THEY looked at the facts a good deal after this; and one of the first consequences of their doing so was that Pemberton stuck it out, in his friends parlance, for the purpose. Morgan made the facts so vivid and so droll, and at the same time so bald and so ugly, that there was fascination in talking them over with him, just as there would have been heartlessness in leaving him alone with them. Now that the pair had such perceptions in common it was useless for them to pretend they didn't judge such people; but the very judgement and the exchange of perceptions created another tie. Morgan had never been so interesting as now that he himself was made plainer by the sidelight of these confidences. What came out in it most was the small fine passion of his pride. He had plenty of that, Pemberton felt—so much that one might perhaps wisely wish for it some early bruises. He would have liked his people to have a spirit and had waked up to the sense of their perpetually eating humble-pie. His mother would consume any amount, and his father would consume even more than his mother. He had a theory that Ulick had wriggled out of an "affair" at Nice: there had once been a flurry at home, a regular panic, after which they all went to bed and took medicine, not to be accounted for on any other supposition. Morgan had a romantic imagination, fed by poetry and history, and he would have liked those who "bore his name"—as he used to say to Pemberton with the humour that made his queer delicacies manly—to carry themselves with an air. But their one idea was to get in with people who didn't want them and to take snubs as if they were honourable scars. Why people didn't want them more he didn't know—that was people's own affair; after all they weren't superficially repulsive, they were a hundred times cleverer than most of the dreary grandees, the "poor swells" they rushed about Europe to catch up with. "After all they *are* amusing—they are!" he used to pronounce with the wisdom of the ages. To which Pemberton always replied: "Amusing—the great Moreen troupe? Why

they're altogether delightful; and if it weren't for the hitch that
you and I (feeble performers!) make in the *ensemble* they'd carry
everything before them."

What the boy couldn't get over was the fact that this particular
blight seemed, in a tradition of self-respect, so undeserved and
so arbitrary. No doubt people had a right to take the line they
liked, but why should *his* people have liked the line of pushing
and toadying and lying and cheating? What had their forefathers—
all decent folk, so far as he knew—done to them, or what had *he*
done to them? Who had poisoned their blood with the fifth-rate
social ideal, the fixed idea of making smart acquaintances and
getting into the *monde chic,* especially when it was foredoomed to
failure and exposure? They showed so what they were after; that
was what made the people they wanted not want *them.* And never
a wince for dignity, never a throb of shame at looking each other
in the face, never any independence or resentment or disgust. If
his father or his brother would only knock some one down once or
twice a year! Clever as they were they never guessed the impression they made. They were good-natured, yes—as good-natured as
Jews at the doors of clothing-shops! But was that the model one
wanted one's family to follow? Morgan had dim memories of an
old grandfather, the maternal, in New York, whom he had been
taken across the ocean at the age of five to see: a gentleman with
a high neck-cloth and a good deal of pronunciation, who wore a
dress-coat in the morning, which made one wonder what he wore
in the evening, and had, or was supposed to have, "property" and
something to do with the Bible Society. It couldn't have been but
that *he* was a good type. Pemberton himself remembered Mrs.
Clancy, a widowed sister of Mr. Moreen's, who was as irritating
as a moral tale and had paid a fortnight's visit to the family at Nice
shortly after he came to live with them. She was "pure and refined," as Amy said over the banjo, and had the air of not knowing what they meant when they talked, and of keeping something
rather important back. Pemberton judged that what she kept back
was an approval of many of their ways; therefore it was to be sup-

posed that she too was of a good type, and that Mr. and Mrs.
Moreen and Ulick and Paula and Amy might easily have been of
a better one if they would.

But that they wouldn't was more and more perceptible from day
to day. They continued to "chivey," as Morgan called it, and in
due time became aware of a variety of reasons for proceeding to
Venice. They mentioned a great many of them—they were always
strikingly frank and had the brightest friendly chatter, at the late
foreign breakfast in especial, before the ladies had made up their
faces, when they leaned their arms on the table, had something
to follow the *demi-tasse*, and, in the heat of familiar discussion as
to what they "really ought" to do, fell inevitably into the languages in which they could *tutoyer*. Even Pemberton liked them
then; he could endure even Ulick when he heard him give his little
flat voice for the "sweet sea-city." That was what made him have
a sneaking kindness for them—that they were so out of the work-
aday world and kept him so out of it. The summer had waned
when, with cries of ecstasy, they all passed out on the balcony
that overhung the Grand Canal. The sunsets then were splendid
and the Dorringtons had arrived. The Dorringtons were the only
reason they hadn't talked of at breakfast; but the reasons they
didn't talk of at breakfast always came out in the end. The Dorringtons on the other hand came out very little; or else when they
did they stayed—as was natural—for hours, during which periods
Mrs. Moreen and the girls sometimes called at their hotel (to see
if they had returned) as many as three times running. The gon-
dola was for the ladies, as in Venice too there were "days," which
Mrs. Moreen knew in their order an hour after she arrived. She
immediately took one herself, to which the Dorringtons never
came, though on a certain occasion when Pemberton and his pupil
were together at Saint Mark's—where, taking the best walks they
had ever had and haunting a hundred churches, they spent a great
deal of time—they saw the old lord turn up with Mr. Moreen and
Ulick, who showed him the dim basilica as if it belonged to them.
Pemberton noted how much less, among its curiosities, Lord Dor-
rington carried himself as a man of the world; wondering too

whether, for such services, his companions took a fee from him. The autumn at any rate waned, the Dorringtons departed, and Lord Verschoyle, the eldest son, had proposed neither for Amy nor for Paula.

One sad November day, while the wind roared round the old palace and the rain lashed the lagoon, Pemberton, for exercise and even somewhat for warmth—the Moreens were horribly frugal about fires; it was a cause of suffering to their inmate—walked up and down the big bare *sala* with his pupil. The scagliola floor was cold, the high battered casements shook in the storm, and the stately decay of the place was unrelieved by a particle of furniture. Pemberton's spirits were low, and it came over him that the fortune of the Moreens was now even lower. A blast of desolation, a portent of disgrace and disaster, seemed to draw through the comfortless hall. Mr. Moreen and Ulick were in the Piazza, looking out for something, strolling drearily, in mackintoshes, under the arcades; but still, in spite of mackintoshes, unmistakeable men of the world. Paula and Amy were in bed—it might have been thought they were staying there to keep warm. Pemberton looked askance at the boy at his side, to see to what extent he was conscious of these dark omens. But Morgan, luckily for him, was now mainly conscious of growing taller and stronger and indeed of being in his fifteenth year. This fact was intensely interesting to him and the basis of a private theory—which, however, he had imparted to his tutor—that in a little while he should stand on his own feet. He considered that the situation would change—that in short he should be "finished," grown up, producible in the world of affairs and ready to prove himself of sterling ability. Sharply as he was capable at times of analysing, as he called it, his life, there were happy hours when he remained, as he also called it— and as the name, really, of their right ideal—"jolly" superficial; the proof of which was his fundamental assumption that he should presently go to Oxford, to Pemberton's college, and aided and abetted by Pemberton, do the most wonderful things. It depressed the young man to see how little in such a project he took account of ways and means: in other connexions he mostly kept to the measure. Pemberton tried to imagine the Moreens at Oxford and fortunately failed; yet unless they were to adopt it as a residence there would be no *modus vivendi* for Morgan. How could he live without an allowance, and where was the allowance to come from? He, Pemberton, might live on Morgan; but how could Morgan live on *him?* What was to become of him anyhow? Somehow the fact that he was a big boy now, with better prospects of health, made the question of his future more difficult. So long as he was markedly frail the great consideration he inspired seemed enough of an answer to it. But at the bottom of Pemberton's heart was the recognition of his probably being strong enough to live and not yet strong enough to struggle or to thrive. Morgan himself at any rate was in the first flush of the rosiest consciousness of adolescence, so that the beating of the tempest seemed to him after all but the voice of life and the challenge of fate. He had on his shabby little overcoat, with the collar up, but was enjoying his walk.

It was interrupted at last by the appearance of his mother at the end of the *sala*. She beckoned him to come to her, and while Pemberton saw him, complaisant, pass down the long vista and over the damp false marble, he wondered what was in the air. Mrs. Moreen said a word to the boy and made him go into the room she had quitted. Then, having closed the door after him, she directed her steps swiftly to Pemberton. There *was* something in the air, but his wildest flight of fancy wouldn't have suggested what it proved to be. She signified that she had made a pretext to get Morgan out of the way, and then she enquired—without hesitation—if the young man could favour her with the loan of three louis. While, before bursting into a laugh, he stared at her with surprise, she declared that she was awfully pressed for the money; she was desperate for it—it would save her life.

"Dear lady, *c'est trop fort!*" Pemberton laughed in the manner and with the borrowed grace of idiom that marked the best colloquial, the best anecdotic, moments of his friends themselves. "Where in the world do you suppose I should get three louis, *du train dont vous allez?*"

"I thought you worked—wrote things. Don't they pay you?"

"Not a penny."

"Are you such a fool as to work for nothing?"

"You ought surely to know that."

Mrs. Moreen stared, then she coloured a little. Pemberton saw she had quite forgotten the terms—if "terms" they could be called —that he had ended by accepting from herself; they had burdened her memory as little as her conscience. "Oh yes, I see what you mean—you've been very nice about that; but why drag it in so often?" She had been perfectly urbane with him ever since the rough scene of explanation in his room the morning he made her accept *his* "terms"—the necessity of his making his case known to Morgan. She had felt no resentment after seeing there was no danger Morgan would take the matter up with her. Indeed, attributing this immunity to the good taste of his influence with the boy, she had once said to Pemberton "My dear fellow, it's an immense comfort you're a gentleman." She repeated this in substance now. "Of course you're a gentleman—that's a bother the less!" Pemberton reminded her that he had not "dragged in" anything that wasn't already in as much as his foot was in his shoe; and she also repeated her prayer that, somewhere and somehow, he would find her sixty francs. He took the liberty of hinting that if he could find them it wouldn't be to lend them to *her*—as to which he consciously did himself injustice, knowing that if he had them he would certainly put them at her disposal. He accused himself, at bottom and not unveraciously, of a fantastic, a demoralised sympathy with her. If misery made strange bedfellows it also made strange sympathies. It was moreover a part of the abasement of living with such people that one had to make vulgar retorts, quite out of one's own tradition of good manners. "Morgan, Morgan, to what pass have I come for you?" he groaned while Mrs. Moreen floated voluminously down the *sala* again to liberate the boy, wailing as she went that everything was too odious.

Before their young friend was liberated there came a thump at the door communicating with the staircase, followed by the apparition of a dripping youth who poked in his head. Pemberton recog-

nised him as the bearer of a telegram and recognised the telegram
as addressed to himself. Morgan came back as, after glancing at
the signature—that of a relative in London—he was reading the
words: "Found jolly job for you, engagement to coach opulent
youth on own terms. Come at once." The answer happily was paid
and the messenger waited. Morgan, who had drawn near, waited
too and looked hard at Pemberton; and Pemberton, after a moment, having met his look, handed him the telegram. It was really
by wise looks—they knew each other so well now—that, while
the telegraph-boy, in his waterproof cape, made a great puddle
on the floor, the thing was settled between them. Pemberton wrote
the answer with a pencil against the frescoed wall, and the messenger departed. When he had gone the young man explained
himself.

"I'll make a tremendous charge; I'll earn a lot of money in a
short time, and we'll live on it."

"Well, I hope the opulent youth will be a dismal dunce—he
probably will," Morgan parenthesised—"and keep you a long
time a-hammering of it in."

"Of course the longer he keeps me the more we shall have for
our old age."

"But suppose *they* don't pay you!" Morgan awfully suggested.

"Oh there are not two such—!" but Pemberton pulled up; he
had been on the point of using too invidious a term. Instead of this
he said "Two such fatalities."

Morgan flushed—the tears came to his eyes. "*Dites toujours*
two such rascally crews!" Then in a different tone he added:
"Happy opulent youth!"

"Not if he's a dismal dunce."

"Oh they're happier then. But you can't have everything, can
you?" the boy smiled.

Pemberton held him fast, hands on his shoulders—he had never
loved him so. "What will become of *you*, what will you do?" He
thought of Mrs. Moreen, desperate for sixty francs.

"I shall become an *homme fait*." And then as if he recognised all the bearings of Pemberton's allusion: "I shall get on with them better when you're not here."

"Ah don't say that—it sounds as if I set you against them!"

"You do—the sight of you. It's all right; you know what I mean. I shall be beautiful. I'll take their affairs in hand; I'll marry my sisters."

"You'll marry yourself!" joked Pemberton; as high, rather tense pleasantry would evidently be the right, or the safest, tone for their separation.

It was, however, not purely in this strain that Morgan suddenly asked: "But I say—how will you get to your jolly job? You'll have to telegraph to the opulent youth for money to come on."

Pemberton bethought himself. "They won't like that, will they?"

"Oh look out for them!"

Then Pemberton brought out his remedy. "I'll go to the American Consul; I'll borrow some money of him—just for the few days, on the strength of the telegram."

Morgan was hilarious. "Show him the telegram—then collar the money and stay!"

Pemberton entered into the joke sufficiently to reply that for Morgan he was really capable of that; but the boy, growing more serious, and to prove he hadn't meant what he said, not only hurried him off to the Consulate—since he was to start that evening, as he had wired to his friend—but made sure of their affair by going with him. They splashed through the tortuous perforations and over the humpbacked bridges, and they passed through the Piazza, where they saw Mr. Moreen and Ulick go into a jeweller's shop. The Consul proved accommodating—Pemberton said it wasn't the letter, but Morgan's grand air—and on their way back they went into Saint Mark's for a hushed ten minutes. Later they took up and kept up the fun of it to the very end; and it seemed to Pemberton a part of that fun that Mrs. Moreen, who was very angry when he had announced her his intention, should charge him, grotesquely and vulgarly and in reference to the loan she had vainly endeavoured to effect, with bolting lest they should "get something out" of him. On the other hand he had to do Mr. Moreen and Ulick the justice to recognise that when on coming in *they* heard the cruel news they took it like perfect men of the world.

VIII

WHEN he got at work with the opulent youth, who was to be taken in hand for Balliol, he found himself unable to say if this aspirant had really such poor parts or if the appearance were only begotten of his own long association with an intensely living little mind. From Morgan he heard half a dozen times: the boy wrote charming young letters, a patchwork of tongues, with indulgent postscripts in the family Volapuk and, in little squares and rounds and crannies of the text, the drollest illustrations—letters that he was divided between the impulse to show his present charge as a vain, a wasted incentive, and the sense of something in them that publicity would profane. The opulent youth went up in due course and failed to pass; but it seemed to add to the presumption that brilliancy was not expected of him all at once that his parents, condoning the lapse, which they good-naturedly treated as little as possible as if it were Pemberton's, should have sounded the rally again, begged the young coach to renew the siege.

The young coach was now in a position to lend Mrs. Moreen three louis, and he sent her a post-office order even for a larger amount. In return for this favour he received a frantic scribbled line from her: "Implore you to come back instantly—Morgan dreadfully ill." They were on the rebound, once more in Paris—often as Pemberton had seen them depressed he had never seen them crushed—and communication was therefore rapid. He wrote to the boy to ascertain the state of his health, but awaited the answer in vain. He accordingly, after three days, took an abrupt leave of the opulent youth and, crossing the Channel, alighted at the small hotel, in the quarter of the Champs Élysées, of which

Mrs. Moreen had given him the address. A deep if dumb dissatisfaction with this lady and her companions bore him company: they couldn't be vulgarly honest, but they could live at hotels, in velvety *entresols,* amid a smell of burnt pastilles, surrounded by the most expensive city in Europe. When he had left them in Venice it was with an irrepressible suspicion that something was going to happen; but the only thing that could have taken place was again their masterly retreat. "How is he? where is he?" he asked of Mrs. Moreen; but before she could speak these questions were answered by the pressure round his neck of a pair of arms, in shrunken sleeves, which still were perfectly capable of an effusive young foreign squeeze.

"Dreadfully ill—I don't see it!" the young man cried. And then to Morgan: "Why on earth didn't you relieve me? Why didn't you answer my letter?"

Mrs. Moreen declared that when she wrote he was very bad, and Pemberton learned at the same time from the boy that he had answered every letter he had received. This led to the clear inference that Pemberton's note had been kept from him so that the game to be practised should not be interfered with. Mrs. Moreen was prepared to see the fact exposed, as Pemberton saw the moment he faced her that she was prepared for a good many other things. She was prepared above all to maintain that she had acted from a sense of duty, that she was enchanted she had got him over, whatever they might say, and that it was useless of him to pretend he didn't know in all his bones that his place at such a time was with Morgan. He had taken the boy away from them and now had no right to abandon him. He had created for himself the gravest responsibilities and must at least abide by what he had done.

"Taken him away from you?" Pemberton exclaimed indignantly.

"Do it—do it for pity's sake; that's just what I want. I can't stand *this*—and such scenes. They're awful frauds—poor dears!" These words broke from Morgan, who had intermitted his embrace, in a key which made Pemberton turn quickly to him and see that he had suddenly seated himself, was breathing in great pain and was very pale.

"*Now* do you say he's not in a state, my precious pet?" shouted his mother, dropping on her knees before him with clasped hands, but touching him no more than if he had been a gilded idol. "It will pass—it's only for an instant; but don't say such dreadful things!"

"I'm all right—all right," Morgan panted to Pemberton, whom he sat looking up at with a strange smile, his hands resting on either side on the sofa.

"Now do you pretend I've been dishonest, that I've deceived?" Mrs. Moreen flashed at Pemberton as she got up.

"It isn't *he* says it, it's I!" the boy returned, apparently easier but sinking back against the wall; while his restored friend, who had sat down beside him, took his hand and bent over him.

"Darling child, one does what one can; there are so many things to consider," urged Mrs. Moreen. "It's his *place*—his only place. You see *you* think it is now."

"Take me away—take me away," Morgan went on, smiling to Pemberton with his white face.

"Where shall I take you, and how—oh *how,* my boy?" the young man stammered, thinking of the rude way in which his friends in London held that, for his convenience, with no assurance of prompt return, he had thrown them over; of the just resentment with which they would already have called in a successor, and of the scant help to finding fresh employment that resided for him in the grossness of his having failed to pass his pupil.

"Oh we'll settle that. You used to talk about it," said Morgan. "If we can only go all the rest's a detail."

"Talk about it as much as you like, but don't think you can attempt it. Mr. Moreen would never consent—it would be so *very* hand-to-mouth," Pemberton's hostess beautifully explained to him. Then to Morgan she made it clearer: "It would destroy our peace, it would break our hearts. Now that he's back it will be all the same again. You'll have your life, your work and your freedom, and we'll all be happy as we used to be. You'll bloom and grow perfectly well, and we won't have any more silly experiments, will we? They're too absurd. It's Mr. Pemberton's place—every one in his place. You in yours, your papa in his, me in mine—*n'est-ce pas, chéri?* We'll all forget how foolish we've been and have lovely times."

She continued to talk and to surge vaguely about the little draped stuffy salon while Pemberton sat with the boy, whose colour gradually came back; and she mixed up her reasons, hinting that there were going to be changes, that the other children might scatter (who knew?—Paula had her ideas) and that then it might be fancied how much the poor old parent-birds would want the little nestling. Morgan looked at Pemberton, who wouldn't let him move; and Pemberton knew exactly how he felt at hearing himself called a little nestling. He admitted that he had had one or two bad days, but he protested afresh against the wrong of his mother's having made them the ground of an appeal to poor Pemberton. Poor Pemberton could laugh now, apart from the comicality of Mrs. Moreen's mustering so much philosophy for her defence—she seemed to shake it out of her agitated petticoats, which knocked over the light gilt chairs—so little did their young companion, *marked,* unmistakeably marked at the best, strike him as qualified to repudiate any advantage.

He himself was in for it at any rate. He should have Morgan on his hands again indefinitely; though indeed he saw the lad had a private theory to produce which would be intended to smooth this down. He was obliged to him for it in advance; but the suggested amendment didn't keep his heart rather from sinking, any more than it prevented him from accepting the prospect on the spot, with some confidence moreover that he should do so even better if he could have a little supper. Mrs. Moreen threw out more hints about the changes that were to be looked for, but she was such a mixture of smiles and shudders—she confessed she was very nervous—that he couldn't tell if she were in high feather or only in hysterics. If the family was really at last going to pieces why shouldn't she recognise the necessity of pitching Morgan into some sort of lifeboat? This presumption was fostered by the fact that they were established in luxurious quarters in the capital of pleasure; that was exactly where they naturally *would* be established in view of going to pieces. Moreover didn't she mention that Mr. Moreen and the others were enjoying themselves at the opera with Mr. Granger, and wasn't *that* also precisely where one would look for them on the eve of a smash? Pemberton gathered that Mr. Granger was a rich vacant American—a big bill with a flourishy heading and no items; so that one of Paula's "ideas" was probably that this time she hadn't missed fire—by which straight shot indeed she would have shattered the general cohesion. And if the cohesion was to crumble what would become of poor Pemberton? He felt quite enough bound up with them to figure to his alarm as a dislodged block in the edifice.

It was Morgan who eventually asked if no supper had been ordered for him; sitting with him below, later, at the dim delayed meal, in the presence of a great deal of corded green plush, a plate of ornamental biscuit and an aloofness marked on the part of the waiter. Mrs. Moreen had explained that they had been obliged to secure a room for the visitor out of the house; and Morgan's consolation—he offered it while Pemberton reflected on the nastiness of luke-warm sauces—proved to be, largely, that this circumstance would facilitate their escape. He talked of their escape —recurring to it often afterwards—as if they were making up a "boy's book" together. But he likewise expressed his sense that there was something in the air, that the Moreens couldn't keep it up much longer. In point of fact, as Pemberton was to see, they kept it up for five or six months. All the while, however, Morgan's contention was designed to cheer him. Mr. Moreen and Ulick, whom he had met the day after his return, accepted that return like perfect men of the world. If Paula and Amy treated it even with less formality an allowance was to be made for them, inasmuch as Mr. Granger hadn't come to the opera after all. He had only placed his box at their service, with a bouquet for each of the party; there was even one apiece, embittering the thought of his profusion, for Mr. Moreen and Ulick. "They're all like that," was Morgan's comment; "at the very last, just when we think we've landed them they're back in the deep sea!"

Morgan's comments in these days were more and more free; they even included a large recognition of the extraordinary tenderness with which he had been treated while Pemberton was away. Oh yes, they couldn't do enough to be nice to him, to show him they had him on their mind and make up for his loss. That was just what made the whole thing so sad and caused him to rejoice after all in Pemberton's return—he had to keep thinking of their affection less, had less sense of obligation. Pemberton laughed out at this last reason, and Morgan blushed and said "Well, dash it, you know what I mean." Pemberton knew perfectly what he meant; but there were a good many things that—dash it too!—it didn't make any clearer. This episode of his second sojourn in Paris stretched itself out wearily, with their resumed readings and wanderings and maunderings, their potterings on the quays, their hauntings of the museums, their occasional lingerings in the Palais Royal when the first sharp weather came on and there was a comfort in warm emanations, before Chevet's wonderful succulent window. Morgan wanted to hear all about the opulent youth—he took an immense interest in him. Some of the details of his opulence—Pemberton could spare him none of them—evidently fed the boy's appreciation of all his friend had given up to come back to him; but in addition to the greater reciprocity established by that heroism he had always his little brooding theory, in which there was a frivolous gaiety too, that their long probation was drawing to a close. Morgan's conviction that the Moreens couldn't go on much longer kept pace with the unexpended impetus with which, from month to month, they did go on. Three weeks after Pemberton had rejoined them they went on to another hotel, a dingier one than the first; but Morgan rejoiced that his tutor had at least still not sacrificed the advantage of a room outside. He clung to the romantic utility of this when the day, or rather the night, should arrive for their escape.

For the first time, in this complicated connexion, our friend felt his collar gall him. It was, as he had said to Mrs. Moreen in Venice, *trop fort*—everything was *trop fort*. He could neither really throw off his blighting burden nor find in it the benefit of a pacified conscience or of a rewarded affection. He had spent all the money accruing to him in England, and he saw his youth going and that he was getting nothing back for it. It was all very well of Morgan to count it for reparation that he should now settle on him permanently—there was an irritating flaw in such a view. He saw what the boy had in his mind; the conception that as his friend had had the generosity to come back he must show his gratitude by giving him his life. But the poor friend didn't desire the gift—what could he do with Morgan's dreadful little life? Of course at the same time that Pemberton was irritated he remembered the reason, which was very honourable to Morgan and which dwelt simply in his making one so forget that he was no more than a patched urchin. If one dealt with him on a different basis one's misadventures were one's own fault. So Pemberton waited in a queer confusion of yearning and alarm for the catastrophe which was held to hang over the house of Moreen, of which he certainly at moments felt the symptoms brush his cheek and as to which he wondered much in what form it would find its liveliest effect.

Perhaps it would take the form of sudden dispersal—a frightened *sauve qui peut*, a scuttling into selfish corners. Certainly they were less elastic than of yore; they were evidently looking for something they didn't find. The Dorringtons hadn't re-appeared, the princes had scattered; wasn't that the beginning of the end? Mrs. Moreen had lost her reckoning of the famous "days"; her social calendar was blurred—it had turned its face to the wall. Pemberton suspected that the great, the cruel discomfiture had been the unspeakable behaviour of Mr. Granger, who seemed not to know what he wanted, or, what was much worse, what *they* wanted. He kept sending flowers, as if to bestrew the path of his retreat, which was never the path of a return. Flowers were all very well, but—Pemberton could complete the proposition. It was now positively conspicuous that in the long run the Moreens were a social failure; so that the young man was almost grateful the run had not been short. Mr. Moreen indeed was still occasionally able to get away on business and, what was more surprising, was likewise able to get back. Ulick had no club, but you couldn't have discovered it from his appearance, which was as much as ever that of a person looking at life from the window of such an institution; therefore Pemberton was doubly surprised at an answer he once heard him make his mother in the desperate tone of a man familiar with the worst privations. Her question Pemberton had not quite caught; it appeared to be an appeal for a suggestion as to whom they might get to take Amy. "Let the Devil take her!" Ulick snapped; so that Pemberton could see that they had not only lost their amiability but had ceased to believe in themselves. He could also see that if Mrs. Moreen was trying to get people to take her children she might be regarded as closing the hatches for the storm. But Morgan would be the last she would part with.

One winter afternoon—it was a Sunday—he and the boy walked far together in the Bois de Boulogne. The evening was so splendid, the cold lemon-coloured sunset so clear, the stream of carriages and pedestrians so amusing and the fascination of Paris so great, that they stayed out later than usual and became aware that they should have to hurry home to arrive in time for dinner. They hurried accordingly, arm-in-arm, good-humoured and hungry, agreeing that there was nothing like Paris after all and that after everything too that had come and gone they were not yet sated with innocent pleasures. When they reached the hotel they found that, though scandalously late, they were in time for all the dinner they were likely to sit down to. Confusion reigned in the apartments of the Moreens—very shabby ones this time, but the best in the house—and before the interrupted service of the table, with objects displaced almost as if there had been a scuffle and a great wine-stain from an overturned bottle, Pemberton couldn't blink the fact that there had been a scene of the last proprietary firmness. The storm had come—they were all seeking refuge. The hatches were down, Paula and Amy were invisible—they had never tried the most casual art upon Pemberton, but he felt they had enough of an eye to him not to wish to meet him as young ladies whose frocks had been confiscated—and Ulick appeared to have jumped overboard. The host and his staff, in a word, had ceased to "go on" at the pace of their guests, and the air of embarrassed detention, thanks to a pile of gaping trunks in the passage, was strangely commingled with the air of indignant withdrawal.

When Morgan took all this in—and he took it in very quickly —he coloured to the roots of his hair. He had walked from his infancy among difficulties and dangers, but he had never seen a public exposure. Pemberton noticed in a second glance at him that the tears had rushed into his eyes and that they were tears of a new and untasted bitterness. He wondered an instant, for the boy's sake, whether he might successfully pretend not to understand. Not successfully, he felt, as Mr. and Mrs. Moreen, dinnerless by their extinguished hearth, rose before him in their little dishonoured salon, casting about with glassy eyes for the nearest port in such a storm. They were not prostrate but were horribly white, and Mrs. Moreen had evidently been crying. Pemberton quickly learned however that her grief was not for the loss of her dinner, much as she usually enjoyed it, but the fruit of a blow that struck even deeper, as she made all haste to explain. He would see for himself, so far as that went, how the great change had come, the dreadful bolt had fallen, and how they would now all have to turn themselves about. Therefore cruel as it was to them to part with their darling she must look to him to carry a little further the influence he had so fortunately acquired with the boy—to induce his young charge to follow him into some modest retreat. They depended on him—that was the fact—to take their delightful child temporarily under his protection: it would leave Mr. Moreen and herself so much more free to give the proper attention (too little, alas! had been given) to the readjustment of their affairs.

"We trust you—we feel we *can*," said Mrs. Moreen, slowly rubbing her plump white hands and looking with compunction hard at Morgan, whose chin, not to take liberties, her husband stroked with a tentative paternal forefinger.

"Oh yes—we feel that we *can*. We trust Mr. Pemberton fully, Morgan," Mr. Moreen pursued.

Pemberton wondered again if he might pretend not to understand; but everything good gave way to the intensity of Morgan's understanding. "Do you mean he may take me to live with him for ever and ever?" cried the boy. "May take me away, away, anywhere he likes?"

"For ever and ever? *Comme vous-y-allez!*" Mr. Moreen laughed indulgently. "For as long as Mr. Pemberton may be so good."

"We've struggled, we've suffered," his wife went on; "but you've made him so your own that we've already been through the worst of the sacrifice."

Morgan had turned away from his father—he stood looking at Pemberton with a light in his face. His sense of shame for their common humiliated state had dropped; the case had another side —the thing was to clutch at *that*. He had a moment of boyish joy, scarcely mitigated by the reflexion that with this unexpected consecration of his hope—too sudden and too violent; the turn taken was away from a *good* boy's book—the "escape" was left on their hands. The boyish joy was there an instant, and Pemberton was almost scared at the rush of gratitude and affection that broke through his first abasement. When he stammered "My dear fellow, what do you say to *that?*" how could one not say something enthusiastic? But there was more need for courage at something else that immediately followed and that made the lad sit down quickly on the nearest chair. He had turned quite livid and had raised his hand to his left side. They were all three looking at him, but Mrs. Moreen suddenly bounded forward. "Ah his darling little heart!" she broke out; and this time, on her knees before him and without respect for the idol, she caught him ardently in her arms. "You walked him too far, you hurried him too fast!" she hurled over her shoulder at Pemberton. Her son made no protest, and the next instant, still holding him, she sprang up with her face convulsed and with the terrified cry "Help, help! he's going, he's gone!" Pemberton saw with equal horror, by Morgan's own stricken face, that he was beyond their wildest recall. He pulled him half out of his mother's hands, and for a moment, while they held him together, they looked all their dismay into each other's eyes. "He couldn't stand it with his weak organ," said Pemberton —"the shock, the whole scene, the violent emotion."

"But I thought he *wanted* to go to you!" wailed Mrs. Moreen.

"I *told* you he didn't, my dear," her husband made answer. Mr. Moreen was trembling all over and was in his way as deeply affected as his wife. But after the very first he took his bereavement as a man of the world.

THE BEAST IN THE JUNGLE

See p. 221.

I

WHAT determined the speech that startled him in the course of their encounter scarcely matters, being probably but some words spoken by himself quite without intention—spoken as they lingered and slowly moved together after their renewal of acquaintance. He had been conveyed by friends an hour or two before to the house at which she was staying; the party of visitors at the other house, of whom he was one, and thanks to whom it was his theory, as always, that he was lost in the crowd, had been invited over to luncheon. There had been after luncheon much dispersal, all in the interest of the original motive, a view of Weatherend itself and the fine things, intrinsic features, pictures, heirlooms, treasures of all the arts, that made the place almost famous; and the great rooms were so numerous that guests could wander at their will, hang back from the principal group and in cases where they took such matters with the last seriousness give themselves up to mysterious appreciations and measurements. There were persons to be observed, singly or in couples, bending toward objects in out-of-the-way corners with their hands on their knees and their heads nodding quite as with the emphasis of an excited sense of smell. When they were two they either mingled their sounds of ecstasy or melted into silences of even deeper import, so that there were aspects of the occasion that gave it for Marcher much the air of the "look round," previous to a sale highly advertised, that excites or quenches, as may be, the dream of acquisition. The dream of acquisition at Weatherend would have had to be wild indeed, and John Marcher found himself, among such suggestions, disconcerted almost equally by the presence of those who knew too much and by that of those who knew nothing. The great rooms caused so much poetry and history to press upon him that he needed some straying apart to feel in a proper relation with them, though this impulse was not, as happened, like the gloating of some of his companions, to be compared to the movements of a dog sniffing a cupboard. It had an issue promptly enough in a direction that was not to have been calculated.

It led, briefly, in the course of the October afternoon, to his closer meeting with May Bartram, whose face, a reminder, yet not quite a remembrance, as they sat much separated at a very long table, had begun merely by troubling him rather pleasantly. It affected him as the sequel of something of which he had lost the beginning. He knew it, and for the time quite welcomed it, as a continuation, but didn't know what it continued, which was an interest or an amusement the greater as he was also somehow aware—yet without a direct sign from her—that the young woman herself hadn't lost the thread. She hadn't lost it, but she wouldn't give it back to him, he saw, without some putting forth of his hand for it; and he not only saw that, but saw several things more, things odd enough in the light of the fact that at the moment some accident of grouping brought them face to face he was still merely fumbling with the idea that any contact between them in the past would have had no importance. If it had had no importance he scarcely knew why his actual impression of her should so seem to have so much; the answer to which, however, was that in such a life as they all appeared to be leading for the moment one could but take things as they came. He was satisfied, without in the least being able to say why, that this young lady might roughly have ranked in the house as a poor relation; satisfied also that she was not there on a brief visit, but was more or less a part of the establishment—almost a working, a remunerated part. Didn't she enjoy at periods a protection that she paid for by helping, among other services, to show the place and explain it, deal with the tiresome people, answer questions about the dates of the building, the styles of the furniture, the authorship of the pictures, the favourite haunts of the ghost? It wasn't that she looked as if you could have given her shillings—it was impossible to look less so. Yet

when she finally drifted toward him, distinctly handsome, though
ever so much older—older than when he had seen her before—
it might have been as an effect of her guessing that he had, within
the couple of hours, devoted more imagination to her than to all
the others put together, and had thereby penetrated to a kind of
truth that the others were too stupid for. She *was* there on harder
terms than any one; she was there as a consequence of things suffered, one way and another, in the interval of years; and she remembered him very much as she was remembered—only a good
deal better.

By the time they at last thus came to speech they were alone
in one of the rooms—remarkable for a fine portrait over the
chimney-place—out of which their friends had passed, and the
charm of it was that even before they had spoken they had practically arranged with each other to stay behind for talk. The charm,
happily, was in other things too—partly in there being scarce a
spot at Weatherend without something to stay behind for. It was
in the way the autumn day looked into the high windows as it
waned; the way the red light, breaking at the close from under a
low sombre sky, reached out in a long shaft and played over old
wainscots, old tapestry, old gold, old colour. It was most of all perhaps in the way she came to him as if, since she had been turned
on to deal with the simpler sort, he might, should he choose to
keep the whole thing down, just take her mild attention for a part
of her general business. As soon as he heard her voice, however,
the gap was filled up and the missing link supplied; the slight
irony he divined in her attitude lost its advantage. He almost
jumped at it to get there before her. "I met you years and years
ago in Rome. I remember all about it." She confessed to disappointment—she had been so sure he didn't; and to prove how well
he did he began to pour forth the particular recollections that
popped up as he called for them. Her face and her voice, all at
his service now, worked the miracle—the impression operating
like the torch of a lamplighter who touches into flame, one by one,
a long row of gas-jets. Marcher flattered himself the illumination
was brilliant, yet he was really still more pleased on her showing

him, with amusement, that in his haste to make everything right
he had got most things rather wrong. It hadn't been at Rome—it
had been at Naples; and it hadn't been eight years before—it had
been more nearly ten. She hadn't been, either, with her uncle and
aunt, but with her mother and her brother; in addition to which
it was not with the Pembles *he* had been, but with the Boyers,
coming down in their company from Rome—a point on which she
insisted, a little to his confusion, and as to which she had her evidence in hand. The Boyers she had known, but didn't know the
Pembles, though she had heard of them, and it was the people he
was with who had made them acquainted. The incident of the
thunderstorm that had raged round them with such violence as to
drive them for refuge into an excavation—this incident had not
occurred at the Palace of the Cæsars, but at Pompeii, on an occasion when they had been present there at an important find.

He accepted her amendments, he enjoyed her corrections,
though the moral of them was, she pointed out, that he *really*
didn't remember the least thing about her; and he only felt it as
a drawback that when all was made strictly historic there didn't
appear much of anything left. They lingered together still, she
neglecting her office—for from the moment he was so clever she
had no proper right to him—and both neglecting the house, just
waiting as to see if a memory or two more wouldn't again breathe
on them. It hadn't taken them many minutes, after all, to put
down on the table, like the cards of a pack, those that constituted
their respective hands; only what came out was that the pack
was unfortunately not perfect—that the past, invoked, invited,
encouraged, could give them, naturally, no more than it had. It
had made them anciently meet—her at twenty, him at twenty-
five; but nothing was so strange, they seemed to say to each other,
as that, while so occupied, it hadn't done a little more for them.
They looked at each other as with the feeling of an occasion
missed; the present would have been so much better if the other,
in the far distance, in the foreign land, hadn't been so stupidly
meagre. There weren't apparently, all counted, more than a dozen
little old things that had succeeded in coming to pass between

them; trivialities of youth, simplicities of freshness, stupidities of ignorance, small possible germs, but too deeply buried—too deeply (didn't it seem?) to sprout after so many years. Marcher could only feel he ought to have rendered her some service—saved her from a capsized boat in the Bay or at least recovered her dressing-bag, filched from her cab in the streets of Naples by a lazzarone with a stiletto. Or it would have been nice if he could have been taken with fever all alone at his hotel, and she could have come to look after him, to write to his people, to drive him out in convalescence. *Then* they would be in possession of the something or other that their actual show seemed to lack. It yet somehow presented itself, this show, as too good to be spoiled; so that they were reduced for a few minutes more to wondering a little helplessly why—since they seemed to know a certain number of the same people—their reunion had been so long averted. They didn't use that name for it, but their delay from minute to minute to join the others was a kind of confession that they didn't quite want it to be a failure. Their attempted supposition of reasons for their not having met but showed how little they knew of each other. There came in fact a moment when Marcher felt a positive pang. It was vain to pretend she was an old friend, for all the communities were wanting, in spite of which it was as an old friend that he saw she would have suited him. He had new ones enough—was surrounded with them for instance on the stage of the other house; as a new one he probably wouldn't have so much as noticed her. He would have liked to invent something, get her to make-believe with him that some passage of a romantic or critical kind *had* originally occurred. He was really almost reaching out in imagination—as against time—for something that would do, and saying to himself that if it didn't come this sketch of a fresh start would show for quite awkwardly bungled. They would separate, and now for no second or no third chance. They would have tried and not succeeded. Then it was, just at the turn, as he afterwards made it out to himself, that, everything else failing, she herself decided to take up the case and, as it were, save the situation. He felt as soon as she spoke that she had been consciously keeping back what she said and hoping to get on without it; a scruple in her that immensely touched him when, by the end of three or four minutes more, he was able to measure it. What she brought out, at any rate, quite cleared the air and supplied the link—the link it was so odd he should frivolously have managed to lose.

"You know you told me something I've never forgotten and that again and again has made me think of you since; it was that tremendously hot day when we went to Sorrento, across the bay, for the breeze. What I allude to was what you said to me, on the way back, as we sat under the awning of the boat enjoying the cool. Have you forgotten?"

He had forgotten and was even more surprised than ashamed. But the great thing was that he saw in this no vulgar reminder of any "sweet" speech. The vanity of women had long memories, but she was making no claim on him of a compliment or a mistake. With another woman, a totally different one, he might have feared the recall possibly even of some imbecile "offer." So, in having to say that he had indeed forgotten, he was conscious rather of a loss than of a gain; he already saw an interest in the matter of her mention. "I try to think—but I give it up. Yet I remember the Sorrento day."

"I'm not very sure you do," May Bartram after a moment said; "and I'm not very sure I ought to want you to. It's dreadful to bring a person back at any time to what he was ten years before. If you've lived away from it," she smiled, "so much the better."

"Ah if *you* haven't why should I?" he asked.

"Lived away, you mean, from what I myself was?"

"From what *I* was. I was of course an ass," Marcher went on; "but I would rather know from you just the sort of ass I was than —from the moment you have something in your mind—not know anything."

Still, however, she hesitated. "But if you've completely ceased to be that sort—?"

"Why I can then all the more bear to know. Besides, perhaps I haven't."

"Perhaps. Yet if you haven't," she added, "I should suppose you'd remember. Not indeed that *I* in the least connect with my impression the invidious name you use. If I had only thought you foolish," she explained, "the thing I speak of wouldn't so have remained with me. It was about yourself." She waited as if it might come to him; but as, only meeting her eyes in wonder, he gave no sign, she burnt her ships. "Has it ever happened?" *This is what startled him on p. 1.*

Then it was that, while he continued to stare, a light broke for him and the blood slowly came to his face, which began to burn with recognition. "Do you mean I told you—?" But he faltered, lest what came to him shouldn't be right, lest he should only give himself away.

"It was something about yourself that it was natural one shouldn't forget—that is if one remembered you at all. That's why I ask you," she smiled, "if the thing you then spoke of has ever come to pass?"

Oh then he saw, but he was lost in wonder and found himself embarrassed. This, he also saw, made her sorry for him, as if her allusion had been a mistake. It took him but a moment, however, to feel it hadn't been, much as it had been a surprise. After the first little shock of it her knowledge on the contrary began, even if rather strangely, to taste sweet to him. She was the only other person in the world then who would have it, and she had had it all these years, while the fact of his having so breathed his secret had unaccountably faded from him. No wonder they couldn't have met as if nothing had happened. "I judge," he finally said, "that I know what you mean. Only I had strangely enough lost any sense of having taken you so far into my confidence."

"Is it because you've taken so many others as well?"

"I've taken nobody. Not a creature since then."

"So that I'm the only person who knows?"

"The only person in the world."

"Well," she quickly replied, "I myself have never spoken. I've never, never repeated of you what you told me." She looked at him so that he perfectly believed her. Their eyes met over it in such a way that he was without a doubt. "And I never will."

She spoke with an earnestness that, as if almost excessive, put him at ease about her possible derision. Somehow the whole question was a new luxury to him—that is from the moment she was in possession. If she didn't take the sarcastic view she clearly took the sympathetic, and that was what he had had, in all the long time, from no one whomsoever. What he felt was that he couldn't at present have begun to tell her, and yet could profit perhaps exquisitely by the accident of having done so of old. "Please don't then. We're just right as it is."

"Oh I am," she laughed, "if you are!" To which she added: "Then you do still feel in the same way?"

It was impossible he shouldn't take to himself that she was really interested, though it all kept coming as perfect surprise. He had thought of himself so long as abominably alone, and lo he wasn't alone a bit. He hadn't been, it appeared, for an hour—since those moments on the Sorrento boat. It was *she* who had been, he seemed to see as he looked at her—she who had been made so by the graceless fact of his lapse of fidelity. To tell her what he had told her—what had it been but to ask something of her? something that she had given, in her charity, without his having, by a remembrance, by a return of the spirit, failing another encounter, so much as thanked her. What he had asked of her had been simply at first not to laugh at him. She had beautifully not done so for ten years, and she was not doing so now. So he had endless gratitude to make up. Only for that he must see just how he had figured to her. "What, exactly, was the account I gave—?"

"Of the way you did feel? Well, it was very simple. You said you had had from your earliest time, as the deepest thing within you, the sense of being kept for something rare and strange, possibly prodigious and terrible, that was sooner or later to happen to you, that you had in your bones the foreboding and the conviction of, and that would perhaps overwhelm you."

"Do you call that very simple?" John Marcher asked.

She thought a moment. "It was perhaps because I seemed, as you spoke, to understand it."

"You do understand it?" he eagerly asked.

Again she kept her kind eyes on him. "You still have the belief?"

"Oh!" he exclaimed helplessly. There was too much to say.

"Whatever it's to be," she clearly made out, "it hasn't yet come."

He shook his head in complete surrender now. "It hasn't yet come. Only, you know, it isn't anything I'm to *do,* to achieve in the world, to be distinguished or admired for. I'm not such an ass as *that*. It would be much better, no doubt, if I were."

"It's to be something you're merely to suffer?"

"Well, say to wait for—to have to meet, to face, to see suddenly break out in my life; possibly destroying all further consciousness, possibly annihilating me; possibly, on the other hand, only altering everything, striking at the root of all my world and leaving me to the consequences, however they shape themselves."

She took this in, but the light in her eyes continued for him not to be that of mockery. "Isn't what you describe perhaps but the expectation—or at any rate the sense of danger, familiar to so many people—of falling in love?"

John Marcher wondered. "Did you ask me that before?"

"No—I wasn't so free-and-easy then. But it's what strikes me now."

"Of course," he said after a moment, "it strikes you. Of course it strikes *me*. Of course what's in store for me may be no more than that. The only thing is," he went on, "that I think if it had been that I should by this time know."

"Do you mean because you've *been* in love?" And then as he but looked at her in silence: "You've been in love, and it hasn't meant such a cataclysm, hasn't proved the great affair?"

"Here I am, you see. It hasn't been overwhelming."

"Then it hasn't been love," said May Bartram.

"Well, I at least thought it was. I took it for that—I've taken it till now. It was agreeable, it was delightful, it was miserable," he explained. "But it wasn't strange. It wasn't what *my* affair's to be."

"You want something all to yourself—something that nobody else knows or *has* known?"

"It isn't a question of what I 'want'—God knows I don't want anything. It's only a question of the apprehension that haunts me —that I live with day by day."

He said this so lucidly and consistently that he could see it further impose itself. If she hadn't been interested before she'd have been interested now. "Is it a sense of coming violence?"

Evidently now too again he liked to talk of it. "I don't think of it as—when it does come—necessarily violent. I only think of it as natural and as of course above all unmistakeable. I think of it simply as *the* thing. *The* thing will of itself appear natural."

"Then how will it appear strange?"

Marcher bethought himself. "It won't—to *me*."

"To whom then?"

"Well," he replied, smiling at last, "say to you."

"Oh then I'm to be present?"

"Why you *are* present—since you know."

"I see." She turned it over. "But I mean at the catastrophe."

At this, for a minute, their lightness gave way to their gravity; it was as if the long look they exchanged held them together. "It will only depend on yourself—if you'll watch with me."

"Are you afraid?" she asked.

"Don't leave me *now*," he went on.

"Are you afraid?" she repeated.

"Do you think me simply out of my mind?" he pursued instead of answering. "Do I merely strike you as a harmless lunatic?"

"No," said May Bartram. "I understand you. I believe you."

"You mean you feel how my obsession—poor old thing!—may correspond to some possible reality?"

"To some possible reality."

"Then you *will* watch with me?"

She hesitated, then for the third time put her question. "Are you afraid?"

"Did I tell you I was—at Naples?"

"No, you said nothing about it."

"Then I don't know. And I should *like* to know," said John Marcher. "You'll tell me yourself whether you think so. If you'll watch with me you'll see."

"Very good then." They had been moving by this time across the room, and at the door, before passing out, they paused as for the full wind-up of their understanding. "I'll watch with you," said May Bartram.

II

THE fact that she "knew"—knew and yet neither chaffed him nor betrayed him—had in a short time begun to constitute between them a goodly bond, which became more marked when, within the year that followed their afternoon at Weatherend, the opportunities for meeting multiplied. The event that thus promoted these occasions was the death of the ancient lady her great-aunt, under whose wing, since losing her mother, she had to such an extent found shelter, and who, though but the widowed mother of the new successor to the property, had succeeded—thanks to a high tone and a high temper—in not forfeiting the supreme position at the great house. The deposition of this personage arrived but with her death, which, followed by many changes, made in particular a difference for the young woman in whom Marcher's expert attention had recognised from the first a dependent with a pride that might ache though it didn't bristle. Nothing for a long time had made him easier than the thought that the aching must have been much soothed by Miss Bartram's now finding herself able to set up a small home in London. She had acquired property, to an amount that made that luxury just possible, under her aunt's extremely complicated will, and when the whole matter began to be straightened out, which indeed took time, she let him know that the happy issue was at last in view. He had seen her again before that day, both because she had more than once accompanied the ancient lady to town and because he had paid another visit to the friends who so conveniently made of Weatherend one of the charms of their own hospitality. These friends had taken him back there; he had achieved there again with Miss Bartram some quiet detachment; and he had in London succeeded in persuading her to more than one brief absence from her aunt. They went together, on these latter occasions, to the National Gallery and the South Kensington Museum, where, among vivid reminders, they talked of Italy at large—not now attempting to recover, as at first, the taste of their youth and their ignorance. That recovery, the first day at Weatherend, had served its purpose well, had given them quite enough; so that they were, to Marcher's sense, no longer hovering about the headwaters of their stream, but had felt their boat pushed sharply off and down the current.

They were literally afloat together; for our gentleman this was marked, quite as marked as that the fortunate cause of it was just the buried treasure of her knowledge. He had with his own hands dug up this little hoard, brought to light—that is to within reach of the dim day constituted by their discretions and privacies—the object of value the hiding-place of which he had, after putting it into the ground himself, so strangely, so long forgotten. The rare luck of his having again just stumbled on the spot made him indifferent to any other question; he would doubtless have devoted more time to the odd accident of his lapse of memory if he hadn't been moved to devote so much to the sweetness, the comfort, as he felt, for the future, that this accident itself had helped to keep fresh. It had never entered into his plan that any one should "know," and mainly for the reason that it wasn't in him to tell any one. That would have been impossible, for nothing but the amusement of a cold world would have waited on it. Since, however, a mysterious fate had opened his mouth betimes, in spite of him, he would count that a compensation and profit by it to the utmost. That the right person *should* know tempered the asperity of his secret more even than his shyness had permitted him to imagine; and May Bartram was clearly right, because—well, because there she was. Her knowledge simply settled it; he would have been sure enough by this time had she been wrong. There was that in his situation, no doubt, that disposed him too much to see her as a mere confidant, taking all her light for him from the fact—the fact only—of her interest in his predicament; from her mercy, sympathy, seriousness, her consent not to regard him as the funniest of the funny. Aware, in fine, that her price for him was just in her giving him this constant sense of his being admirably spared, he was careful to remember that she had also a life of her own, with things that might happen to *her,* things that in friendship one should likewise take account of. Something fairly remarkable came to pass with him, for that matter, in this connexion—something represented by a certain passage of his consciousness, in the suddenest way, from one extreme to the other.

He had thought himself, so long as nobody knew, the most disinterested person in the world, carrying his concentrated burden, his perpetual suspense, ever so quietly, holding his tongue about it, giving others no glimpse of it nor of its effect upon his life, asking of them no allowance and only making on his side all those that were asked. He hadn't disturbed people with the queerness of their having to know a haunted man, though he had had moments of rather special temptation on hearing them say they were forsooth "unsettled." If they were as unsettled as he was—he who had never been settled for an hour in his life—they would know what it meant. Yet it wasn't, all the same, for him to make them, and he listened to them civilly enough. This was why he had such good—though possibly such rather colourless—manners; this was why, above all, he could regard himself, in a greedy world, as decently—as in fact perhaps even a little sublimely—unselfish. Our point is accordingly that he valued this character quite sufficiently to measure his present danger of letting it lapse, against which he promised himself to be much on his guard. He was quite ready, none the less, to be selfish just a little, since surely no more charming occasion for it had come to him. "Just a little," in a word, was just as much as Miss Bartram, taking one day with another, would let him. He never would be in the least coercive, and would keep well before him the lines on which consideration for her— the very highest—ought to proceed. He would thoroughly establish the heads under which her affairs, her requirements, her peculiarities—he went so far as to give them the latitude of that name—would come into their intercourse. All this naturally was a sign of how much he took the intercourse itself for granted. There was nothing more to be done about *that*. It simply existed; had sprung into being with her first penetrating question to him in the autumn light there at Weatherend. The real form it should have taken on the basis that stood out large was the form of their marrying. But the devil in this was that the very basis itself put marrying out of the question. His conviction, his apprehension, his obsession, in short, wasn't a privilege he could invite a woman to share; and that consequence of it was precisely what was the matter with him. Something or other lay in wait for him, amid the twists and the turns of the months and the years, like a crouching beast in the jungle. It signified little whether the crouching beast were destined to slay him or to be slain. The definite point was the inevitable spring of the creature; and the definite lesson from that was that a man of feeling didn't cause himself to be accompanied by a lady on a tiger-hunt. Such was the image under which he had ended by figuring his life.

They had at first, none the less, in the scattered hours spent together, made no allusion to that view of it; which was a sign he was handsomely alert to give that he didn't expect, that he in fact didn't care, always to be talking about it. Such a feature in one's outlook was really like a hump on one's back. The difference it made every minute of the day existed quite independently of discussion. One discussed of course *like* a hunchback, for there was always, if nothing else, the hunchback face. That remained, and she was watching him; but people watched best, as a general thing, in silence, so that such would be predominantly the manner of their vigil. Yet he didn't want, at the same time, to be tense and solemn; tense and solemn was what he imagined he too much showed for with other people. The thing to be, with the one person who knew, was easy and natural—to make the reference rather than be seeming to avoid it, to avoid it rather than be seeming to make it, and to keep it, in any case, familiar, facetious even, rather than pedantic and portentous. Some such consideration as the latter was doubtless in his mind for instance when he wrote pleasantly to Miss Bartram that perhaps the great thing he had so long felt as in the lap of the gods was no more than this circumstance, which touched him so nearly, of her acquiring a house in London. It was the first allusion they had yet again made, needing any other hitherto so little; but when she replied, after having given him the news, that she was by no means satisfied with such a trifle as the climax to so special a suspense, she almost set him wondering if she hadn't even a larger conception of singularity for him than he had for himself. He was at all events destined to become aware little by little, as time went by, that she was all the while looking at his life, judging it, measuring it, in the light of the thing she knew, which grew to be at last, with the consecration of the years, never mentioned between them save as "the real truth" about him. That had always been his own form of reference to it, but she adopted the form so quietly that, looking back at the end of a period, he knew there was no moment at which it was traceable that she had, as he might say, got inside his idea, or exchanged the attitude of beautifully indulging for that of still more beautifully believing him.

It was always open to him to accuse her of seeing him but as the most harmless of maniacs, and this, in the long run—since it covered so much ground—was his easiest description of their friendship. He had a screw loose for her, but she liked him in spite of it and was practically, against the rest of the world, his kind wise keeper, unremunerated but fairly amused and, in the absence of other near ties, not disreputably occupied. The rest of the world of course thought him queer, but she, she only, knew how, and above all why, queer; which was precisely what enabled her to dispose the concealing veil in the right folds. She took his gaiety from him—since it had to pass with them for gaiety—as she took everything else; but she certainly so far justified by her unerring touch his finer sense of the degree to which he had ended by convincing her. *She* at least never spoke of the secret of his life except as "the real truth about you," and she had in fact a wonderful way of making it seem, as such, the secret of her own life too. That was in fine how he so constantly felt her as allowing for him; he couldn't on the whole call it anything else. He allowed for himself, but she, exactly, allowed still more; partly because, better placed for a sight of the matter, she traced his unhappy perversion through reaches of its course into which he could scarce follow it. He knew how he felt, but, besides knowing that, she knew how he *looked* as well; he knew each of the things of importance he was insidiously kept from doing, but she could add up the amount they made, understand how much, with a lighter weight on his spirit, he might have done, and thereby establish how, clever as he was, he fell short. Above all she was in the secret of the difference between the forms he went through—those of his little office under Government, those of caring for his modest patrimony, for his library, for his garden in the country, for the people in London whose invitations he accepted and repaid—and the detachment that reigned beneath them and that made of all behaviour, all that could in the least be called behaviour, a long act of dissimulation. What it had come to was that he wore a mask painted with the social simper, out of the eye-holes of which there looked eyes of an expression not in the least matching the other features. This the stupid world, even after years, had never more than half-discovered. It was only May Bartram who had, and she achieved, by an art indescribable, the feat of at once—or perhaps it was only alternately—meeting the eyes from in front and mingling her own vision, as from over his shoulder, with their peep through the apertures.

So while they grew older together she did watch with him, and so she let this association give shape and colour to her own existence. Beneath *her* forms as well detachment had learned to sit, and behaviour had become for her, in the social sense, a false account of herself. There was but one account of her that would have been true all the while and that she could give straight to nobody, least of all to John Marcher. Her whole attitude was a virtual statement, but the perception of that only seemed called to take its place for him as one of the many things necessarily crowded out of his consciousness. If she had moreover, like himself, to make sacrifices to their real truth, it was to be granted that her compensation might have affected her as more prompt and more natural. They had long periods, in this London time, during which, when they were together, a stranger might have listened to them without in the least pricking up his ears; on the other hand the real truth was equally liable at any moment to rise to the surface, and the auditor would then have wondered indeed what they were talking about. They had from an early hour made up their mind that society was, luckily, unintelligent, and the margin allowed them by this had fairly become one of their commonplaces. Yet there were still moments when the situation turned almost fresh—usually under the effect of some expression drawn from herself. Her expressions doubtless repeated themselves, but her intervals were generous. "What saves us, you know, is that we answer so completely to so usual an appearance: that of the man and woman whose friendship has become such a daily habit—or almost—as to be at last indispensable." That for instance was a remark she had frequently enough had occasion to make, though she had given it at different times different developments. What we are especially concerned with is the turn it happened to take from her one afternoon when he had come to see her in honour of her birthday. This anniversary had fallen on a Sunday, at a season of thick fog and general outward gloom; but he had brought her his customary offering, having known her now long enough to have established a hundred small traditions. It was one of his proofs to himself, the present he made her on her birthday, that he hadn't sunk into real selfishness. It was mostly nothing more than a small trinket, but it was always fine of its kind, and he was regularly careful to pay for it more than he thought he could afford. "Our habit saves you at least, don't you see? because it makes you, after all, for the vulgar, indistinguishable from other men. What's the most inveterate mark of men in general? Why the capacity to spend endless time with dull women—to spend it I won't say without being bored, but without minding that they are, without being driven off at a tangent by it; which comes to the same thing. I'm your dull woman, a part of the daily bread for which you pray at church. That covers your tracks more than anything."

"And what covers yours?" asked Marcher, whom his dull woman could mostly to this extent amuse. "I see of course what you mean by your saving me, in this way and that, so far as other people are concerned—I've seen it all along. Only what is it that saves *you?* I often think, you know, of that."

She looked as if she sometimes thought of that too, but rather in a different way. "Where other people, you mean, are concerned?"

"Well, you're really so in with me, you know—as a sort of result of my being so in with yourself. I mean of my having such an immense regard for you, being so tremendously mindful of all you've done for me. I sometimes ask myself if it's quite fair. Fair I mean to have so involved and—since one may say it—interested you. I almost feel as if you hadn't really had time to do anything else."

"Anything else but be interested?" she asked. "Ah what else does one ever want to be? If I've been 'watching' with you, as we long ago agreed I was to do, watching's always in itself an absorption."

"Oh certainly," John Marcher said, "if you hadn't had your curiosity—! Only doesn't it sometimes come to you as time goes on that your curiosity isn't being particularly repaid?"

May Bartram had a pause. "Do you ask that, by any chance, because you feel at all that yours isn't? I mean because you have to wait so long."

Oh he understood what she meant! "For the thing to happen that never does happen? For the beast to jump out? No, I'm just where I was about it. It isn't a matter as to which I can *choose*, I can decide for a change. It isn't one as to which there *can* be a change. It's in the lap of the gods. One's in the hands of one's law —there one is. As to the form the law will take, the way it will operate, that's its own affair."

"Yes," Miss Bartram replied; "of course one's fate's coming, of course it *has* come in its own form and its own way, all the while. Only, you know, the form and the way in your case were to have been—well, something so exceptional and, as one may say, so particularly *your* own."

Something in this made him look at her with suspicion. "You say 'were to *have* been,' as if in your heart you had begun to doubt."

"Oh!" she vaguely protested.

"As if you believe," he went on, "that nothing will now take place."

She shook her head slowly but rather inscrutably. "You're far from my thought."

He continued to look at her. "What then is the matter with you?"

"Well," she said after another wait, "the matter with me is simply that I'm more sure than ever my curiosity, as you call it, will be but too well repaid."

They were frankly grave now; he had got up from his seat, had turned once more about the little drawing-room to which, year after year, he brought his inevitable topic; in which he had, as he might have said, tasted their intimate community with every sauce, where every object was as familiar to him as the things of his own house and the very carpets were worn with his fitful walk very much as the desks in old counting-houses are worn by the elbows of generations of clerks. The generations of his nervous moods had been at work there, and the place was the written history of his whole middle life. Under the impression of what his friend had just said he knew himself, for some reason, more aware of these things; which made him, after a moment, stop again before her. "Is it possibly that you've grown afraid?"

"Afraid?" He thought, as she repeated the word, that his question had made her, a little, change colour; so that, lest he should have touched on a truth, he explained very kindly: "You remember that that was what you asked *me* long ago—that first day at Weatherend."

"Oh yes, and you told me you didn't know—that I was to see for myself. We've said little about it since, even in so long a time."

"Precisely," Marcher interposed—"quite as if it were too delicate a matter for us to make free with. Quite as if we might find, on pressure, that I *am* afraid. For then," he said, "we shouldn't, should we? quite know what to do."

She had for the time no answer to this question. "There have been days when I thought you were. Only, of course," she added, "there have been days when we have thought almost anything."

"Everything. Oh!" Marcher softly groaned as with a gasp, half-spent, at the face, more uncovered just then than it had been for a long while, of the imagination always with them. It had always had its incalculable moments of glaring out, quite as with the very eyes of the very Beast, and, used as he was to them, they could still draw from him the tribute of a sigh that rose from the depths of his being. All they had thought, first and last, rolled over him; the past seemed to have been reduced to mere barren speculation. This in fact was what the place had just struck him as so full of—the simplification of everything but the state of suspense. That remained only by seeming to hang in the void surrounding it. Even his original fear, if fear it had been, had lost itself in the desert. "I judge, however," he continued, "that you see I'm not afraid now."

"What I see, as I make it out, is that you've achieved something almost unprecedented in the way of getting used to danger. Living with it so long and so closely you've lost your sense of it; you know it's there, but you're indifferent, and you cease even, as of old, to have to whistle in the dark. Considering what the danger is," May Bartram wound up, "I'm bound to say I don't think your attitude could well be surpassed."

John Marcher faintly smiled. "It's heroic?"

"Certainly—call it that."

It was what he would have liked indeed to call it. "I *am* then a man of courage?"

"That's what you were to show me."

He still, however, wondered. "But doesn't the man of courage know what he's afraid of—or *not* afraid of? I don't know *that*, you see. I don't focus it. I can't name it. I only know I'm exposed."

"Yes, but exposed—how shall I say?—so directly. So intimately. That's surely enough."

"Enough to make you feel then—as what we may call the end and the upshot of our watch—that I'm not afraid?"

"You're not afraid. But it isn't," she said, "the end of our watch. That is it isn't the end of yours. You've everything still to see."

"Then why haven't *you?*" he asked. He had had, all along, today, the sense of her keeping something back, and he still had it. As this was his first impression of that it quite made a date. The case was the more marked as she didn't at first answer; which in turn made him go on. "You know something I don't." Then his voice, for that of a man of courage, trembled a little. "You know what's to happen." Her silence, with the face she showed, was almost a confession—it made him sure. "You know, and you're afraid to tell me. It's so bad that you're afraid I'll find out."

All this might be true, for she did look as if, unexpectedly to her, he had crossed some mystic line that she had secretly drawn round her. Yet she might, after all, not have worried; and the real climax was that he himself, at all events, needn't. "You'll never find out."

III

It was all to have made, none the less, as I have said, a date; which came out in the fact that again and again, even after long intervals, other things that passed between them wore in relation to this hour but the character of recalls and results. Its immediate effect had been indeed rather to lighten insistence—almost to provoke a reaction; as if their topic had dropped by its own weight and as if moreover, for that matter, Marcher had been visited by one of his occasional warnings against egotism. He had kept up, he felt, and very decently on the whole, his consciousness of the importance of not being selfish, and it was true that he had never sinned in that direction without promptly enough trying to press the scales the other way. He often repaired his fault, the season permitting, by inviting his friend to accompany him to the opera;

and it not infrequently thus happened that, to show he didn't wish her to have but one sort of food for her mind, he was the cause of her appearing there with him a dozen nights in the month. It even happened that, seeing her home at such times, he occasionally went in with her to finish, as he called it, the evening, and, the better to make his point, sat down to the frugal but always careful little supper that awaited his pleasure. His point was made, he thought, by his not eternally insisting with her on himself; made for instance, at such hours, when it befell that, her piano at hand and each of them familiar with it, they went over passages of the opera together. It chanced to be on one of these occasions, however, that he reminded her of her not having answered a certain question he had put to her during the talk that had taken place between them on her last birthday. "What is it that saves *you?*" —saved her, he meant, from that appearance of variation from the usual human type. If he had practically escaped remark, as she pretended, by doing, in the most important particular, what most men do—find the answer to life in patching up an alliance of a sort with a woman no better than himself—how had she escaped it, and how could the alliance, such as it was, since they must suppose it had been more or less noticed, have failed to make her rather positively talked about?

"I never said," May Bartram replied, "that it hadn't made me a good deal talked about."

"Ah well then you're not 'saved.' "

"It hasn't been a question for me. If you've had your woman I've had," she said, "my man."

"And you mean that makes you all right?"

Oh it was always as if there were so much to say! "I don't know why it shouldn't make me—humanly, which is what we're speaking of—as right as it makes you."

"I see," Marcher returned. " 'Humanly,' no doubt, as showing that you're living for something. Not, that is, just for me and my secret."

May Bartram smiled. "I don't pretend it exactly shows that

I'm not living for you. It's my intimacy with you that's in question."

He laughed as he saw what she meant. "Yes, but since, as you say, I'm only, so far as people make out, ordinary, you're—aren't you?—no more than ordinary either. You help me to pass for a man like another. So if I *am*, as I understand you, you're not compromised. Is that it?"

She had another of her waits, but she spoke clearly enough. "That's it. It's all that concerns me—to help you to pass for a man like another."

He was careful to acknowledge the remark handsomely. "How kind, how beautiful, you are to me! How shall I ever repay you?"

She had her last grave pause, as if there might be a choice of ways. But she chose. "By going on as you are."

It was into this going on as he was that they relapsed, and really for so long a time that the day inevitably came for a further sounding of their depths. These depths, constantly bridged over by a structure firm enough in spite of its lightness and of its occasional oscillation in the somewhat vertiginous air, invited on occasion, in the interest of their nerves, a dropping of the plummet and a measurement of the abyss. A difference had been made moreover, once for all, by the fact that she had all the while not appeared to feel the need of rebutting his charge of an idea within her that she didn't dare to express—a charge uttered just before one of the fullest of their later discussions ended. It had come up for him then that she "knew" something and that what she knew was bad—too bad to tell him. When he had spoken of it as visibly so bad that she was afraid he might find it out, her reply had left the matter too equivocal to be let alone and yet, for Marcher's special sensibility, almost too formidable again to touch. He circled about it at a distance that alternately narrowed and widened and that still wasn't much affected by the consciousness in him that there was nothing she could "know," after all, any better than he did. She had no source of knowledge he hadn't equally—except of course that she might have finer nerves. That was what women

had where they were interested; they made out things, where
people were concerned, that the people often couldn't have made
out for themselves. Their nerves, their sensibility, their imagination, were conductors and revealers, and the beauty of May Bartram was in particular that she had given herself so to his case.
He felt in these days what, oddly enough, he had never felt before, the growth of a dread of losing her by some catastrophe—
some catastrophe that yet wouldn't at all be *the* catastrophe:
partly because she had almost of a sudden begun to strike him as
more useful to him than ever yet, and partly by reason of an appearance of uncertainty in her health, coincident and equally new.
It was characteristic of the inner detachment he had hitherto so
successfully cultivated and to which our whole account of him is a
reference, it was characteristic that his complications, such as they
were, had never yet seemed so as at this crisis to thicken about
him, even to the point of making him ask himself if he were, by
any chance, of a truth, within sight or sound, within touch or
reach, within the immediate jurisdiction, of the thing that waited.

When the day came, as come it had to, that his friend confessed
to him her fear of a deep disorder in her blood, he felt somehow the
shadow of a change and the chill of a shock. He immediately began
to imagine aggravations and disasters, and above all to think of
her peril as the direct menace for himself of personal privation.
This indeed gave him one of those partial recoveries of equanimity
that were agreeable to him—it showed him that what was still first
in his mind was the loss she herself might suffer. "What if she
should have to die before knowing, before seeing—?" It would
have been brutal, in the early stages of her trouble, to put that
question to her; but it had immediately sounded for him to his
own concern, and the possibility was what most made him sorry
for her. If she did "know," moreover, in the sense of her having
had some—what should he think?—mystical irresistible light,
this would make the matter not better, but worse, inasmuch as
her original adoption of his own curiosity had quite become the
basis of her life. She had been living to see what would *be* to be
seen, and it would quite lacerate her to have to give up before the

accomplishment of the vision. These reflexions, as I say, quickened his generosity; yet, make them as he might, he saw himself, with the lapse of the period, more and more disconcerted. It lapsed for him with a strange steady sweep, and the oddest oddity was that it gave him, independently of the threat of much inconvenience, almost the only positive surprise his career, if career it could be called, had yet offered him. She kept the house as she had never done; he had to go to her to see her—she could meet him nowhere now, though there was scarce a corner of their loved old London in which she hadn't in the past, at one time or another, done so; and he found her always seated by her fire in the deep old-fashioned chair she was less and less able to leave. He had been struck one day, after an absence exceeding his usual measure, with her suddenly looking much older to him than he had ever thought of her being; then he recognised that the suddenness was all on his side—he had just simply and suddenly noticed. She looked older because inevitably, after so many years, she *was* old, or almost; which was of course true in still greater measure of her companion. If she was old, or almost, John Marcher assuredly was, and yet it was her showing of the lesson, not his own, that brought the truth home to him. His surprises began here; when once they had begun they multiplied; they came rather with a rush: it was as if, in the oddest way in the world, they had all been kept back, sown in a thick cluster, for the late afternoon of life, the time at which for people in general the unexpected has died out.

One of them was that he should have caught himself—for he *had* so done—*really* wondering if the great accident would take form now as nothing more than his being condemned to see this charming woman, this admirable friend, pass away from him. He had never so unreservedly qualified her as while confronted in thought with such a possibility; in spite of which there was small doubt for him that as an answer to his long riddle the mere effacement of even so fine a feature of his situation would be an abject anti-climax. It would represent, as connected with his past attitude, a drop of dignity under the shadow of which his existence could only become the most grotesque of failures. He had been far from holding it a failure—long as he had waited for the appearance that was to make it a success. He had waited for quite another thing, not for such a thing as that. The breath of his good faith came short, however, as he recognised how long he had waited, or how long at least his companion had. That she, at all events, might be recorded as having waited in vain—this affected him sharply, and all the more because of his at first having done little more than amuse himself with the idea. It grew more grave as the gravity of her condition grew, and the state of mind it produced in him, which he himself ended by watching as if it had been some definite disfigurement of his outer person, may pass for another of his surprises. This conjoined itself still with another, the really stupefying consciousness of a question that he would have allowed to shape itself had he dared. What did everything mean—what, that is, did *she* mean, she and her vain waiting and her probable death and the soundless admonition of it all—unless that, at this time of day, it was simply, it was overwhelmingly too late? He had never at any stage of his queer consciousness admitted the whisper of such a correction; he had never till within these last few months been so false to his conviction as not to hold that what was to come to him had time, whether *he* struck himself as having it or not. That at last, at last, he certainly hadn't it, to speak of, or had it but in the scantiest measure—such, soon enough, as things went with him, became the inference with which his old obsession had to reckon: and this it was not helped to do by the more and more confirmed appearance that the great vagueness casting the long shadow in which he had lived had, to attest itself, almost no margin left. Since it was in Time that he was to have met his fate, so it was in Time that his fate was to have acted; and as he waked up to the sense of no longer being young, which was exactly the sense of being stale, just as that, in turn, was the sense of being weak, he waked up to another matter beside. It all hung together; they were subject, he and the great vagueness, to an equal and indivisible law. When the possibilities themselves had accordingly turned stale, when the secret of the gods had grown faint, had perhaps even quite evaporated, that, and that only, was failure. It wouldn't have been failure to be bankrupt, dishonoured, pilloried, hanged; it was failure not to be anything. And so, in the dark valley into which his path had taken its unlooked-for twist, he wondered not a little as he groped. He didn't care what awful crash might overtake him, with what ignominy or what monstrosity he might yet be associated—since he wasn't after all too utterly old to suffer—if it would only be decently proportionate to the posture he had kept, all his life, in the threatened presence of it. He had but one desire left—that he shouldn't have been "sold."

IV

THEN it was that, one afternoon, while the spring of the year was young and new she met all in her own way his frankest betrayal of these alarms. He had gone in late to see her, but evening hadn't settled and she was presented to him in that long fresh light of waning April days which affects us often with a sadness sharper than the greyest hours of autumn. The week had been warm, the spring was supposed to have begun early, and May Bartram sat, for the first time in the year, without a fire; a fact that, to Marcher's sense, gave the scene of which she formed part a smooth and ultimate look, an air of knowing, in its immaculate order and cold meaningless cheer, that it would never see a fire again. Her own aspect—he could scarce have said why—intensified this note. Almost as white as wax, with the marks and signs in her face as numerous and as fine as if they had been etched by a needle, with soft white draperies relieved by a faded green scarf on the delicate tone of which the years had further refined, she was the picture of a serene and exquisite but impenetrable sphinx, whose head, or indeed all whose person, might have been powdered with silver. She was a sphinx, yet with her white petals and green fronds she might have been a lily too—only an artificial lily, wonderfully imitated and constantly kept, without dust or stain, though not exempt from a slight droop and a complexity of faint creases, under some clear glass bell. The perfection of household care, of high polish and finish, always reigned in her rooms, but they now looked most as if everything had been wound up, tucked in, put away, so that she might sit with folded hands and with nothing more to do. She was "out of it," to Marcher's vision; her work was over; she communicated with him as across some gulf or from some island of rest that she had already reached, and it made him feel strangely abandoned. Was it—or rather wasn't it—that if for so long she had been watching with him the answer to their question must have swum into her ken and taken on its name, so that her occupation was verily gone? He had as much as charged her with this in saying to her, many months before, that she even then knew something she was keeping from him. It was a point he had never since ventured to press, vaguely fearing as he did that it might become a difference, perhaps a disagreement, between them. He had in this later time turned nervous, which was what he in all the other years had never been; and the oddity was that his nervousness should have waited till he had begun to doubt, should have held off so long as he was sure. There was something, it seemed to him, that the wrong word would bring down on his head, something that would so at least ease off his tension. But he wanted not to speak the wrong word; that would make everything ugly. He wanted the knowledge he lacked to drop on him, if drop it could, by its own august weight. If she was to forsake him it was surely for her to take leave. This was why he didn't directly ask her again what she knew; but it was also why, approaching the matter from another side, he said to her in the course of his visit: "What do you regard as the very worst that at this time of day *can* happen to me?"

He had asked her that in the past often enough; they had, with the odd irregular rhythm of their intensities and avoidances, exchanged ideas about it and then had seen the ideas washed away by cool intervals, washed like figures traced in sea-sand. It had ever been the mark of their talk that the oldest allusions in it required but a little dismissal and reaction to come out again, sounding for the hour as new. She could thus at present meet his enquiry quite freshly and patiently. "Oh yes, I've repeatedly thought, only it always seemed to me of old that I couldn't quite make up my mind. I thought of dreadful things, between which it was difficult to choose; and so must you have done."

"Rather! I feel now as if I had scarce done anything else. I appear to myself to have spent my life in thinking of nothing *but* dreadful things. A great many of them I've at different times named to you, but there were others I couldn't name."

"They were too, too dreadful?"

"Too, too dreadful—some of them."

She looked at him a minute, and there came to him as he met it an inconsequent sense that her eyes, when one got their full clearness, were still as beautiful as they had been in youth, only beautiful with a strange cold light—a light that somehow was a part of the effect, if it wasn't rather a part of the cause, of the pale hard sweetness of the season and the hour. "And yet," she said at last, "there are horrors we've mentioned."

It deepened the strangeness to see her, as such a figure in such a picture, talk of "horrors," but she was to do in a few minutes something stranger yet—though even of this he was to take the full measure but afterwards—and the note of it already trembled. It was, for the matter of that, one of the signs that her eyes were having again the high flicker of their prime. He had to admit, however, what she said. "Oh yes, there were times when we did go far." He caught himself in the act of speaking as if it all were over. Well, he wished it were; and the consummation depended for him clearly more and more on his friend.

But she had now a soft smile. "Oh far—!"

It was oddly ironic. "Do you mean you're prepared to go further?"

She was frail and ancient and charming as she continued to look at him, yet it was rather as if she had lost the thread. "Do you consider that we went far?"

"Why I thought it the point you were just making—that we *had* looked most things in the face."

"Including each other?" She still smiled. "But you're quite right. We've had together great imaginations, often great fears; but some of them have been unspoken."

"Then the worst—we haven't faced that. I *could* face it, I believe, if I knew what you think it. I feel," he explained, "as if I had lost my power to conceive such things." And he wondered if he looked as blank as he sounded. "It's spent."

"Then why do you assume," she asked, "that mine isn't?"

"Because you've given me signs to the contrary. It isn't a question for you of conceiving, imagining, comparing. It isn't a question now of choosing." At last he came out with it. "You know something I don't. You've shown me that before."

These last words had affected her, he made out in a moment, exceedingly, and she spoke with firmness. "I've shown you, my dear, nothing."

He shook his head. "You can't hide it."

"Oh, oh!" May Bartram sounded over what she couldn't hide. It was almost a smothered groan.

"You admitted it months ago, when I spoke of it to you as of something you were afraid I should find out. Your answer was that I couldn't, that I wouldn't, and I don't pretend I have. But you had something therefore in mind, and I now see how it must have been, how it still is, the possibility that, of all possibilities, has settled itself for you as the worst. This," he went on, "is why I appeal to you. I'm only afraid of ignorance to-day—I'm not afraid of knowledge." And then as for a while she said nothing: "What makes me sure is that I see in your face and feel here, in this air and amid these appearances, that you're out of it. You've done. You've had your experience. You leave me to my fate."

Well, she listened, motionless and white in her chair, as on a decision to be made, so that her manner was fairly an avowal, though still, with a small fine inner stiffness, an imperfect surrender. "It *would* be the worst," she finally let herself say. "I mean the thing I've never said."

It hushed him a moment. "More monstrous than all the monstrosities we've named?"

"More monstrous. Isn't that what you sufficiently express," she asked, "in calling it the worst?"

Marcher thought. "Assuredly—if you mean, as I do, something that includes all the loss and all the shame that are thinkable."

"It would if it *should* happen," said May Bartram. "What we're speaking of, remember, is only my idea."

"It's your belief," Marcher returned. "That's enough for me. I feel your beliefs are right. Therefore if, having this one, you give me no more light on it, you abandon me."

"No, no!" she repeated. "I'm with you—don't you see?—still." And as to make it more vivid to him she rose from her chair—a movement she seldom risked in these days—and showed herself, all draped and all soft, in her fairness and slimness. "I haven't forsaken you."

It was really, in its effort against weakness, a generous assurance, and had the success of the impulse not, happily, been great, it would have touched him to pain more than to pleasure. But the cold charm in her eyes had spread, as she hovered before him, to all the rest of her person, so that it was for the minute almost a recovery of youth. He couldn't pity her for that; he could only take her as she showed—as capable even yet of helping him. It was as if, at the same time, her light might at any instant go out; wherefore he must make the most of it. There passed before him with intensity the three or four things he wanted most to know; but the question that came of itself to his lips really covered the others. "Then tell me if I shall consciously suffer."

She promptly shook her head. "Never!"

It confirmed the authority he imputed to her, and it produced on him an extraordinary effect. "Well, what's better than that? Do you call that the worst?"

"You think nothing is better?" she asked.

She seemed to mean something so special that he again sharply wondered, though still with the dawn of a prospect of relief. "Why not, if one doesn't *know?*" After which, as their eyes, over his question, met in a silence, the dawn deepened and something to his purpose came prodigiously out of her very face. His own, as he took it in, suddenly flushed to the forehead, and he gasped with the force of a perception to which, on the instant, everything fitted. The sound of his gasp filled the air; then he became articulate. "I see—if I don't suffer!"

In her own look, however, was doubt. "You see what?"

"Why what you mean—what you've always meant."

She again shook her head. "What I mean isn't what I've always meant. It's different."

"It's something new?"

She hung back from it a little. "Something new. It's not what you think. I see what you think."

His divination drew breath then; only her correction might be wrong. "It isn't that I *am* a blockhead?" he asked between faintness and grimness. "It isn't that it's all a mistake?"

"A mistake?" she pityingly echoed. *That* possibility, for her, he saw, would be monstrous; and if she guaranteed him the immunity from pain it would accordingly not be what she had in mind. "Oh no," she declared; "it's nothing of that sort. You've been right."

Yet he couldn't help asking himself if she weren't, thus pressed, speaking but to save him. It seemed to him he should be most in a hole if his history should prove all a platitude. "Are you telling me the truth, so that I shan't have been a bigger idiot than I can bear to know? I *haven't* lived with a vain imagination, in the most besotted illusion? I haven't waited but to see the door shut in my face?"

She shook her head again. "However the case stands *that* isn't the truth. Whatever the reality, it *is* a reality. The door isn't shut. The door's open," said May Bartram.

"Then something's to come?"

She waited once again, always with her <u>cold sweet eyes</u> on him. "It's never too late." She had, with her gliding step, diminished the distance between them, and she stood nearer to him, close to him, a minute, as if still charged with the unspoken. Her movement might have been for some finer emphasis of what she was at once hesitating and deciding to say. He had been standing by the chimney-piece, fireless and sparely adorned, a small perfect old

French clock and two morsels of rosy Dresden constituting all its furniture; and her hand grasped the shelf while she kept him waiting, grasped it a little as for support and encouragement. She only kept him waiting, however; that is he only waited. It had become suddenly, from her movement and attitude, beautiful and vivid to him that she had something more to give him; her wasted face delicately shone with it—it glittered almost as with the white lustre of silver in her expression. She was right, incontestably, for what he saw in her face was the truth, and strangely, without consequence, while their talk of it as dreadful was still in the air, she appeared to present it as inordinately soft. This, prompting bewilderment, made him but gape the more gratefully for her revelation, so that they continued for some minutes silent, her face shining at him, her contact imponderably pressing, and his stare all kind but all expectant. The end, none the less, was that what he had expected failed to come to him. Something else took place instead, which seemed to consist at first in the mere closing of her eyes. She gave way at the same instant to a slow fine shudder, and though he remained staring—though he stared in fact but the harder—turned off and regained her chair. It was the end of what she had been intending, but it left him thinking only of that.

"Well, you don't say—?"

She had touched in her passage a bell near the chimney and had sunk back strangely pale. "I'm afraid I'm too ill."

"Too ill to tell me?" It sprang up sharp to him, and almost to his lips, the fear she might die without giving him light. He checked himself in time from so expressing his question, but she answered as if she had heard the words.

"Don't you know—now?"

"'Now'—?" She had spoken as if some difference had been made within the moment. But her maid, quickly obedient to her bell, was already with them. "I know nothing." And he was afterwards to say to himself that he must have spoken with odious impatience, such an impatience as to show that, supremely disconcerted, he washed his hands of the whole question.

"Oh!" said May Bartram.

"Are you in pain?" he asked as the woman went to her.

"No," said May Bartram.

Her maid, who had put an arm round her as if to take her to her room, fixed on him eyes that appealingly contradicted her; in spite of which, however, he showed once more his mystification. "What then has happened?"

She was once more, with her companion's help, on her feet, and, feeling withdrawal imposed on him, he had blankly found his hat and gloves and had reached the door. Yet he waited for her answer. "What *was* to," she said.

V

HE CAME back the next day, but she was then unable to see him, and as it was literally the first time this had occurred in the long stretch of their acquaintance he turned away, defeated and sore, almost angry—or feeling at least that such a break in their custom was really the beginning of the end—and wandered alone with his thoughts, especially with the one he was least able to keep down. She was dying and he would lose her; she was dying and his life would end. He stopped in the Park, into which he had passed, and stared before him at his recurrent doubt. Away from her the doubt pressed again; in her presence he had believed her, but as he felt his forlornness he threw himself into the explanation that, nearest at hand, had most of a miserable warmth for him and least of a cold torment. She had deceived him to save him—to put him off with something in which he should be able to rest. What could the thing that was to happen to him be, after all, but just this thing that had begun to happen? Her dying, her death, his consequent solitude—*that* was what he had figured as the Beast in the Jungle, that was what had been in the lap of the gods. He had had her word for it as he left her—what else on earth could she have meant? It wasn't a thing of a monstrous order; not a fate rare and distinguished; not a stroke of fortune that overwhelmed and immortalised; it had only the stamp of the common doom. But poor

Marcher at this hour judged the commom doom sufficient. It would serve his turn, and even as the consummation of infinite waiting he would bend his pride to accept it. He sat down on a bench in the twilight. He hadn't been a fool. Something had *been,* as she had said, to come. Before he rose indeed it had quite struck him that the final fact really matched with the long avenue through which he had had to reach it. As sharing his suspense and as giving herself all, giving her life, to bring it to an end, she had come with him every step of the way. He had lived by her aid, and to leave her behind would be cruelly, damnably to miss her. What could be more overwhelming than that?

Well, he was to know within the week, for though she kept him a while at bay, left him restless and wretched during a series of days on each of which he asked about her only again to have to turn away, she ended his trial by receiving him where she had always received him. Yet she had been brought out at some hazard into the presence of so many of the things that were, consciously, vainly, half their past, and there was scant service left in the gentleness of her mere desire, all too visible, to check his obsession and wind up his long trouble. That was clearly what she wanted, the one thing more for her own peace while she could still put out her hand. He was so affected by her state that, once seated by her chair, he was moved to let everything go; it was she herself therefore who brought him back, took up again, before she dismissed him, her last word of the other time. She showed how she wished to leave their business in order. "I'm not sure you understood. You've nothing to wait for more. It *has* come."

Oh how he looked at her! "Really?"

"Really."

"The thing that, as you said, *was* to?"

"The thing that we began in our youth to watch for."

Face to face with her once more he believed her; it was a claim to which he had so abjectly little to oppose. "You mean that it has come as a positive definite occurrence, with a name and a date?"

"Positive. Definite. I don't know about the 'name,' but oh with a date!"

He found himself again too helplessly at sea. "But come in the night—come and passed me by?"

May Bartram had her strange faint smile. "Oh no, it hasn't passed you by!"

"But if I haven't been aware of it and it hasn't touched me—-?"

"Ah your not being aware of it"—and she seemed to hesitate an instant to deal with this—"your not being aware of it is the strangeness *in* the strangeness. It's the wonder *of* the wonder." She spoke as with the softness almost of a sick child, yet now at last, at the end of all, with the perfect straightness of a sibyl. She visibly knew that she knew, and the effect on him was of something co-ordinate, in its high character, with the law that had ruled him. It was the true voice of the law; so on her lips would the law itself have sounded. "It *has* touched you," she went on. "It has done its office. It has made you all its own."

"So utterly without my knowing it?"

"So utterly without your knowing it." His hand, as he leaned to her, was on the arm of her chair, and, dimly smiling always now, she placed her own on it. "It's enough if *I* know it."

"Oh!" he confusedly breathed, as she herself of late so often had done.

"What I long ago said is true. You'll never know now, and I think you ought to be content. You've *had* it," said May Bartram.

"But had what?"

"Why what was to have marked you out. The proof of your law. It has acted. I'm too glad," she then bravely added, "to have been able to see what it's *not*."

He continued to attach his eyes to her, and with the sense that it was all beyond him, and that *she* was too, he would still have sharply challenged her hadn't he so felt it an abuse of her weakness to do more than take devoutly what she gave him, take it hushed as to a revelation. If he did speak, it was out of the fore-knowledge of his loneliness to come. "If you're glad of what it's 'not' it might then have been worse?"

She turned her eyes away, she looked straight before her; with which after a moment: "Well, you know our fears."

He wondered. "It's something then we never feared?"

On this slowly she turned to him. "Did we ever dream, with all our dreams, that we should sit and talk of it thus?"

He tried for a little to make out that they had; but it was as if their dreams, numberless enough, were in solution in some thick cold mist through which thought lost itself. "It might have been that we couldn't talk?"

"Well"—she did her best for him—"not from this side. This, you see," she said, "is the *other* side."

"I think," poor Marcher returned, "that all sides are the same to me." Then, however, as she gently shook her head in correction: "We mightn't, as it were, have got across—?"

"To where we are—no. We're *here*"—she made her weak emphasis.

"And much good does it do us!" was her friend's frank comment.

"It does us the good it can. It does us the good that *it* isn't here. It's past. It's behind," said May Bartram. "Before—" but her voice dropped.

He had got up, not to tire her, but it was hard to combat his yearning. She after all told him nothing but that his light had failed—which he knew well enough without her. "Before—?" he blankly echoed.

"Before, you see, it was always to *come*. That kept it present."

"Oh I don't care what comes now! Besides," Marcher added, "it seems to me I liked it better present, as you say, than I can like it absent with *your* absence."

"Oh mine!"—and her pale hands made light of it.

"With the absence of everything." He had a dreadful sense of standing there before her for—so far as anything but this proved, this bottomless drop was concerned—the last time of their life. It rested on him with a weight he felt he could scarce bear, and this weight it apparently was that still pressed out what remained in him of speakable protest. "I believe you; but I can't begin to pretend I understand. *Nothing,* for me, is past; nothing *will* pass till I pass myself, which I pray my stars may be as soon as possible. Say, however," he added, "that I've eaten my cake, as you contend, to the last crumb—how can the thing I've never felt at all be the thing I was marked out to feel?"

She met him perhaps less directly, but she met him unperturbed. "You take your 'feelings' for granted. You were to suffer your fate. That was not necessarily to know it."

"How in the world—when what is such knowledge but suffering?"

She looked up at him a while in silence. "No—you don't understand."

"I suffer," said John Marcher.

"Don't, don't!"

"How can I help at least *that?*"

"*Don't!*" May Bartram repeated.

She spoke it in a tone so special, in spite of her weakness, that he stared an instant—stared as if some light, hitherto hidden, had shimmered across his vision. Darkness again closed over it, but the gleam had already become for him an idea. "Because I haven't the right—?"

"Don't *know*—when you needn't," she mercifully urged. "You needn't—for we shouldn't."

"Shouldn't?" If he could but know what she meant!

"No—it's too much."

"Too much?" he still asked but, with a mystification that was the next moment of a sudden to give way. Her words, if they meant something, affected him in this light—the light also of her wasted face—as meaning *all,* and the sense of what knowledge had been for herself came over him with a rush which broke through into a question. "Is it of that then you're dying?"

She but watched him, gravely at first, as to see, with this, where he was, and she might have seen something or feared something that moved her sympathy. "I would live for you still—if I could." Her eyes closed for a little, as if, withdrawn into herself, she were for a last time trying. "But I can't!" she said as she raised them again to take leave of him.

She couldn't indeed, as but too promptly and sharply appeared, and he had no vision of her after this that was anything but darkness and doom. They had parted for ever in that strange talk; access to her chamber of pain, rigidly guarded, was almost wholly forbidden him; he was feeling now moreover, in the face of doctors, nurses, the two or three relatives attracted doubtless by the presumption of what she had to "leave," how few were the rights, as they were called in such cases, that he had to put forward, and how odd it might even seem that their intimacy shouldn't have given him more of them. The stupidest fourth cousin had more, even though she had been nothing in such a person's life. She had been a feature of features in *his,* for what else was it to have been so indispensable? Strange beyond saying were the ways of existence, baffling for him the anomaly of his lack, as he felt it to be, of producible claim. A woman might have been, as it were, everything to him, and it might yet present him in no connexion that any one seemed held to recognise. If this was the case in these closing weeks it was the case more sharply on the occasion of the last offices rendered, in the great grey London cemetery, to what had been mortal, to what had been precious, in his friend. The concourse at her grave was not numerous, but he saw himself treated as scarce more nearly concerned with it than if there had been a thousand others. He was in short from this moment face to face with the fact that he was to profit extraordinarily little by the interest May Bartram had taken in him. He couldn't quite have said what he expected, but he hadn't surely expected this approach to a double privation. Not only had her interest failed him, but he seemed to feel himself unattended—and for a reason he couldn't seize—by the distinction, the dignity, the propriety, if nothing else, of the man markedly bereaved. It was as if in the view of society he had not *been* markedly bereaved, as if there still failed some sign or proof of it, and as if none the less his character could never be affirmed nor the deficiency ever made up. There were moments as the weeks went by when he would have liked, by some almost aggressive act, to take his stand on the intimacy of his loss, in order that it *might* be questioned and his retort, to the relief of his spirit, so recorded; but the moments of an irritation more helpless followed fast on these, the moments during which, turning things over with a good conscience but with a bare horizon, he found himself wondering if he oughn't to have begun, so to speak, further back.

He found himself wondering indeed at many things, and this last speculation had others to keep it company. What could he have done, after all, in her lifetime, without giving them both, as it were, away? He couldn't have made known she was watching him, for that would have published the superstition of the Beast. This was what closed his mouth now—now that the Jungle had been threshed to vacancy and that the Beast had stolen away. It sounded too foolish and too flat; the difference for him in this particular, the extinction in his life of the element of suspense, was such as in fact to surprise him. He could scarce have said what the effect resembled; the abrupt cessation, the positive prohibition, of music perhaps, more than anything else, in some place all adjusted and all accustomed to sonority and to attention. If he could at any rate have conceived lifting the veil from his image at some moment of the past (what had he done, after all, if not lift it to *her?*) so to do this to-day, to talk to people at large of the Jungle cleared and confide to them that he now felt it as safe, would have been not only to see them listen as to a goodwife's tale, but really to hear himself tell one. What it presently came to in truth was that poor Marcher waded through his beaten grass, where no life stirred, where no breath sounded, where no evil eye seemed to gleam from a possible lair, very much as if vaguely looking for the Beast, and still more as if acutely missing it. He walked about in an existence that had grown strangely more spacious and, stopping fitfully in places where the undergrowth of life struck him as closer, asked himself yearningly, wondered secretly and sorely, if it would have lurked here or there. It would have at all events *sprung;* what was at least complete was his belief in the truth itself of the assurance given him. The change from his old sense to his new was absolute and final: what was to happen *had* so absolutely and finally happened that he was as little able to know a fear for his future as to know a hope; so absent in short was any question of anything still to come. He was to live entirely with the other question, that of his unidentified past, that of his having to see his fortune impenetrably muffled and masked.

The torment of this vision became then his occupation; he couldn't perhaps have consented to live but for the possibility of guessing. She had told him, his friend, not to guess; she had forbidden him, so far as he might, to know, and she had even in a sort denied the power in him to learn: which were so many things, precisely, to deprive him of rest. It wasn't that he wanted, he argued for fairness, that anything past and done should repeat itself; it was only that he shouldn't, as an anticlimax, have been taken sleeping so sound as not to be able to win back by an effort of thought the lost stuff of consciousness. He declared to himself at moments that he would either win it back or have done with consciousness for ever; he made this idea his one motive in fine, made it so much his passion that none other, to compare with it, seemed ever to have touched him. The lost stuff of consciousness became thus for him as a strayed or stolen child to an unappeasable father; he hunted it up and down very much as if he were knocking at doors and enquiring of the police. This was the spirit in which, inevitably, he set himself to travel; he started on a journey that was to be as long as he could make it; it danced before him that, as the other side of the globe couldn't possibly have less to say to him, it might, by a possibility of suggestion, have more. Before he quitted London, however, he made a pilgrimage to May Bartram's grave, took his way to it through the endless avenues of the grim suburban metropolis, sought it out in the wilderness of tombs, and, though he had come but for the renewal of the act of farewell, found himself, when he had at last stood by it, beguiled into long intensities. He stood for an hour, powerless to turn away and yet powerless to penetrate the darkness of death; fixing with his eyes her inscribed name and date, beating his forehead against the fact of the secret they kept, drawing his breath, while he waited, as if some sense would in pity of him rise from the stones. He kneeled on the stones, however, in vain; they kept what they concealed; and if the face of the tomb did become a face for him it was because her two names became a pair of eyes that didn't know him. He gave them a last long look, but no palest light broke.

VI

HE stayed away, after this, for a year; he visited the depths of Asia, spending himself on scenes of romantic interest, of superlative sanctity; but what was present to him everywhere was that for a man who had known what *he* had known the world was vulgar and vain. The state of mind in which he had lived for so many years shone out to him, in reflexion, as a light that coloured and refined, a light beside which the glow of the East was garish cheap and thin. The terrible truth was that he had lost—with everything else—a distinction as well; the things he saw couldn't help being common when he had become common to look at them. He was simply now one of them himself—he was in the dust, without a peg for the sense of difference; and there were hours when, before the temples of gods and the sepulchres of kings, his spirit turned for nobleness of association to the barely discriminated slab in the London suburb. That had become for him, and more intensely with time and distance, his one witness of a past glory. It was all that was left to him for proof or pride, yet the past glories of Pharaohs were nothing to him as he thought of it. Small wonder then that he came back to it on the morrow of his return. He was drawn there this time as irresistibly as the other, yet with a confidence, almost, that was doubtless the effect of the many months that had elapsed. He had lived, in spite of himself, into his change of feeling, and in wandering over the earth had wandered, as might be said, from the circumference to the centre of his desert. He had settled to his safety and accepted perforce his extinction; figuring to himself, with some colour, in the likeness of certain little old men he remembered to have seen, of whom, all meagre and wizened as they might look, it was related that they had in their time fought twenty duels or been loved by ten princesses. They indeed had been wondrous for others while

he was but wondrous for himself; which, however, was exactly
the cause of his haste to renew the wonder by getting back, as he
might put it, into his own presence. That had quickened his steps
and checked his delay. If his visit was prompt it was because he
had been separated so long from the part of himself that alone he
now valued.

It's accordingly not false to say that he reached his goal with
a certain elation and stood there again with a certain assurance.
The creature beneath the sod *knew* of his rare experience, so that,
strangely now, the place had lost for him its mere blankness of expression. It met him in mildness—not, as before, in mockery; it
wore for him the air of conscious greeting that we find, after absence, in things that have closely belonged to us and which seem
to confess of themselves to the connexion. The plot of ground,
the graven tablet, the tended flowers affected him so as belonging
to him that he resembled for the hour a contented landlord re-
viewing a piece of property. Whatever had happened—well, had
happened. He had not come back this time with the vanity of that
question, his former worrying "what, *what?*" now practically so
spent. Yet he would none the less never again so cut himself off
from the spot; he would come back to it every month, for if he did
nothing else by its aid he at least held up his head. It thus grew
for him, in the oddest way, a positive resource; he carried out his
idea of periodical returns, which took their place at last among
the most inveterate of his habits. What it all amounted to, oddly
enough, was that in his finally so simplified world this garden of
death gave him the few square feet of earth on which he could still
most live. It was as if, being nothing anywhere else for any one,
nothing even for himself, he were just everything here, and if
not for a crowd of witnesses or indeed for any witness but John
Marcher, then by clear right of the register that he could scan
like an open page. The open page was the tomb of his friend,
and *there* were the facts of the past, there the truth of his life,
there the backward reaches in which he could lose himself. He
did this from time to time with such effect that he seemed to wander through the old years with his hand in the arm of a companion

who was, in the most extraordinary manner, his other, his younger self; and to wander, which was more extraordinary yet, round and round a third presence—not wandering she, but stationary, still, whose eyes, turning with his revolution, never ceased to follow him, and whose seat was his point, so to speak, of orientation. Thus in short he settled to live—feeding all on the sense that he once *had* lived, and dependent on it not alone for a support but for an identity.

It sufficed him in its way for months and the year elapsed; it would doubtless even have carried him further but for an accident, superficially slight, which moved him, quite in another direction, with a force beyond any of his impressions of Egypt or of India. It was a thing of the merest chance—the turn, as he afterwards felt, of a hair, though he was indeed to live to believe that if light hadn't come to him in this particular fashion it would still have come in another. He was to live to believe this, I say, though he was not to live, I may not less definitely mention, to do much else. We allow him at any rate the benefit of the conviction, struggling up for him at the end, that, whatever might have happened or not happened, he would have come round of himself to the light. The incident of an autumn day had put the match to the train laid from of old by his misery. With the light before him he knew that even of late his ache had only been smothered. It was strangely drugged, but it throbbed; at the touch it began to bleed. And the touch, in the event, was the face of a fellow mortal. This face, one grey afternoon when the leaves were thick in the alleys, looked into Marcher's own, at the cemetery, with an expression like the cut of a blade. He felt it, that is, so deep down that he winced at the steady thrust. The person who so mutely assaulted him was a figure he had noticed, on reaching his own goal, absorbed by a grave a short distance away, a grave apparently fresh, so that the emotion of the visitor would probably match it for frankness. This fact alone forbade further attention, though during the time he stayed he remained vaguely conscious of his neighbour, a middle-aged man apparently, in mourning, whose bowed back, among the clustered monuments and mortuary yews, was constantly presented. Marcher's theory that these were elements in contact with which he himself revived, had suffered, on this occasion, it may be granted, a marked, an excessive check. The autumn day was dire for him as none had recently been, and he rested with a heaviness he had not yet known on the low stone table that bore May Bartram's name. He rested without power to move, as if some spring in him, some spell vouchsafed, had suddenly been broken for ever. If he could have done that moment as he wanted he would simply have stretched himself on the slab that was ready to take him, treating it as a place prepared to receive his last sleep. What in all the wide world had he now to keep awake for? He stared before him with the question, and it was then that, as one of the cemetery walks passed near him, he caught the shock of the face.

His neighbour at the other grave had withdrawn, as he himself, with force enough in him, would have done by now, and was advancing along the path on his way to one of the gates. This brought him close, and his pace was slow, so that—and all the more as there was a kind of hunger in his look—the two men were for a minute directly confronted. Marcher knew him at once for one of the deeply stricken—a perception so sharp that nothing else in the picture comparatively lived, neither his dress, his age, nor his presumable character and class; nothing lived but the deep ravage of the features he showed. He *showed* them—that was the point; he was moved, as he passed, by some impulse that was either a signal for sympathy or, more possibly, a challenge to an opposed sorrow. He might already have been aware of our friend, might at some previous hour have noticed in him the smooth habit of the scene, with which the state of his own senses so scantly consorted, and might thereby have been stirred as by an overt discord. What Marcher was at all events conscious of was in the first place that the image of scarred passion presented to him was conscious too—of something that profaned the air; and in the second that, roused, startled, shocked, he was yet the next moment looking after it, as it went, with envy. The most extraordinary thing that had happened to him—though he had given that name to other matters as well—took place, after his immediate vague stare, as a consequence of this impression. The stranger passed, but the raw glare of his grief remained, making our friend wonder in pity what wrong, what wound it expressed, what injury not to be healed. What had the man *had,* to make him by the loss of it so bleed and yet live?

Something—and this reached him with a pang—that *he,* John Marcher, hadn't; the proof of which was precisely John Marcher's arid end. No passion had ever touched him, for this was what passion meant; he had survived and maundered and pined, but where had been *his* deep ravage? The extraordinary thing we speak of was the sudden rush of the result of this question. The sight that had just met his eyes named to him, as in letters of quick flame, something he had utterly, insanely missed, and what he had missed made these things a train of fire, made them mark themselves in an anguish of inward throbs. He had seen *outside* of his life, not learned it within, the way a woman was mourned when she had been loved for herself: such was the force of his conviction of the meaning of the stranger's face, which still flared for him as a smoky torch. It hadn't come to him, the knowledge, on the wings of experience; it had brushed him, jostled him, upset him, with the disrespect of chance, the insolence of accident. Now that the illumination had begun, however, it blazed to the zenith, and what he presently stood there gazing at was the sounded void of his life. He gazed, he drew breath, in pain; he turned in his dismay, and, turning, he had before him in sharper incision than ever the open page of his story. The name on the table smote him as the passage of his neighbour had done, and what it said to him, full in the face, was that *she* was what he had missed. This was the awful thought, the answer to all the past, the vision at the dread clearness of which he grew as cold as the stone beneath him. Everything fell together, confessed, explained, overwhelmed; leaving him most of all stupefied at the blindness he had cherished. The fate he had been marked for he had met with a vengeance—he had emptied the cup to the lees; he had been the man of his time, *the* man, to whom nothing on earth was to have happened. That was the rare stroke—that was his visitation. So he saw it, as we say, in pale horror, while the pieces fitted and fitted. So *she* had seen it while he didn't, and so she served at this hour to drive the truth home. It was the truth, vivid and monstrous, that all the while he had waited the wait was itself his portion. This the companion of his vigil had at a given moment made out, and she had then offered him the chance to baffle his doom. One's doom, however, was never baffled, and on the day she told him his own had come down she had seen him but stupidly stare at the escape she offered him.

The escape would have been to love her; then, *then* he would have lived. *She* had lived—who could say now with what passion?—since she had loved him for himself; whereas he had never thought of her (ah how it hugely glared at him!) but in the chill of his egotism and the light of her use. Her spoken words came back to him—the chain stretched and stretched. The Beast had lurked indeed, and the Beast, at its hour, had sprung; it had sprung in that twilight of the cold April when, pale, ill, wasted, but all beautiful, and perhaps even then recoverable, she had risen from her chair to stand before him and let him imaginably guess. It had sprung as he didn't guess; it had sprung as she hopelessly turned from him, and the mark, by the time he left her, had fallen where it *was* to fall. He had justified his fear and achieved his fate; he had failed, with the last exactitude, of all he was to fail of; and a moan now rose to his lips as he remembered she had prayed he mightn't know. This horror of waking—*this* was knowledge, knowledge under the breath of which the very tears in his eyes seemed to freeze. Through them, none the less, he tried to fix it and hold it; he kept it there before him so that he might feel the pain. That at least, belated and bitter, had something of the taste of life. But the bitterness suddenly sickened him, and it was as if, horribly, he saw, in the truth, in the cruelty of his image, what had been appointed and done. He saw the Jungle of his life and saw the lurking Beast; then, while he looked, perceived it, as by a stir of the air, rise, huge and hideous, for the leap that was to settle him. His eyes darkened—it was close; and, instinctively turning, in his hallucination, to avoid it, he flung himself, face down, on the tomb.

THE BIRTHPLACE

I

IT SEEMED to them at first, the offer, too good to be true, and
their friend's letter, addressed to them to feel, as he said, the
ground, to sound them as to inclinations and possibilities, had
almost the effect of a brave joke at their expense. Their friend,
Mr. Grant-Jackson, a highly preponderant pushing person, great
in discussion and arrangement, abrupt in overture, unexpected,
if not perverse, in attitude, and almost equally acclaimed and objected to in the wide midland region to which he had taught, as the
phrase was, the size of his foot—their friend had launched his
bolt quite out of the blue and had thereby so shaken them as to
make them fear almost more than hope. The place had fallen vacant by the death of one of the two ladies, mother and daughter,
who had discharged its duties for fifteen years; the daughter was
staying on alone, to accommodate, but had found, though extremely mature, an opportunity of marriage that involved retire-
ment, and the question of the new incumbents was not a little
pressing. The want thus determined was of a united couple of
some sort, of the right sort, a pair of educated and competent sisters possibly preferred, but a married pair having its advantages
if other qualifications were marked. Applicants, candidates, be-
siegers of the door of every one supposed to have a voice in the
matter, were already beyond counting, and Mr. Grant-Jackson,
who was in his way diplomatic and whose voice, though not perhaps of the loudest, possessed notes of insistence, had found his
preference fixing itself on some person or brace of persons who
had been decent and dumb. The Gedges appeared to have struck
him as waiting in silence—though absolutely, as happened, no
busybody had brought them, far away in the North, a hint either

of bliss or of danger; and the happy spell, for the rest, had obviously been wrought in him by a remembrance which, though now scarcely fresh, had never before borne any such fruit.

Morris Gedge had for a few years, as a young man, carried on a small private school of the order known as preparatory, and had happened then to receive under his roof the small son of the great man, who was not at that time so great. The little boy, during an absence of his parents from England, had been dangerously ill, so dangerously that they had been recalled in haste, though with inevitable delays, from a far country—they had gone to America, with the whole continent and the great sea to cross again—and had got back to find the child saved, but saved, as couldn't help coming to light, by the extreme devotion and perfect judgement of Mrs. Gedge. Without children of her own she had particularly attached herself to this tiniest and tenderest of her husband's pupils, and they had both dreaded as a dire disaster the injury to their little enterprise that would be caused by their losing him. Nervous anxious sensitive persons, with a pride—as they were for that matter well aware—above their position, never, at the best, to be anything but dingy, they had nursed him in terror and had brought him through in exhaustion. Exhaustion, as befell, had thus overtaken them early and had for one reason and another managed to assert itself as their permanent portion. The little boy's death would, as they said, have done for them, yet his recovery hadn't saved them; with which it was doubtless also part of a shy but stiff candour in them that they didn't regard themselves as having in a more indirect manner laid up treasure. Treasure was not to be, in any form whatever, of their dreams or of their waking sense; and the years that followed had limped under their weight, had now and then rather grievously stumbled, had even barely escaped laying them in the dust. The school hadn't prospered, had but dwindled to a close. Gedge's health had failed and still more every sign in him of a capacity to publish himself as practical. He had tried several things, he had tried many, but the final appearance was of their having tried him not less. They mostly, at the time I speak of, were trying his successors, while he found himself, with an effect of dull felicity that had come in this case from the mere postponement of change, in charge of the grey town-library of Blackport-on-Dwindle, all granite, fog and female fiction. This was a situation in which his general intelligence—admittedly his strong point—was doubtless imaged, around him, as feeling less of a strain than that mastery of particulars in which he was recognised as weak.

It was at Blackport-on-Dwindle that the silver shaft reached and pierced him; it was as an alternative to dispensing dog's-eared volumes the very titles of which, on the lips of innumerable glib girls, were a challenge to his nerves, that the wardenship of so different a temple presented itself. The stipend named exceeded little the slim wage at present paid him, but even had it been less the interest and the honour would have struck him as determinant. The shrine at which he was to preside—though he had always lacked occasion to approach it—figured to him as the most sacred known to the steps of men, the early home of the supreme poet, the Mecca of the English-speaking race. The tears came into his eyes sooner still than into his wife's while he looked about with her at their actual narrow prison, so grim with enlightenment, so ugly with industry, so turned away from any dream, so intolerable to any taste. He felt as if a window had opened into a great green woodland, a woodland that had a name all glorious, immortal, that was peopled with vivid figures, each of them renowned, and that gave out a murmur, deep as the sound of the sea, which was the rustle in forest shade of all the poetry, the beauty, the colour of life. It would be prodigious that of this transfigured world *he* should keep the key. No—he couldn't believe it, not even when Isabel, at sight of his face, came and helpfully kissed him. He shook his head with a strange smile. "We shan't get it. Why should we? It's perfect."

"If we don't he'll simply have been cruel; which is impossible when he has waited all this time to be kind." Mrs. Gedge did believe—she *would;* since the wide doors of the world of poetry had suddenly pushed back for them it was in the form of poetic justice that they were first to know it. She had her faith in their patron; it was sudden, but now complete. "He remembers—that's all; and that's our strength."

"And what's *his?*" Gedge asked. "He may want to put us through, but that's a different thing from being able. What are our special advantages?"

"Well, that we're just the thing." Her knowledge of the needs of the case was as yet, thanks to scant information, of the vaguest, and she had never, more than her husband, stood on the sacred spot; but she saw herself waving a nicely-gloved hand over a collection of remarkable objects and saying to a compact crowd of gaping awestruck persons: "And now, please, *this* way." She even heard herself meeting with promptness and decision an occasional enquiry from a visitor in whom audacity had prevailed over awe. She had once been with a cousin, years before, to a great northern castle, and that was the way the housekeeper had taken them round. And it was not moreover, either, that she thought of herself as a housekeeper: she was well above that, and the wave of her hand wouldn't fail to be such as to show it. This and much else she summed up as she answered her mate. "Our special advantages are that you're a gentleman."

"Oh!" said Gedge as if he had never thought of it, and yet as if too it were scarce worth thinking of.

"I see it all," she went on; "they've *had* the vulgar—they find they don't do. We're poor and we're modest, but any one can see what we are."

Gedge wondered. "Do you mean—?" More modest than she, he didn't know quite what she meant.

"We're refined. We know how to speak."

"Do we?"—he still, suddenly, wondered.

But she was from the first surer of everything than he; so that when a few weeks more had elapsed and the shade of uncertainty —though it was only a shade—had grown almost to sicken him, her triumph was to come with the news that they were fairly named. "We're on poor pay, though we manage"—she had at the present juncture contended for her point. "But we're highly cultivated, and for them to get *that*, don't you see? without getting too much with it in the way of pretensions and demands, must be precisely their dream. We've no social position, but we don't *mind* that we haven't, do we? a bit; which is because we know the difference between realities and shams. We hold to reality, and that gives us common sense, which the vulgar have less than anything and which yet must be wanted there, after all, as well as anywhere else."

Her companion followed her, but musingly, as if his horizon had within a few moments grown so great that he was almost lost in it and required a new orientation. The shining spaces surrounded him; the association alone gave a nobler arch to the sky. "Allow that we hold also a little to the romance. It seems to me that that's the beauty. We've missed it all our life, and now it's come. We shall be at headquarters for it. We shall have our fill of it."

She looked at his face, at the effect in it of these prospects, and her own lighted as if he had suddenly grown handsome. "Certainly —we shall live as in a fairy-tale. But what I mean is that we shall give, in a way—and so gladly—quite as much as we get. With all the rest of it we're for instance neat." Their letter had come to them at breakfast, and she picked a fly out of the butter-dish. "It's the way we'll *keep* the place"—with which she removed from the sofa to the top of the cottage-piano a tin of biscuits that had refused to squeeze into the cupboard. At Blackport they were in lodgings—of the lowest description, she had been known to declare with a freedom felt by Blackport to be slightly invidious. The Birthplace—and that itself, after such a life, was exaltation —wouldn't be lodgings, since a house close beside it was set apart for the warden, a house joining on to it as a sweet old parsonage is often annexed to a quaint old church. It would all together be their home, and such a home as would make a little world that they would never want to leave. She dwelt on the gain, for that matter, to their income; as obviously, though the salary was not a change for the better, the house given them would make all the difference. He assented to this, but absently, and she was almost impatient at the range of his thoughts. It was as if something, for him—the very swarm of them—veiled the view; and he presently of himself showed what it was.

"What I can't get over is its being such a man—!" He almost, from inward emotion, broke down.

"Such a man—?"

"Him, *him*, HIM—!" It was too much.

"Grant-Jackson? Yes, it's a surprise, but one sees how he has been meaning, all the while, the right thing by us."

"I mean *Him*," Gedge returned more coldly; "our becoming familiar and intimate—for that's what it will come to. We shall just live with Him."

"Of course—it *is* the beauty." And she added quite gaily: "The more we do the more we shall love Him."

"No doubt—but it's rather awful. The more we *know* Him," Gedge reflected, "the more we shall love Him. We don't as yet, you see, know Him so very tremendously."

"We do so quite as well, I imagine, as the sort of people they've had. And that probably isn't—unless you care, as we do—so awfully necessary. For there are the facts."

"Yes—there are the facts."

"I mean the principal ones. They're all that the people—the people who come—want."

"Yes—they must be all *they* want."

"So that they're all that those who've been in charge have needed to know."

"Ah," he said as if it were a question of honour, "*we* must know everything."

She cheerfully acceded: she had the merit, he felt, of keeping the case within bounds. "Everything. But about him personally," she added, "there isn't, is there? so very very much."

"More, I believe, than there used to be. They've made discoveries."

It was a grand thought. "Perhaps *we* shall make some!"

"Oh I shall be content to be a little better up in what has been done." And his eyes rested on a shelf of books, half of which, little worn but much faded, were of the florid "gift" order and belonged to the house. Of those among them that were his own most were common specimens of the reference sort, not excluding an old Bradshaw and a catalogue of the town-library. "We've not even a Set of our own. Of the Works," he explained in quick repudiation of the sense, perhaps more obvious, in which she might have taken it.

As a proof of their scant range of possessions this sounded almost abject, till the painful flush with which they met on the admission melted presently into a different glow. It was just for that kind of poorness that their new situation was, by its intrinsic charm, to console them. And Mrs. Gedge had a happy thought. "Wouldn't the Library more or less have them?"

"Oh no, we've nothing of that sort: for what do you take us?" This, however, was but the play of Gedge's high spirits: the form both depression and exhilaration most frequently took with him being a bitterness on the subject of the literary taste of Blackport. No one was so deeply acquainted with it. It acted with him in fact as so lurid a sign of the future that the charm of the thought of removal was sharply enhanced by the prospect of escape from it. The institution he served didn't of course deserve the particular reproach into which his irony had flowered; and indeed if the several Sets in which the Works were present were a trifle dusty, the dust was a little his own fault. To make up for that now he had the vision of immediately giving his time to the study of them; he saw himself indeed, inflamed with a new passion, earnestly commenting and collating. Mrs. Gedge, who had suggested that, till their move should come, they ought to read Him regularly of an evening—certain as they were to do it still more when in closer quarters with Him—Mrs. Gedge felt also, in her degree, the spell; so that the very happiest time of their anxious life was perhaps to have been the series of lamplight hours, after supper, in which, alternately taking the book, they declaimed, they almost performed, their beneficent author. He became speedily more than their author—their personal friend, their universal light, their final authority and divinity. Where in the world, they were already asking themselves, would they have been without Him? By the time their appointment arrived in form their relation to Him had immensely developed. It was amusing to Morris Gedge that he had so lately blushed for his ignorance, and he made this remark to his wife during the last hour they were able to give their study before proceeding, across half the country, to the scene of their romantic future. It was as if, in deep close throbs, in cool after-waves that broke of a sudden and bathed his mind, all posses-sion and comprehension and sympathy, all the truth and the life and the story, had come to him, and come, as the newspapers said, to stay. "It's absurd," he didn't hesitate to say, "to talk of our not 'knowing.' So far as we don't it's because we're dunces. He's *in* the thing, over His ears, and the more we get into it the more we're with Him. I seem to myself at any rate," he declared, "to *see* Him in it as if He were painted on the wall."

"Oh *doesn't* one rather, the dear thing? And don't you feel where it is?" Mrs. Gedge finely asked. "We see Him because we love Him—that's what we do. How can we not, the old darling—with what He's doing for us? There's no light"—she had a senten-tious turn—"like true affection."

"Yes, I suppose that's it. And yet," her husband mused, "I see, confound me, the faults."

"That's because you're so critical. You see them, but you don't mind them. You see them, but you forgive them. You mustn't mention them *there*. We shan't, you know, be there for *that*."

"Dear no!" he laughed: "we'll chuck out any one who hints at them."

II

IF THE sweetness of the preliminary months had been great, great too, though almost excessive as agitation, was the wonder of fairly being housed with Him, of treading day and night in the footsteps He had worn, of touching the objects, or at all events the surfaces, the substances, over which His hands had played, which His arms, His shoulders had rubbed, of breathing the air—or something not too unlike it—in which His voice had sounded. They had had a little at first their bewilderments, their disconcertedness; the place was both humbler and grander than they had exactly pre-figured, more at once of a cottage and of a museum, a little more archaically bare and yet a little more richly official. But the sense was strong with them that the point of view, for the inevitable ease of the connexion, patiently, indulgently awaited them; in addi-tion to which, from the first evening, after closing-hour, when the last blank pilgrim had gone, the mere spell, the mystic pres-ence—as if they had had it quite to themselves—were all they could have desired. They had received, at Grant-Jackson's behest and in addition to a table of instructions and admonitions by the number and in some particulars by the nature of which they found themselves slightly depressed, various little guides, manuals, trav-ellers' tributes, literary memorials and other catch-penny publica-tions; which, however, were to be for the moment swallowed up in the interesting episode of the induction or initiation appointed for them in advance at the hands of several persons whose relation to the establishment was, as superior to their own, still more of-ficial, and at those in especial of one of the ladies who had for so many years borne the brunt. About the instructions from above, about the shilling books and the well-known facts and the full-blown legend, the supervision, the subjection, the submission, the view as of a cage in which he should circulate and a groove in which he should slide, Gedge had preserved a certain play of mind; but all power of reaction appeared suddenly to desert him in the presence of his so visibly competent predecessor and as an effect of her good offices. He had not the resource, enjoyed by his wife, of seeing himself, with impatience, attired in black silk of a make characterised by just the right shade of austerity; so that this firm smooth expert and consummately respectable middle-aged person had him somehow, on the whole ground, completely at her mercy.

It was evidently something of a rueful moment when, as a lesson —she being for the day or two still in the field—he accepted Miss Putchin's suggestion of "going round" with her and with the suc-cessive squads of visitors she was there to deal with. He appreci-

ated her method—he saw there had to *be* one; he admired her as
succinct and definite; for there were the facts, as his wife had said
at Blackport, and they were to be disposed of in the time; yet he
felt a very little boy as he dangled, more than once, with Mrs.
Gedge, at the tail of the human comet. The idea had been that
they should by this attendance more fully embrace the possible
accidents and incidents, so to put it, of the relation to the great
public in which they were to find themselves; and the poor man's
excited perception of the great public rapidly became such as to
resist any diversion meaner than that of the admirable manner of
their guide. It wandered from his gaping companions to that of the
priestess in black silk, whom he kept asking himself if either he or
Isabel could hope by any possibility ever remotely to resemble;
then it bounded restlessly back to the numerous persons who revealed to him as it had never yet been revealed the happy power
of the simple to hang upon the lips of the wise. The great thing
seemed to be—and quite surprisingly—that the business was easy
and the strain, which as a strain they had feared, moderate; so
that he might have been puzzled, had he fairly caught himself in
the act, by his recognising as the last effect of the impression an
odd absence of the power really to rest in it, an agitation deep
within him that vaguely threatened to grow. "It isn't, you see,
so very complicated," the black silk lady seemed to throw off, with
everything else, in her neat crisp cheerful way; in spite of which
he already, the very first time—that is after several parties had
been in and out and up and down—went so far as to wonder if
there weren't more in it than she imagined. She was, so to speak,
kindness itself—was all encouragement and reassurance; but it
was just her slightly coarse redolence of these very things that, on
repetition, before they parted, dimmed a little, as he felt, the light
of his acknowledging smile. This again she took for a symptom of
some pleading weakness in him—he could never be as brave as
she; so that she wound up with a few pleasant words from the very
depth of her experience. "You'll get into it, never fear—it will
come; and then you'll feel as if you had never done anything else."
He was afterwards to know that, on the spot, at this moment, he

must have begun to wince a little at such a menace; that he might come to feel as if he had never done anything but what Miss Putchin did loomed for him, in germ, as a penalty to pay. The support she offered, none the less, continued to strike him; she put the whole thing on so sound a basis when she said: "You see they're so nice about it—they take such an interest. And they never do a thing they shouldn't. That was always everything to mother and me." "They," Gedge had already noticed, referred constantly and hugely, in the good woman's talk, to the millions who shuffled through the house; the pronoun in question was for ever on her lips, the hordes it represented filled her consciousness, the addition of their numbers ministered to her glory. Mrs. Gedge promptly fell in. "It must be indeed delightful to see the effect on so many and to feel that one may perhaps do something to make it—well, permanent." But he was kept silent by his becoming more sharply aware that this was a new view, for him, of the reference made, that he had never thought of the quality of the place as derived from Them, but from Somebody Else, and that They, in short, seemed to have got into the way of crowding Him out. He found himself even a little resenting this for Him—which perhaps had something to do with the slightly invidious cast of his next enquiry.

"And are They always, as one might say—a—stupid?"

"Stupid!" She stared, looking as if no one *could* be such a thing in such a connexion. No one had ever been anything but neat and cheerful and fluent, except to be attentive and unobjectionable and, so far as was possible, American.

"What I mean is," he explained, "is there any perceptible proportion that take an interest in Him?"

His wife stepped on his toe; she deprecated levity. But his mistake fortunately was lost on their friend. "That's just why they come, that they take such an interest. I sometimes think they take more than about anything else in the world." With which Miss Putchin looked about at the place. "It *is* pretty, don't you think, the way they've got it now?" This, Gedge saw, was a different "They"; it applied to the powers that were—the people who had appointed him, the governing, visiting Body, in respect to which he was afterwards to remark to Mrs. Gedge that a fellow—it was the difficulty—didn't know "where to have her." His wife, at a loss, questioned at that moment the necessity of having her anywhere, and he said, good-humouredly "Of course; it's all right." He was in fact content enough with the last touches their friend had given the picture. "There are many who know all about it when they come, and the Americans often are tremendously up. Mother and me really enjoyed"—it was her only slip—"the interest of the Americans. We've sometimes had ninety a day, and all wanting to see and hear everything. But you'll work them off; you'll see the way—it's all experience." She came back for his comfort to that. She came back also to other things: she did justice to the considerable class who arrived positive and primed. "There are those who know more about it than you do. But *that* only comes from their interest."

"Who know more about what?" Gedge enquired.

"Why about the place. I mean they have their ideas—of what everything is, and *where* it is, and what it isn't and where it *should* be. They do ask questions," she said, yet not so much in warning as in the complacency of being herself seasoned and sound; "and they're down on you when they think you go wrong. As if you ever could! You know too much," she astutely smiled; "or you *will*."

"Oh you mustn't know *too* much, must you?" And Gedge now smiled as well. He knew, he thought, what he meant.

"Well, you must know as much as anybody else. I claim at any rate that I do," Miss Putchin declared. "They never really caught me out."

"I'm very certain of *that*"—and Mrs. Gedge had an elation almost personal.

"Surely," he said, "I don't want to be caught out." She rejoined that in such a case he would have *Them* down on him, and he saw that this time she meant the powers above. It quickened his sense of all the elements that were to reckon with, yet he felt at the same time that the powers above were not what he should most fear.

"I'm glad," he observed, "that they ever ask questions; but I happened to notice, you know, that no one did to-day."

"Then you missed several—and no loss. There were three or four put to me too silly to remember. But of course they mostly *are* silly."

"You mean the questions?"

She laughed with all her cheer. "Yes, sir; I don't mean the answers."

Whereupon, for a moment snubbed and silent, he felt like one of the crowd. Then it made him slightly vicious. "I didn't know but you meant the people in general—till I remembered that I'm to understand from you that *they're* wise, only occasionally breaking down."

It wasn't really till then, he thought, that she lost patience; and he had had, much more than he meant no doubt, a cross-questioning air. "You'll see for yourself." Of which he was sure enough. He was in fact so ready to take this that she came round to full accommodation, put it frankly that every now and then they broke out—not the silly, oh no, the intensely enquiring. "We've had quite lively discussions, don't you know, about well-known points. They want it all *their* way, and I know the sort that are going to as soon as I see them. That's one of the things you do—you get to know the sorts. And if it's what you're afraid of—their taking you up," she was further gracious enough to say, "you needn't mind a bit. What *do* they know, after all, when for us it's our life? I've never moved an inch, because, you see, I shouldn't have been here if I didn't know where I was. No more will *you* be a year hence— you know what I mean, putting it impossibly—if *you* don't. I expect you do, in spite of your fancies." And she dropped once more to bed-rock. "There are the facts. Otherwise where would any of us be? That's all you've got to go upon. A person, however cheeky, can't have them *his* way just because he takes it into his head. There can only be *one* way, and," she gaily added as she took leave of them, "I'm sure it's quite enough!"

III

GEDGE not only assented eagerly—one way *was* quite enough if it were the right one—but repeated it, after this conversation, at odd moments, several times over to his wife. "There can only be one way, one way," he continued to remark—though indeed much as if it were a joke; till she asked him how many more he supposed she wanted. He failed to answer this question, but resorted to another repetition. "There are the facts, the facts," which perhaps, however, he kept a little more to himself, sounding it at intervals in different parts of the house. Mrs. Gedge was full of comment on their clever introductress, though not restrictively save in the matter of her speech, "Me and mother," and a general tone—which certainly was not their sort of thing. "I don't know," he said, "perhaps it comes with the place, since speaking in immortal verse doesn't seem to come. It must be, one seems to see, one thing or the other. I dare say that in a few months I shall also be at it—'me an the wife.' "

Why not 'me and the missus' at once?" Mrs. Gedge resentfully enquired. "I don't think," she observed at another time, "that I quite know what's the matter with you."

"It's only that I'm excited, awfully excited—as I don't see how one can't be. You wouldn't have a fellow drop into this berth as into an appointment at the Post Office. Here on the spot it goes to my head—how can that be helped? But we shall live into it, and perhaps," he said with an implication of the other possibility that was doubtless but part of his fine ecstasy, "we shall live through it." The place acted on his imagination—how, surely, shouldn't it? And his imagination acted on his nerves, and these things together, with the general vividness and the new and complete immersion, made rest for him almost impossible, so that he could scarce go to bed at night and even during the first week more than once rose in the small hours to move about, up and down, with his lamp—standing, sitting, listening, wondering, in the stillness, as if positively to recover some echo, to surprise some secret, of the *genius loci*. He couldn't have explained it—and didn't in fact need to explain it, at least to himself, since the impulse simply held him and shook him; but the time after closing, the time above all after the people—Them, as he felt himself on the way habitually to put it, predominant, insistent, all in the foreground—brought him, or ought to have brought him, he seemed to see, nearer to the enshrined Presence, enlarging the opportunity for communion and intensifying the sense of it. These nightly prowls, as he called them, were disquieting to his wife, who had no disposition to share in them, speaking with decision of the whole place as just the place to be forbidding after dark. She rejoiced in the distinctness, contiguous though it was, of their own little residence, where she trimmed the lamp and stirred the fire and heard the kettle sing, repairing the while the omissions of the small domestic who slept out; she foresaw herself, with some promptness, drawing rather sharply the line between her own precinct and that in which the great spirit might walk. It would be with them, the great spirit, all day—even if indeed on her making that remark, and in just that form, to her husband, he replied with a queer "But will he though?" And she vaguely imaged the development of a domestic antidote after a while, precisely, in the shape of curtains more markedly drawn and everything most modern and lively, tea, "patterns," the newspapers, the female fiction itself that they had reacted against at Blackport, quite defiantly cultivated.

These possibilities, however, were all right, as her companion said it was, all the first autumn—they had arrived at summer's end; and he might have been more than content with a special set of his own that he had access to from behind, passing out of their low door for the few steps between it and the Birthplace. With his lamp ever so carefully guarded and his nursed keys that made him free of treasures, he crossed the dusky interval so often that she began to qualify it as a habit that "grew." She spoke of it almost as if he had taken to drink, and he humoured that view of it by allowing the cup to be strong. This had been in truth altogether his immediate sense of it; strange and deep for him the spell of silent sessions before familiarity and, to some small extent, disappointment had set in. The exhibitional side of the establishment had struck him, even on arrival, as qualifying too much its character; he scarce knew what he might best have looked for, but the three or four rooms bristled overmuch, in the garish light of day, with busts and relics, not even ostensibly always *His,* old prints and old editions, old objects fashioned in His likeness, furniture "of the time" and autographs of celebrated worshippers. In the quiet hours and the deep dusk, none the less, under the play of the shifted lamp and that of his own emotion, these things too recovered their advantage, ministered to the mystery, or at all events to the impression, seemed consciously to offer themselves as personal to the poet. Not one of them was really or unchallengeably so, but they had somehow, through long association, got, as Gedge always phrased it, into the secret, and it was about the secret he asked them while he restlessly wandered. It wasn't till months had elapsed that he found how little they had to tell him, and he was quite at his ease with them when he knew they were by no means where his sensibility had first placed them. They were as out of it as he; only, to do them justice, they had made him immensely feel. And still, too, it was not they who had done that most, since his sentiment had gradually cleared itself to deep, to deeper refinements.

The Holy of Holies of the Birthplace was the low, the sublime Chamber of Birth, sublime because, as the Americans usually said —unlike the natives they mostly found words—it was so pathetic; and pathetic because it was—well, really nothing else in the world that one could name, number or measure. It was as empty as a shell of which the kernel has withered, and contained neither busts nor prints nor early copies; it contained only the Fact—*the* Fact itself—which, as he stood sentient there at midnight, our friend, holding his breath, allowed to sink into him. He *had* to take it as the place where the spirit would most walk and where He would therefore be most to be met, with possibilities of recognition and reciprocity. He hadn't, most probably—*He* hadn't—much inhabited the room, as men weren't apt, as a rule, to convert to their later use and involve in their wider fortune the scene itself of their nativity. But as there were moments when, in the conflict of theories, the sole certainty surviving for the critic threatened to be that He had not—unlike other successful men—*not* been born, so Gedge, though little of a critic, clung to the square feet of space that connected themselves, however feebly, with the positive appearance. He was little of a critic—he was nothing of one; he hadn't pretended to the character before coming, nor come to pretend to it; also, luckily for him, he was seeing day by day how little use he could possibly have for it. It would be to him, the attitude of a high expert, distinctly a stumbling-block, and that he rejoiced, as the winter waned, in his ignorance, was one of the propositions he betook himself, in his odd manner, to enunciating to his wife. She denied it, for hadn't she in the first place been present, wasn't she still present, at his pious, his tireless study of everything connected with the subject?—so present that she had herself learned more about it than had ever seemed likely. Then in the second place he wasn't to proclaim on the house-tops any point at which he might be weak, for who knew, if it should get abroad that they were ignorant, what effect might be produced—?

"On the attraction"—he took her up—"of the Show?"

He had fallen into the harmless habit of speaking of the place as the "Show"; but she didn't mind this so much as to be diverted by it. "No; on the attitude of the Body. You know they're pleased with us, and I don't see why you should want to spoil it. We got in by a tight squeeze—you know we've had evidence of that, and that it was about as much as our backers could manage. But we're proving a comfort to them, and it's absurd of you to question your suitability to people who were content with the Putchins."

"I don't, my dear," he returned, "question anything; but if I should do so it would be precisely because of the greater advantage constituted for the Putchins by the simplicity of their spirit. They were kept straight by the quality of their ignorance—which was denser even than mine. It was a mistake in us from the first to have attempted to correct or to disguise ours. We should have waited simply to become good parrots, to learn our lesson—all on the spot here, so little of it is wanted—and squawk it off."

"Ah 'squawk,' love—what a word to use about Him!"

"It isn't about Him—nothing's about Him. None of Them care tuppence about Him. The only thing They care about is this empty shell—or rather, for it isn't empty, the extraneous preposterous stuffing of it."

"Preposterous?"—he made her stare with this as he hadn't yet done.

At sight of her look, however—the gleam, as it might have been, of a queer suspicion—he bent to her kindly and tapped her cheek. "Oh it's all right. We *must* fall back on the Putchins. Do you remember what she said?—'They've made it so pretty now.' They *have* made it pretty, and it's a first-rate show. It's a first-rate show and a first-rate billet, and He was a first-rate poet, and you're a first-rate woman—to put up so sweetly, I mean, with my nonsense."

She appreciated his domestic charm and she justified that part of his tribute which concerned herself. "I don't care how much of your nonsense you talk to me, so long as you *keep* it all for me and don't treat *Them* to it."

"The pilgrims? No," he conceded—"it isn't fair to Them. They mean well."

"What complaint have we after all to make of Them so long as They don't break off bits—as They used, Miss Putchin told us, so awfully—in order to conceal them about Their Persons? She broke Them at least of that."

"Yes," Gedge mused again; "I wish awfully she hadn't!"

"You'd like the relics destroyed, removed? That's all that's wanted!"

"There *are* no relics."

"There won't be any *soon*—unless you take care." But he was already laughing, and the talk wasn't dropped without his having patted her once more. An impression or two nevertheless remained with her from it, as he saw from a question she asked him on the morrow. "What did you mean yesterday about Miss Putchin's simplicity—it's keeping her 'straight'? Do you mean mentally?"

Her "mentally" was rather portentous, but he practically confessed. "Well, it kept her up. I mean," he amended, laughing, "it kept her down."

It was really as if she had been a little uneasy. "You consider there's a danger of your being affected? You know what I mean— of its going to your head. You do know," she insisted as he said nothing. "Through your caring for him so. You'd certainly be right in that case about its having been a mistake for you to plunge so deep." And then as his listening without reply, though with his look a little sad for her, might have denoted that, allowing for extravagance of statement, he saw there was something in it: "Give up your prowls. Keep it for daylight. Keep it for *Them*."

"Ah," he smiled, "if one could! My prowls," he added, "are what I most enjoy. They're the only time, as I've told you before, that I'm really with *Him*. Then I don't see the place. He isn't the place."

"I don't care for what you 'don't see,'" she returned with vivacity; "the question is of what you do see."

Well, if it was, he waited before meeting it. "Do you know what I sometimes do?" And then as she waited too: "In the Birthroom there, when I look in late, I often put out my light. That makes it better."

"Makes what—?"

"Everything."

"What is it then you see in the dark?"

"Nothing!" said Morris Gedge.

"And what's the pleasure of that?"

"Well, what the American ladies say. It's so fascinating!"

IV

THE autumn was brisk, as Miss Putchin had told them it would be, but business naturally fell off with the winter months and the short days. There was rarely an hour indeed without a call of some sort, and they were never allowed to forget that they kept the shop in all the world, as they might say, where custom was least fluctuating. The seasons told on it, as they tell on travel, but no other influence, consideration or convulsion to which the population of the globe is exposed. This population, never exactly in simultaneous hordes, but in a full swift and steady stream, passed through the smoothly-working mill and went, in its variety of degrees duly impressed and edified, on its artless way. Gedge gave himself up, with much ingenuity of spirit, to trying to keep in relation with it; having even at moments, in the early time, glimpses of the chance that the impressions gathered from so rare an opportunity for contact with the general mind might prove as interesting as anything else in the connexion. Types, classes, nationalities, manners, diversities of behaviour, modes of seeing, feeling, of expression, would pass before him and become for him, after a fashion, the experience of an untravelled man. His journeys had been short and saving, but poetic justice again seemed inclined to work for him in placing him just at the point in all Europe perhaps where the confluence of races was thickest. The theory at any rate carried him on, operating helpfully for the term of his anxious beginnings and gilding in a manner—it was the way he characterised the case to his wife—the somewhat stodgy gingerbread of their daily routine. They hadn't known many people and their visiting-list was small—which made it again poetic justice that they should be visited on such a scale. They dressed and were at home, they were under arms and received, and except for the offer of refreshment—and Gedge had his view that there would eventually be a *buffet* farmed out to a great firm—their hospitality would have made them princely if mere hospitality ever did. Thus they were launched, and it was interesting; so that from having been ready to drop, originally, with fatigue they emerged as even-winded and strong in the legs as if they had had an Alpine holiday. This experience, Gedge opined, also represented, as a gain, a like seasoning of the spirit— by which he meant a certain command of impenetrable patience.

The patience was needed for the particular feature of the ordeal

that, by the time the lively season was with them again, had dis-
engaged itself as the sharpest—the immense assumption of veraci-
ties and sanctities, of the general soundness of the legend, with
which every one arrived. He was well provided certainly for meeting it, and he gave all he had, yet he had sometimes the sense of a
vague resentment on the part of his pilgrims at his not ladling out
their fare with a bigger spoon. An irritation had begun to grumble
in him during the comparatively idle months of winter when a pilgrim would turn up singly. The pious individual, entertained for
the half-hour, had occasionally seemed to offer him the promise
of beguilement or the semblance of a personal relation; it came
back again to the few pleasant calls he had received in the course
of a life almost void of social amenity. Sometimes he liked the
person, the face, the speech: an educated man, a gentleman, not
one of the herd; a graceful woman, vague, accidental, unconscious
of him, but making him wonder, while he hovered, who she was.
These chances represented for him light yearnings and faint flut-
ters; they acted indeed within him to a special, an extraordinary
tune. He would have liked to talk with such stray companions,
to talk with them *really*, to talk with them as he might have talked
had he met them where he couldn't meet them—at dinner, in the
"world," on a visit at a country-house. Then he could have said—
and about the shrine and the idol always—things he couldn't say
now. The form in which his irritation first came to him was that of
his feeling obliged to say to them—to the single visitor, even when
sympathetic, quite as to the gaping group—the particular things,
a dreadful dozen or so, that they expected. If he had thus arrived
at characterising these things as dreadful the reason touched the
very point that, for a while turning everything over, he kept dodging, not facing, trying to ignore. The point was that he was on
his way to become two quite different persons, the public and the
private—as to which it would somehow have to be managed that
these persons should live together. He was splitting into halves,
unmistakeably—he who, whatever else he had been, had at least
always been so entire and in his way so solid. One of the halves,

or perhaps even, since the split promised to be rather unequal, one of the quarters, was the keeper, the showman, the priest of the idol; the other piece was the poor unsuccessful honest man he had always been.

There were moments when he recognised this primary character as he had never done before; when he in fact quite shook in his shoes at the idea that it perhaps had in reserve some supreme assertion of its identity. It was honest, verily, just by reason of the possibility. It was poor and unsuccessful because here it was just on the verge of quarrelling with its bread and butter. Salvation would be of course—the salvation of the showman—rigidly to *keep* it on the verge; not to let it, in other words, overpass by an inch. He might count on this, he said to himself, if there weren't any public—if there weren't thousands of people demanding of him what he was paid for. He saw the approach of the stage at which they would affect him, the thousands of people—and perhaps even more the earnest individual—as coming really to see if he were earning his wage. Wouldn't he soon begin to fancy them in league with the Body, practically deputed by it—given, no doubt, a kindled suspicion—to look in and report observations? It was the way he broke down with the lonely pilgrim that led to his first heart-searchings—broke down as to the courage required for damping an uncritical faith. What they all most wanted was to feel that everything was "just as it was"; only the shock of having to part with that vision was greater than any individual could bear unsupported. The bad moments were upstairs in the Birthroom, for here the forces pressing on the very edge assumed a dire intensity. The mere expression of eye, all-credulous, omnivorous and fairly moistening in the act, with which many persons gazed about, might eventually make it difficult for him to remain fairly civil. Often they came in pairs—sometimes one had come before—and then they explained to each other. He in that case never corrected; he listened, for the lesson of listening: after which he would remark to his wife that there was no end to what he was learning. He saw that if he should really ever break down it would be with her he would begin. He had given her hints and digs enough, but she was so inflamed with appreciation that she either didn't feel them or pretended not to understand.

This was the greater complication that, with the return of the spring and the increase of the public, her services were more required. She took the field with him from an early hour; she was present with the party above while he kept an eye, and still more an ear, on the party below; and how could he know, he asked himself, what she might say to them and what she might suffer *Them* to say—or in other words, poor wretches, to believe—while removed from his control? Some day or other, and before too long, he couldn't but think, he must have the matter out with her—the matter, namely, of the *morality* of their position. The morality of women was special—he was getting lights on that. Isabel's conception of her office was to cherish and enrich the legend. It was already, the legend, very taking, but what was she there for but to make it more so? She certainly wasn't there to chill any natural piety. If it was all in the air—all in their "eye," as the vulgar might say—that He *had* been born in the Birthroom, where was the value of the sixpences they took? where the equivalent they had engaged to supply? "Oh dear, yes—just about *here*"; and she must tap the place with her foot. "Altered? Oh dear, no— save in a few trifling particulars; you see the place—and isn't that just the charm of it?—quite as *He* saw it. Very poor and homely, no doubt; but that's just what's so wonderful." He didn't want to hear her, and yet he didn't want to give her her head; he didn't want to make difficulties or to snatch the bread from her mouth. But he must none the less give her a warning before they had gone *too* far. That was the way, one evening in June, he put it to her; the affluence, with the finest weather, having lately been of the largest and the crowd all day fairly gorged with the story. "We mustn't, you know, go *too* far."

The odd thing was that she had now ceased even to be conscious of what troubled him—she was so launched in her own career. "Too far for what?"

"To save our immortal souls. We mustn't, love, tell too many lies."

She looked at him with dire reproach. "Ah now are you going to begin again?"

"I never *have* begun; I haven't wanted to worry you. But, you know, we don't know anything about it." And then as she stared, flushing: "About His having been born up there. About anything really. Not the least little scrap that would weigh in any other connexion as evidence. So don't rub it in so."

"Rub it in how?"

"That He *was* born—" But at sight of her face he only sighed. "Oh dear, oh dear!"

"Don't you think," she replied cuttingly, "that He was born anywhere?"

He hesitated—it was such an edifice to shake. "Well, we don't know. There's very little *to* know. He covered His tracks as no other human being has ever done."

She was still in her public costume and hadn't taken off the gloves she made a point of wearing as a part of that uniform; she remembered how the rustling housekeeper in the Border castle, on whom she had begun modelling herself, had worn them. She seemed official and slightly distant. "To cover His tracks He must have had to exist. Have we got to give *that* up?"

"No, I don't ask you to give it up *yet*. But there's very little to go upon."

"And is that what I'm to tell Them in return for everything?"

Gedge waited—he walked about. The place was doubly still after the bustle of the day, and the summer evening rested on it as a blessing, making it, in its small state and ancientry, mellow and sweet. It was good to be there and it would be good to stay. At the same time there was something incalculable in the effect on one's nerves of the great gregarious density. This was an attitude that had nothing to do with degrees and shades, the attitude of wanting all or nothing. And you couldn't talk things over with it. You could only do that with friends, and then but in cases where you were sure the friends wouldn't betray you.

"Couldn't you adopt," he replied at last, "a slightly more discreet method? What we can say is that things have been *said;*

that's all *we* have to do with. 'And is this really'—when they jam
their umbrellas into the floor—'the very *spot* where He was born?'
'So it has, from a long time back, been described as being.'
Couldn't one meet Them, to be decent a little, in some such way
as that?"

She looked at him very hard. "Is that the way *you* meet them?"

"No; I've kept on lying—without scruple, without shame."

"Then why do you haul me up?"

"Because it has seemed to me we might, like true companions,
work it out a little together."

This was not strong, he felt, as, pausing with his hands in his
pockets, he stood before her; and he knew it as weaker still after
she had looked at him a minute. "Morris Gedge, I propose to be
your true companion, and I've come here to stay. That's all I've
got to say." It was not, however, for "You had better try yourself
and see," she presently added. "Give the place, give the story
away, by so much as a look, and—well, I'd allow you about nine
days. Then you'd see."

He feigned, to gain time, an innocence. "They'd take it so ill?"
And then as she said nothing: "They'd turn and rend me? They'd
tear me to pieces?"

But she wouldn't make a joke of it. "They wouldn't *have* it, simply."

"No—They wouldn't. That's what I say. They won't."

"You had better," she went on, "begin with Grant-Jackson.
But even that isn't necessary. It would get to him, it would get to
the Body, like wildfire."

"I see," said poor Gedge. And indeed for the moment he did
see, while his companion followed up what she believed her advantage.

"Do you consider it's *all* a fraud?"

"Well, I grant you there was somebody. But the details are
naught. The links are missing. The evidence—in particular about
that room upstairs, in itself our Casa Santa—is *nil*. It was so awfully long ago." Which he knew again sounded weak.

"Of course it was awfully long ago—that's just the beauty and the interest. Tell Them, *tell* Them," she continued, "that the evidence is *nil*, and I'll tell Them something else." She spoke it with such meaning that his face seemed to show a question, to which she was on the spot of replying "I'll tell Them you're a—" She stopped, however, changing it. "I'll tell Them exactly the opposite. And I'll find out what you say—it won't take long—to do it. If we tell different stories *that* possibly may save us."

"I see what you mean. It would perhaps, as an oddity, have a success of curiosity. It might become a draw. Still, They but want broad masses." And he looked at her sadly. "You're no more than one of Them."

"If it's being no more than one of Them to love it," she answered, "then I certainly am. And I'm not ashamed of my company."

"To love *what?*" said Morris Gedge.

"To love to think He was born there."

"You think too much. It's bad for you." He turned away with his chronic moan. But it was without losing what she called after him.

"I decline to let the place down." And what was there indeed to say? They *were* there to keep it up.

V

HE KEPT it up through the summer, but with the queerest consciousness, at times, of the want of proportion between his secret rage and the spirit of those from whom the friction came. He said to himself—so sore his sensibility had grown—that They were gregariously ferocious at the very time he was seeing Them as individually mild. He said to himself that They were mild only because *he* was—he flattered himself that he was divinely so, considering what he might be; and that he should, as his wife had warned him, soon enough have news of it were he to deflect by a hair's breadth from the line traced for him. *That* was the collective fatuity—that it was capable of turning on the instant both to a general and to a particular resentment. Since the least breath of discrimination would get him the sack without mercy, it was absurd, he reflected, to speak of his discomfort as light. He was gagged, he was goaded, as in omnivorous companies he doubtless sometimes showed by a strange silent glare. They'd get him the sack for that as well, if he didn't look out; therefore wasn't it in effect ferocity when you mightn't even hold your tongue? They wouldn't let you off with silence—They insisted on your committing yourself. It was the pound of flesh—They *would* have it; so under his coat he bled. But a wondrous peace, by exception, dropped on him one afternoon at the end of August. The pressure had, as usual, been high, but it had diminished with the fall of day, and the place was empty before the hour for closing. Then it was that, within a few minutes of this hour, there presented themselves a pair of pilgrims to whom in the ordinary course he would have remarked that they were, to his regret, too late. He was to wonder afterwards why the course had at sight of the visitors—a gentleman and a lady, appealing and fairly young—shown for him as other than ordinary; the consequence sprang doubtless from something rather fine and unnameable, something for example in the tone of the young man or in the light of his eye, after hearing the statement on the subject of the hour. "Yes, we know it's late; but it's just, I'm afraid, *because* of that. We've had rather a notion of escaping the crowd—as I suppose you mostly have one now; and it was really on the chance of finding you alone—!"

These things the young man said before being quite admitted, and they were words any one might have spoken who hadn't taken the trouble to be punctual or who desired, a little ingratiatingly, to force the door. Gedge even guessed at the sense that might lurk in them, the hint of a special tip if the point were stretched. There were no tips, he had often thanked his stars, at the Birthplace; there was the charged fee and nothing more; everything else was out of order, to the relief of a palm not formed by nature as a scoop. Yet in spite of everything, in spite especially of the almost audible chink of the gentleman's sovereigns, which might in another case exactly have put him out, he presently found him-

self, in the Birthroom, access to which he had gracefully enough
granted, almost treating the visit as personal and private. The
reason—well, the reason would have been, if anywhere, in something naturally persuasive on the part of the couple; unless it had
been rather again, in the way the young man, once he was in the
place, met the caretaker's expression of face, held it a moment
and seemed to wish to sound it. That they were Americans was
promptly clear, and Gedge could very nearly have told what kind;
he had arrived at the point of distinguishing kinds, though the
difficulty might have been with him now that the case before him
was rare. He saw it suddenly in the light of the golden midland
evening which reached them through low old windows, saw it with
a rush of feeling, unexpected and smothered, that made him a moment wish to keep it before him as a case of inordinate happiness.
It made him feel old shabby poor, but he watched it no less intensely for its doing so. They were children of fortune, of the
greatest, as it might seem to Morris Gedge, and they were of
course lately married; the husband, smooth-faced and soft, but
resolute and fine, several years older than the wife, and the wife
vaguely, delicately, irregularly, but mercilessly pretty. Somehow
the world was theirs; they gave the person who took the sixpences
at the Birthplace such a sense of the high luxury of freedom as he
had never had. The thing was that the world was theirs not simply
because they had money—he had seen rich people enough—but
because they could in a supreme degree think and feel and say
what they liked. They had a nature and a culture, a tradition, a
facility of some sort—and all producing in them an effect of positive beauty—that gave a light to their liberty and an ease to their
tone. These things moreover suffered nothing from the fact that
they happened to be in mourning; this was probably worn for
some lately-deceased opulent father—if not some delicate mother
who would be sure to have been a part of the source of the beauty;
and it affected Gedge, in the gathered twilight and at his odd
crisis, as the very uniform of their distinction.

He couldn't quite have said afterwards by what steps the point
had been reached, but it had become at the end of five minutes a

part of their presence in the Birthroom, a part of the young man's look, a part of the charm of the moment, and a part above all of a strange sense within him of "Now or never!" that Gedge had suddenly, thrillingly, let himself go. He hadn't been definitely conscious of drifting to it; he had been, for that, too conscious merely of thinking how different, in all their range, were such a united couple from another united couple known to him. They were everything he and his wife weren't; this was more than anything else the first lesson of their talk. Thousands of couples of whom the same was true certainly had passed before him, but none of whom it was true with just that engaging intensity. And just *because* of their transcendent freedom; that was what, at the end of five minutes, he saw it all come back to. The husband, who had been there at some earlier time, had his impression, which he wished now to make his wife share. But he already, Gedge could see, hadn't concealed it from her. A pleasant irony in fine our friend seemed to taste in the air—he who hadn't yet felt free to taste his own.

"I think you weren't here four years ago"—that was what the young man had almost begun by remarking. Gedge liked his remembering it, liked his frankly speaking to him; all the more that he had offered, as it were, no opening. He had let them look about below and then had taken them up, but without words, without the usual showman's song, of which he would have been afraid. The visitors didn't ask for it; the young man had taken the matter out of his hands by himself dropping for the benefit of the young woman a few detached remarks. What Gedge oddly felt was that these remarks were not inconsiderate of him; he had heard others, both of the priggish order and the crude, that might have been called so. And as the young man hadn't been aided to this cognition of him as new, it already began to make for them a certain common ground. The ground became immense when the visitor presently added with a smile: "There was a good lady, I recollect, who had a great deal to say."

It was the gentleman's smile that had done it; the irony *was* there. "Ah there had been a great deal said." And Gedge's look at his interlocutor doubtless showed his sense of being sounded. It was extraordinary of course that a perfect stranger should have guessed the travail of his spirit, should have caught the gleam of his inner commentary. That probably leaked in spite of him out of his poor old eyes. "Much of it, in such places as this," he heard himself adding, "is of course said very irresponsibly." *Such places as this!*—he winced at the words as soon as he had uttered them.

There was no wincing, however, on the part of his pleasant companions. "Exactly so; the whole thing becomes a sort of stiff smug convention—like a dressed-up sacred doll in a Spanish church—which you're a monster if you touch."

"A monster," Gedge assented, meeting his eyes.

The young man smiled, but he thought looking at him a little harder. "A blasphemer."

"A blasphemer."

It seemed to do his visitor good—he certainly *was* looking at him harder. Detached as he was he was interested—he was at least amused. "Then you don't claim or at any rate don't insist—? I mean you personally."

He had an identity for him, Gedge felt, that he couldn't have had for a Briton, and the impulse was quick in our friend to testify to this perception. "I don't insist to *you*."

The young man laughed. "It really—I assure you if I may—wouldn't do any good. I'm too awfully interested."

"Do you mean," his wife lightly enquired, "in—a—pulling it down? That's rather in what you've said to me."

"Has he said to you," Gedge intervened, though quaking a little, "that he would like to pull it down?"

She met, in her free sweetness, this appeal with such a charm! "Oh perhaps not quite the *house*—!"

"Good. You see we live on it—I mean *we* people."

The husband laughed, but had now so completely ceased to look about him that there seemed nothing left for him but to talk avowedly with the caretaker. "I'm interested," he explained, "in what I think *the* interesting thing—or at all events the eternally tormenting one. The fact of the abysmally little that, in proportion, we know."

"In proportion to what?" his companion asked.

"Well, to what there must have been—to what in fact there *is*—to wonder about. That's the interest; it's immense. He escapes us like a thief at night, carrying off—well, carrying off everything. And people pretend to catch Him like a flown canary, over whom you can close your hand, and put Him back in the cage. He won't *go* back; he won't *come* back. He's not"—the young man laughed —"such a fool! It makes Him the happiest of all great men."

He had begun by speaking to his wife, but had ended, with his friendly, his easy, his indescribable competence, for Gedge—poor Gedge who quite held his breath and who felt, in the most unexpected way, that he had somehow never been in such good society. The young wife, who for herself meanwhile had continued to look about, sighed out, smiled out—Gedge couldn't have told which—her little answer to these remarks. "It's rather a pity, you know, that He *isn't* here. I mean as Goethe's at Weimar. For Goethe *is* at Weimar."

"Yes, my dear; that's Goethe's bad luck. There he sticks. *This* man isn't anywhere. I defy you to catch Him."

"Why not say, beautifully," the young woman laughed, "that, like the wind, He's everywhere?"

It wasn't of course the tone of discussion, it was the tone of pleasantry, though of better pleasantry, Gedge seemed to feel, and more within his own appreciation, than he had ever listened to; and this was precisely why the young man could go on without the effect of irritation, answering his wife but still with eyes for their companion. "I'll be hanged if He's *here!*"

It was almost as if he were taken—that is, struck and rather held —by their companion's unruffled state, which they hadn't meant to ruffle, but which suddenly presented its interest, perhaps even projected its light. The gentleman didn't know, Gedge was afterwards to say to himself, how that hypocrite was inwardly all of a tremble, how it seemed to him his fate was being literally pulled down on his head. He was trembling for the moment certainly too much to speak; abject he might be, but he didn't want his voice to have the absurdity of a quaver. And the young woman —charming creature!—still had another word. It was for the guardian of the spot, and she made it in her way delightful. They had remained in the Holy of Holies, where she had been looking for a minute, with a ruefulness just marked enough to be pretty, at the queer old floor. "Then if you say it *wasn't* in this room He was born—well, what's the use?"

"What's the use of what?" her husband asked. "The use, you mean, of our coming here? Why the place is charming in itself. And it's also interesting," he added to Gedge, "to know how you get on."

Gedge looked at him a moment in silence, but answering the young woman first. If poor Isabel, he was thinking, could only have been like that!—not as to youth, beauty, arrangement of hair or picturesque grace of hat—these things he didn't mind; but as to sympathy, facility, light perceptive, and yet not cheap, detachment! "I don't say it wasn't—but I don't say it *was*."

"Ah but doesn't that," she returned, "come very much to the same thing? And don't They want also to see where He had His dinner and where He had His tea?"

"They want everything," said Morris Gedge. "They want to see where He hung up His hat and where He kept His boots and where His mother boiled her pot."

"But if you don't show them—?"

"They show *me*. It's in all their little books."

"You mean," the husband asked, "that you've only to hold your tongue?"

"I try to," said Gedge.

"Well," his visitor smiled, "I see you *can*."

Gedge hesitated. "I can't."

"Oh well," said his friend, "what does it matter?"

"I do speak," he continued. "I can't sometimes not."

"Then how do you get on?"

Gedge looked at him more abjectly, to his own sense, than ever at any one—even at Isabel when she frightened him. "I don't get on. I speak," he said—"since I've spoken to *you*."

"Oh *we* shan't hurt you!" the young man reassuringly laughed.

The twilight meanwhile had sensibly thickened, the end of the visit was indicated. They turned together out of the upper room and came down the narrow stair. The words just exchanged might have been felt as producing an awkwardness which the young woman gracefully felt the impulse to dissipate. "You must rather wonder why we've come." And it was the first note for Gedge of a further awkwardness—as if he had definitely heard it make the husband's hand, in a full pocket, begin to fumble.

It was even a little awkwardly that the husband still held off. "Oh we like it as it is. There's always *something*." With which they had approached the door of egress.

"What is there, please?" asked Morris Gedge, not yet opening the door, since he would fain have kept the pair on, and conscious only for a moment after he had spoken that his question was just having for the young man too dreadfully wrong a sound. This personage wondered yet feared, and had evidently for some minutes been putting himself a question; so that, with his preoccupation, the caretaker's words had represented to him inevitably: "What is there, please, for *me?*" Gedge already knew with it moreover that he wasn't stopping him in time. He had uttered that challenge to show he himself wasn't afraid, and he must have had in consequence, he was subsequently to reflect, a lamentable air of waiting.

The visitor's hand came out. "I hope I may take the liberty—?" What afterwards happened our friend scarcely knew, for it fell into a slight confusion, the confusion of a queer gleam of gold—a sovereign fairly thrust at him; of a quick, almost violent motion on his own part, which, to make the matter worse, might well have sent the money rolling on the floor; and then of marked blushes all round and a sensible embarrassment; producing indeed in turn rather oddly and ever so quickly an increase of communion. It was as if the young man had offered him money to make up to him for having, as it were, led him on, and then, perceiving the mistake, but liking him the better for his refusal, had wanted to obliterate this aggravation of his original wrong. He had done so, presently, while Gedge got the door open, by saying the best thing he could, and by saying it frankly and gaily. "Luckily it doesn't at all affect the *work!*"

The small town-street, quiet and empty in the summer eventide, stretched to right and left, with a gabled and timbered house or two, and fairly seemed to have cleared itself to congruity with the historic void over which our friends, lingering an instant to converse, looked at each other. The young wife, rather, looked about a moment at all there wasn't to be seen, and then, before Gedge had found a reply to her husband's remark, uttered, evidently in the interest of conciliation, a little question of her own that she tried to make earnest. "It's our unfortunate ignorance, you mean, that doesn't?"

"Unfortunate or fortunate. I like it so," said the husband. " 'The play's the thing.' Let the author alone."

Gedge, with his key on his forefinger, leaned against the door-post, took in the stupid little street and was sorry to see them go —they seemed so to abandon him. "That's just what They won't do—nor let *me* do. It's all I want—to let the author alone. Practically"—he felt himself getting the last of his chance— "there *is* no author; that is for us to deal with. There are all the immortal people—*in* the work; but there's nobody else."

"Yes," said the young man—"that's what it comes to. There should really, to clear the matter up, be no such Person."

"As you say," Gedge returned, "it's what it comes to. There *is* no such Person."

The evening air listened, in the warm thick midland stillness, while the wife's little cry rang out. "But *wasn't* there—?"

"There was somebody," said Gedge against the door-post. "But They've killed Him. And, dead as He is, They keep it up, They do it over again, They kill Him every day."

He was aware of saying this so grimly—more than he wished —that his companions exchanged a glance and even perhaps looked as if they felt him extravagant. That was really the way Isabel had warned him all the others would be looking if he should talk to Them as he talked to *her*. He liked, however, for that matter, to hear how he should sound when pronounced incapable through deterioration of the brain. "Then if there's no author, if there's nothing to be said but that there isn't anybody," the young woman smilingly asked, "why in the world should there be a house?"

"There shouldn't," said Morris Gedge.

Decidedly, yes, he affected the young man. "Oh, I don't say, mind you, that you should pull it down!"

"Then where would you *go?*" their companion sweetly enquired.

"That's what my wife asks," Gedge returned.

"Then keep it up, keep it up!" And the husband held out his hand.

"That's what my wife says," Gedge went on as he shook it.

The young woman, charming creature, emulated the other visitor; she offered their remarkable friend her handshake. "Then mind your wife."

The poor man faced her gravely. "I would if she were such a wife as you!"

VI

IT HAD made for him, all the same, an immense difference; it had given him an extraordinary lift, so that a certain sweet aftertaste of his freedom might a couple of months later have been suspected of aiding to produce for him another and really a more considerable adventure. It was an absurd way to reason, but he had been, to his imagination, for twenty minutes in good society —that being the term that best described for him the company of people to whom he hadn't to talk, as he phrased it, rot. It was his title to good society that he had, in his doubtless awkward way affirmed; and the difficulty was just that, having affirmed it, he couldn't take back the affirmation. Few things had happened to him in life, that is few that were agreeable, but at least *this* had, and he wasn't so constructed that he could go on as if it hadn't. It was going on as if it had, however, that landed him,

alas! in the situation unmistakeably marked by a visit from
Grant-Jackson late one afternoon toward the end of October. This
had been the hour of the call of the young Americans. Every day
that hour had come round something of the deep throb of it, the
successful secret, woke up; but the two occasions were, of a truth,
related only by being so intensely opposed. The secret had been
successful in that he had said nothing of it to Isabel, who, occupied in their own quarter while the incident lasted, had neither
heard the visitors arrive nor seen them depart. It was on the other
hand scarcely successful in guarding itself from indirect betrayals.
There were two persons in the world at least who felt as he did;
they were persons also who had treated him, benignly, as feeling
after *their* style; who had been ready in fact to overflow in gifts
as a sign of it, and though they were now off in space they were
still with him sufficiently in spirit to make him play, as it were,
with the sense of their sympathy. This in turn made him, as he
was perfectly aware, more than a shade or two reckless, so that, in
his reaction from that gluttony of the public for false facts which
had from the first tormented him, he fell into the habit of sailing,
as he would have said, too near the wind, or in other words—all in
presence of the people—of washing his hands of the legend. He
had crossed the line—he knew it; he had struck wild—They drove
him to it; he had substituted, by a succession of uncontrollable
profanities, an attitude that couldn't be understood for an attitude
that but too evidently *had* been.

This was of course the franker line, only he hadn't taken it,
alas! for frankness—hadn't in the least really adopted it at all,
but had been simply himself caught up and disposed of by it,
hurled by his fate against the bedizened walls of the temple, quite
in the way of a priest possessed to excess of the god, or, more vulgarly, that of a blind bull in a china-shop—an animal to which he
often compared himself. He had let himself fatally go, in fine, just
for irritation, for rage, having, in his predicament, nothing whatever to do with frankness—a luxury reserved for quite other situations. It had always been his view that one lived to learn; he had
learned something every hour of his life, though people mostly

never knew what, in spite of its having generally been—hadn't it?—at somebody's expense. What he was at present continually learning was the sense of a form of words heretofore so vain— the famous "false position" that had so often helped out a phrase. One used names in that way without knowing what they were worth; then of a sudden, one fine day, their meaning grew bitter in the mouth. This was a truth with the relish of which his fire- side hours were occupied, and he was aware of how much it ex- posed a man to look so perpetually as if something had disagreed with him. The look to be worn at the Birthplace was properly the beatific, and when once it had fairly been missed by those who took it for granted, who indeed paid sixpence for it—like the table-wine in provincial France it was *compris*—one would be sure to have news of the remark.

News accordingly was what Gedge had been expecting—and what he knew, above all, had been expected by his wife, who had a way of sitting at present as with an ear for a certain knock. She didn't watch him, didn't follow him about the house, at the public hours, to spy upon his treachery; and that could touch him even though her averted eyes went through him more than her fixed. Her mistrust was so perfectly expressed by her manner of showing she trusted that he never felt so nervous, never tried so to keep straight, as when she most let him alone. When the crowd thick- ened and they had of necessity to receive together he tried him- self to get off by allowing her as much as possible the word. When people appealed to him he turned to her—and with more of cere- mony than their relation warranted: he couldn't help *this* either, if it seemed ironic—as to the person most concerned or most com- petent. He flattered himself at these moments that no one would have guessed her being his wife; especially as, to do her justice, she met his manner with a wonderful grim bravado—grim, so to say, for himself, grim by its outrageous cheerfulness for the simple-minded. The lore she *did* produce for them, the associa- tions of the sacred spot she developed, multiplied, embroidered; the things in short she said and the stupendous way she said them! She wasn't a bit ashamed, since why need virtue be ever ashamed?

It *was* virtue, for it put bread into his mouth—he meanwhile on his side taking it out of hers. He had seen Grant-Jackson on the October day in the Birthplace itself—the right setting of course for such an interview; and what had occurred was that, precisely, when the scene had ended and he had come back to their own sitting-room, the question she put to him for information was: "Have you settled it that I'm to starve?"

She had for a long time said nothing to him so straight—which was but a proof of her real anxiety; the straightness of Grant-Jackson's visit, following on the very slight sinuosity of a note shortly before received from him, made tension show for what it was. By this time, really, however, his decision had been taken; the minutes elapsing between his reappearance at the domestic fireside and his having, from the other threshold, seen Grant-Jackson's broad well-fitted back, the back of a banker and a patriot, move away, had, though few, presented themselves to him as supremely critical. They formed, as it were, the hinge of his door, that door actually ajar so as to show him a possible fate beyond it, but which, with his hand, in a spasm, thus tightening on the knob, he might either open wide or close partly or altogether. He stood at autumn dusk in the little museum that constituted the vestibule of the temple, and there, as with a concentrated push at the crank of a windlass, he brought himself round. The portraits on the walls seemed vaguely to watch for it; it was in their august presence—kept dimly august for the moment by Grant-Jackson's impressive check of his application of a match to the vulgar gas—that the great man had uttered, as if it said all, his "You know, my dear fellow, really—!" He had managed it with the special tact of a fat man, always, when there *was* any, very fine; he had got the most out of the time, the place, the setting, all the little massed admonitions and symbols; confronted there with his victim on the spot that he took occasion to name afresh as, to *his* piety and patriotism, the most sacred on earth, he had given it to be understood that in the first place he was lost in amazement and that in the second he expected a single warning now to suffice. Not to insist too much moreover on the question of gratitude, he would let his remonstrance rest, if need be, solely on the question of taste. *As* a matter of taste alone—! But he was surely not to be obliged to follow that up. Poor Gedge indeed would have been sorry to oblige him, for he saw it was exactly to the atrocious taste of unthankfulness the allusion was made. When he said he wouldn't dwell on what the fortunate occupant of the post owed him for the stout battle originally fought on his behalf, he simply meant he *would*. That was his tact—which, with everything else that has been mentioned, in the scene, to help, really had the ground to itself. The day *had* been when Gedge couldn't have thanked him enough—though he had thanked him, he considered, almost fulsomely—and nothing, nothing that he could coherently or reputably name, had happened since then. From the moment he was pulled up, in short, he had no case, and if he exhibited, instead of one, only hot tears in his eyes, the mystic gloom of the temple either prevented his friend from seeing them or rendered it possible that they stood for remorse. He had dried them, with the pads formed by the base of his bony thumbs, before he went in to Isabel. This was the more fortunate as, in spite of her enquiry, prompt and pointed, he but moved about the room looking at her hard. Then he stood before the fire a little with his hands behind him and his coat-tails divided, quite as the person in permanent possession. It was an indication his wife appeared to take in; but she put nevertheless presently another question. "You object to telling me what he said?"

"He said 'You know, my dear fellow, really—!'"

"And is that all?"

"Practically. Except that I'm a thankless beast."

"Well!" she responded, not with dissent.

"You mean that I *am?*"

"Are those the words he used?" she asked with a scruple.

Gedge continued to think. "The words he used were that I give away the Show and that, from several sources, it has come round to Them."

"As of course a baby would have known!" And then as her husband said nothing: "Were *those* the words he used?"

"Absolutely. He couldn't have used better ones."

"Did he call it," Mrs. Gedge enquired, "the 'Show'?"

"Of course he did. The Biggest on Earth."

She winced, looking at him hard—she wondered, but only for a moment. "Well, it *is*."

"Then it's something," Gedge went on, "to have given *that* away. But," he added, "I've taken it back."

"You mean you've been convinced?"

"I mean I've been scared."

"At last, at last!" she gratefully breathed.

"Oh it was easily done. It was only two words. But here I am."

Her face was now less hard for him. "And what two words?"

" 'You know, Mr. Gedge, that it simply won't do.' That was all. But it was the way such a man says them."

"I'm glad then," Mrs. Gedge frankly averred, "that he *is* such a man. How did you ever think it *could* do?"

"Well, it was my critical sense. I didn't ever know I had one —till They came and (by putting me here) waked it up in me. Then I had somehow, don't you see? to live with it; and I seemed to feel that, with one thing and another, giving it time and in the long run, it might, it *ought* to, come out on top of the heap. Now that's where, he says, it simply won't 'do.' So I must put it—I *have* put it—at the bottom."

"A very good place then for a critical sense!" And Isabel, more placidly now, folded her work. "*If*, that is, you can only keep it there. If it doesn't struggle up again."

"It can't struggle." He was still before the fire, looking round at the warm low room, peaceful in the lamplight, with the hum of the kettle for the ear, with the curtain drawn over the leaded casement, a short moreen curtain artfully chosen by Isabel for the effect of the olden time, its virtue of letting the light within show ruddy to the street. "It's dead," he went on; "I killed it just now."

He really spoke so that she wondered. "Just now?"

"There in the other place—I strangled it, poor thing, in the dark. If you'll go out and see, there must be blood. Which, indeed," he added, "on an altar of sacrifice, is all right. But the place is for ever spattered."

"I don't want to go out and see." She locked her hands over the needlework folded on her knee, and he knew, with her eyes on him, that a look he had seen before was in her face. "You're off your head, you know, my dear, in a way." Then, however, more cheeringly: "It's a good job it hasn't been too late."

"Too late to get it under?"

"Too late for Them to give you the second chance that I thank God you accept."

"Yes, if it *had* been—!" And he looked away as through the ruddy curtain and into the chill street. Then he faced her again. "I've scarcely got over my fright yet. I mean," he went on, "for you."

"And I mean for *you*. Suppose what you had come to announce to me now were that we had *got* the sack. How should I enjoy, do you think, seeing you turned out? Yes, out *there!*" she added as his eyes again moved from their little warm circle to the night of early winter on the other side of the pane, to the rare quick footsteps, to the closed doors, to the curtains drawn like their own, behind which the small flat town, intrinsically dull, was sitting down to supper.

He stiffened himself as he warmed his back; he held up his head, shaking himself a little as if to shake the stoop out of his shoulders, but he had to allow she was right. "What would have become of us?"

"What indeed? We should have begged our bread—or I should be taking in washing."

He was silent a little. "I'm too old. I should have begun sooner."

"Oh God forbid!" she cried.

"The pinch," he pursued, "is that I can do nothing else."

"Nothing whatever!" she agreed with elation.

"Whereas here—if I cultivate it—I perhaps *can* still lie. But I must cultivate it."

"Oh you old dear!" And she got up to kiss him.

"I'll do my best," he said.

VII

"Do you remember us?" the gentleman asked and smiled—with the lady beside him smiling too; speaking so much less as an earnest pilgrim or as a tiresome tourist than as an old acquaintance. It was history repeating itself as Gedge had somehow never expected, with almost everything the same except that the evening was now a mild April-end, except that the visitors had put off mourning and showed all their bravery—besides showing, as he doubtless did himself, though so differently, for a little older; except, above all, that—oh seeing them again suddenly affected him not a bit as the thing he'd have supposed it. "We're in England again and we were near; I've a brother at Oxford with whom we've been spending a day, so that we thought we'd come over." This the young man pleasantly said while our friend took in the queer fact that he must himself seem to them rather coldly to gape. They had come in the same way at the quiet close; another August had passed, and this was the second spring; the Birthplace, given the hour, was about to suspend operations till the morrow; the last lingerer had gone and the fancy of the visitors was once more for a look round by themselves. This represented surely no greater presumption than the terms on which they had last parted with him seemed to warrant; so that if he did inconsequently stare it was just in fact because he was so supremely far from having forgotten them. But the sight of the pair luckily had a double effect, and the first precipitated the second—the second being really his sudden vision that everything perhaps depended for him on his recognising no complication. He must go straight on, since it was what had for more than a year now so handsomely answered; he must brazen it out consistently, since that only was what his dignity was at last reduced to. He mustn't be afraid in one way any more than he had been in another; besides which it came over him to the point of his flushing for it that their visit, in its essence, must have been for himself. It was good society again, and *they* were the same. It wasn't for him therefore to behave as if he couldn't meet them.

These deep vibrations, on Gedge's part, were as quick as they were deep; they came in fact all at once, so that his response, his declaration that it was all right—"Oh *rather;* the hour doesn't matter for *you!*"—had hung fire but an instant; and when they were well across the threshold and the door closed behind them, housed in the twilight of the temple, where, as before, the votive offerings glimmered on the walls, he drew the long breath of one who might by a self-betrayal have done something too dreadful. For what had brought them back was indubitably not the glamour of the shrine itself—since he had had a glimpse of their analysis of that quantity; but their critical (not to say their sentimental) interest in the queer case of the priest. Their call was the tribute of curiosity, of sympathy, of a compassion really, as such things went, exquisite—a tribute *to* that queerness which entitled them to the frankest welcome. They had wanted, for the generous wonder of it, to judge how he was getting on, how such a man in such a place *could;* and they had doubtless more than half-expected to see the door opened by somebody who had succeeded him. Well, somebody *had*—only with a strange equivocation; as they would have, poor things, to make out themselves, an embarrassment for which he pitied them. Nothing could have been more odd, but verily it was this troubled vision of their possible bewilderment, and this compunctious view of such a return for their amenity, that practically determined in him his tone. The lapse of the months had but made their name familiar to him; they had on the other occasion inscribed it, among the thousand names, in the current public register, and he had since then, for reasons of his own, reasons of feeling, again and again turned back to it. It was nothing in itself; it told him nothing—"Mr. and Mrs. B. D. Hayes, New York"—one of those American labels that were just like every other American label and that were precisely the most remarkable thing about people reduced to achieving an identity in such other ways. They could be Mr. and Mrs. B. D. Hayes and yet could be, with all presumptions missing—well, what these callers were. It had quickly enough indeed cleared the situation a little further that his friends had absolutely, the other time, as it came back to him, warned him of his original danger, their anxiety about which had been the last note sounded among them. What he was afraid of, with this reminiscence, was that, finding him still safe, they would, the next thing, definitely congratulate him and perhaps even, no less candidly, ask him how he had managed. It was with the sense of nipping some such enquiry in the bud that, losing no time and holding himself with a firm grip, he began on the spot, downstairs, to make plain to them how he had managed. He routed the possibility of the question in short by the assurance of his answer. "Yes, yes, I'm still here; I suppose it *is* in a manner to one's profit that one does, such as it is, one's best." He did his best on the present occasion, did it with the gravest face he had ever worn and a soft serenity that was like a large damp sponge passed over their previous meeting—over everything in it, that is, but the fact of its pleasantness.

"We stand here, you see, in the old living-room, happily still to be reconstructed in the mind's eye, in spite of the havoc of time, which we have fortunately of late years been able to arrest. It was of course rude and humble, but it must have been snug and quaint, and we have at least the pleasure of knowing that the tradition in respect to the features that do remain is delightfully uninterrupted. Across that threshold He habitually passed; through those low windows, in childhood, He peered out into the world that He was to make so much happier by the gift to it of His genius; over the boards of this floor—that is over *some* of them, for we mustn't be carried away!—his little feet often pattered; and the beams of this ceiling (we must really in some places take care of *our* heads!) he endeavoured, in boyish strife, to jump up and touch. It's not often that in the early home of genius and renown the whole tenor of existence is laid so bare, not often that we are able to retrace, from point to point and from step to step, its connexion with objects, with influences—to build it round

again with the little solid facts out of which it sprang. This therefore, I need scarcely remind you, is what makes the small space
between these walls—so modest to measurement, so insignificant
of aspect—unique on all the earth. *There's nothing like it,*" Morris
Gedge went on, insisting as solemnly and softly, for his bewildered
hearers, as over a pulpit-edge; "there's nothing at all like it anywhere in the world. There's nothing, only reflect, for the combina-
tion of greatness and, as we venture to say, of intimacy. You may
find elsewhere perhaps absolutely fewer changes, but where shall
you find a *Presence* equally diffused, uncontested and undisturbed? Where in particular shall you find, on the part of the abid-
ing spirit, an equally towering eminence? You may find elsewhere
eminence of a considerable order, but where shall you find *with*
it, don't you see, changes after all so few and the contemporary
element caught so, as it were, in the very fact?" His visitors, at
first confounded but gradually spellbound, were still gaping with
the universal gape—wondering, he judged, into what strange
pleasantry he had been suddenly moved to explode, and yet beginning to see in him an intention beyond a joke, so that they
started, at this point, they almost jumped, when, by as rapid a
transition, he made, toward the old fireplace, a dash that seemed
to illustrate precisely the act of eager catching. "It is in this old
chimney-corner, the quaint inglenook of our ancestors—just there
in the far angle, where His little stool was placed, and where, I
dare say, if we could look close enough, we should find the hearth-
stone scraped with His little feet—that we see the inconceivable
child gazing into the blaze of the old oaken logs and making out
there pictures and stories, see Him conning, with curly bent head,
His well-worn hornbook, or poring over some scrap of an ancient
ballad, some page of some such rudely-bound volume of chronicles
as lay, we may be sure, in His father's window-seat."

It was, he even himself felt at this moment, wonderfully done;
no auditors, for all his thousands, had ever yet so inspired him.
The odd slightly alarmed shyness in the two faces, as if in a
drawing-room, in their "good society" exactly, some act incon-
gruous, something grazing the indecent, had abruptly been per-

petrated, the painful reality of which stayed itself before coming home—the visible effect on his friends in fine wound him up as to the sense that *they* were worth the trick. It came of itself now—he had got it so by heart; but perhaps really it had never come so well, with the staleness so disguised, the interest so renewed and the clerical unction demanded by the priestly character so successfully distilled. Mr. Hayes of New York had more than once looked at his wife, and Mrs. Hayes of New York had more than once looked at her husband—only, up to now, with a stolen glance, with eyes it hadn't been easy to detach from the remarkable countenance by the aid of which their entertainer held them. At present, however, after an exchange less furtive, they ventured on a sign that they hadn't been appealed to in vain. "Charming, charming, Mr. Gedge!" Mr. Hayes broke out. "We feel that we've caught you in the mood."

His wife hastened to assent—it eased the tension. "It *would* be quite the way; except," she smiled, "that you'd be too dangerous. You've really a genius!"

Gedge looked at her hard, but yielding no inch, even though she touched him there at a point of consciousness that quivered. This was the prodigy for him, and had been, the year through—that he did it all, he found, easily, did it better than he had done anything else in life; with so high and broad an effect, in truth, an inspiration so rich and free, that his poor wife now, literally, had been moved more than once to fresh fear. She had had her bad moments, he knew, after taking the measure of his new direction—moments of readjusted suspicion in which she wondered if he hadn't simply adopted another, a different perversity. There would be more than one fashion of giving away the Show, and wasn't *this* perhaps a question of giving it away by excess? He could dish them by too much romance as well as by too little; she hadn't hitherto fairly grasped that there might *be* too much. It was a way like another, at any rate, of reducing the place to the absurd; which reduction, if he didn't look out, would reduce *them* again to the prospect of the streets, and this time surely without appeal. It all depended indeed—he knew she knew that—

on how much Grant-Jackson and the others, how much the Body, in a word, would take. He knew she knew what he himself held it would take—that he considered no limit could be imputed to the quantity. They simply wanted it piled up, and so did every one else; wherefore if no one reported him as before why were They to be uneasy? It was in consequence of idiots tempted to reason that he had been dealt with before; but as there was now no form of idiocy that he didn't systematically flatter, goading it on really to its *own* private doom, who was ever to pull the string of the guillotine? The axe was in the air—yes; but in a world gorged to satiety there were no revolutions. And it had been vain for Isabel to ask if the other thunder-growl also hadn't come out of the blue. There was actually proof positive that the winds were now at rest. How could they be more so?—he appealed to the receipts. These were golden days—the Show had never so flourished. So he had argued, so he was arguing still—and, it had to be owned, with every appearance in his favour. Yet if he inwardly winced at the tribute to his plausibility rendered by his flushed friends, this was because he felt in it the real ground of his optimism. The charming woman before him acknowledged his "genius" as he himself had had to do. He had been surprised at his facility until he had grown used to it. Whether or no he had, as a fresh menace to his future, found a new perversity, he had found a vocation much older, evidently, than he had at first been prepared to recognise. He had done himself injustice. He liked to be brave because it came so easy; he could measure it off by the yard. It was in the Birthroom, above all, that he continued to do this, having ushered up his companions without, as he was still more elated to feel, the turn of a hair. She might take it as she liked, but he had had the lucidity—all, that is, for his own safety—to meet without the grace of an answer the homage of her beautiful smile. She took it apparently, and her husband took it, but as a part of his odd humour, and they followed him aloft with faces now a little more responsive to the manner in which on *that* spot he would naturally come out. He came out, according to the word of his assured private receipt, "strong." He missed a little, in truth, the usual round-eyed question from them—the inveterate artless cue with which, from moment to moment, clustered troops had for a year obliged him. Mr. and Mrs. Hayes were from New York, but it was a little like singing, as he had heard one of his Americans once say about something, to a Boston audience. He did none the less what he could, and it was ever his practice to stop still at a certain spot in the room and, after having secured attention by look and gesture, suddenly shoot off: "Here!"

They always understood, the good people—he could fairly love them now for it; they always said breathlessly and unanimously "There?" and stared down at the designated point quite as if some trace of the grand event were still to be made out. This movement produced he again looked round. "Consider it well: *the* spot of earth—!" "Oh but it isn't *earth!*" the boldest spirit—there was always a boldest—would generally pipe out. Then the guardian of the Birthplace would be truly superior—as if the unfortunate had figured the Immortal coming up, like a potato, through the soil. "I'm not suggesting that He was born on the bare ground. He was born *here!*"—with an uncompromising dig of his heel. "There ought to be a brass, with an inscription, let in." "Into the floor?" —it always came. "Birth and burial: seedtime, summer, autumn!" —that always, with its special right cadence, thanks to his unfailing spring, came too. "Why not as well as into the pavement of the church?—you've *seen* our grand old church?" The former of which questions nobody ever answered—abounding, on the other hand, to make up, in relation to the latter. Mr. and Mrs. Hayes even were at first left dumb by it—not indeed, to do them justice, having uttered the word that called for it. They had uttered no word while he kept the game up, and (though that made it a little more difficult) he could yet stand triumphant before them after he had finished with his flourish. Only then it was that Mr. Hayes of New York broke silence.

"Well, if we wanted to see I think I may say we're quite satisfied. As my wife says, it *would* seem your line." He spoke now, visibly, with more ease, as if a light had come: though he made no joke of it, for a reason that presently appeared. They were coming down the little stair, and it was on the descent that his companion added her word.

"Do you know what we half *did* think—?" And then to her husband: "Is it dreadful to tell him?" They were in the room below, and the young woman, also relieved, expressed the feeling with gaiety. She smiled as before at Morris Gedge, treating him as a person with whom relations were possible, yet remaining just uncertain enough to invoke Mr. Hayes's opinion. "We *have* awfully wanted—from what we had heard." But she met her husband's graver face; he was not quite out of the wood. At this she was slightly flurried—but she cut it short. "You must know—don't you?—that, with the crowds who listen to you, we'd have heard."

He looked from one to the other, and once more again, with force, something came over him. They had kept him in mind, they were neither ashamed nor afraid to show it, and it was positively an interest on the part of this charming creature and this keen cautious gentleman, an interesting resisting oblivion and surviving separation, that had governed their return. Their other visit had been the brightest thing that had ever happened to him, but this was the gravest; so that at the end of a minute something broke in him and his mask dropped of itself. He chucked, as he would have said, consistency; which, in its extinction, left the tears in his eyes. His smile was therefore queer. "Heard how I'm going it?"

The young man, though still looking at him hard, felt sure, with this, of his own ground. "Of course you're tremendously talked about. You've gone round the world."

"You've heard of me in America?"

"Why almost of nothing else!"

"That was what made us feel—!" Mrs. Hayes contributed.

"That you must see for yourselves?" Again he compared, poor Gedge, their faces. "Do you mean I excite—a—scandal?"

"Dear no! Admiration. You renew so," the young man observed, "the interest."

"Ah there it is!" said Gedge with eyes of adventure that seemed to rest beyond the Atlantic.

"They listen, month after month, when they're out here, as you must have seen; then they go home and talk. But they sing your praise."

Our friend could scarce take it in. "Over *there!*"

"Over there. I think you must be even in the papers."

"Without abuse?"

"Oh we don't abuse every one."

Mrs. Hayes, in her beauty, it was clear, stretched the point. "They rave about you."

"Then they *don't* know?"

"Nobody knows," the young man declared; "it wasn't any one's knowledge, at any rate, that made us uneasy."

"It was your own? I mean your own sense?"

"Well, call it that. We remembered, and we wondered what had happened. So," Mr. Hayes now frankly laughed, "we came to see."

Gedge stared through his film of tears. "Came from America to see *me?*"

"Oh a part of the way. But we wouldn't, in England, have missed you."

"And now we *haven't!*" the young woman soothingly added.

Gedge still could only gape at the candour of the tribute. But he tried to meet them—it was what was least poor for him—in their own key. "Well, how do you like it?"

Mrs. Hayes, he thought—if their answer were important—laughed a little nervously. "Oh you see."

Once more he looked from one to the other. "It's too beastly easy, you know."

Her husband raised his eyebrows. "You conceal your art. The emotion—yes; that must be easy; the general tone must flow. But about your facts—you've so many: how do you get *them* through?"

Gedge wondered. "You think I get too many—?"

At this they were amused together. "That's just what we came to see!"

"Well, you know, I've felt my way; I've gone step by step; you wouldn't believe how I've tried it on. *This*—where you see me—is where I've come out." After which, as they said nothing: "You hadn't thought I *could* come out?"

Again they just waited, but the husband spoke: "Are you so awfully sure you *are* out?"

Gedge drew himself up in the manner of his moments of emotion, almost conscious even that, with his sloping shoulders, his long lean neck and his nose so prominent in proportion to other matters, he resembled the more a giraffe. It was now at last he really caught on. "I *may* be in danger again—and the danger is what has moved you? Oh!" the poor man fairly moaned. His appreciation of it quite weakened him, yet he pulled himself together. "You've your view of my danger?"

It was wondrous how, with that note definitely sounded, the air was cleared. Lucid Mr. Hayes, at the end of a minute, had put the thing in a nutshell. "I don't know what you'll think of us—for being so beastly curious."

"I think," poor Gedge grimaced, "you're only too beastly kind."

"It's all your own fault," his friend returned, "for presenting us (who are not idiots, say) with so striking a picture of a crisis. At our other visit, you remember," he smiled, "you created an anxiety for the opposite reason. Therefore if *this* should again be a crisis for you, you'd really give us the case with an ideal completeness."

"You make me wish," said Morris Gedge, "that it might be one."

"Well, don't try—for our amusement—to bring one on. I don't see, you know, how you can have much margin. Take care—take care."

Gedge did it pensive justice. "Yes, that was what you said a year ago. You did me the honour to be uneasy—as my wife was."

Which determined on the young woman's part an immediate question. "May I ask then if Mrs. Gedge is now at rest?"

"No—since you do ask. *She* fears at least that I go too far; she doesn't believe in my margin. You see we *had* our scare after your visit. They came down."

His friends were all interest. "Ah! They came down?"

"Heavy. They brought *me* down. That's *why*—"

"Why you *are* down?" Mrs. Hayes sweetly demanded.

"Ah but my dear man," her husband interposed, "you're not down; you're *up!* You're only up a different tree, but you're up at the tip-top."

"You mean I take it too high?"

"That's exactly the question," the young man answered; "and the possibility, as matching your first danger, is just what we felt we couldn't, if you didn't mind, miss the measure of."

Gedge gazed at him. "I feel that I know what you at bottom *hoped.*"

"We at bottom 'hope,' surely, that you're all right?"

"In spite of the fool it makes of every one?"

Mr. Hayes of New York smiled. "Say *because* of that. We only ask to believe every one *is* a fool!"

"Only you haven't been, without reassurance, able to imagine fools of the size that my case demands?" And Gedge had a pause while, as if on the chance of some proof, his companion waited. "Well, I won't pretend to you that your anxiety hasn't made me, doesn't threaten to make me, a bit nervous; though I don't quite understand it if, as you say, people but rave about me."

"Oh *that* report was from the other side; people in our country so very easily rave. You've seen small children laugh to shrieks when tickled in a new place. So there are amiable millions with us who are but small shrieking children. They perpetually present new places for the tickler. What we've seen in further lights," Mr. Hayes good-humouredly pursued, "is your people *here*—the Committee, the Board, or whatever the powers to whom you're responsible."

"Call them my friend Grant-Jackson then—my original backer, though I admit for that reason perhaps my most formidable critic. It's with him practically I deal; or rather it's by him I'm dealt with—*was* dealt with before. I stand or fall by him. But he has given me my head."

"Mayn't he then want you," Mrs. Hayes enquired, "just to show as flagrantly running away."

"Of course—I see what you mean. I'm riding, blindly, for a fall, and They're watching (to be tender of me!) for the smash that may come of itself. It's Machiavellic—but everything's possible. And what did you just now mean," Gedge asked—"especially if you've only heard of my prosperity—by your 'further lights'?"

His friends for an instant looked embarrassed, but Mr. Hayes came to the point. "We've heard of your prosperity, but we've also, remember, within a few minutes, heard *you.*"

"I was determined you *should,*" said Gedge. "I'm good then —but I overdo?" His strained grin was still sceptical.

Thus challenged, at any rate, his visitor pronounced. "Well, if you don't; if at the end of six months more it's clear that you haven't overdone; then, *then*—"

"Then what?"

"Then it's great."

"But it is great—greater than anything of the sort ever was. I overdo, thank goodness, yes; or I would if it were a thing you *could.*"

"Oh well, if there's *proof* that you can't—!" With which and an expressive gesture Mr. Hayes threw up his fears.

His wife, however, for a moment seemed unable to let them go. "Don't They want then *any* truth?—none even for the mere look of it?"

"The look of it," said Morris Gedge, "is what I give!"

It made them, the others, exchange a look of their own. Then she smiled. "Oh, well, if they think so—!"

"You at least don't? You're like my wife—which indeed, I remember," Gedge added, "is a similarity I expressed a year ago the wish for! At any rate I frighten *her.*"

The young husband, with an "Ah wives are terrible!" smoothed it over, and their visit would have failed of further excuse had not at this instant a movement at the other end of the room suddenly engaged them. The evening had so nearly closed in, though Gedge, in the course of their talk, had lighted the lamp nearest them, that they had not distinguished, in connexion with the opening of the door of communication to the warden's lodge, the appearance of another person, an eager woman who in her impatience had barely paused before advancing. Mrs. Gedge—her identity took but a few seconds to become vivid—was upon them, and she had not been too late for Mr. Hayes's last remark. Gedge saw at once that she had come with news; no need even, for that certitude, of her quick retort to the words in the air—"You may say as well, sir, that they're often, poor wives, terrified!" She knew nothing of the friends whom, at so unnatural an hour, he was showing about; but there was no livelier sign for him that this didn't matter than the possibility with which she intensely charged her "Grant-Jackson, to see you at once!"—letting it, so to speak, fly in his face.

"He has been with you?"

"Only a minute—he's there. But it's you he wants to see."

He looked at the others. "And what does he want, dear?"

"God knows! There it is. It's his horrid hour—it *was* that other time."

She had nervously turned to the others, overflowing to them, in her dismay, for all their strangeness—quite, as he said to himself, like a woman of the people. She was the bareheaded goodwife talking in the street about the row in the house, and it was in this character that he instantly introduced her: "My dear doubting wife, who will do her best to entertain you while I wait upon our friend." And he explained to her as he could his now protesting companions—"Mr. and Mrs. Hayes of New York, who have been here before." He knew, without knowing why, that her announcement chilled him; he failed at least to see why it should chill him so much. His good friends had themselves been visibly affected by it, and heaven knew that the depths of brooding fancy in him were easily stirred by contact. If they had wanted a crisis they accordingly had found one, albeit they had already asked leave to retire before it. This he wouldn't have. "Ah no, you must really see!"

"But we shan't be able to bear it, you know," said the young woman, "if it *is* to turn you out."

Her crudity attested her sincerity, and it was the latter, doubtless, that instantly held Mrs. Gedge. "It *is* to turn us out."

"Has he told you that, madam?" Mr. Hayes enquired of her—it being wondrous how the breath of doom had drawn them together.

"No, not told me; but there's something in him there—I mean in his awful manner—that matches too well with other things. We've seen," said the poor pale lady, "other things enough."

The young woman almost clutched her. "Is his manner very awful?"

"It's simply the manner," Gedge interposed, "of a very great man."

"Well, very great men," said his wife, "are very awful things."

"It's exactly," he laughed, "what we're finding out! But I mustn't keep him waiting. Our friends here," he went on, "are directly interested. You mustn't, mind you let them go until we know."

Mr. Hayes, however, held him; he found himself stayed. "We're so directly interested that I want you to understand this. If anything happens—"

"Yes?" said Gedge, all gentle as he faltered.

"Well, *we* must set you up."

Mrs. Hayes quickly abounded. "Oh *do* come to us!"

Again he could but take them in. They were really wonderful folk. And with it all but Mr. and Mrs. Hayes! It affected even Isabel through her alarm; though the balm, in a manner, seemed to foretell the wound. He had reached the threshold of his own quarters; he stood there as at the door of the chamber of judgement. But he laughed; at least he could be gallant in going up for sentence. "Very good then—I'll come to you!"

This was very well, but it didn't prevent his heart, a minute later, at the end of the passage, from thumping with beats he could count. He had paused again before going in; on the other side of this second door his poor future was to be let loose at him. It was

broken, at best, and spiritless, but wasn't Grant-Jackson there
like a beast-tamer in a cage, all tights and spangles and circus attitudes, to give it a cut with the smart official whip and make it
spring at him? It was during this moment that he fully measured
the effect for his nerves of the impression made on his so oddly
earnest friends—whose earnestness he verily, in the spasm of this
last effort, came within an ace of resenting. They had upset him by
contact; he was afraid literally of meeting his doom on his knees;
it wouldn't have taken much more, he absolutely felt, to make him
approach with his forehead in the dust the great man whose wrath
was to be averted. Mr. and Mrs. Hayes of New York had brought
tears to his eyes, but was it to be reserved for Grant-Jackson to
make him cry like a baby? He wished, yes, while he palpitated, that
Mr. and Mrs. Hayes of New York hadn't had such an eccentricity
of interest, for it seemed somehow to come from *them* that he was
going so fast to pieces. Before he turned the knob of the door, however, he had another queer instant; making out that it had been,
strictly, his case that was interesting, his funny power, however
accidental, to show as in a picture the attitude of others—not his
poor pale personality. It was this latter quantity, none the less,
that was marching to execution. It is to our friend's credit that he
believed, as he prepared to turn the knob, that he was going to
be hanged; and it's certainly not less to his credit that his wife, on
the chance, had his supreme thought. Here it was that—possibly
with his last articulate breath—he thanked his stars, such as they
were, for Mr. and Mrs. Hayes of New York. At least they would
take care of her.

They were doing that certainly with some success when he returned to them ten minutes later. She sat between them in the
beautified Birthplace, and he couldn't have been sure afterwards
that each wasn't holding her hand. The three together had at any
rate the effect of recalling to him—it was too whimsical—some picture, a sentimental print, seen and admired in his youth, a "Waiting for the Verdict," a "Counting the Hours," or something of that
sort; humble respectability in suspense about humble innocence.
He didn't know how he himself looked, and he didn't care; the

great thing was that he wasn't crying—though he might have been; the glitter in his eyes was assuredly dry, though that there *was* a glitter, or something slightly to bewilder, the faces of the others as they rose to meet him sufficiently proved. His wife's eyes pierced his own, but it was Mrs. Hayes of New York who spoke. "*Was* it then for that—?"

He only looked at them at first—he felt he might now enjoy it. "Yes, it was for 'that.' I mean it was about the way I've been going on. He came to speak of it."

"And he's gone?" Mr. Hayes permitted himself to enquire.

"He's gone."

"It's over?" Isabel hoarsely asked.

"It's over."

"Then we go?"

This it was that he enjoyed. "No, my dear; we stay."

There was fairly a triple gasp; relief took time to operate. "Then why did he come?"

"In the fulness of his kind heart and of *Their* discussed and decreed satisfaction. To express Their sense—!"

Mr. Hayes broke into a laugh, but his wife wanted to know. "Of the grand work you're doing?"

"Of the way I polish it off. They're most handsome about it. The receipts, it appears, speak—"

He was nursing his effect; Isabel intently watched him and the others hung on his lips. "Yes, speak—?"

"Well, volumes. They tell the truth."

At this Mr. Hayes laughed again. "Oh *they* at least do?"

Near him thus once more Gedge knew their intelligence as one —which was so good a consciousness to get back that his tension now relaxed as by the snap of a spring and he felt his old face at ease. "So you can't say," he continued, "that we don't want it."

"I bow to it," the young man smiled. "It's what I said then. It's *great*."

"It's great," said Morris Gedge. "It couldn't be greater."

His wife still watched him; her irony hung behind. "Then we're just as we were?"

"No, not as we were."

She jumped at it. "Better?"

"Better. They give us a rise."

"Of income?"

"Of our sweet little stipend—by a vote of the Committee. That's what, as Chairman, he came to announce."

The very echoes of the Birthplace were themselves, for the instant, hushed; the warden's three companions showed in the conscious air a struggle for their own breath. But Isabel, almost with a shriek, was the first to recover hers. "They double us?"

"Well—call it that. 'In recognition.' There you are." Isabel uttered another sound—but this time inarticulate; partly because Mrs. Hayes of New York had already jumped at her to kiss her. Mr. Hayes meanwhile, as with too much to say, but put out his hand, which our friend took in silence. So Gedge had the last word. "And there *you* are!"

THE JOLLY CORNER

I

"Every one asks me what I 'think' of everything," said Spencer Brydon; "and I make answer as I can—begging or dodging the question, putting them off with any nonsense. It wouldn't matter to any of them really," he went on, "for, even were it possible to meet in that stand-and-deliver way so silly a demand on so big a subject, my 'thoughts' would still be almost altogether about something that concerns only myself." He was talking to Miss Staverton, with whom for a couple of months now he had availed himself of every possible occasion to talk; this disposition and this resource, this comfort and support, as the situation in fact presented itself, having promptly enough taken the first place in the considerable array of rather unattenuated surprises attending his so strangely belated return to America. Everything was somehow a surprise; and that might be natural when one had so long and so consistently neglected everything, taken pains to give surprises so much margin for play. He had given them more than thirty years—thirty-three, to be exact; and they now seemed to him to have organised their performance quite on the scale of that licence. He had been twenty-three on leaving New York—he was fifty-six today: unless indeed he were to reckon as he had sometimes, since his repatriation, found himself feeling; in which case he would have lived longer than is often allotted to man. It would have taken a century, he repeatedly said to himself, and said also to Alice Staverton, it would have taken a longer absence and a more averted mind than those even of which he had been guilty, to pile up the differences, the newnesses, the queernesses, above all the bignesses, for the better or the worse, that at present assaulted his vision wherever he looked.

The great fact all the while however had been the incalculability; since he *had* supposed himself, from decade to decade, to be allowing, and in the most liberal and intelligent manner, for brilliancy of change. He actually saw that he had allowed for nothing; he missed what he would have been sure of finding, he found what he would never have imagined. Proportions and values were upside-down; the ugly things he had expected, the ugly things of his far-away youth, when he had too promptly waked up to a sense of the ugly—these uncanny phenomena placed him rather, as it happened, under the charm; whereas the "swagger" things, the modern, the monstrous, the famous things, those he had more particularly, like thousands of ingenuous enquirers every year, come over to see, were exactly his sources of dismay. They were as so many set traps for displeasure, above all for reaction, of which his restless tread was constantly pressing the spring. It was interesting, doubtless, the whole show, but it would have been too disconcerting hadn't a certain finer truth saved the situation. He had distinctly not, in this steadier light, come over *all* for the monstrosities; he had come, not only in the last analysis but quite on the face of the act, under an impulse with which they had nothing to do. He had come—putting the thing pompously—to look at his "property," which he had thus for a third of a century not been within four thousand miles of; or, expressing it less sordidly, he had yielded to the humour of seeing again his house on the jolly corner, as he usually, and quite fondly, described it—the one in which he had first seen the light, in which various members of his family had lived and had died, in which the holidays of his over-schooled boyhood had been passed and the few social flowers of his chilled adolescence gathered, and which, alienated then for so long a period, had, through the successive deaths of his two brothers and the termination of old arrangements, come wholly into his hands. He was the owner of another, not quite so "good" —the jolly corner having been, from far back, superlatively extended and consecrated; and the value of the pair represented his main capital, with an income consisting, in these later years, of their respective rents which (thanks precisely to their original excellent type) had never been depressingly low. He could live in "Europe," as he had been in the habit of living, on the product of these flourishing New York leases, and all the better since, that of the second structure, the mere number in its long row, having within a twelvemonth fallen in, renovation at a high advance had proved beautifully possible.

These were items of property indeed, but he had found himself since his arrival distinguishing more than ever between them. The house within the street, two bristling blocks westward, was already in course of reconstruction as a tall mass of flats; he had acceded, some time before, to overtures for this conversion—in which, now that it was going forward, it had been not the least of his astonishments to find himself able, on the spot, and though without a previous ounce of such experience, to participate with a certain intelligence, almost with a certain authority. He had lived his life with his back so turned to such concerns and his face addressed to those of so different an order that he scarce knew what to make of this lively stir, in a compartment of his mind never yet penetrated, of a capacity for business and a sense for construction. These virtues, so common all round him now, had been dormant in his own organism—where it might be said of them perhaps that they had slept the sleep of the just. At present, in the splendid autumn weather—the autumn at least was a pure boon in the terrible place—he loafed about his "work" undeterred, secretly agitated; not in the least "minding" that the whole proposition, as they said, was vulgar and sordid, and ready to climb ladders, to walk the plank, to handle materials and look wise about them, to ask questions, in fine, and challenge explanations and really "go into" figures.

It amused, it verily quite charmed him; and, by the same stroke, it amused, and even more, Alice Staverton, though perhaps charming her perceptibly less. She wasn't however going to be better off for it, as *he* was—and so astonishingly much: nothing was now likely, he knew, ever to make her better off than she found herself, in the afternoon of life, as the delicately frugal possessor and tenant of the small house in Irving Place to which she had subtly managed to cling through her almost unbroken New York career. If he knew the way to it now better than to any other address among the dreadful multiplied numberings which seemed to him to reduce the whole place to some vast ledger-page, overgrown, fantastic, of ruled and criss-crossed lines and figures—if he had formed, for his consolation, that habit, it was really not a little because of the charm of his having encountered and recognised, in the vast wilderness of the wholesale, breaking through the mere gross generalisation of wealth and force and success, a small still scene where items and shades, all delicate things, kept the sharpness of the notes of a high voice perfectly trained, and where economy hung about like the scent of a garden. His old friend lived with one maid and herself dusted her relics and trimmed her lamps and polished her silver; she stood off, in the awful modern crush, when she could, but she sallied forth and did battle when the challenge was really to "spirit," the spirit she after all confessed to, proudly and a little shyly, as to that of the better time, that of *their* common, their quite far-away and antediluvian social period and order. She made use of the street-cars when need be, the terrible things that people scrambled for as the panic-stricken at sea scramble for the boats; she affronted, inscrutably, under stress, all the public concussions and ordeals; and yet, with that slim mystifying grace of her appearance, which defied you to say if she were a fair young woman who looked older through trouble, or a fine smooth older one who looked young through successful indifference; with her precious reference, above all, to memories and histories into which he could enter, she was as exquisite for him as some pale pressed flower (a rarity to begin with), and, failing other sweetnesses, she was a sufficient reward of his effort. They had communities of knowledge, "their" knowledge (this discriminating possessive was always on her lips) of presences of the other age, presences all overlaid, in his case, by the experience of a man and the freedom of a wanderer, overlaid by pleasure, by infidelity, by passages of life that were strange and dim to her, just by "Europe" in short, but still unobscured, still exposed and cherished, under that pious visitation of the spirit from which she had never been diverted.

She had come with him one day to see how his "apartment-house" was rising; he had helped her over gaps and explained to her plans, and while they were there had happened to have, before her, a brief but lively discussion with the man in charge, the representative of the building-firm that had undertaken his work. He had found himself quite "standing-up" to this personage over a failure on the latter's part to observe some detail of one of their noted conditions, and had so lucidly urged his case that, besides ever so prettily flushing, at the time, for sympathy in his triumph, she had afterwards said to him (though to a slightly greater effect of irony) that he had clearly for too many years neglected a real gift. If he had but stayed at home he would have anticipated the inventor of the sky-scraper. If he had but stayed at home he would have discovered his genius in time really to start some new variety of awful architectural hare and run it till it burrowed in a gold-mine. He was to remember these words, while the weeks elapsed, for the small silver ring they had sounded over the queerest and deepest of his own lately most disguised and most muffled vibrations.

It had begun to be present to him after the first fortnight, it had broken out with the oddest abruptness, this particular wanton wonderment: it met him there—and this was the image under which he himself judged the matter, or at least, not a little, thrilled and flushed with it—very much as he might have been met by some strange figure, some unexpected occupant, at a turn of one of the dim passages of an empty house. The quaint analogy quite hauntingly remained with him, when he didn't indeed rather improve it by a still intenser form: that of his opening a door behind which he would have made sure of finding nothing, a door into a room shuttered and void, and yet so coming, with a great suppressed start, on some quite erect confronting presence, something planted in the middle of the place and facing him through the dusk. After that visit to the house in construction he walked with his companion to see the other and always so much the better one, which in the eastward direction formed one of the corners, the "jolly" one precisely, of the street now so generally dishonoured and disfigured in its westward reaches, and of the comparatively conservative Avenue. The Avenue still had pretensions, as Miss Staverton said, to decency; the old people had mostly gone, the old names were unknown, and here and there an old association seemed to stray, all vaguely, like some very aged person, out too late, whom you might meet and feel the impulse to watch or follow, in kindness, for safe restoration to shelter.

They went in together, our friends; he admitted himself with his key, as he kept no one there, he explained, preferring, for his reasons, to leave the place empty, under a simple arrangement with a good woman living in the neighbourhood and who came for a daily hour to open windows and dust and sweep. Spencer Brydon had his reasons and was growingly aware of them; they seemed to him better each time he was there, though he didn't name them all to his companion, any more than he told her as yet how often, how quite absurdly often, he himself came. He only let her see for the present, while they walked through the great blank rooms, that absolute vacancy reigned and that, from top to bottom, there was nothing but Mrs. Muldoon's broomstick, in a corner, to tempt the burglar. Mrs. Muldoon was then on the premises, and she loquaciously attended the visitors, preceding them from room to room and pushing back shutters and throwing up sashes—all to show them, as she remarked, how little there was to see. There was little indeed to see in the great gaunt shell where the main dispositions and the general apportionment of space, the style of an age of ampler allowances, had nevertheless for its master their honest pleading message, affecting him as some good old servant's, some lifelong retainer's appeal for a character, or even for a retiring-pension; yet it was also a remark of Mrs. Muldoon's that, glad as she was to oblige him by her noonday round, there was a request she greatly hoped he would never make of her. If he should wish her for any reason to come in after dark she would just tell him, if he "plased," that he must ask it of somebody else.

The fact that there was nothing to see didn't militate for the worthy woman against what one *might* see, and she put it frankly to Miss Staverton that no lady could be expected to like, could she? "craping up to thim top storeys in the ayvil hours." The gas and the electric light were off the house, and she fairly evoked a gruesome vision of her march through the great grey rooms—so many of them as there were too!—with her glimmering taper. Miss Staverton met her honest glare with a smile and the profession that she herself certainly would recoil from such an adventure. Spencer Brydon meanwhile held his peace—for the moment; the question of the "evil" hours in his old home had already become too grave for him. He had begun some time since to "crape," and he knew just why a packet of candles addressed to that pursuit had been stowed by his own hand, three weeks before, at the back of a drawer of the fine old sideboard that occupied, as a "fix-ture," the deep recess in the dining-room. Just now he laughed at his companions—quickly however changing the subject; for the reason that, in the first place, his laugh struck him even at that moment as starting the odd echo, the conscious human reso-nance (he scarce knew how to qualify it) that sounds made while he was there alone sent back to his ear or his fancy; and that, in the second, he imagined Alice Staverton for the instant on the point of asking him, with a divination, if he ever so prowled. There were divinations he was unprepared for, and he had at all events averted enquiry by the time Mrs. Muldoon had left them, passing on to other parts.

There was happily enough to say, on so consecrated a spot, that could be said freely and fairly; so that a whole train of decla-rations was precipitated by his friend's having herself broken out, after a yearning look round: "But I hope you don't mean they want you to pull *this* to pieces!" His answer came, promptly, with his re-awakened wrath: it was of course exactly what they wanted, and what they were "at" him for, daily, with the iteration of people who couldn't for their life understand a man's liability to decent feelings. He had found the place, just as it stood and beyond what he could express, an interest and a joy. There were

values other than the beastly rent-values, and in short, in short—!
But it was thus Miss Staverton took him up. "In short you're to
make so good a thing of your sky-scraper that, living in luxury on
those ill-gotten gains, you can afford for a while to be sentimental
here!" Her smile had for him, with the words, the particular mild
irony with which he found half her talk suffused; an irony without bitterness and that came, exactly, from her having so much
imagination—not, like the cheap sarcasms with which one heard
most people, about the world of "society," bid for the reputation
of cleverness, from nobody's really having any. It was agreeable
to him at this very moment to be sure that when he had answered,
after a brief demur, "Well yes: so, precisely, you may put it!"
her imagination would still do him justice. He explained that even
if never a dollar were to come to him from the other house he
would nevertheless cherish this one; and he dwelt, further, while
they lingered and wandered, on the fact of the stupefaction he was
already exciting, the positive mystification he felt himself create.

He spoke of the value of all he read into it, into the mere sight
of the walls, mere shapes of the rooms, mere sound of the floors,
mere feel, in his hand, of the old silver-plated knobs of the several
mahogany doors, which suggested the pressure of the palms of the
dead; the seventy years of the past in fine that these things represented, the annals of nearly three generations, counting his grandfather's, the one that had ended there, and the impalpable ashes
of his long-extinct youth, afloat in the very air like microscopic
motes. She listened to everything; she was a woman who answered
intimately but who utterly didn't chatter. She scattered abroad
therefore no cloud of words; she could assent, she could agree,
above all she could encourage, without doing that. Only at the last
she went a little further than he had done himself. "And then how
do you know? You may still, after all, want to live here." It rather
indeed pulled him up, for it wasn't what he had been thinking, at
least in her sense of the words. "You mean I may decide to stay on
for the sake of it?"

"Well, *with* such a home—!" But, quite beautifully, she had
too much tact to dot so monstrous an *i*, and it was precisely an

illustration of the way she didn't rattle. How could any one—of any wit—insist on any one else's "wanting" to live in New York?

"Oh," he said, "I *might* have lived here (since I had my opportunity early in life); I might have put in here all these years. Then everything would have been different enough—and, I dare say, 'funny' enough. But that's another matter. And then the beauty of it—I mean of my perversity, of my refusal to agree to a 'deal'—is just in the total absence of a reason. Don't you see that if I had a reason about the matter at all it would *have* to be the other way, and would then be inevitably a reason of dollars? There are no reasons here *but* of dollars. Let us therefore have none whatever—not the ghost of one."

They were back in the hall then for departure, but from where they stood the vista was large, through an open door, into the great square main saloon, with its almost antique felicity of brave spaces between windows. Her eyes came back from that reach and met his own a moment. "Are you very sure the 'ghost' of one doesn't, much rather, serve—?"

He had a positive sense of turning pale. But it was as near as they were then to come. For he made answer, he believed, between a glare and a grin: "Oh ghosts—of course the place must swarm with them! I should be ashamed of it if it didn't. Poor Mrs. Muldoon's right, and it's why I haven't asked her to do more than look in."

Miss Staverton's gaze again lost itself, and things she didn't utter, it was clear, came and went in her mind. She might even for the minute, off there in the fine room, have imagined some element dimly gathering. Simplified like the death-mask of a handsome face, it perhaps produced for her just then an effect akin to the stir of an expression in the "set" commemorative plaster. Yet whatever her impression may have been she produced instead a vague platitude. "Well, if it were only furnished and lived in—!"

She appeared to imply that in case of its being still furnished he might have been a little less opposed to the idea of a return. But she passed straight into the vestibule, as if to leave her words behind her, and the next moment he had opened the house-door and was standing with her on the steps. He closed the door and, while he re-pocketed his key, looking up and down, they took in the comparatively harsh actuality of the Avenue, which reminded him of the assault of the outer light of the Desert on the traveller emerging from an Egyptian tomb. But he risked before they stepped into the street his gathered answer to her speech. "For me it *is* lived in. For me it *is* furnished." At which it was easy for her to sigh "Ah yes—!" all vaguely and discreetly; since his parents and his favourite sister, to say nothing of other kin, in numbers, had run their course and met their end there. That represented, within the walls, ineffaceable life.

It was a few days after this that, during an hour passed with her again, he had expressed his impatience of the too flattering curiosity—among the people he met—about his appreciation of New York. He had arrived at none at all that was socially producible, and as for that matter of his "thinking" (thinking the better or the worse of anything there) he was wholly taken up with one subject of thought. It was mere vain egoism, and it was moreover, if she liked, a morbid obsession. He found all things come back to the question of what he personally might have been, how he might have led his life and "turned out," if he had not so, at the outset, given it up. And confessing for the first time to the intensity within him of this absurd speculation—which but proved also, no doubt, the habit of too selfishly thinking—he affirmed the impotence there of any other source of interest, any other native appeal. "What would it have made of me, what would it have made of me? I keep for ever wondering, all idiotically; as if I could possibly know! I see what it has made of dozens of others, those I meet, and it positively aches within me, to the point of exasperation, that it would have made something of me as well. Only I can't make out *what*, and the worry of it, the small rage of curiosity never to be satisfied, brings back what I remember to have felt, once or twice, after judging best, for reasons, to burn some important letter unopened. I've been sorry, I've hated it—

I've never known what was in the letter. You may of course say it's a trifle—!"

"I don't say it's a trifle," Miss Staverton gravely interrupted.

She was seated by her fire, and before her, on his feet and restless, he turned to and fro between this intensity of his idea and a fitful and unseeing inspection, through his single eye-glass, of the dear little old objects on her chimney-piece. Her interruption made him for an instant look at her harder. "I shouldn't care if you did!" he laughed, however; "and it's only a figure, at any rate, for the way I now feel. *Not* to have followed my perverse young course—and almost in the teeth of my father's curse, as I may say; not to have kept it up, so, 'over there,' from that day to this, without a doubt or a pang; not, above all, to have liked it, to have loved it, so much, loved it, no doubt, with such an abysmal conceit of my own preference: some variation from *that*, I say, must have produced some different effect for my life and for my 'form.' I should have stuck here—if it had been possible; and I was too young, at twenty-three, to judge, *pour deux sous,* whether it *were* possible. If I had waited I might have seen it was, and then I might have been, by staying here, something nearer to one of these types who have been hammered so hard and made so keen by their conditions. It isn't that I admire them so much— the question of any charm in them, or of any charm, beyond that of the rank money-passion, exerted by their conditions *for* them, has nothing to do with the matter: it's only a question of what fantastic, yet perfectly possible, development of my own nature I mayn't have missed. It comes over me that I had then a strange *alter ego* deep down somewhere within me, as the full-blown flower is in the small tight bud, and that I just took the course, I just transferred him to the climate, that blighted him for once and for ever."

"And you wonder about the flower," Miss Staverton said. "So do I, if you want to know; and so I've been wondering these several weeks. I believe in the flower," she continued, "I feel it would have been quite splendid, quite huge and monstrous."

"Monstrous above all!" her visitor echoed; "and I imagine, by the same stroke, quite hideous and offensive."

"You don't believe that," she returned; "if you did you wouldn't wonder. You'd know, and that would be enough for you. What you feel—and what I feel *for* you—is that you'd have had power."

"You'd have liked me that way?" he asked.

She barely hung fire. "How should I not have liked you?"

"I see. You'd have liked me, have preferred me, a billionaire!"

"How should I not have liked you?" she simply again asked.

He stood before her still—her question kept him motionless. He took it in, so much there was of it; and indeed his not otherwise meeting it testified to that. "I know at least what I am," he simply went on; "the other side of the medal's clear enough. I've not been edifying—I believe I'm thought in a hundred quarters to have been barely decent. I've followed strange paths and worshipped strange gods; it must have come to you again and again —in fact you've admitted to me as much—that I was leading, at any time these thirty years, a selfish frivolous scandalous life. And you see what it has made of me."

She just waited, smiling at him. "You see what it has made of *me*."

"Oh you're a person whom nothing can have altered. You were born to be what you are, anywhere, anyway: you've the perfection nothing else could have blighted. And don't you see how, without my exile, I shouldn't have been waiting till now—?" But he pulled up for the strange pang.

"The great thing to see," she presently said, "seems to me to be that it has spoiled nothing. It hasn't spoiled your being here at last. It hasn't spoiled this. It hasn't spoiled your speaking—" She also however faltered.

He wondered at everything her controlled emotion might mean. "Do you believe then—too dreadfully!—that I *am* as good as I might ever have been?"

"Oh no! Far from it!" With which she got up from her chair and was nearer to him. "But I don't care," she smiled.

"You mean I'm good enough?"

She considered a little. "Will you believe it if I say so? I mean will you let that settle your question for you?" And then as if making out in his face that he drew back from this, that he had some idea which, however absurd, he couldn't yet bargain away: "Oh you don't care either—but very differently: you don't care for anything but yourself."

Spencer Brydon recognised it—it was in fact what he had absolutely professed. Yet he importantly qualified. "*He* isn't myself. He's the just so totally other person. But I do want to see him," he added. "And I can. And I shall."

Their eyes met for a minute while he guessed from something in hers that she divined his strange sense. But neither of them otherwise expressed it, and her apparent understanding, with no protesting shock, no easy derision, touched him more deeply than anything yet, constituting for his stifled perversity, on the spot, an element that was like breatheable air. What she said however was unexpected. "Well, *I've* seen him."

"You—?"

"I've seen him in a dream."

"Oh a 'dream'—!" It let him down.

"But twice over," she continued. "I saw him as I see you now."

"You've dreamed the same dream—?"

"Twice over," she repeated. "The very same."

This did somehow a little speak to him, as it also gratified him. "You dream about me at that rate?"

"Ah about *him!*" she smiled.

His eyes again sounded her. "Then you know all about him." And as she said nothing more: "What's the wretch like?"

She hesitated, and it was as if he were pressing her so hard that, resisting for reasons of her own, she had to turn away. "I'll tell you some other time!"

II

It was after this that there was most of a virtue for him, most of a cultivated charm, most of a preposterous secret thrill, in the particular form of surrender to his obsession and of address to what he more and more believed to be his privilege. It was what in these weeks he was living for—since he really felt life to begin but after Mrs. Muldoon had retired from the scene and, visiting the ample house from attic to cellar, making sure he was alone, he knew himself in safe possession and, as he tacitly expressed it, let himself go. He sometimes came twice in the twenty-four hours; the moments he liked best were those of gathering dusk, of the short autumn twilight; this was the time of which, again and again, he found himself hoping most. Then he could, as seemed to him, most intimately wander and wait, linger and listen, feel his fine attention, never in his life before so fine, on the pulse of the great vague place: he preferred the lampless hour and only wished he might have prolonged each day the deep crepuscular spell. Later—rarely much before midnight, but then for a considerable vigil—he watched with his glimmering light; moving slowly, holding it high, playing it far, rejoicing above all, as much as he might, in open vistas, reaches of communication between rooms and by passages; the long straight chance or show, as he would have called it, for the revelation he pretended to invite. It was practice he found he could perfectly "work" without exciting remark; no one was in the least the wiser for it; even Alice Staverton, who was moreover a well of discretion, didn't quite fully imagine.

He let himself in and let himself out with the assurance of calm proprietorship; and accident so far favoured him that, if a fat Avenue "officer" had happened on occasion to see him entering at eleven-thirty, he had never yet, to the best of his belief, been noticed as emerging at two. He walked there on the crisp November nights, arrived regularly at the evening's end; it was as easy to do this after dining out as to take his way to a club or to his hotel. When he left his club, if he hadn't been dining out, it was ostensibly to go to his hotel; and when he left his hotel, if he had spent a part of the evening there, it was ostensibly to go to his club. Everything was easy in fine; everything conspired and promoted: there was truly even in the strain of his experience something that glossed over, something that salved and simplified, all the rest of consciousness. He circulated, talked, renewed, loosely and pleasantly, old relations—met indeed, so far as he could, new expectations and seemed to make out on the whole that in spite of the career, of such different contacts, which he had spoken of to Miss Staverton as ministering so little, for those who might have watched it, to edification, he was positively rather liked than not. He was a dim secondary social success—and all with people who had truly not an idea of him. It was all mere surface sound, this murmur of their welcome, this popping of their corks—just as his gestures of response were the extravagant shadows, emphatic in proportion as they meant little, of some game of *ombres chinoises*. He projected himself all day, in thought, straight over the bristling line of hard unconscious heads and into the other, the real, the waiting life; the life that, as soon as he had heard behind him the click of his great house-door, began for him, on the jolly corner, as beguilingly as the slow opening bars of some rich music follows the tap of the conductor's wand.

He always caught the first effect of the steel point of his stick on the old marble of the hall pavement, large black-and-white squares that he remembered as the admiration of his childhood and that had then made in him, as he now saw, for the growth of an early conception of style. This effect was the dim reverberating tinkle as of some far-off bell hung who should say where?—in the depths of the house, of the past, of that mystical other world that might have flourished for him had he not, for weal or woe, abandoned it. On this impression he did ever the same thing; he put his stick noiselessly away in a corner—feeling the place once more in the likeness of some great glass bowl, all precious concave crystal, set delicately humming by the play of a moist finger round its edge. The concave crystal held, as it were, this mystical other world, and the indescribably fine murmur of its rim was the sigh there, the scarce audible pathetic wail to his strained ear, of all the old baffled forsworn possibilities. What he did therefore by this appeal of his hushed presence was to wake them into such measure of ghostly life as they might still enjoy. They were shy, all but unappeasably shy, but they weren't really sinister; at least they weren't as he had hitherto felt them—before they had taken the Form he so yearned to make them take, the Form he at moments saw himself in the light of fairly hunting on tiptoe, the points of his evening-shoes, from room to room and from storey to storey.

That was the essence of his vision—which was all rank folly, if one would, while he was out of the house and otherwise occupied, but which took on the last verisimilitude as soon as he was placed and posted. He knew what he meant and what he wanted; it was as clear as the figure on a cheque presented in demand for cash. His *alter ego* "walked"—that was the note of his image of him, while his image of his motive for his own odd pastime was the desire to waylay him and meet him. He roamed, slowly, warily, but all restlessly, he himself did—Mrs. Muldoon had been right, absolutely, with her figure of their "craping"; and the presence he watched for would roam restlessly too. But it would be as cautious and as shifty; the conviction of its probable, in fact its already quite sensible, quite audible evasion of pursuit grew for him from night to night, laying on him finally a rigour to which nothing in his life had been comparable. It had been the theory of many superficially-judging persons, he knew, that he was wasting that life in a surrender to sensations, but he had tasted of no pleasure so fine as his actual tension, had been introduced to no sport that demanded at once the patience and the nerve of this stalking of a creature more subtle, yet at bay perhaps more formidable, than any beast of the forest. The terms, the comparisons, the very practices of the chase positively came again into play; there were even moments when passages of his occasional experience as a sportsman, stirred memories, from his younger time, of moor and mountain and desert, revived for him—and to the increase of his keenness—by the tremendous force of analogy. He found himself at moments—once he had placed his single light on some mantel-shelf or in some recess—stepping back into shelter or shade, effacing himself behind a door or in an embrasure, as he had sought of old the vantage of rock and tree; he found himself holding his breath and living in the joy of the instant, the supreme suspense created by big game alone.

He wasn't afraid (though putting himself the question as he believed gentlemen on Bengal tiger-shoots or in close quarters with the great bear of the Rockies had been known to confess to having put it); and this indeed—since here at least he might be frank!—because of the impression, so intimate and so strange, that he himself produced as yet a dread, produced certainly a strain, beyond the liveliest he was likely to feel. They fell for him into categories, they fairly became familiar, the signs, for his own perception, of the alarm his presence and his vigilance created; though leaving him always to remark, portentously, on his probably having formed a relation, his probably enjoying a consciousness, unique in the experience of man. People enough, first and last, had been in terror of apparitions, but who had ever before so turned the tables and become himself, in the apparitional world, an incalculable terror? He might have found this sublime had he quite dared to think of it; but he didn't too much insist, truly, on that side of his privilege. With habit and repetition he gained to an extraordinary degree the power to penetrate the dusk of distances and the darkness of corners, to resolve back into their innocence the treacheries of uncertain light, the evil-looking forms taken in the gloom by mere shadows, by accidents of the air, by shifting effects of perspective; putting down his dim luminary he could still wander on without it, pass into other rooms and, only knowing it was there behind him in case of need, see his way about, visually project for his purpose a comparative clearness. It made him feel, this acquired faculty, like some monstrous stealthy cat; he wondered if he would have glared at these moments with large shining yellow eyes, and what it mightn't verily be, for the poor hard-pressed *alter ego,* to be confronted with such a type.

He liked however the open shutters; he opened everywhere

those Mrs. Muldoon had closed, closing them as carefully afterwards, so that she shouldn't notice: he liked—oh this he did like,
and above all in the upper rooms!—the sense of the hard silver
of the autumn stars through the window-panes, and scarcely less
the flare of the street-lamps below, the white electric lustre which
it would have taken curtains to keep out. This was human actual
social; this was of the world he had lived in, and he was more
at his ease certainly for the countenance, coldly general and impersonal, that all the while and in spite of his detachment it
seemed to give him. He had support of course mostly in the rooms
at the wide front and the prolonged side; it failed him considerably in the central shades and the parts at the back. But if he
sometimes, on his rounds, was glad of his optical reach, so none
the less often the rear of the house affected him as the very jungle
of his prey. The place was there more subdivided; a large "extension" in particular, where small rooms for servants had been
multiplied, abounded in nooks and corners, in closets and passages, in the ramifications especially of an ample back staircase
over which he leaned, many a time, to look far down—not deterred from his gravity even while aware that he might, for a
spectator, have figured some solemn simpleton playing at hide-
and-seek. Outside in fact he might himself make that ironic *rap-
prochement;* but within the walls, and in spite of the clear windows, his consistency was proof against the cynical light of New
York.

It had belonged to that idea of the exasperated consciousness
of his victim to become a real test for him; since he had quite put
it to himself from the first that, oh distinctly! he could "cultivate"
his whole perception. He had felt it as above all open to cultivation—which indeed was but another name for his manner of
spending his time. He was bringing it on, bringing it to perfection,
by practice; in consequence of which it had grown so fine that
he was now aware of impressions, attestations of his general pos-
tulate, that couldn't have broken upon him at once. This was the
case more specifically with a phenomenon at last quite frequent
for him in the upper rooms, the recognition—absolutely unmis-

takeable, and by a turn dating from a particular hour, his resumption of his campaign after a diplomatic drop, a calculated absence of three nights—of his being definitely followed, tracked at a distance carefully taken and to the express end that he should the less confidently, less arrogantly, appear to himself merely to pursue. It worried, it finally quite broke him up, for it proved, of all the conceivable impressions, the one least suited to his book. He was kept in sight while remaining himself—as regards the essence of his position—sightless, and his only recourse then was in abrupt turns, rapid recoveries of ground. He wheeled about, retracing his steps, as if he might so catch in his face at least the stirred air of some other quick revolution. It was indeed true that his fully dislocalised thought of these manœuvres recalled to him Pantaloon, at the Christmas farce, buffeted and tricked from behind by ubiquitous Harlequin; but it left intact the influence of the conditions themselves each time he was re-exposed to them, so that in fact this association, had he suffered it to become constant, would on a certain side have but ministered to his intenser gravity. He had made, as I have said, to create on the premises the baseless sense of a reprieve, his three absences; and the result of the third was to confirm the after-effect of the second.

On his return, that night—the night succeeding his last intermission—he stood in the hall and looked up the staircase with a certainty more intimate than any he had yet known. "He's *there*, at the top, and waiting—not, as in general, falling back for disappearance. He's holding his ground, and it's the first time—which is a proof, isn't it? that something has happened for him." So Brydon argued with his hand on the banister and his foot on the lowest stair; in which position he felt as never before the air chilled by his logic. He himself turned cold in it, for he seemed of a sudden to know what now was involved. "Harder pressed?—yes, he takes it in, with its thus making clear to him that I've come, as they say, 'to stay.' He finally doesn't like and can't bear it, in the sense, I mean, that his wrath, his menaced interest, now balances with his dread. I've hunted him till he has 'turned': that, up there, is what has happened—he's the fanged or the antlered animal brought at last to bay." There came to him, as I say—but determined by an influence beyond my notation!—the acuteness of this certainty; under which however the next moment he had broken into a sweat that he would as little have consented to attribute to fear as he would have dared immediately to act upon it for enterprise. It marked none the less a prodigious thrill, a thrill that represented sudden dismay, no doubt, but also represented, and with the selfsame throb, the strangest, the most joyous, possibly the next minute almost the proudest, duplication of consciousness.

"He has been dodging, retreating, hiding, but now, worked up to anger, he'll fight!"—this intense impression made a single mouthful, as it were, of terror and applause. But what was wondrous was that the applause, for the felt fact, was so eager, since, if it was his other self he was running to earth, this ineffable identity was thus in the last resort not unworthy of him. It bristled there—somewhere near at hand, however unseen still—as the hunted thing, even as the trodden worm of the adage *must* at last bristle; and Brydon at this instant tasted probably of a sensation more complex than had ever before found itself consistent with sanity. It was as if it would have shamed him that a character so associated with his own should triumphantly succeed in just skulking, should to the end not risk the open, so that the drop of this danger was, on the spot, a great lift of the whole situation. Yet with another rare shift of the same subtlety he was already trying to measure by how much more he himself might now be in peril of fear; so rejoicing that he could, in another form, actively inspire that fear, and simultaneously quaking for the form in which he might passively know it.

The apprehension of knowing it must after a little have grown in him, and the strangest moment of his adventure perhaps, the most memorable or really most interesting, afterwards, of his crisis, was the lapse of certain instants of concentrated conscious *combat*, the sense of a need to hold on to something, even after the manner of a man slipping and slipping on some awful incline; the vivid impulse, above all, to move, to act, to charge, somehow and upon something—to show himself, in a word, that he wasn't afraid. The state of "holding-on" was thus the state to which he was momentarily reduced; if there had been anything, in the great vacancy, to seize, he would presently have been aware of having clutched it as he might under a shock at home have clutched the nearest chair-back. He had been surprised at any rate—of this he *was* aware—into something unprecedented since his original appropriation of the place; he had closed his eyes, held them tight, for a long minute, as with that instinct of dismay and that terror of vision. When he opened them the room, the other con-tiguous rooms, extraordinarily, seemed lighter—so light, almost, that at first he took the change for day. He stood firm, however that might be, just where he had paused; his resistance had helped him—it was as if there were something he had tided over. He knew after a little what this was—it had been in the imminent danger of flight. He had stiffened his will against going; without this he would have made for the stairs, and it seemed to him that, still with his eyes closed, he would have descended them, would have known how, straight and swiftly, to the bottom.

Well, as he had held out, here he was—still at the top, among the more intricate upper rooms and with the gauntlet of the oth-ers, of all the rest of the house, still to run when it should be his time to go. He would go at his time—only at his time: didn't he go every night very much at the same hour? He took out his watch —there was light for that: it was scarcely a quarter past one, and he had never withdrawn so soon. He reached his lodgings for the most part at two—with his walk of a quarter of an hour. He would wait for the last quarter—he wouldn't stir till then; and he kept his watch there with his eyes on it, reflecting while he held it that this deliberate wait, a wait with an effort, which he recognised, would serve perfectly for the attestation he desired to make. It would prove his courage—unless indeed the latter might most be proved by his budging at last from his place. What he mainly felt now was that, since he hadn't originally scuttled, he had his dig-nities—which had never in his life seemed so many—all to pre-serve and to carry aloft. This was before him in truth as a physical image, an image almost worthy of an age of greater romance. That remark indeed glimmered for him only to glow the next instant with a finer light; since what age of romance, after all, could have matched either the state of his mind or, "objectively," as they said, the wonder of his situation? The only difference would have been that, brandishing his dignities over his head as in a parchment scroll, he might then—that is in the heroic time—have proceeded downstairs with a drawn sword in his other grasp.

At present, really, the light he had set down on the mantel of the next room would have to figure his sword; which utensil, in the course of a minute, he had taken the requisite number of steps to possess himself of. The door between the rooms was open, and from the second another door opened to a third. These rooms, as he remembered, gave all three upon a common corridor as well, but there was a fourth, beyond them, without issue save through the preceding. To have moved, to have heard his step again, was appreciably a help; though even in recognising this he lingered once more a little by the chimney-piece on which his light had rested. When he next moved, just hesitating where to turn, he found himself considering a circumstance that, after his first and comparatively vague apprehension of it, produced in him the start that often attends some pang of recollection, the violent shock of having ceased happily to forget. He had come into sight of the door in which the brief chain of communication ended and which he now surveyed from the nearer threshold, the one not directly facing it. Placed at some distance to the left of this point, it would have admitted him to the last room of the four, the room without other approach or egress, had it not, to his intimate conviction, been closed *since* his former visitation, the matter probably of a quarter of an hour before. He stared with all his eyes at the wonder of the fact, arrested again where he stood and again holding his breath while he sounded its sense. Surely it had been *subsequently* closed—that is it had been on his previous passage indubitably open!

He took it full in the face that something had happened between—that he couldn't not have noticed before (by which he meant on his original tour of all the rooms that evening) that such a barrier had exceptionally presented itself. He had indeed since that moment undergone an agitation so extraordinary that it might have muddled for him any earlier view; and he tried to convince himself that he might perhaps then have gone into the room and, inadvertently, automatically, on coming out, have drawn the door after him. The difficulty was that this exactly was what he never did; it was against his whole policy, as he might have said, the essence of which was to keep vistas clear. He had them from the first, as he was well aware, quite on the brain: the strange apparition, at the far end of one of them, of his baffled "prey" (which had become by so sharp an irony so little the term now to apply!) was the form of success his imagination had most cherished, projecting into it always a refinement of beauty. He had known fifty times the start of perception that had afterwards dropped; had fifty times gasped to himself "There!" under some fond brief hallucination. The house, as the case stood, admirably lent itself; he might wonder at the taste, the native architecture of the particular time, which could rejoice so in the multiplication of doors—the opposite extreme to the modern, the actual almost complete proscription of them; but it had fairly contributed to provoke this obsession of the presence encountered telescopically, as he might say, focussed and studied in diminishing perspective and as by a rest for the elbow.

It was with these considerations that his present attention was charged—they perfectly availed to make what he saw portentous. He *couldn't*, by any lapse, have blocked that aperture; and if he hadn't, if it was unthinkable, why what else was clear but that there had been another agent? Another agent?—he had been catching, as he felt, a moment back, the very breath of him; but when had he been so close as in this simple, this logical, this completely personal act? It was so logical, that is, that one might have *taken* it for personal; yet for what did Brydon take it, he asked himself, while, softly panting, he felt his eyes almost leave their sockets. Ah this time at last they *were*, the two, the opposed projections of him, in presence; and this time, as much as one would, the question of danger loomed. With it rose, as not before, the question of courage—for what he knew the blank face of the door to say to him was "Show us how much you have!" It stared, it glared back at him with that challenge; it put to him the two alternatives: should he just push it open or not? Oh to have this consciousness was to *think*—and to think, Brydon knew, as he stood there, was, with the lapsing moments, not to have acted! Not to have acted—that was the misery and the pang—was even still not to act; was in fact *all* to feel the thing in another, in a new and terrible way. How long did he pause and how long did he debate? There was presently nothing to measure it; for his vibration had already changed—as just by the effect of its intensity. Shut up there, at bay, defiant, and with the prodigy of the thing palpably proveably *done,* thus giving notice like some stark signboard—under that accession of accent the situation itself had turned; and Brydon at last remarkably made up his mind on what it had turned to.

It had turned altogether to a different admonition; to a supreme hint, for him, of the value of Discretion! This slowly dawned, no doubt—for it could take its time; so perfectly, on his threshold, had he been stayed, so little as yet had he either advanced or retreated. It was the strangest of all things that now when, by his taking ten steps and applying his hand to a latch, or even his shoulder and his knee, if necessary, to a panel, all the hunger of his prime need might have been met, his high curiosity crowned, his unrest assuaged—it was amazing, but it was also exquisite and rare, that insistence should have, at a touch, quite dropped from him. Discretion—he jumped at that; and yet not, verily, at such a pitch, because it saved his nerves or his skin, but because, much more valuably, it saved the situation. When I say he "jumped" at it I feel the consonance of this term with the fact that—at the end indeed of I know not how long—he did move again, he crossed straight to the door. He wouldn't touch it—it seemed now that he might *if* he would: he would only just wait there a little, to show, to prove, that he wouldn't. He had thus another station, close to the thin partition by which revelation was denied him; but with his eyes bent and his hands held off in a mere intensity of stillness. He listened as if there had been something to hear, but this attitude, while it lasted, was his own communication. "If you won't then—good: I spare you and I give up. You affect me as by the appeal positively for pity: you convince me that for reasons rigid and sublime—what do I know?—we both of us should have suffered. I respect them then, and, though moved and privileged as, I believe, it has never been given to man, I retire, I renounce—never, on my honour, to try again. So rest for ever— and let *me!*"

That, for Brydon was the deep sense of this last demonstration —solemn, measured, directed, as he felt it to be. He brought it to a close, he turned away; and now verily he knew how deeply he had been stirred. He retraced his steps, taking up his candle, burnt, he observed, well-nigh to the socket, and marking again, lighten it as he would, the distinctness of his footfall; after which, in a moment, he knew himself at the other side of the house. He did here what he had not yet done at these hours—he opened half a casement, one of those in the front, and let in the air of the night; a thing he would have taken at any time previous for a sharp rupture of his spell. His spell was broken now, and it didn't matter—broken by his concession and his surrender, which made it idle henceforth that he should ever come back. The empty street —its other life so marked even by the great lamplit vacancy—was within call, within touch; he stayed there as to be in it again, high above it though he was still perched; he watched as for some comforting common fact, some vulgar human note, the passage of a scavenger or a thief, some night-bird however base. He would have blessed that sign of life; he would have welcomed positively the slow approach of his friend the policeman, whom he had hitherto only sought to avoid, and was not sure that if the patrol had come into sight he mightn't have felt the impulse to get into relation with it, to hail it, on some pretext, from his fourth floor.

The pretext that wouldn't have been too silly or too compromising, the explanation that would have saved his dignity and kept his name, in such a case, out of the papers, was not definite to him: he was so occupied with the thought of recording his Discretion—

as an effect of the vow he had just uttered to his intimate adversary —that the importance of this loomed large and something had overtaken all ironically his sense of proportion. If there had been a ladder applied to the front of the house, even one of the vertiginous perpendiculars employed by painters and roofers and sometimes left standing overnight, he would have managed somehow, astride of the window-sill, to compass by outstretched leg and arm that mode of descent. If there had been some such uncanny thing as he had found in his room at hotels, a workable fire-escape in the form of notched cable or a canvas shoot, he would have availed himself of it as a proof—well, of his present delicacy. He nursed that sentiment, as the question stood, a little in vain, and even—at the end of he scarce knew, once more, how long— found it, as by the action on his mind of the failure of response of the outer world, sinking back to vague anguish. It seemed to him he had waited an age for some stir of the great grim hush; the life of the town was itself under a spell—so unnaturally, up and down the whole prospect of known and rather ugly objects, the blankness and the silence lasted. Had they ever, he asked himself, the hard-faced houses, which had begun to look livid in the dim dawn, had they ever spoken so little to any need of his spirit? Great builded voids, great crowded stillnesses put on, often, in the heart of cities, for the small hours, a sort of sinister mask, and it was of this large collective negation that Brydon presently became conscious—all the more that the break of day was, almost incredibly, now at hand, proving to him what a night he had made of it.

He looked again at his watch, saw what had become of his time-values (he had taken hours for minutes—not, as in other tense situations, minutes for hours) and the strange air of the streets was but the weak, the sullen flush of a dawn in which everything was still locked up. His choked appeal from his own open window had been the sole note of life, and he could but break off at last as for a worse despair. Yet while so deeply demoralised he was capable again of an impulse denoting—at least by his present measure—extraordinary resolution; of retracing his steps to the spot where he had turned cold with the extinction of his last pulse of doubt as to there being in the place another presence than his own. This required an effort strong enough to sicken him; but he had his reason, which over-mastered for the moment everything else. There was the whole of the rest of the house to traverse, and how should he screw himself to that if the door he had seen closed were at present open? He could hold to the idea that the closing had practically been for him an act of mercy, a chance offered him to descend, depart, get off the ground and never again profane it. This conception held together, it worked; but what it meant for him depended now clearly on the amount of forbearance his recent action, or rather his recent inaction, had engendered. The image of the "presence," whatever it was, waiting there for him to go —this image had not yet been so concrete for his nerves as when he stopped short of the point at which certainty would have come to him. For, with all his resolution, or more exactly with all his dread, he did stop short—he hung back from really seeing. The risk was too great and his fear too definite: it took at this moment an awful specific form.

He knew—yes, as he had never known anything—that, *should* he see the door open, it would all too abjectly be the end of him. It would mean that the agent of his shame—for his shame was the deep abjection—was once more at large and in general possession; and what glared him thus in the face was the act that this would determine for him. It would send him straight about to the window he had left open, and by that window, be long ladder and dangling rope as absent as they would, he saw himself uncontrollably in- sanely fatally take his way to the street. The hideous chance of this he at least could avert; but he could only avert it by recoiling in time from assurance. He had the whole house to deal with, this fact was still there; only he now knew that uncertainty alone could start him. He stole back from where he had checked himself —merely to do so was suddenly like safety—and, making blindly for the greater staircase, left gaping rooms and sounding passages behind. Here was the top of the stairs, with a fine large dim de- scent and three spacious landings to mark off. His instinct was all for mildness, but his feet were harsh on the floors, and, strangely, when he had in a couple of minutes become aware of this, it counted somehow for help. He couldn't have spoken, the tone of his voice would have scared him, and the common conceit or resource of "whistling in the dark" (whether literally or figuratively) have appeared basely vulgar; yet he liked none the less to hear himself go, and when he had reached his first landing—taking it all with no rush, but quite steadily—that stage of success drew from him a gasp of relief.

The house, withal, seemed immense, the scale of space again inordinate; the open rooms to no one of which his eyes deflected, gloomed in their shuttered state like mouths of caverns; only the high skylight that formed the crown of the deep well created for him a medium in which he could advance, but which might have been, for queerness of colour, some watery under-world. He tried to think of something noble, as that his property was really grand, a splendid possession; but this nobleness took the form too of the clear delight with which he was finally to sacrifice it. They might come in now, the builders, the destroyers—they might come as soon as they would. At the end of two flights he had dropped to another zone, and from the middle of the third, with only one more left, he recognised the influence of the lower windows, of half-drawn blinds, of the occasional gleam of street-lamps, of the glazed spaces of the vestibule. This was the bottom of the sea, which showed an illumination of its own and which he even saw paved—when at a given moment he drew up to sink a long look over the banisters—with the marble squares of his childhood. By that time indubitably he felt, as he might have said in a commoner cause, better; it had allowed him to stop and draw breath, and the ease increased with the sight of the old black-and-white slabs. But what he most felt was that now surely, with the element of impunity pulling him as by hard firm hands, the case was settled for what he might have seen above had he dared that last look. The closed door, blessedly remote now, was still closed—and he had only in short to reach that of the house.

He came down further, he crossed the passage forming the access to the last flight; and if here again he stopped an instant it was almost for the sharpness of the thrill of assured escape. It made him shut his eyes—which opened again to the straight slope of the remainder of the stairs. Here was impunity still, but impunity almost excessive; inasmuch as the side-lights and the high fan-tracery of the entrance were glimmering straight into the hall; an appearance produced, he the next instant saw, by the fact that the vestibule gaped wide, that the hinged halves of the inner door had been thrown far back. Out of that again the *question* sprang at him, making his eyes, as he felt, half-start from his head, as they had done, at the top of the house, before the sign of the other door. If he had left that one open, hadn't he left this one closed, and wasn't he now in *most* immediate presence of some inconceivable occult activity? It was as sharp, the question, as a knife in his side, but the answer hung fire still and seemed to lose itself in the vague darkness to which the thin admitted dawn, glimmering archwise over the whole outer door, made a semicircular margin, a cold silvery nimbus that seemed to play a little as he looked— to shift and expand and contract.

It was as if there had been something within it, protected by indistinctness and corresponding in extent with the opaque surface behind, the painted panels of the last barrier to his escape, of which the key was in his pocket. The indistinctness mocked him even while he stared, affected him as somehow shrouding or challenging certitude, so that after faltering an instant on his step he let himself go with the sense that here *was* at last something to meet, to touch, to take, to know—something all unnatural and dreadful, but to advance upon which was the condition for him either of liberation or of supreme defeat. The penumbra, dense and dark, was the virtual screen of a figure which stood in it as still as some image erect in a niche or as some black-vizored sentinel guarding a treasure. Brydon was to know afterwards, was to recall and make out, the particular thing he had believed during the rest of his descent. He saw, in its great grey glimmering margin, the central vagueness diminish, and he felt it to be taking the very form toward which, for so many days, the passion of his curiosity had yearned. It gloomed, it loomed, it was something, it was somebody, the prodigy of a personal presence.

Rigid and conscious, spectral yet human, a man of his own substance and stature waited there to measure himself with his power to dismay. This only could it be—this only till he recognised, with his advance, that what made the face dim was the pair of raised hands that covered it and in which, so far from being offered in defiance, it was buried as for dark deprecation. So Brydon, before him, took him in; with every fact of him now, in the higher light, hard and acute—his planted stillness, his vivid truth, his grizzled bent head and white masking hands, his queer actuality of evening-dress, of dangling double eye-glass, of gleaming silk lappet and white linen, of pearl button and gold watch-guard and polished shoe. No portrait by a great modern master could have presented him with more intensity, thrust him out of his frame with more art, as if there had been "treatment," of the consummate sort, in his every shade and salience. The revulsion, for our friend, had become, before he knew it, immense—this drop, in the act of apprehension, to the sense of his adversary's inscrutable manœuvre. That meaning at least, while he gaped, it offered him; for he could but gape at his other self in this other anguish, gape as a proof that *he*, standing there for the achieved, the enjoyed, the triumphant life, couldn't be faced in his triumph. Wasn't the proof in the splendid covering hands, strong and completely spread?—so spread and so intentional that, in spite of a special verity that surpassed every other, the fact that one of these hands had lost two fingers, which were reduced to stumps, as if accidentally shot away, the face was effectually guarded and saved.

"Saved," though, *would* it be?—Brydon breathed his wonder till the very impunity of his attitude and the very insistence of his eyes produced, as he felt, a sudden stir which showed the next instant as a deeper portent, while the head raised itself, the betrayal of a braver purpose. The hands, as he looked, began to move, to open; then, as if deciding in a flash, dropped from the face and left it uncovered and presented. Horror, with the sight, had leaped into Brydon's throat, gasping there in a sound he couldn't utter; for the bared identity was too hideous as *his*, and his glare was the passion of his protest. The face, *that* face, Spencer Brydon's?—he searched it still, but looking away from it in dismay and denial, falling straight from his height of sublimity. It was unknown, inconceivable, awful, disconnected from any possibility—! He had been "sold," he inwardly moaned, stalking such game as this: the presence before him was a presence, the horror within him a horror, but the waste of his nights had been only grotesque and the success of his adventure an irony. Such an identity fitted his at *no* point, made its alternative monstrous. A thousand times yes, as it came upon him nearer now—the face was the face of a stranger. It came upon him nearer now, quite as one of those expanding fantastic images projected by the magic lantern of childhood; for the stranger, whoever he might be, evil, odious, blatant, vulgar, had advanced as for aggression, and he knew himself give ground. Then harder pressed still, sick with the force of his shock, and falling back as under the hot breath and the roused passion of a life larger than his own, a rage of personality before which his own collapsed, he felt the whole vision turn to darkness and his very feet give way. His head went round; he was going; he had gone.

III

WHAT had next brought him back, clearly—though after how long?—was Mrs. Muldoon's voice, coming to him from quite near, from so near that he seemed presently to see her as kneeling on the ground before him while he lay looking up at her; himself not wholly on the ground, but half-raised and upheld—conscious, yes, of tenderness of support and, more particularly, of a head pillowed in extraordinary softness and faintly refreshing fragrance. He considered, he wondered, his wit but half at his service; than another face intervened, bending more directly over him, and he finally knew that Alice Staverton had made her lap an ample and perfect cushion to him, and that she had to this end seated herself on the lowest degree of the staircase, the rest of his long person remaining stretched on his old black-and-white slabs. They were cold, these marble squares of his youth; but *he* somehow was not, in this rich return of consciousness—the most wonderful hour, little by little, that he had ever known, leaving him, as it did, so gratefully, so abysmally passive, and yet as with a treasure of intelligence waiting all round him for quiet appropriation; dissolved, he might call it, in the air of the place and producing the golden glow of a late autumn afternoon. He had come back, yes—come back from further away than any man but himself had ever travelled; but it was strange how with this sense what he had come back *to* seemed really the great thing, and as if his prodigious journey had been all for the sake of it. Slowly but surely his consciousness grew, his vision of his state thus completing itself: he had been miraculously *carried* back—lifted and carefully borne as from where he had been picked up, the uttermost end of an interminable grey passage. Even with this he was suffered to rest, and what had now brought him to knowledge was the break in the long mild motion.

It had brought him to knowledge, to knowledge—yes, this was the beauty of his state; which came to resemble more and more that of a man who has gone to sleep on some news of a great inheritance, and then, after dreaming it away, after profaning it with matters strange to it, has waked up again to serenity of certitude and has only to lie and watch it grow. This was the drift of his patience—that he had only to let it shine on him. He must moreover, with intermissions, still have been lifted and borne; since why and how else should he have known himself, later on, with the afternoon glow intenser, no longer at the foot of his stairs—situated as these now seemed at that dark other end of his tunnel—but on a deep window-bench of his high saloon, over which had been spread, couch-fashion, a mantle of soft stuff lined with grey fur that was familiar to his eyes and that one of his hands kept fondly feeling as for its pledge of truth. Mrs. Muldoon's face had gone, but the other, the second he had recognised, hung over him in a way that showed how he was still propped and pillowed. He took it all in, and the more he took it the more it seemed to suffice: he was as much at peace as if he had had food and drink. It was the two women who had found him, on Mrs. Muldoon's having plied, at her usual hour, her latch-key—and on her having above all arrived while Miss Staverton still lingered near the house. She had been turning away, all anxiety, from worrying the vain bell-handle—her calculation having been of the hour of the good woman's visit; but the latter, blessedly, had come up while she was still there, and they had entered together. He had then lain, beyond the vestibule, very much as he was lying now—quite, that is, as he appeared to have fallen, but all so wondrously without bruise or gash; only in a depth of stupor. What he most took in, however, at present, with the steadier clearance, was that Alice Staverton had for a long unspeakable moment not doubted he was dead.

"It must have been that I *was*." He made it out as she held him. "Yes—I can only have died. You brought me literally to life. Only," he wondered, his eyes rising to her, "only, in the name of all the benedictions, how?"

It took her but an instant to bend her face and kiss him, and something in the manner of it, and in the way her hands clasped and locked his head while he felt the cool charity and virtue of her lips, something in all this beatitude somehow answered everything. "And now I keep you," she said.

"Oh keep me, keep me!" he pleaded while her face still hung over him: in response to which it dropped again and stayed close, clingingly close. It was the seal of their situation—of which he tasted the impress for a long blissful moment in silence. But he came back. "Yet how did you know—?"

"I was uneasy. You were to have come, you remember—and you had sent no word."

"Yes, I remember—I was to have gone to you at one today." It caught on to their "old" life and relation—which were so near and so far. "I was still out there in my strange darkness—where was it, what was it? I must have stayed there so long." He could but wonder at the depth and the duration of his swoon.

"Since last night?" she asked with a shade of fear for her possible indiscretion.

"Since this morning—it must have been: the cold dim dawn of today. Where have I been," he vaguely wailed, "where have I been?" He felt her hold him close, and it was as if this helped him now to make in all security his mild moan. "What a long dark day!"

All in her tenderness she had waited a moment. "In the cold dim dawn?" she quavered.

But he had already gone on piecing together the parts of the whole prodigy. "As I didn't turn up you came straight—?"

She barely cast about. "I went first to your hotel—where they told me of your absence. You had dined out last evening and hadn't been back since. But they appeared to know you had been at your club."

"So you had the idea of *this*—?"

"Of what?" she asked in a moment.

"Well—of what has happened."

"I believed at least you'd have been here. I've known, all along," she said, "that you've been coming."

" 'Known' it—?"

"Well, I've believed it. I said nothing to you after that talk we had a month ago—but I felt sure. I knew you *would*," she declared.

"That I'd persist, you mean?"

"That you'd see him."

"Ah but I didn't!" cried Brydon with his long wail. "There's somebody—an awful beast; whom I brought, too horribly, to bay. But it's not me."

At this she bent over him again, and her eyes were in his eyes. "No—it's not you." And it was as if, while her face hovered, he might have made out in it, hadn't it been so near, some particular meaning blurred by a smile. "No, thank heaven," she repeated— "it's not you! Of course it wasn't to have been."

"Ah but it *was*," he gently insisted. And he stared before him now as he had been staring for so many weeks. "I was to have known myself."

"You couldn't!" she returned consolingly. And then reverting, and as if to account further for what she had herself done, "But it wasn't only *that*, that you hadn't been at home," she went on. "I waited till the hour at which we had found Mrs. Muldoon that day of my going with you; and she arrived, as I've told you, while, failing to bring any one to the door, I lingered in my despair on the steps. After a little, if she hadn't come, by such a mercy, I should have found means to hunt her up. But it wasn't," said Alice Staverton, as if once more with her fine intention—"it wasn't only that."

His eyes, as he lay, turned back to her. "What more then?"

She met it, the wonder she had stirred. "In the cold dim dawn, you say? Well, in the cold dim dawn of this morning I too saw you."

"Saw *me*—?"

"Saw *him*," said Alice Staverton. "It must have been at the same moment."

He lay an instant taking it in—as if he wished to be quite reasonable. "At the same moment?"

"Yes—in my dream again, the same one I've named to you. He came back to me. Then I knew it for a sign. He had come to you."

At this Brydon raised himself; he had to see her better. She helped him when she understood his movement, and he sat up, steadying himself beside her there on the window-bench and with his right hand grasping her left. "*He* didn't come to me."

"You came to yourself," she beautifully smiled.

"Ah I've come to myself now—thanks to you, dearest. But this brute, with his awful face—this brute's a black stranger. He's none of *me*, even as I *might* have been," Brydon sturdily declared.

But she kept the clearness that was like the breath of infallibility. "Isn't the whole point that you'd have been different?"

He almost scowled for it. "As different as *that*—?"

Her look again was more beautiful to him than the things of this world. "Haven't you exactly wanted to know *how* different? So this morning," she said, "you appeared to me."

"Like *him?*"

"A black stranger!"

"Then how did you know it was I?"

"Because, as I told you weeks ago, my mind, my imagination, had worked so over what you might, what you mightn't have been—to show you, you see, how I've thought of you. In the midst of that you came to me—that my wonder might be answered. So I knew," she went on; "and believed that, since the question held you too so fast, as you told me that day, you too would see for yourself. And when this morning I again saw I knew it would be because you had—and also then, from the first moment, because you somehow wanted me. *He* seemed to tell me of that. So why," she strangely smiled, "shouldn't I like him?"

It brought Spencer Brydon to his feet. "You 'like' that horror—?"

"I *could* have liked him. And to me," she said, "he was no horror. I had accepted him."

" 'Accepted'—?" Brydon oddly sounded.

"Before, for the interest of his difference—yes. And as *I* didn't disown him, as *I* knew him—which you at last, confronted with him in his difference, so cruelly didn't, my dear—well, he must have been, you see, less dreadful to me. And it may have pleased him that I pitied him."

She was beside him on her feet, but still holding his hand—still with her arm supporting him. But though it all brought for him thus a dim light, "You 'pitied' him?" he grudgingly, resentfully asked.

"He has been unhappy; he has been ravaged," she said.

"And haven't I been unhappy? Am not I—you've only to look at me!—ravaged?"

"Ah I don't say I like him *better,*" she granted after a thought. "But he's grim, he's worn—and things have happened to him. He doesn't make shift, for sight, with your charming monocle."

"No"—it struck Brydon: "I couldn't have sported mine 'down-town.' They'd have guyed me there."

"His great convex pince-nez—I saw it, I recognised the kind —is for his poor ruined sight. And his poor right hand—!"

"Ah!" Brydon winced—whether for his proved identity or for his lost fingers. Then, "He has a million a year," he lucidly added. "But he hasn't you."

"And he isn't—no, he isn't—*you!*" she murmured as he drew her to his breast.

Rinehart Editions